MESSAGE FROM A KILLER

Driving to the Tot Lot, Mariah felt dread edging her awareness. Would anything unpleasant be waiting for her at the tiny yellow brick building?

She parked in the rear lot and walked observantly across the playground. Her passing scan revealed nothing unusual. She pulled her key ring from her purse and approached the rear door. Despite herself, she found her heart thumping. She stopped short.

A small pane in the door had been broken away just above the lock.

Mariah tried the door.

It was open.

Mariah moved slowly through the building. At the doorway to each room, she held her breath. The interiors seemed undisturbed, but she felt her anxiety increase. She was certain something somewhere was wrong. She was trembling, damp and shaky-kneed.

When she reached her office, Mariah was relieved to find that everything was as she had left it on Friday. But then, in the middle of her desk, she saw it.

It was a message, written in letters shaped from yellow molding clay.

IT'S ALL GOING TO HAPPEN AGAIN!

CHILD'S CRY

DIMITRI GAT

ZEBRA BOOKS
KENSINGTON PUBLISHING CORP.

ZEBRA BOOKS are published by

Kensington Publishing Corp.
850 Third Avenue
New York, NY 10022

First Printing: April, 1995

Printed in the United States of America

One

Driving to the Tot Lot (DAY-CARE *EXTRAORDINAIRE!*) at 6:15 A.M. on a splendid September morning, Mariah Sullivan recalled that had it not been for her Uncle Edgar, she wouldn't own this place. Years ago he had appeared in his nieces' and nephews' lives with the unpredictability of natural disasters. He was a bit of a disaster himself, with his loud voice and even louder ties. Not to mention his clumsiness. He stumbled often and broke china— somehow always the most expensive. Her cousins were impatient with him. But Mariah in those days was too forbearing; she hated to make anyone unhappy. Maybe Uncle Edgar sensed her soft heart. He always visted longest with her.

Against her will he became her investment adviser. He overflowed with stock tips and ins to "Godzilla-big real estate deals." He insisted from time to time that she ante in with him and twelve years ago she allowed him to persuade her to take two flyers on what he described as "high *po*-tential growth issues." When those trial investments went sour, she found her own name for them: "silly stocks." Though she knew better, when he once more came forward enthusiastically, she bought several thousand shares of a third stock, Electronic Development International, for a few dollars each. Afterwards, she threw the certificates into the bottom of her bureau.

Some time later cancer crawled to Uncle Edgar and carried him off. Though she wept sincerely, amid her sorrow she found some small relief in knowing that he would no longer loom large and loud-tied in her doorway, the newest "pure mone-e-ey machine, Mariah!" on his lips, and her too unassertive to turn him down.

Then the trouble had come and she'd needed every penny she could find. With little hope, she took her Electronic Development International certificates to a local stockbroker. She remembered how shiny broker Jim Chesty's skull was and how the mustache he wore curved across his thin lip like a woolly bear; he put one in mind of a pitchman at a county fair. She timidly put her certificates on the edge of his desk. "These worth anything at all?" she asked.

He picked them up. "EDI. *EDI?*" He glanced up at her. "Joker, huh?"

"Not really. I don't know much—"

"Mrs. Erris, EDI is hotter than rocket exhaust. It was fifty-two on the big board yesterday. What'd you pay?"

"I think a dollar and a half. Five years ago."

Jim Chesty's pale eyes widened in awe behind his aviator glasses. "Present . . . at the *creation*," he whispered. "Then you have the four splits coming to you too."

Thanks to the generosity of another uncle with whom she was living at the time, she needed to sell only some shares to see her through her difficulties. Seven years passed before she liquidated the rest. Wanting her own day-care center had become her career focus, and she said a fond goodbye to the last of Uncle Ed's silly stock, although there was nothing silly about the proceeds that she distributed to the commercial real estate agent, the bank, the architect, and the contractor.

Then the Tot Lot had opened, one year ago today.

She turned to seven-year-old Clarisse, pulled for the day from second grade—a rare occurrence—to help celebrate. "Remember when I opened the Tot Lot, Clarisse?"

"I remember you wondered if any kids were gonna come." Clarisse's wide, toothy grin was a replica of Mariah's.

They came, in time. Right after the first ads ran in the *Borough Reminder* and the *Announcer*, four children were enrolled. All were just over the three-month minimum age. Some older children arrived in early October when arrangements elsewhere failed or parents heard early warnings of inadequate attention or unsuitable peers in their chosen day care centers. Word of mouth was working. Mariah hoped news had also spread about her skills and her staff's competency. Whatever, something good happened. By the beginning of the new year the Tot Lot had a full enrollment of thirty-five. She could be a little smug about now having a waiting list.

It had been a long, difficult journey.

"You gonna tell everybody I helped make the cake?" Clarisse asked.

"*And* about how you loaded the beaters before you licked them," Mariah grinned.

"You wouldn't do that . . ."

"You were a big help, sweet. I'll tell the world. Don't worry."

Mariah swung her van around the corner. Halfway down the block, the Tot Lot sat back on its two-acre plot, lawn and curving drive in front, Cyclone-fenced playground behind. She admired the tidy glass and yellow brick structure that she had seen grow from an architect's rough sketches to a hole in the ground to a metal skeleton and finally to the fully furnished functional building before her.

Her eyes moved over the familiar extended portico protecting the drive as it straightened by the front doors, then to the wide thermal windows, where . . .

"Uh oh," she murmured.

"What 'uh oh'?" Clarisse asked, now all eyes.

"White printing on the windows." Mariah read it to herself: *Tot Lot Kids Are Abused.*

" 'Tot Lot kids are . . .' What's the last word mean, Mom?"

"It means treated badly. Whoever wrote that is 'abusing' the Tot Lot."

What a thoughtless, stupid prank, she thought as she parked the van and hurried inside with Clarisse. The cake and decorations could wait in the van. Thank goodness she made it a policy to get to work forty-five minutes before the first children arrived! She filled a bucket, tossed in a sponge, and started out the front door, Clarisse in her wake. She would get that writing off there—and fast.

As she'd guessed, the message had been written with a bar of soap. She would make short work of it. She wet the sponge and raised it, the warm water steaming in the cool air.

"Well, would you look at that!" came a voice behind her.

Mariah turned to see one of her employees, Rochelle Camwell. Though middle-aged, Rochelle had kept her figure. She wore her heavy blond hair in a single pigtail that often hung down over her big heart. She loved children and had worked with them earlier in Clarion City, where Mariah once had lived. Rochelle had fifteen years of child-care experience and admitted she preferred managing toddlers to "those pimply, rude creatures they grow up to be."

"Look fast," Mariah ordered. "It'll be gone in seconds." She turned back to the window and raised the sponge.

"You're in quite a hurry," Rochelle said.

Mariah glanced toward the older woman as she continued to scrub. "Well, wouldn't *you* be? For goodness' sakes! It's not the kind of message you want on the windows of a day-care center."

Rochelle's solid face shifted thoughtfully. "Certainly not. But I wouldn't do it myself. I'd wait till Molly or Randi got in and have one of them handle the job."

From time to time Rochelle, whose intuitions about personality were as accurate as Bureau of Standards measurements, nudged Mariah about the flaws in her management style. While she never directly said her boss should be more forceful and assign more responsibility, she dropped frequent hints. Nor was she above giving orders to the younger women saying they came directly from Mariah. It wasn't surprising the woman was questioning Mariah's decision not to delegate a messy job.

But Rochelle couldn't dream what a sensitive issue abuse was with Mariah.

While sluicing off the last of the faded white smear, it occurred to Mariah that she should have asked Rochelle to do the cleanup. For once her reason wasn't lack of assertiveness; she had worked successfully to reduce that. It was guilt, damn it! Guilt she *should not* feel.

Two

Mariah had divided the Tot Lot children into three groups: Sleep and Creep, Walk and Talk, and Chatter and Batter. Ages newborn through nine. Her good judgment had allowed her to make some good hires that matched the groups.

Single mother Randi Monroe, poor but patient, was content to work with the newborns in exchange for the enrollment of her two toddlers and a modest stipend. "They're scholarship kids, I guess," she said about her Gert and Dan. "Only *I'm* paying the scholarships." Randi diapered, bottled, and nurtured with the help of one aide. No problems in Sleep and Creep.

Rochelle, the toddler lover, handled Walk and Talk. Though never a mother, she was a devout disciple of discipline; she ran a tight ship. Her stock of stories, games, and songs was endless. She sang a clear alto and played a decent Sony keyboard. She had persuaded Nikki Herakis, a neighbor high school graduate, to sign on as her

"Tot Lot Apprentice," a position the older woman conceived in an inspired moment. Mariah should have thought of it. Given a chance to learn mothering skills firsthand, Nikki was happy to work for only slightly more than the minimum wage. One of her friends was waiting for the next apprentice opening.

College-educated Molly Dolman supervised the current enrollment of eight older children, Mariah helping out when necessary. Dolly was a skilled improviser, comfortable in leading group activities or in guiding the independent. This group's children came and went irregularly, dropped off and picked up by parents and cooperative school buses. When the Tot Lot opened, Mariah put in place rigid controls over who came and went and with whom. She dreaded losing a child.

She had two floaters, Grace Kleingold and Deidre Williamson, women in their early forties who moved among the groups to help out according to the mix at different times of day. Both had married young and their children had already left the nest. They kept busy at the Tot Lot while their husbands hung in at jobs and aimed for early retirement. Grace was a chatty blonde, Deidre a dreamy redhead who loved to read aloud and tell stories, which she embellished with florid dramatic gestures that her audience gleefully anticipated.

Mariah did everything else. That included most record keeping and finances, updating the business plan, tax paying, scheduling, billing, ordering supplies, readying meals and snacks, snipping at the red tape of licensing and certification, conferring with parents, and occasionally expelling—always a tact test. Whenever the unexpected happened, it was Mariah to the front line. All that was a small price to pay for a finally successful career and a stable life for her and Clarisse.

The party to celebrate the anniversary of the Tot Lot was scheduled for three. Aside from the babies who stayed with an aide, all the children were brought to the central room. Their wide eyes settled excitedly on Mariah's cake. She had sweated last night to bake, cut, and assemble it—an iced model of the Tot Lot building in devil's food, her and Clarisse's favorite.

Unbidden, her daughter stood up and faced the two noisy groups. "This is a party for a *place!*" she said defiantly. "You can have a party for a place, you know."

Her brashness hadn't been inherited from her, Mariah thought. Credit Rudy Erris, her ex. Even after seven years of divorce she still couldn't bring herself to credit him with much else, except taking a few decent photographs of her and autumn landscapes. Maybe there really never had been much more than that to the man.

Christopher Orel waved his hand and said, "You can have a party for *God*, too!" As the other children took up the theme of parties-not-for-people, for dogs, goldfish, the USA, Mariah again felt the uneasiness Christopher sparked in her. He was a polite boy, fond of talking about God and Jesus as though they lived just down the block. That was to be expected of a child of newly reborn, enthusiastic Christians. She had nearly refused to admit him when a nervous Audrey Orel had most unexpectedly brought him to the Tot Lot doorstep with humble apologies regarding the past. Her posture was one of trust, proven beyond doubt by her wish to enroll her son. Pondering, Mariah had accepted Christopher, knowing that in so doing she, Audrey, and Audrey's husband, Truman, were forming a pact with great, healing meaning for all of them.

Rochelle and Molly had taken over organizing the singing of "Happy Birthday" to the Tot Lot with the promise of cake and milk to follow. While there were disagreements about who would sit closest to the cake, there were none about who was to blow out the single candle. "Ms. Sullivan! Ms. Sullivan!" they all piped in childish treble. As the singing wound down and Mariah was about to test her lung power, the phone beside her warbled. She answered, "Tot Lot. Day-care *extraordinaire!* Good afternoon."

"A year since you put me out of business!" a woman growled.

Mariah recognized the voice. It was Delsy Comorra, a nasty, spiteful lady by any measure. She lowered her voice and turned away from the party. "The Tot Lot didn't put you out of business, Delsy," she said evenly. She wanted to add that what *had* was the woman's slovenly, ignorant, and largely incompetent ways. Mariah's candidness had improved over what it had been. Not yet quite *that* much, however. For years Delsy's in-home center had flourished in a seller's market before the state had come up with stricter guidelines and parents had become more discerning. Before day care had become one of the competitive growth areas of the 1990s.

"The hell it didn't," Delsy barked. "The hell *you* didn't!"

Mariah wished she had enough audacity to tell the woman off. Instead she said, "What do you want, Delsy?"

"Just wanted to make sure you don't gloat too much!" She hung up.

Mariah knew Delsy had been drinking. She struggled to push memories of the woman and her year-old threats out of her mind. She put down the phone and managed a smile as she turned back to the party.

The children were staring expectantly at her. Patience wasn't a tot's strong suit. She huffed and puffed and blew the candle out.

Molly's vibrato carried clearly over the cacophany. She pointed a drill sergeant finger at two of her older children. "Alex and Christine will help with the serving. Ms. Sullivan gets the first piece."

"And I get the second 'cause I'm *hers!*" Clarisse shouted.

The party was a success, never mind the usual small quarrels and minor spills. After four o'clock, parents began to appear. School buses dropped off another six children. A typical day wound toward its conclusion. Mariah didn't always stay till the Tot Lot closed. This evening, however, she had some accounting to do. Clariesse had her own desk and play area in the office. Nikki Herakis was scheduled to see to the final departures.

Locking up after seven, Mariah found herself strolling her little empire from storage room to kitchen to bathrooms to nap spaces. She smelled the odors of the day: used and fresh diapers, paste, cake, oranges and the faint sweet musk of the young. She strolled the playground with its steel and wooden play apparatus, looking absently for lost items of clothing or plastic toys that had escaped the roundup. She stood in a corner of the Cyclone fence and watched the sun through the leaves, golden beams barring the scuffed grass. "Watch me race!" Clarisse cried and sped away through the sunlight and shadow of her mother's peaceable kingdom.

That evening after Clarisse was asleep, Mariah found herself pacing the condo. At first she didn't want to admit what was niggling at her. In time, though, she accepted that the soaped message was behind her nervousness. TOT LOT KIDS ARE ABUSED! Of all the things that a prankster could have written, why *that?* Just an odd coincidence, but disturbing considering all that had gone before . . .

She shook off thoughts of the past and resumed her evening's plan to make cookies for home and Tot Lot. She bustled in the kitchen wearing earphones whose wires ran up through a plastic loop hanging from the ceiling and off to the CD player. She was combining two of her favorite hobbies, cooking and music. Tonight's program was mixed, as usual. Some re-issued Bix Biederbeck, early Pogues, and Mahler's Seventh. The recipes were for fudge bars and coconut clusters.

She had just put the fudge bars in the oven when the phone rang. She picked it up to hear a familiar voice—but an unwelcome and unexpected one nonetheless. "Rudy," she breathed. Her ex-husband. "Where are you?"

"In town. I want to talk to you."

"You're here in Madison?" Her heart sank. She wondered how he had found her.

"Yeah, Helga and me. We're renting a big old white elephant house on the North Side and—"

"What do you want?"

"I told you. I want to talk to you."

Mariah twisted inwardly. There was no reason for them to talk. All the papers had been signed more than seven years ago. He had renounced custody and visiting rights before Clarisse was born—at Helga's suggestion, she was sure. Her stomach knotted as some of her residual timidity clashed with her will. She made herself say what she had learned was the magic word, though she still wasn't as quick with it as she ought to be. "No," she said softly. And hung up.

The phone rang again at once. She let it roll over to the answering machine. While she listened, Rudy told the device that he needed to talk to her *tout de suite*. If she didn't call him at this number to arrange a time, she'd wish she had. Mariah gasped in the silence. What did he mean by *that?*

What was going on? He hadn't spoken to her in years and she was glad. Sighing heavily, she checked the fudge bars. Something had been different in his tone of voice. It was more menacing than she remembered. And what about his threat? Why had he moved to Madison, of all places, with thousands of cities from which to choose? So it seemed she wasn't yet totally rid of him. He knew how much trouble she used to have saying no. Hadn't he used it to define their marriage until . . . Well, she wasn't going to dredge up all *that* at this hour. She wasn't going to turn back to any of what had happened eight years ago. It was too personal, too draining. And she was much more in charge of her life than she had been in those bad old days. She was tougher, too—and proud of it! Rudy Erris could go pound salt!

When the coconut clusters were done and cooled, she packed them in a tin and went up to the bathroom. She took her time doing her face, giving herself the once-over in the wide mirror over the double sinks. She was thirty-two and told herself she didn't look it. Sure, the laugh and frown lines were etching in for the duration, but her skin was still good. It wasn't far removed from the creamy Irish smoothness of her early twenties. She treated her skin well, spending more than she should on balms and aloes and avoiding excessive exposure to the sun. The four years she had spent restoring herself under Ireland's clouds had helped much.

Her heart-shaped face, featuring wide-set brown eyes, was framed by thick black hair with enough body, she thought in frustrated moments, to suit the fussiest sheep.

But it *did* keep its shape. She had managed to keep hers, too, even after having Clarisse, but she wasn't so foolish as to think some body parts weren't shifting, bowing to that ol' devil gravity. But so far so good. She wished she wasn't so concerned about her appearance. Why couldn't she buy into all that stuff about inner beauty and intellect being more important? No dice. She figured they had her—they being the media, high (and not so high) fashion moguls, maybe some of her friends, and of course the proverbial old wives. And whispering low, out of earshot of earnest feminists, a little voice suggested that a little vanity was probably part of the primal package.

She checked on Clarisse, still sleeping with her Glow-worm. What a pair the two of them would make when together they went off to college! She adjusted her daughter's quilt and went into her own bedroom, sinking into bed with a smile. One year of the Tot Lot. In a way, the little celebration that afternoon had marked the end of a seven-year odyssey. Seven years! The biblical time span for wandering. And hadn't she wandered! Having no home to return to, she had fashioned one here in Madison—and a life to go with it. Yes, she was indeed home at last.

In fact, she had much to celebrate. Why so subdued, then? she asked herself. She knew why: the soaped warning, the calls from Delsy and Rudy. She shivered. Please, please, no trouble now, now that she had at long last rebuilt her life.

Three

She had to admit, she was uneasy driving to the Tot Lot the next morning, tinned cookies on the seat beside her. It seemed her nerves were still shaky. By now she doubted they'd ever be wholly right again. She held her breath as the van passed the day-care center's drive and she scanned the building's front. Nothing marred the sweep of glass. Thank goodness! She swung the van around the building to the small parking lot, deciding to use the back door this morning.

She opened the padlock on the fence gate and started to cross the playground. If the autumn breeze hadn't been stirring, she might have missed what hung above. A whirl of white from above caught her glance. She looked up into the tree's branches and cried out hoarsely.

The effigy of a small girl dangled on the end of a rope, tied into a hangman's knot. The circling figure's stirring white jumper skirt had caught her eye. She stared up to see more. White sneakers dangled below matching tights.

A red blouse covered the narrow chest, across which a blue sash was angled. It read: WILL THIS BE YOUR KID? A large doll's head drooped on the loosely stuffed neck. The monstrosity was crowned with a blond wig in which two golden barrettes winked sinisterly in the sun.

Mariah felt light-headed. She sank down, edging toward a faint. She barely caught herself in time to put a hand down on the cool, spongy grass. She squatted and drew deep breaths. The red rush receded, replaced with anxiety. Who had done this. *Why?* A fleeting, taunting answer presented itself, then was banished. No, that was impossible! The true answer surely lay much closer to Madison. In fact, she had a very good idea who . . .

She smothered her anxious speculations. The important thing now was to get that damned thing *down* before the day's first arrivals. The problem was, the Tot Lot didn't own a ladder long enough to reach up there. She stood, hands on hips, and watched the effigy circle. Even from about thirty feet she saw how much care had been taken in the horror's construction. At a glance it looked like a human child. WILL THIS BE YOUR KID? How dreadful and cruel to hang such a thing!

She fought off her vague fears and ran for the office. She rushed down the hall, heart pounding. She had to get that thing off the property! Her shaking finger twice punched the wrong sequence phoning Don Susann, her handyman. Her palm was clammy on the receiver.

Mrs. Susann answered and told her Don wasn't home, having gone out for a paper. Mariah groaned inwardly. "Have him come over to the Tot Lot right away! It's an emergency."

"Don't know if he has anything lined up for this morning," Mrs. Susann said, not grasping her caller's anxiety.

Mariah hesitated. It was so *hard* for her to exert her

will. But she was learning that to do so was absolutely essential if one was to be an effective person. "Maybe he could put any other appointments off for a little while? I really need him! It's an emergency. And—tell him to bring his longest ladder!"

Mariah hung up the phone and rushed for the art supplies. On a square of poster board she quickly lettered with a thick felt-tipped pen: REAR DOOR CLOSED. USE DRIVEWAY ENTRANCE. She grabbed a child's easel and rushed out to the parking lot drive, setting up the easel in the middle of the asphalt and resting the sign on it. There! That should turn them away. Lord, her heart was pounding! She couldn't resist angling around for another look at that dangling *thing*. Don absolutely *had* to arrive quickly and cut it down.

She said nothing to the staff. When Randi Monroe, her two tots in tow, asked what was wrong with the back door, she said, "Jammed. Don's on his way here to fix it." She tried to hold onto her composure as the rituals of arrival began. All the while she was wondering where in heaven Don was. What was he? A *New York Times* reader who journeyed to the city for his copy? She paced her office, grateful for the established routines that made her presence unnecessary. She *was* a good administrator. She shouldn't forget that when things got rocky. *Where* was Don?

Ten minutes later she welcomed his be-laddered truck like she was a famine victim greeting a food convoy. In minutes she had him at work under the tree. She strode the front hall, welcoming latecomers. Now she was able to crank up her warmest smile. She practiced it on Mickey Donaldson, a black attorney who clearly wanted the best for his five-year-old daughter Shanala. "Good morning, Mr. Donaldson," she said.

"Halloween early this year, looks like," he said.

"Pardon?"

"Somebody rushin' the season, I'd say. Hangin' spooky things out back in your tree."

"In the playground?"

He nodded. "When I saw the sign I pulled into the parking lot to circle . . ." He paused.

"What—did you see?" She fought for an expression of polite concern, not the anxious dismay that rushed through her like a flash flood.

"Somethin' you better get out of your tree. That's all."

"I'll look into it." She tried a confident smile.

"I wouldn't waste any time if I was you," he said.

"I see." She studied his face, behind gold-rimmed glasses. Was there speculation in those intelligent eyes? Had he seen the banner? WILL THIS BE YOUR KID? His Shanala? Did he doubt Mariah? The Tot Lot? Suddenly she felt that she couldn't face him. She spun away before her face flamed with guilt she hadn't earned. "Thank you, Mr. Donaldson," she said. "I'll get on it right away."

After Don finished pulling down the effigy, she had him put it in her van. When he left, she went out and examined it. The head was standard doll plastic. The rest was made of cloth stuffed with rags. She studied the careful stitching of the arms and legs and joins to the torso. It looked like a woman's work.

Which fit in nicely with her growing suspicions.

Yesterday's message she had thought a random prank, the work of idiot teenagers or prepubescent boys. Today she understood that the soaped letters and the effigy were in no way coincidental. She also thought it curious that she had recently taken a surly phone call from a most unpleasant woman . . .

She left the Tot Lot early. As she drove to the other

end of the borough, she remembered the first time she had met Delsy Comorra, now more than a year ago. The wide woman had come at her across the brand-new Tot Lot office floor with a churning waddle while workers *whanged* and *clanged* at finishing touches. She had put meaty hands atop her hips and growled, "So *you're* the bitch who's killing my business!"

She went on from there. Her theme: Mariah's opening the Tot Lot was a personal vendetta against her in-home day-care center, "where I been doing a good business for years, not three miles from here!" She characterized Mariah as "rich and eggheaded," while she was "just folks," doing the best she could in these tough times.

Though Mariah hated confrontations and wasn't good at them, she had learned at some cost that always to avoid them was unwise. She started to color and broke out in a sweat. She loathed the last clinging cords of her timidity, but couldn't completely wriggle free of them, even with this behemoth in her face. Nonetheless, she launched a counterattack. She claimed that there was room for two day-care centers in Morgan Borough, her anger contained like steam in a pressure cooker. She knew she should have opened the vents, shouted back, and told Delsy that she was a vulgar clown, but couldn't quite do it. Almost, though. Some day . . .

Possibly because Mariah had met her rudeness with civility, Delsy dared breach a proposal that her day-care center and the Tot Lot merge. Mariah simply couldn't allow that. She had no trouble mouthing a firm no and clinging determinedly to it.

Enraged, Delsy put spread palms big as platters on her desk and leaned forward threateningly. "You open this place without taking care of me first, you'll be damned sorry!"

"What does that mean, Mrs. Comorra?"

"It means your little Irish ass will fry!"

"You—"

"You don't take care of me now, one day you'll be one miserable little . . . I swear to God." She raised a platter palm. *"Swear to God!"*

So she had sworn—and nothing had happened. Another bluffer caught out, Mariah remembered thinking during the Tot Lot's first few days. As the days turned to weeks and then months, she'd discounted the woman's threats altogether. Then two weeks ago she heard through the grapevine that Delsy's day-care center had closed. Too few enrollees and some hard-to-answer questions asked by the day-care regulatory board had put the last nails in her commercial coffin. It seemed to Mariah that a lot of pieces from their separate lives were falling into place to form a sinister bridge between them.

Mariah slowed the van about halfway to her destination. Maybe this wasn't the best approach, to burst in unannounced. She tried always to consider people's feelings, even people like Delsy Comorra. Maybe the woman wasn't even home, in which case Mariah was wasting time and gas. A phone call seemed to make sense. She pulled over by a phone kiosk. After two rings she heard the big woman's rough voice. She told her she wanted to talk to her immediately.

" 'Immediately,' huh? Such fancy palaver!" Delsy teased. "The queen wants to visit the peasant. So come on. Get your skinny butt over here. I'm looking forward to it!"

Mariah hung up, wondering why she had called. Was it that she didn't want to offend Delsy? *Offend* Delsy? How could she? How could *anyone?* She had a hide as resistant as shark skin. Mariah bit her teeth, upset with herself. She had called Delsy to ask her permission to act. That was a mistake. She ought to always act as she wanted, even if it meant people like Delsy wouldn't like her. She had to keep reminding herself not to live her life trying to please. She was fighting steadily to change that part of her personality. Her intuition told her that she could never get full control of her life until, like St. George, she slew that dragon once and for all.

The Comorras lived in a rambling turn-of-the-century frame house falling to ruin. A wooden sign driven into the lawn, reading WEE PEOPLE DAY CARE, had been defaced with black spray paint. The door was opened by a young woman wearing a wraparound corduroy robe. She carried a baby on her hip that was screaming almost as loudly as the heavy metal music from the boom box on the table. She wore no wedding ring. ''Yeah?'' she said in greeting.

''I'm Mariah Sullivan. I came—''

''She's in the bedroom,'' the woman shouted over the rock percussion. Her face carried a layer of fat that softened its features. She had the look of an overgrown baby. Only her small black eyes reflected what betrayals her seventeen years had brought her. They were narrow, guarded, and cynical. She tossed her head, indicating the direction Mariah should go. And stared at her as she went.

On her excursion through the downstairs, Mariah saw remnants of Wee People: cleared spaces, scattered toys, and TV sets in three rooms. She found her steps faltering. No, she had to go through with it. She had to summon her strength. She simply couldn't allow Delsy Camorra's vendetta to continue. It had to be stopped—and now!

Delsy was in a king-sized bed, a mountain of woman under a spread drawn up to her waist. She wore fawn-colored pajamas broad enough to look the work of a sailmaker. She was even heavier than she had been a year ago. Her brown eyes peered out amid fatty slabs like rodents in hiding. On the bedside were a telephone, prescription bottles, and an open pint of Silver Satin blended whiskey. No glass was in sight.

Mariah felt herself grow still more nervous. Why did so much of living require confrontation? She had tried to prepare a statement of sorts. Now, face to face with the heap that was Delsy, she felt her words flying away like imps. There was no question in her mind that the most important battles people fought in life were within themselves.

"So? What brings you here, Queenie? Finally decided to make a deal with me?"

Mariah approached the bedside. The room's heavy, stale air bore a distant hint of excrement. She made herself look straight into the fleshy cave where Delsy's eyes skulked. "I came to tell you to cut it out!"

Delsy blinked. "Cut what out?"

"You know." Mariah wouldn't lower herself to describe the mischiefs for which she was certain this woman was responsible. She said only, "The things you did yesterday and today at the Tot Lot."

Delsy frowned and shook her head. "I haven't been to the friggin' Tot Lot for more than a year. I drove by it once. That was enough. It almost made me puke! All clean and yellow. Like something out of the *Wizard of Oz*." She heaved her bulk up higher on the mound of pillows. "The Tot Lot can *rot in hell* as far as I'm concerned."

Mariah took a deep breath. "You threatened me a year ago," she said in a level voice. "You swore to God that I'd be sorry if I ever opened the Tot Lot. Well, I opened it. A year later—a couple of weeks ago—your day-care center went out of business. So you decided to do what you threatened. Yesterday early you wrote on my windows with soap. And you phoned me. Last night or this morning you hung a dummy from my playground tree."

"So I had a buzz on, gave you a ding-a-ling and pulled your chain." Delsy frowned. "What the hell is that *other* stuff you're talking about?" Her question came as a shout.

Mariah chose not to shout back, though maybe this was one of those occasions that called for it. She was still on somewhat unfamiliar ground when it came to venting her emotions. She said, "I'm telling you to stop harassing the Tot Lot. No more soapy messages! No more dummies hanging in trees!"

Delsy growled out a laugh. "I don't know where you're coming from with that bull. But if you think I hung anything in a tree, you're cuckoo!"

"I'm *certain* you did."

Delsy growled. "Here's your 'certain,' Queenie!" With a vigorous thrust of her heavy arm she threw her bed covers down to the foot of the bed.

Her left leg was in a thigh-to-ankle cast!

She clanged the exposed metal bedpan with a beringed hand. "I can't even get up to take a crap, you think I'm over at the Tot Lot climbing *trees?*"

Brassy voice booming, Delsy explained that last week she had been drinking more than usual and had taken a tumble down the stairs. Since coming home from the hospital, she hadn't been anywhere but where Mariah now saw her. She put her head back on the pillow. "Look of you, I'd say you got some trouble over at your precious Tot Lot, skinny." She grinned, looking happier now, Mariah guessed, than she had since her accident. "Pardon my French if I say you friggin' *deserve* it. Now why don't you beat it and go play detective somewhere else?"

Mariah stood red-faced as some of the anger she felt

finally catalyzed her tongue. "I'm not sure I believe you. I wouldn't trust you as far as I could throw you. And that wouldn't be very far, would it?"

"Well, listen to you!"

"And I'm not sure a broken leg disqualifies you, Delsy. Maybe you have a friend with a ladder—"

"Bag it!"

"I'll bag it when I'm through!" Mariah said hotly, though at the moment she had nothing more to say. She glared at the woman, then turned to go.

Delsy frowned thoughtfully. "Hang on." Her eyes narrowed as Mariah turned again to face her. Delsy continued, "If it turns out that you get more trouble than you can handle, give me a call. Maybe we can still be partners. I'll take care of your troubles for half interest in the Tot Lot. How's that sound?" She smiled broadly.

"I'll handle my own troubles," Mariah said evenly.

Delsy's hearty laughter shook the vast bed. "Yeah, yeah! And I'll hit cleanup for the Yankees!"

Mariah turned again and headed for the door.

"Hey, Queenie, don't forget. You get more trouble you can't handle, who do you call? Delsy!" Her wheezing laughter followed Mariah until she left the house.

In the car Mariah sat shaking, damp with sweat. Confrontations! She was going to continue to face them until she felt herself their mistress. She had learned the hard way that there was nothing to be gained from backing down.

She stared down the street, seeing traffic move but not really noticing it. Though Delsy was out of action, who could say that she hadn't ordered someone else up the ladder with the effigy. Nothing about being bedridden kept her from using a needle and thread, did it? As moments passed, however, Mariah found herself putting

some distance between her suspicions and Delsy. While
it was possible the big woman was indeed responsible,
something about her flippant attitude made her much less
a suspect now than she had been in the hothouse of
Mariah's imagination.

But if not her, then? . . . Maybe the harrowing events of
years ago had conditioned Mariah to overreact. Pranksters
sometimes fastened on a particular person or place to do
their mischief. They could keep at it until they were caught
or bored. After all, how serious was the situation, she
asked herself. Some soap on a window and a stuffed
figure on a rope. She was making much out of little. She
started the van and pulled out.

Yet she couldn't put Delsy completely out of her suspicions. She sensed the woman's capacity for misbehavior
was as huge as her bulk. She had the potential, certainly.
Mariah mulled over their recent conversation. One phrase
clung in her mind, refusing to be dislodged.

More trouble.

Friday night Mariah and Clarisse planned an outing with
Clarisse's friend Jennifer "Jeeter" McRae and her mother,
Rita. Jeeter and Clarisse met in first grade and clung to
each other with the single-minded mania that only children
could muster. Jeeter was quiet and introverted. That meant
Clarisse, the little show-stopper, could play leader and
love it. Jeeter's good-natured capacity for taking orders
seemed boundless. Whatever the dynamic, both kids loved
being together and kept asking about the ritual that would
make them blood sisters.

Spending two hours with Rita McRae explained her
daughter's long silences: the girl couldn't get a word in.
Rita *talked*. She was wound tight with a thick spring. Her

answer to life's problems was *energy*. Go get 'em! Tilt hard enough at those windmills and down they'd come. She had the perfect job for a fast-talking go-getter. She sold advertising services for a big local agency and made a good living because she simply outhustled her competitors. "Want some advice for success in life, Mariah Sullivan?" she asked. "Persist, persist, *persist!*" Her persistence fell short two years ago when her husband left her "for a twenty-year-old, big everywhere except in the brain." Adjusting to that, she finally came to a conclusion not unlike Mariah's own: she wasn't sure how much she really needed a man in her life.

For the most part Rita handled challenges with skill and directness. She explained how she dealt with negative thoughts and the emotional snares of the past. She would touch her thumb and forefinger together. "Got those troubles right here!" She would raise her fingers to her lips and "Send them off! Send them out! *Pooof!*" And she would blow them away "*Pooof* them high and far and they'll never float back!"

For Mariah, making friends wasn't easy. She always made the mistake of thinking that every new person in her life was filled with virtues. As time passed, she was inevitably disappointed. Her grandest error in this area was Rudy Erris. At first he had seemed to be everything a woman could want: intelligent, industrious, and generous. Time proved to her great regret that he actually possessed none of those qualities. All that he could do well, so far as she could tell, was buy camera equipment and take photos, in that order. But by then she had married him. That lesson made her more cautious when evaluating all subsequent acquaintances. Level-headed analysis revealed that she continued to value Rita, with whom she shared the vicissitudes of single parenthood. She had the right stuff. Mariah would judge the depth of the friendship on the basis of when she was able to tell her friend all that had happened to her, beginning with the tragedy eight years ago. Maybe she could show Mariah how to gather even all that together and *pooof* it forever out of her mind.

Tonight it was dinner at Taco Bell and dollar night at the second-run multi-cinema. After the movie Mariah invited Rita in for an espresso. The machine was an unlikely wedding present she had managed to hang onto through it all. She peeled off two narrow slices of lemon rind and put them in the tiny saucers. She poured. Rita took her seat across the tag-sale kitchen table. It was getting to be their little ritual.

As Rita chattered on, Mariah found her attention turning back to the incidents at the Tot Lot. Even if she chose not to share her past, it might be a good idea to let go of some of the present. She knew how easy it was for her to get into a tailspin if she chewed too much on her thoughts. She imagined it was time to see how another pilot might handle the situation. She edged into Rita's monologue with an outline of the recent events and asked her what she thought.

Rita was what Mariah's mother would have called "a comely woman." Which meant a certain regularity of facial features that taken together didn't mean beautiful so much as easy to look at. Her face was round, her jaw firm, lips a bit thin, nose nicely arched, and blue eyes frank. She wore intricate earrings from places like Bali and Portugal, swept her hair up and held it with an assortment of exotic clips and bands. It wasn't her style to be "invisible." She heard Mariah out, narrowed her eyes, and thoughtfully looked up at the darkened kitchen skylight.

"This is how I see it, pal. Couple odd things like that, you can let them slide. Kids, cranks, whatever, they go away. But . . ."

Mariah waited. For someone who talked like a machine gun, Rita got a lot of effect out of a slight pause. "But . . . what?" she asked.

Rita's eyes met hers. "If anything else happens, I think you've got some kind of a problem."

That weekend she tried to see the episodes as little more than thoughtless annoyances. She tried looking at the bigger picture. "Perspective," Rita had urged Friday night. "Don't lose your perspective." As usual, she was right on the money. So many things were right with the Tot Lot, Mariah, and Clarisse. She mustn't allow herself to be knocked off center by mere pranks. The Tot Lot was a new day-care center, years and miles removed from the last one. There was no reason to connect the prosperous present with the painful past.

Sunday evening, Rudy called again. Once more he tried to arrange a meeting. Again she steeled herself and managed to refuse him. When he persisted, she hung up. She stood by the phone feeling guilty. The warbling ring began again at once.

Why was he calling her now after all these years?

Her hand moved, as though on its own, toward the receiver. She was going to let him talk her into meeting him, despite herself. With dismay she understood that a small part of her still wanted to please him, of all people. He and maybe everybody else in the world. She had to fight that!

Just then, the doorbell rang. She turned away from the phone. It was one of Clarisse's schoolboy friends selling chances on five hundred dollars' worth of groceries to benefit midget football. While she bought a chance, the call rolled onto the answering machine. Thank God! But she couldn't expect to be bailed out the next time he called. He *would* call. She knew him. He'd keep after her till he got what he wanted. Until she gave it to him.

Four

Mariah slept poorly and was up with her Monday morning coffee an hour early on another clear September day. She made Clarisse oatmeal and kept it warm in the double boiler. She got out the brown sugar, put it into a small bowl, and stuck in the Goofy spoon. She scooped out an orange, peeled an apple, diced it together with a banana, and stirred in the orange pulp. She set it at Clarisse's place.

She climbed the stairs. "You moving?" she called.

"I'm up and at 'em!" Clarisse said, echoing a line from the old movies she loved to watch.

"I'm going to work. You get on the bus yourself." She paused. "Tell me the rules."

"Mom!"

"Humor me, Miss Smarty!"

"Keep the door locked. Stay in till there are at least two kids waiting at the bus stop. Don't go with anybody except the bus driver."

"Backup?"

"Mrs. Morris, Unit 23."

"Take the blue bus this afternoon and get off at the Tot Lot. Got it?"

"Yeah!"

"Don't forget."

"Mom, give me a break!"

"I'll break *you* if you don't watch that mouth!"

Mariah hated to leave her, hated not to be at home when she finished school. What she really felt wasn't hate. It was guilt. She had in her too much guilt altogether. Unless she could shed most of it she was in for every bit as rough a life as she had experienced up to now. She swallowed. The hardest changes to make were the ones inside yourself!

Driving to the Tot Lot after a weekend she had not found reviving, she felt dread edging her awareness. Would anything unpleasant be waiting for her at the tidy yellow brick building? Or as Rita had implied, was she overreacting to a pair of pranks? Her passing scan revealed nothing unusual. She parked in the rear lot and walked observantly across the playground. She peered up uneasily into the oak. Nothing. Everything looked okay.

She pulled the key ring from her purse and approached the rear door. Despite herself, she found her heart thumping as though she had run up two flights of stairs. And then she stopped short. A small pane in the door had been broken away just above the lock.

Someone had forced their way inside.

Why? Was whoever it was still in there?

She tried the door. It was open. She thought of going inside. No. Bad idea. She stuck her head into the doorway and shouted, "Get out of here!" Then she took a few steps backward. Maybe that hadn't been smart. Whoever was in there might come out this way! She stood feeling foolish and at risk, but heard nothing from inside the building. She shouted again, "Hey, get out!"

While she stood uncertain about what to do, Rochelle Camwell arrived for work. The older woman listened as Mariah explained the situation. "Well, let's go in and see what's going on," she suggested.

"They might still be in there," Mariah said uneasily.

"Not likely. If they came by night, they didn't want company." Rochelle squared her solid shoulders. "Come on. Let's go. See if they trashed the place."

"Oh, Lord, I hope not." Mariah felt a surge of anger. How *dare* they touch one thing in her Tot Lot! "Let's stick together," she said.

"I don't think we have anything to worry about," Rochelle said confidently.

Mariah wondered where the older woman got her fearlessness. It was as though she *knew* whoever had broken in was long gone.

Deliberately talking loudly, they moved through the building. At the doorway of each room, Mariah held her breath. The interiors seemed undisturbed. There was so much that could be tumbled and toppled. So many faucets and taps to open. Rather than calming down at finding nothing out of place, she felt her anxiety increase. She was certain something somewhere was wrong. She was trembling, damp and shaky-kneed. They went to the office last.

Rochelle stood in the doorway calmly adjusting her blond bun while Mariah entered. Everything looked the same as she had left it on Friday. But then she saw it. There in the middle of her desk. *Oh, no!* With a casual move she slid two sheets of typing paper over what she had found.

She turned and walked back to Rochelle. "I can't believe it! Everything's okay," she said. She hoped desperately that her voice wouldn't betray her.

Rochelle had frank gray eyes set in a no-nonsense face. They moved over Mariah's features. "You're white as Goslow's Paste, dear."

"I—don't like any of this!" Mariah said.

"Makes two of us. I'm going to have another look around. God knows, but these days you have to worry they maybe left some kind of dangerous calling card." She moved off with a purposeful stride.

Mariah just made it to her desk chair before her knees gave out. She sagged down, grabbing at the desk edge. A rotating redness rushed into the boundaries of her vision. Fainting? Head below the heart, she remembered from some long-ago first aid instruction. She lowered her head to knee level and took deep breaths. Oh, Lord, what she had just seen! Within a minute the redness had retreated.

Unable to resist, she straightened, and with a ginger thumb and forefinger slid the sheets off the message written in letters shaped from yellow molding clay.

IT'S ALL GOING TO HAPPEN AGAIN!

No, no! It simply could not be! Yet there could be no mistaking the meaning. The past was to be *repeated*. The horrid, dangerous, and violent past from which she was certain she had escaped with an undeservedly scarred reputation and psyche.

She pressed her palms to the desk to steady herself. They left wet smears on the smooth metal. For one panicked moment she thought she was going to lose her sanity. This could not be happening. All that was over.

All over! She couldn't tear her eyes away from the letters. *It's all going to happen again* . . .

Teamed with her shock was desperate curiosity. Who had done this? Who had linked the present with the eight-year-old past?

Parents were beginning to drop off children. Now there was no way she could put on her reassuring, competent smile. Twice she was interrupted by Molly Dolman and Randi Monroe with administrative questions. She sat motionless, giving her responses like an assembly line robot. Neither woman seemed to notice her agitation, thank God.

After staring at the yellow message for nearly an hour, her thoughts swarming and scattering, she exploded. Crying out hoarsely from deep in her throat, she spread her hands and swept the letters together. With suddenly steely fingers she wadded the clay into a ball and flung it with all the strength in her left arm. It stuck on the wall like a yellow growth off to the left of the city day-care license.

Tears started up, but she choked them back. This was business too serious for a descent into helplessness. She had to *think*, despite the emotions that churned up like a hurricane's storm surge, threatening to overwhelm her. One thing was clear. She had her answer. The soaped message and the effigy weren't random pranks. It hadn't been a coincidence after all that the child strung high had been a girl—though she had succeeded well in denying that distant echo.

The day passed slowly. Thank goodness for her staff! Her odd distancing they assumed was preoccupation with business concerns or maybe an early cold in the making. All she was capable of was to show her face wherever children were gathered. She fought a battle against memories that suddenly swept up from her past, with all the accompanying emotions—shame, guilt, embarrassment, and sorrow.

All day her hands were icy, her stomach in a knot. She paced the office, now and then glancing out the tall narrow windows into the playground populated with darting little creatures and watchful adults. The first battle she fought to a marginal victory was that with her emotions. She absolutely *had* to get hold of herself so that she could think rationally about what was happening. Toward late afternoon she had a tenuous grip on herself, one she knew could slip at any moment. Should it, tears and hysteria were certain to follow.

When Clarisse got off the bus Mariah had to shape up. Saying she had a bit of work to do, she asked her daughter if she wouldn't like to play with Gert and Dan Monroe in Randi's group. When she trotted off, Mariah heaved a sigh of relief. That bought her a couple of hours to try to piece things together.

Her first thought had been to call the police, but she'd quickly dropped the idea. How foolish! All she needed was to draw attention to the Tot Lot and herself. She well knew to what disaster that would lead. No, no police. She closed her door and sat at her desk, eyes closed. Out of her shock and surprise one certainty emerged: whoever left the note had known about what had happened in Clarion City eight years ago. She thought at once of Audrey Orel, but she had come in peace bearing the most sincere offering she could make: the weekday custody of her son. Then there was Rudy Erris. Her ex was . . . well, her ex. She didn't imagine he was up to hanging effigies and leaving messages.

Another name came to mind, all too easily. She who had been the core of the long-past disaster. She who had appeared to her not three months ago, as unwelcome a visitation as a victim's ghost to his murderer.

Jacquelyn "Jacky" DuMarr.

She had picked her time well, a Wednesday evening in early June. Later Mariah wondered if she had been watching her, waiting for the perfect moment. Clarisse had gone to play with Jeeter. Enjoying the first really balmy weather, Mariah had left her condo town house door open with the screen door locked. When the chime sounded, she came right out of the kitchen and in an instant was face to face with Jacky, a woman she had been certain she would never see again. Surely she never *wanted* to see her again.

For an instant she didn't recognize the woman. Prison had thinned her, rendered and removed what Mariah had come to think of as the fat of the voluptuary. The leanness shadowed her face, too, save for lips that still held their fleshy bee-stung curves now like a lush oasis amid stark sands. The yellow-blond hair still showed its prison cut. The tailored suit and sensible shoes weren't the old Jacky's style either. Loud flowered prints and dagger heels had been more her fashion. "Mariah," she said.

"Hello, Jacky." Mariah found her voice shaking. "I didn't think I'd ever see you again."

"You know what they say about a bad penny!" Jacky's brassy laugh had lost none of its unpleasant clarion note.

"I thought you were very angry with me," Mariah said. "You said as much after the trial."

Jacquelyn shrugged. "Over the dam. Hey, do I get invited in, or do I have to walk through the screen?"

Mariah didn't want to stand in the same room with the woman, much less to talk to her. But she couldn't just say no. She opened the screen door and Jacky barged in. She gave the condo's first floor a quick glance. "Nice place you got." She sat on the couch. Mariah expected her to light a cigarette, but she made no move toward her purse. Prison had at least done that for her. Who knew what other positive changes, if any, had been made in Jacky's habits. Why was she out of prison? She had been given ten years.

As though reading her mind, Jacky explained, "You're lookin' at a model prisoner, babe, now a paroled offender. I see my parole officer every week and keep myself on the straight and narrow." She motioned for Mariah to sit. That commanding gesture! It brought back unhappy memories that twisted like snakes. They reminded her of how much she had been under this woman's influence, and the world of serious trouble into which she had been led. She had done what Jacky asked—damn her passive personality of those long-gone days!—unquestioningly. She had never suspected that a single indecent thing was going on at J. D. Day Care. If life was one long test of character, she had failed it then. Jacky's unexpected appearance made her wonder if there might not be some more difficult test on the horizon. She stood, one meager act of defiance.

"So I see you're doing pretty good." Jacky leaned back, arms atop the couch back, an all too familiar posture that caused Mariah to groan inwardly.

"I'm just making a living for Clarisse and myself. And a no-frills one at that."

"Sure, sure." Jacky winked like a conspirator. "I came to Madison to stay with my sister, kind of pick up and start over. You must know the feeling. Didn't know what to do with myself. Then I saw your ad, early sign-up for—what is it?—the Tot Lot? Ad looked pretty flashy to me."

"We have to attract an early enrollment for next fall."

Jacky continued. "So I figured you got a big enough operation you probably need people to help you out." She shrugged, palms up, as though in support of the painfully obvious. "So I figured one of your people could be me!"

The nerve! The incredible, outrageous *nerve* . . . Mariah found Jacky's suggestion doubly offensive. First, because eight years ago she had defamed Mariah's character under oath, trying to make the jury believe that she had helped take the photographs. She had made other charges under oath as offensive as spit on the face of Mariah's reputation, all of them an effort to diffuse her guilt by smearing some of it on her employee. The anguish that Mariah had felt over being so accused was crushing. She could not *believe* that one person could do such a thing to another. There was so little duplicity in her that she could not imagine mountains of it in others. When she shared her shock with her attorney Shelly Mortenstein, he growled, "Where'd you grow up, Mariah Sullivan? Goody-goody Land?"

Mariah's second reason for being greatly distressed by Jacky's proposal was that she was clearly prepared to try to take advantage of her intuitive understanding of Mariah's good nature. Though she had attempted a character assassination that cost Mariah her reputation and nearly her sanity—never mind maybe six years of her life—she knew that her former employee would nonetheless not find it easy to refuse her demands. Somehow that insight was almost more infuriating to Mariah than Jacky's perjury. It was as though her former boss held up a huge sign suggesting that Mariah's crippling flaws were still in place despite the years. Well, they weren't! Mariah iced her voice. "I have a complete staff, Jacky."

"Hey, come on! I'm starting over. I'll work for next to nothing. I'm staying with my sister and—"

"I'm afraid it's impossible." Inwardly Mariah was trembling. She absolutely could *not* allow this woman inside the walls of the Tot Lot. She had abused young children. She had been found guilty and sentenced. She was a felon, for goodness sake! And here she was, asking for employment in the same line of work. Asking *her* because she knew she might actually have a chance. Mariah simply could *not* allow it.

Over the next half hour, Jacky worked to break down her defenses. She pleaded with Mariah. She'd work for nothing to get her hand in again. Mariah had nothing to worry about. She had learned her lesson, done her time. She wasn't that way about little kids now. Look how she dressed. She was super straight. She just needed a little break to get started again. That's why she had come to her old friend . . .

Mariah knew her face was flushed. She was perspiring heavily. She would have given a hand not to have this awful woman after her like this. As though sensing Mariah's great discomfort, Jacky pressed her case all the harder. The psychological pressure mounted. Mariah paced while Jacky sat stolidly on the couch. She moved only her arms to gesture imploringly.

Mariah felt herself weakening. She began to tell herself that maybe she could set something up for Jacky, something temporary, something where she'd be supervised so that she would never be alone with any of the children. What was she thinking! *She could not!*

She whirled toward her unwanted visitor. "No, I can't! Absolutely *not!*" she blurted, feeling she was about to burst into tears. "And that's final." She knew her face was scarlet. Her stomach was so knotted she wanted to double over. Yet, yet, she felt a surge of guilt. How could she feel guilty turning down this, this—*creature?*

"Well, well . . ." Jacky's sensuous lips parted in an unpleasant smile. "Aren't you the hard-nosed one?" The brassy laughter pierced Mariah's ears like a skewer. Jacky leaned back, seemingly as relaxed as Mariah was agitated. "Maybe you ought to think again."

Mariah breathed deeply, forced herself to meet the woman's smiling but humorless eyes. "Why should I?"

" 'Cause there's a lot of glass in that Tot Lot of yours. I been by it. People who have lots of glass in their houses should be careful."

Mariah swallowed. "What does that mean?"

"It means that if people knew what happened eight years ago, you'd be finished."

Mariah gasped. "Are you threatening me?"

"If people knew you worked with me at J. D. Day Care . . ."

"You were guilty. *I wasn't!* I was *not* guilty!"

"You think anybody would believe it?"

"It happens to be true! It was you who—"

"Forget the truth. It doesn't matter much nowadays," Jacky said. "It's what people think that counts."

How could this be happening, Mariah asked herself. Jacquelyn DuMarr descending on her out of the past, first with pleas, now with horrid threats. She had so much wanted all that had come before to be locked away in history's cabinet and never again dragged out for analysis or review. Now here was a leaner and likely meaner Jacky pointing out in her rude way how impossible that was.

She saw now behind her former boss's new leanness. Seven years in prison had caused internal changes as well. She sensed a hardness—more, a ruthlessness—in her that made her more than just a mere annoyance. She was a threat and could become a dangerous enemy. Just the same, her threatened blackmail was built on straw. Though

Mariah sometimes forgot, *she had not been guilty*. She had been acquitted. Jacky's threats were built on sand. For that reason she could not submit.

"Please leave now, Jacky." Her voice was firm.

Jacky sat.

"Leave or I'll call the police."

That got a reaction. Jacky rose and glowered. Women on parole didn't need any complaints filed against them. "You could be damn sorry about this!" she hissed. "Damn sorry!"

She showed Jacky to the door. Mariah watched from her small porch as the woman stomped to her car and squealed off down the street.

Mariah hadn't seen Jacky since. But her threat had never quite left Mariah's memory. She nodded in the silence of her office. Who on earth was better qualified to make sure "it's all going to happen again" than the woman who had made it happen in the first place? Mariah could not bear for any part of that horrible past to be repeated, never mind *all* of it. Jacky had to be stopped—and now!

She went to the phone book, then into a maze of governmental listings. She had no idea whom to call. She tried the general prison number. When someone answered, she said, "Could you tell me how to get in touch with the parole office?"

It shortly became clear that finding her way through the bureaucratic maze would take a number of calls. She was making them when someone knocked on the open door. She hung up the phone. Audrey Orel, her son Christopher in tow, stood in the doorway. Audrey was a bit over five feet tall with eyes like agates over which her lids seemed seldom to fall, so intense was her stare. With it came small twitchings of her wrists and regular inward

snorts of breath. Eight years ago she had reminded Mariah
of a badly wired small appliance. When she appeared at
the Tot Lot two months ago, her wiring seemed worse.
Yet she hadn't short-circuited. The reason she continually
vocalized centered on the benefits of having had Jesus
come into her life. He was the rock upon which she now
stood.

Mariah was still uneasy in Audrey's presence. Maybe
it would have been wiser for her to have refused to enroll
Christopher, no matter his parents' pleas. Doing so would
have simplified her emotional life. "We just came by to
tell you how pleased Truman, I, and Christopher are with
the Tot Lot," Audrey chirped in her nervous wren voice.
"Jesus told us to bring him. And He's never wrong, is
He?"

"I'm so happy you're pleased," Mariah said woodenly.

"I love the games with dice!" Christopher said brightly.
He was black-haired like his mother and had his father,
Truman's, gentle air. Mariah's staff and her own observa-
tions had convinced her that he was a sweet boy. And
doubled her determination that no ill whatever befall him.
It's all going to happen again . . . She shuddered inwardly
against dread of the past and for the first time faint concern
for the future as well.

"Jesus told us this was the way to redeem ourselves
for our former vindictiveness." Audrey gave one of her
habitual inward snorts. "That Truman was transferred to
Madison this August was clearly the hand of God, don't
you agree, Mariah?"

"Well . . ."

"How could we be wiping away the ugliness of the
past if it hadn't been for His help?" Audrey moved forward
in her rapid, birdlike stride. Her skin was covered with
fine, tiny wrinkles, as though her face was stretched to

breaking by inner tension. Mariah found herself hoping God could keep her together at least until her son was out of the Tot Lot. "Do you see how He works?" Audrey asked. "What better way for us to exorcise the ugliness of our behavior toward you—"

"You couldn't understand then that neither I nor Jacky had anything to do with what happened to Dotty."

Audrey closed her eyes. "*Please.* Don't speak her name."

"I'm sorry! I—"

"Do you see how He works?" she repeated. "We redeem ourselves and you get to care for our child. Just as you deserved to do all along. It's wonderful! Jesus is wonderful!"

"Yes." Mariah felt her face coloring. Get off it, Audrey. A little goes a long way.

"Jesus loves me!" Christopher said, beaming ear to ear as though God was whispering privately to him at that very moment.

"I'm so glad you stopped by, Audrey. All our reports on Christopher are first rate. He's a wonderful addition to our center."

"I'll be staying in close touch, Mariah," Audrey said. "We must celebrate this inspired work of God at every opportunity."

Mariah nodded, rose, and walked to the doorway. Audrey turned to leave, thank goodness! As the pair passed her, Mariah noted that the older woman looked tired, worn, and fragile. Mariah might have looked that way herself, she thought, if her daughter had been murdered.

Five

Parole Officer Felicia Greene had soot-dark, shiny skin. She looked as though she had seen it all. Mariah guessed this country hadn't given Felicia Greene an inch. She struggled for everything she had, much of the struggle taking place in a part of society Mariah wasn't stupid enough to think she knew very much about. Felicia Greene's profession, which immersed her in corrections and surrounded her with convicted criminals, further extended Mariah's respect for her. The gap between the two women's life experiences couldn't be greater. While Mariah attended prep school and college, Felicia had been enrolled in the school of hard knocks. As they spoke, Mariah distanced herself to listen to the differences between their conversational styles. She couldn't help but smile and feel a little envious. Felicia's tough tones and brusque gestures were miles removed from her habitual politeness and what she often felt were her over-delicate ways.

"Let's recap then, shall we, Ms. Sullivan?" Felicia said

matter-of-factly. "Jacky came to you in the middle of the summer asking for a job. When you refused to give her one, she threatened you."

"Yes."

Felicia glanced down at her notes. "And you think Jacky was responsible for the problems at your day-care center. The 'incidents,' you call them."

"There's no one else it could be."

Felicia folded her arms and leaned forward. She shook her head in disbelief. "All you told me 'bout you working for her. *You* and Jacky Babette DuMarr—as she likes me to call her— *You* workin' for *her?* *You* takin' her jive—"

"What I told you about our past is *confidential*. I don't want you to—"

"Stay cool, Ms. Sullivan. *Stay cool.* I see where you're comin' from. I'm just wondering how you could be workin' for her at her day-care place and not know what she was up to—"

"Don't put me on trial again!" Mariah couldn't control her outburst. She was still raw, sensitive and ashamed about the past.

Felicia raised her palms in a calming gesture. "Easy!" She got up. "Let's go get some coffee."

Bitter coffee dripped from the vending machine in the state corrections department basement. The furniture was shaped plastic, just fine for penguin- or seal-shaped people, but not so great for Mariah's spine. Calmed, she tried to explain to Felicia Greene how years ago Jacky's personality had overwhelmed hers, how she had been passive and naive.

Felicia frowned. "And so you were unaware she was leading the kids off and taking pictures of them naked?"

Mariah shook her head. "I know that's hard to believe.

But it is the truth. Look, I don't want to talk about those days. I just want Jacky to stay away from the Tot Lot."

Felicia nodded. "I'll be talkin' to her. Don't you worry none."

"Thank you!"

"Don't be so quick to thank me."

"I don't see why I shouldn't thank you," Mariah said. "You're doing me a favor."

Felicia took a deep swallow of coffee. She laughed suddenly, a hearty chuckle that shook her big chest. "Ain't this terrible tastin' stuff?"

Mariah laughed in spite of herself.

Felicia smiled up at the stained ceiling tiles. "You want to know why you maybe shouldn't be thankin' me? Tell you why. In the business I'm in you see the worst people— no lie! Every one of them tryin' to con Felicia Greene." She shook her head slowly. "Ain't many that do, by now. I been doin' this fifteen years come January first. You get to know people real good. You get to know who you're going to see again, in say five or ten years. 'Cause they into doin' bad and it's all they'll ever know. And you get to know the ones that learned their lessons."

Mariah waited. Felicia said nothing. She prompted: "And . . ."

"Your Jacky Babette DuMarr. I believe she's one that learned hers."

That Tuesday morning's schedule included a routine conference with Clarisse's second grade teacher at North Madison Elementary School. Ms. Tolliver was perky and wore wide, gold hoop earrings. She also had the energy of her twenty-five years—which was what one wanted in a room filled with seven-year-olds. She had on her desk the files from Clarisse's kindergarten and first grade and reported what Mariah already knew: Clarisse had always behaved well and did better than average work. She had never been a problem to the school or herself.

Ms. Tolliver was effusive with the compliments. Clarisse's present school year looked every bit as promising as her previous two. She rated in the upper tenth percentile in social skills. Ms. Tolliver put down her pencil and smiled. "I wish I had ten like Clarisse in my room," she said. "And believe me, I don't say that to every parent!"

Mariah smiled in turn. "I'll keep my fingers crossed," she said.

"I have a hunch you know there's more to raising a child than just hoping."

Notwithstanding the teacher's earnestness, Mariah got the feeling she was being set up for some unpleasant news. She looked at Ms. Tolliver questioningly.

"I gather you're a single mother, Ms. Sullivan?"

Mariah nodded.

"We have our share of single parent families," Ms. Tolliver said. "Women and men raising children alone. We have a lesbian couple, too, you know, and two church-married gays." She sounded proud of it all, as though the death of the traditional arrangement was to be celebrated. Mariah didn't think being a single parent was all that great, even if the media was now trying to tell her that the traditional family was something of a myth. She hoped Ms. Tolliver would ask her about that. She didn't. Instead she said, "Clarisse has never had a father, has she? I mean, even for a short time?"

"Rudy left when I was four months pregnant." Mariah wanted to add it was also when her life was at its lowest point. To poison the sword a bit more, he had left her for

Helga, a Teutonic juggernaut. "He made it clear he wanted no part of Clarisse," Mariah went on. "He couldn't care less that I gave her my maiden name."

Ms. Tolliver leaned forward a bit. She had rough skin and her thin lips were dry. Mariah thought that came from working in a climate-controlled environment that pumped the germs around in a microbe carousel to give them second and third shots at you. The teacher was getting to it now. "Does Clarisse ever talk about her father?"

"She knows who he is. But it's just factual information. She's never seen him."

Ms. Tolliver smiled and folded her hands. "Sometimes it's not clear just where being a teacher ends. Where you say to yourself this or that is entirely the parents' responsibility. It's a tough call. But having met you, I think it would be a good idea to share—without any commentary from me—what your daughter did and said a few days after school started."

One afternoon Clarisse had "crashed," as Ms. Tolliver put it. She had burst into tears and curled up in a ball. "It happens now and then. They just lose it." She had led Clarisse to the nap space where she could recover and maybe sleep. She helped the girl blow her nose and calmed her down. "That's when she said it," Ms. Tolliver said. "Twice, to make sure I heard her. She said, 'I want a daddy!'"

Leaving the school, Mariah realized April Tolliver was shrewd for her years. She knew far more about which end was up than Mariah had at that age. Had Mariah ever consciously wondered if her daughter dreamed of having a father? Maybe, but only off on a distant edge of her thoughts. Clarisse must have grasped somehow that it would not be a welcome topic of conversation. As though she knew it wasn't Mom's fault that she didn't have a husband. And that sharing her childish wish might upset Mariah.

Since Rudy, she hadn't been within a hundred miles of another husband. After the trial, she had fled Clarion City and Rudy's adultery, her emotions flowing like tattered ribbons in her wake. Then she had been busy caring for an infant and tending to her own emotional scars. No time to chat up the men when you were nursing every two hours. Then she had made her odyssey across Ireland. Irish men? Well, nobody in Ireland ever had to worry about a population explosion. If younger men stayed in the country, they hid themselves well. If they married at all, they married late. They maybe had too much mother, too much church, too much guilt. What they were best at was talking and drinking, two of her weaker suits. After she had come home and voiced her complaints, acquaintances told her she simply hadn't met the right ones. Then she was nearly overwhelmed by caring for Uncle Harry. And so the years had flown . . .

When she thought of Rudy it was easy to convince herself that she was better off alone.

Until now she had never considered what Clarisse might need in terms of nurturing. She sighed as she got behind the wheel of her van. The problem of course was that you couldn't just add water to a capsule and grow the kind of man you wanted. She was only thirty-two, the "professional woman" that so delighted personal column ad writers. She was attractive enough. Yet by now she had learned that there was so much more to pairing and succeeding than exteriors and appearances. An effective relationship was monstrously complicated. And all a woman could bring to the challenge of developing a good one was intuition and a little common sense. Buckshot for hunting rhinos. She wheeled the van around and headed back toward the Tot Lot.

She supposed she should thank April Tolliver for the information about her daughter's deep desire. She had done the right thing. Even though at that moment finding a father for Clarisse and a good husband for herself seemed a lot like one more problem she didn't need.

There was a white van parked in the Tot Lot drive next to the no parking sign. WLIT TV, read the van logo. She was alarmed. Was something wrong? After parking her car she hurried inside. The care sessions were in full swing. All was calm. She heaved a relieved sigh. But in her office she found two men, one sitting, one standing with a video camera and light unit on his shoulder. When she walked in, he swung the camera toward her. The lights blossomed brightly and he began to tape her.

"What are you doing?" she asked indignantly.

"What we do best," the seated man said. "Getting the *image!*"

The camera man said nothing. He adjusted focus slightly. His lights blazed steadily. Behind the glare, Mariah glimpsed the gleaming pate of a shaved head. "What do I have to do to stop him from doing that?" she asked.

"No sense asking Oscar anything. He doesn't talk. They took out his voice box a year ago. Too many days at three packs per." The seated man was about forty. His hair was black, except for a narrow swath of white running back from the right side of his forehead. His features were pointy, cheeks, chin, and nose above all. It protruded like a hawk's beak, its nostrils dark and cavernous. He wore an expensive silk suit—tailored, Mariah imagined. "Guess you know who I am?" He grinned. His teeth were large, squarish, and expensively capped. Amusement hooded his heavy lidded black eyes.

"I'm afraid I don't." Mariah felt some irritation.

"Phil Fontenot. *Inside Track.* Monday nights. Channel 7. Top-rated investigative reporting, broadcast in three states."

Mariah didn't have much time to watch TV. She tried to keep Clarisse away from it, too. Particularly from the kind of smut and slut shows she suspected *Inside Track* to be. She glared at Oscar. "Please stop with the lights, okay?" The lights blazed on, the camera rolled. For the first time, she felt assaulted. *"Please!"*

"All right for now, O.," Fontenot said. The lights died; the video camera light went off.

Mariah felt intruded upon and didn't like it. "What brings you here, if I might ask?"

Fontenot's unpleasant smile widened. "A letter. A big blonde brought it to the station late yesterday—"

"Who was she?" Mariah demanded.

Fontenot shrugged. "Nobody got a good look at her." He rose. "I didn't know what I'd find here at the Tot Lot. What a nice surprise for me!"

Mariah frowned. "What's surprised you?"

"You. Nice brunette with class. The minute you came in here I could smell class."

Mariah felt herself color and put her hands on her hips. "I believe you're working your way onto thin ice, Mr. Fontenot. Let me ask you again why you're here. Something to do with a letter?" She knew by now her face was scarlet. That annoyed her. She shouldn't be bothered by this man.

"Quite a little *billet-doux* she left." His black eyes determinedly sought hers. What was this, Mariah wondered. A test of wills? She stared right back at him. "Said enough to get me over here with an idea of maybe blowing the lid off you and your Tot Lot.''

Fear twitched near her heart like a small animal. ''I can't imagine what you're talking about. What was in this letter?'' She tried to keep her voice firm.

''Some juicy stuff . . .'' He paused. His grin widened. ''From eight, nine years ago. Some newspaper clippings. They had leads like 'Day Care Center from Hell.' And my favorite . . .'' Again the pause and the shameless leer. '' 'Porno Abuse Peaks with Dead Waif.' ''

Mariah's head spun. She grabbed for a chair and realized dimly that she wasn't going to make it. Agonizing memories rushed in like red waves and rolled over her . . .

It had been her new husband Rudy who had hurried her into finding a job. ''You have a college education,'' he would say. ''They're supposed to be worth bucks. How about going out and earning some?'' She ought to have asked him what had happened to his plans for that house construction partnership he had touted before their wedding. Or his brainstorm to use some of his camera skills and expensive equipment to find work as a professional photographer. Hindsight was wonderful stuff. Bingo! every time. Instead of demanding that he carry his share of the responsibilities, she had hustled into the employment arena, where her interests and education had centered on child care.

She went to the state first, but there were too many exams and long delays. All followed regularly by rejection. Only gradually did it dawn on her that the really good jobs went to friends of political friends. She went on to the want ads and employment agencies. She was given three interviews and was turned down each time.

Her inclination was to be more patient, but Rudy was on her every night after she came home from job hunting asking if she had found anything.

So when she was on her way to food shop and saw a help wanted sign beside another reading "J. D. Day Care" she stopped the car. Blond Jacquelyn DuMarr was impressive with her flamboyance and energy. Equally impressive was the crowd of children under only partial control filling the first floor of her house. "I need help and I need it *now*," Jacky had said. As badly as she needed it, she wasn't prepared to pay much. With a better self-image, Mariah might have held out for more money or gone elsewhere. But then, years ago all she thought was how wonderful it would be to be employed. She took the job. Rudy took her out to dinner at Roy Rogers; she paid.

There was much to be done at J. D. Day Care. She was younger and more energetic than the middle-aged women Jacky had gathered as her staff. She also found that she was more knowledgeable than they about children's needs and what ought to happen in a day-care center. While she didn't really assert herself, her actions spoke for her: higher quality snacks that she helped pay for out of her own pocket, more games and art supplies, more organized activities and unplugged TV sets.

There were staff changes. Working with Mariah proved too taxing for some of the women who had been doing as little as they could in exchange for pin money. Jacky seemed willing to let Mariah handle the new hires—some enthusiastic child-loving high school graduates who fit right in with her idea of how things should be done.

Jacky was fond of boasting about her waiting list. It was a day-care center's bragging point. "Since you came to me a year and a half ago, Mariah, my waiting list has expanded by eighty percent!"

Mariah snapped up the praise like a starving fish. Rudy's business ventures had all gone sour. They needed money. He had been after her to push Jacky for a raise. So right then she asked for it.

Jacky looked startled. That day she wore a strange hat made of bird feathers that Mariah imagined broke most of the endangered avian species laws at one blow. "You ought to look at the books to see how much it costs to run this place since I hired you," she said. "It costs money to do things your way. I have to save it somewhere. I just can't pay you any more." She shrugged, her fleshy face in a *moue* of displeasure. "I mean—look at the books!"

"I'd like to do that," Mariah said.

"Any time."

But Jacky never showed the books to Mariah. And Mariah was too timid to ask again. When Rudy confronted her with her failure to get a raise, she agreed to work longer hours at her present rate to bring in more money. Against that promised income increase he went out and bought himself a 500 mm. telephoto lens for his top-of-the-line Nikon SLR.

Despite the pay, Mariah was pleased with her job. Of course, it was the children, with their bright eyes and eagerness, that delighted her days. Dealing with them was so much more enjoyable and easier for her than interacting with adults. Sometimes it seemed that the older people became, the rougher, ruder, and more selfishly they behaved. Or was it more that they were not afraid to try to work their wills and she was? The months flew by, filling her life. J. D. Day Care was open fifty-two weeks a year, the only closings being New Year's Day, Fourth of July, Thanksgiving, and Christmas. Jacky was considering remaining open those days, too, and charging a premium. The question was were there enough Pakistanis,

Koreans, Japanese, and Thai children enrolled who didn't celebrate those holidays to make the change worthwhile

Though she didn't clearly realize it at the time, Mariah was happier at J. D. Day Care than she was at home. To one freshly wed it wasn't obvious that Rudy wasn't keeping his half of the bargain. He was irregularly employed always at jobs like apprentice salesman, heavy equipment operator, and third-shift supervisor. In his mind, these positions were pregnant with possibilities, but in fact his stay in any job ended after two or three months. Always he claimed he was supervised by "assholes." Though he had time on his hands, he didn't clean, cook, or play handyman. Mariah wasn't sure what he did during his unemployed days, only that he wasn't home. When she asked him what he was doing, he told her he was "scoping out the territory."

Often Mariah went to Jacky with suggestions for improving things. Usually she took them, often without deliberation. While she played a minor role with the children, she nonetheless seemed to be completely occupied She had gained weight, her face rounding about her heavy sensuous lips. She seemed supremely satisfied in way that Mariah failed to grasp.

Possibly that was because Mariah had her own agenda It filled her with secret satisfaction. Every one of her successful improvements went down in an expanding résumé. By now it was impressive. She was going to give J. D. Day Care another three months, then go elsewhere to find a better child-care job at a higher salary.

At home there was some wonderful news. She was pregnant! For a few sunny weeks she was delighted with how her life was going.

The horror began with the most trivial thing.

Five-year-old Eddy Swale caught a cold in May.

Mrs. Helen Swale, a huffy woman Mariah would never have nominated for Mother of the Year, got angry at the news of illness because a sick kid meant a day at home for her. She wasn't paid when she was at home. So she took out her anger on poor Eddy. Later under oath she admitted she had grabbed his shoulders and shaken him, shouting, "What the hell do you *do* at day care that makes you catch cold?" Badly frightened, Eddy answered, "I have to be sometimes with no clothes on!" Then he burst into tears because Ms. DuMarr had told him over and over never to talk about his "Quiet Times" with her and her camera.

There was talk before there was action, talk that Mariah never heard. The first faint breeze from the hurricane to come was the sudden resignation of her two teenaged assistants. One day they walked in and claimed they had found other jobs. Thanks for all Mariah had taught them. Sorry for the short notice. Zoom! Gone.

Shortly afterward Jacky announced that Mr. and Mrs. Swale had made a conference appointment. "I want you to sit in, Mariah," she ordered.

Mr. Swale was big and beefy, by day a wrestler of electrical cables and conduits. Mrs. Swale stood short and poised, left foot out like a boxer moving in to jab. She shuffled forward into Jacky's living room office. "We want to know what the hell's going on here!" she growled.

When Mariah first heard the Swales' charges she was astonished. Jacky had made Eddy strip and stand alone or with other boys and girls while she photographed him? What nonsense! Jacky heard them out. For once Mariah was glad the woman was loud and forceful. "That is the biggest bunch of dangerous bullshit I have ever heard!" she roared. "And if I hear any more of it I'm calling my attorney!"

Mrs. Swale, clearly the spokeswoman, said, "You better call your attorney anyway. We've been talking to the Changs. It wasn't easy for them to get it out of their Jasmine. But you sicko, you made her spread for you!"

Jacky flew into a rage that made Helen Swale's anger trivial in comparison. Then she threw the couple out. "And forget sending your kid to J. D. anymore. He's outta here!"

Five minutes later Jacky was still bristling and muttering. Mariah felt terrible for her. To have those kinds of false charges leveled at Jacky could jeopardize J. D. Day Care altogether. "The ideas kids get into their heads!" Mariah said. "Lord knows where they get them. And one accusation leads to another. Children are extremely susceptible to leading questions." She cast a questioning glance at her boss. "Maybe you *should* get an attorney. Accusations like that can cause big trouble."

"The hell with shysters! The hell with the Swales, too. They can take their lying little geek's bull and shove it!"

"But if Jasmine—"

"I'll handle it, Mariah." Jacky drew a deep breath and squared her shoulders. "I don't have a thing to worry about. My hands are *clean!* "

That night Mariah told Rudy what had happened. "Some loonies," he said about the Swales. Then he thought for a moment. "You've never seen your boss with a camera, have you?"

"Of course not!"

"Hey, keep your eyes open. You never know. It's a crazy world." He touched his pocket, a familiar gesture. "You got any money?"

Mariah made a face. "Just a few dollars. I was going to go out and pick up some milk. I'm trying to eat better. The gynecologist said—"

"Yeah, sure. Do it." He tossed his big shoulder, a characteristic move. Even pestering her for a few dollars, he was still a handsome dog in her eyes, with his thick head of blond hair, the wide forehead and Superman chin. She sighed inwardly. And she was still as malleable as clay in his hands. She trusted him with her life, which she had vowed at the altar to give to him. What was a few dollars in light of that commitment? She gave him the money and a happy smile.

Six

Jacky drew Mariah into her defense of J. D. Day Care Center. She asked her to handle the phones for the next few days. The first calls she took were from a half dozen parents who, in clipped voices, withdrew their children. Others were nameless abusers calling down the wrath of God and society upon her and Jacky, but not giving their names. It was so unfair! Neither Jacky nor she had done anything wrong. They would just have to wait till the undeserved rumormongering died down.

Then the media entered the picture. She found the first article tucked away in the borough section of the local paper. "Officials Investigate Charges against Day-Care Center," the headline read. The article said that the state licensing board and the police were investigating charges of sexual abuse and corruption of minors. She rushed to Jacky's office crying, "None of this is true! What investigation?"

Jacky didn't quite meet her glance. "I been getting

some calls when you weren't around," she allowed. "And some visitors at home."

Mariah was indignant. "Why don't they give it up? One hysterical little boy . . ."

Jacky stood up, solid as a pillar. "I gave them what for, don't you worry. But cops are cops and government snoops are all the same. Who knows what it'll take to get them out of our hair?"

Mariah was relieved to see and hear the old abrasive "give-'em-hell" Jacky. For a brief moment she had actually wondered . . .

A reporter called her at home. She was about to hang up on him when he asked, "How do you feel your position has been affected by the cops finding that trunk of photos?"

"Finding . . . what?"

"For a lady in deep shit, you don't seem to know the score," the reporter said. "The cops had a warrant. They found your trunk."

"I don't own a trunk!" Mariah snapped.

"And *I* never went to a dirty movie," the reporter said with a rough chuckle.

Mariah slammed the receiver down with a choked cry. What trunk? *What was going on?*

When Rudy came home she told him about the calls. "I'll be a son-of-a-bitch!" he said.

"What should I do about all this?" Mariah asked. "I'm really getting nervous."

He moved closer, always light on his feet. He chucked her gently under the chin and made her look up into his dark brown eyes. "You do one goddamned thing wrong, babe?"

"No, of course not. I—"

"Then you got nothing whatever to worry about!"

After that he went out for the evening.

The next week at the center was a nightmare. While some children had withdrawn, other parents in doubt about the rumors were anxious to be reassured. Jacky seemed never to be around when they pressed close to express their concerns. "The rumors are the worst kind of unfounded gossip. Everything at J. D. Day Care is *all right*," Mariah said over and over to dozens of faces. Parents could trust the staff—absolutely!

Children sensed their parents' uncertainty and the mood within the center. There were more than the normal number of quarrels and fights and fewer extended periods of concentration. Stories and games that had delighted in earlier months now led to long looks out the windows and unexplained crying fits. Supervising was stressful and exhausting.

Part of the cause was the shortage of staff. The departure of Mariah's two trusted high school graduates and her inability to find anyone to take their places meant that she, Jacky, and Conchita Rico tried to run things. Jacky proved to be part of the problem. Her periods of distraction were now deeper and more frequent. She left too much in Mariah's hands. Rather than confront her with the situation, Mariah tried to work harder and get Conchita to do the same. The two women found themselves rushing from crises to minor emergencies like critters on a treadmill with no time to be thorough or careful. Mariah was so exhausted that she felt on the edge of a breakdown. She began to take shortcuts with her grooming and dress. She adopted a daily uniform of sorts, dark brown slacks, one of her collection of short-sleeved white blouses, and sneakers. She pulled her hair together with the same polka-dot kerchief.

One Friday afternoon, she felt that she couldn't bear

J. D. Day Care for another moment. When the place settled down temporarily, she told Conchita she had to take a short walk. She walked down the block to the deserted park. She eased down on a bench. She couldn't afford to be away for more than ten minutes. In her fatigue she found her eyes closing. Very much against her wishes, she fell asleep. When a passing street sweeper startled her with a sprinkling of spray, she sprang up drowsy and bewildered. Her watch told her she had been asleep a half hour. She rushed back to Jacky's house.

She found Conchita and an assembly of children standing in rows. The white-faced woman was counting, Mariah sensed not for the first time. As she rushed into the room, Conchita said, "One is missing! They were out in the yard. A toilet started overflowing and I—"

Mariah bolted outside into the middle of Jacky's yard, where she searched frantically in all directions. Where was the child? She shouted, "Past time to go inside!" And watched for the slightest motion with the eagerness of a cat outside a mouse hole. The late May sunlight angled down through the shading branches of the sole tree, a huge oak. What the light seemed to illuminate most was the inadequate fencing.

She broke into a hurried scuttle that carried her past all the possible hiding places. Maybe the child had gone inside unnoticed. She rushed back. Where was Jacky? Where the *hell* was Jacky, with a kid maybe missing? She found no missing child in the house. Maybe he or she had only hidden beyond finding. She prayed that was so.

Conchita was so shaken that she couldn't figure out the identity of the missing child. When Mariah got back to the assembly, Conchita was staring at a list. Mariah told her it was out of date and filled with cross-outs and add-ons as well. She scanned the twenty-seven children. Which one was missing?

"Anybody know who isn't here?" she asked.

A voice piped up, "Dotty. Dotty's not here."

Dotty Orel! Oh, Lord! She *had* been there earlier, before Mariah had gone for a walk, she was sure of it.

Jacky lumbered into the room. "What's happening? Why the lineup?"

"Dotty Orel isn't here!" Mariah's voice was shrill. "She's missing!"

Conchita muttered in Spanish and blessed herself.

Jacky cursed. She moved front and center to the group. "Listen up, little people!" she ordered. "Any of you see where Dotty went?"

There was a chorus of Nos and head shakings.

"Listen, we need to find her," Jacky insisted. "Help us if you can. This is important!"

"This is a game, huh?" Elmore Thurgood asked. He was a five-year-old with round eyes and creamy brown skin. "You know where she is."

Mariah asked, "Why do you say that, Elmore?"

" 'Cause *you* helped her over the fence."

Elmore had been at the other end of the yard, and just caught a glimpse of the disappearing Dotty and "the lady who helped her over the fence." At the edge of panic over the missing girl Mariah told him it wasn't she he had seen. At this his eyes widened. "Saw you," he insisted.

"You didn't!"

"Saw you!"

"No!"

Jacky looked at Mariah strangely. "Cool it!" she ordered.

Mariah said, "Jacky, I don't like this!"

"You think I do, you twit?" She pressed a clenched fist to her heavy lips. "We gotta call the cops."

"No!" Mariah felt her world crumbling.

"Well, *we* can't find Dotty, can we?" Jacky asked.

Mariah found her eyes on Elmore, now chatting with the others about having seen her go off with Dotty. She wanted to shriek at him to be still.

"And we've got to call the Orels." Jacky turned her face to the ceiling and threw up meaty arms. "I can't friggin' be*lieve* this!"

How many times since that afternoon had Mariah regretted losing it at that moment! Maybe it wouldn't have happened if she hadn't been exhausted from weeks of overwork. She scarcely remembered her cries. She bolted, Jacky's orders to come back falling on her deaf ears. She found herself in her car careening through city streets then onto the expressway and out into the country. She was alternately laughing and bawling. Radio blasting, she howled along with rockers and folkies. She didn't know where she went. She came back to herself in the parking lot of an interstate truck stop. It was past midnight when she drove home drained and exhausted. She trembled so much that she couldn't hold her toothbrush. Crawling into bed, she didn't wake Rudy. She didn't want to bother him with her troubles; he never liked to be awakened after falling asleep.

The days after Dotty's disappearance forever stirred in her memory, recollections popping up here and there. Above all she remembered her defenselessness, made worse by her habit of trying to please everyone. Conscientious, she went back to the day-care center the next day. Audrey and Truman Orel were there, frantic about their child who hadn't yet been found. Audrey was nearly

hysterical and made wild accusations about Jacky and
Mariah. She was ugly in her rage and obscenity. Repeatedly she said that she "should have pulled Dotty out of
here the minute she heard the rumors." Truman, a slightly
built man with a delicate face, made sincere threats
through clenched teeth. He promised lawsuits and physical violence—or worse—should his Dotty not be found.

Two anxious days passed in which the last tatters of
order and control were torn away from J. D. Day Care.
Conchita disappeared. Left to Mariah and Jacky were a
half-dozen children whose parents' ignorance or indifference still delivered them to the doorstep. Mariah tried
hard to persuade herself that things weren't as bad as they
seemed. She didn't believe the accusations about her boss
photographing the children. Possibly a relative had come
and taken Dotty away, the result of some kind of family
dispute that the Orels weren't willing to make public. She
hoped desperately that in the end everything would be
all right.

The police found Dotty in the woods two miles from
J. D. Day Care. She had been mutilated with what they
said was a cleaver or machete and strangled with a rope
fashioned into a hangman's knot. Jacky phoned the news
to Mariah. After hearing it, she threw down the receiver,
screamed and clutched handfuls of hair. She tore at them
like a madwoman and howled out bitter tears. The child
was dead; her worst fear had been realized.

And now what was going to happen?

The media pounced on J. D. Day Care like hunting
cats. Where *had* they found those photographs of her and
Jacky together? Reporters clustered around Jacky's house
like swarming bees. The big woman locked them out.
They fell upon the few parents who came and went,
mikes and cameras aimed like arrows. They tried to shove

in when a child changed hands. Jacky overflowed with curses. When it was time to close the center for the day, Mariah was in despair. She couldn't face that *horde*. She had been a wreck for the last two days. A look in the bathroom mirror showed a disheveled, flushed creature on the verge of lunacy. She couldn't take much more.

Jacky went on the offensive. She rummaged in her attic and came down with an automatic shotgun. She opened the front door and fired two blasts over the heads of the hovering. They dove for cover. Shortly afterward, both women were on their way in separate cars. Mariah sped home. She badly needed Rudy's advice and consolation.

But Rudy wasn't home.

The phone rang on and off for the next two hours. She ignored it while she paced and waited in vain for her husband's return.

She sank down in a chair and pressed a clenched fist to her cheek. First the accusations about the lewd photography. Now one of *her* children had been abducted and murdered. Poor innocent Dotty Orel! She was distraught past tears. She stared wide-eyed at the wall. A chill surged through her. Lurking behind it, like a long shadow on a summer day, were the words of little Elmore.

I saw you . . .

She had to talk to somebody! She picked up the phone and called Jacky. She began to excitedly explain how bewildered and upset she was. Jacky cut her short. "Got a pencil?" She gave her an address. "Be there tomorrow. Ten in the morning."

"But what about the center?"

"Figure it out. I closed it down."

"You *closed* it?"

"Till further notice."

Thinking about it, Mariah realized nothing else could

be done. "What's this address, Jacky? Why should I go there?"

"It's where our attorney has his office. His name's Sally Silver. You'll *love* him."

"Why do we need an attorney? We didn't do anything."

"Wise up, Mariah!"

Mariah slept a total of twenty minutes that night. Her mind darted among triple concerns. First and worst was the murder. Who had abducted and killed pretty Dotty Orel? How was that tragedy going to affect her life? What would the Orels do and say? What about the police?

Then there was the matter of the accusations against Jacky—and her. Yes, *her!* Had something innocent that her boss did in past weeks been misinterpreted until it seemed to parallel a small part of the Swales' claims? One of the angry parents on the phone had said not only Eddy and Jasmine had been "fouled," but three other children "and counting," he snarled. Mariah had dismissed his charges as a symptom of mass hysteria. But now she wasn't sure . . .

There was a third very good reason why she didn't sleep.

Rudy didn't come home that night.

When morning finally came, Mariah found her way to Sally Silver's office. The attorney was a nervous little man with bad pores and a string tie. His sentences and movements were choppy and abrupt. He reminded Mariah of a caged rodent. He occupied a single-room office, one half of which once had the outline of a legal library. Time had disarrayed the bulky volumes and heaped papers in yellowing moguls atop available flat surfaces. He swept two chairs free. Jacky sank her ample bottom down and bellowed, "We didn't do a goddamned thing!"

The next twenty minutes' conversation Mariah found

baffling. To her it seemed both Attorney Silver and Jacky were speaking out of both sides of their mouths. One moment they were amplifying Jacky's and Mariah's guiltless positions, the next talking about accusations, evidence, and pleas. The more they talked, the more upset Mariah became. She wanted all this trouble to simply go away with Silver's help. It didn't sound as though that was going to happen unless they went to court. Unless they went to trial!

She couldn't bear this another moment. She jumped up. "I can't listen to you two going on like this. I didn't *do* anything to need a defense strategy for!"

"Sit down!" Jacky commanded.

Mariah sat.

Her boss leaned her bulk forward. "You knew about my Quiet Times with them," she said softly.

Mariah blinked. "Well, sure, but . . ."

"Maybe you kinda closed your eyes, huh? I mean, you never said anything, never asked any questions . . ." She turned to Silver. "She knew, Sally. She went along with it."

"Went along with *what?* If you're saying I knew you were taking smutty pictures—and I'm not saying you were—I didn't know anything about it. *Nothing!*" She hesitated. "And what about Dotty Orel?"

Jacky turned a cynical gaze toward her. "I'm clean on that one." She paused meaningfully. "How about *you?*"

Mariah stared at her blankly. What was she trying to say? That she had something to do with Dotty's death? She opened her mouth to shape a denial.

Jacky looked back at Sally Silver. "Couple times I had a real good idea she was peeping in on us. Getting her kicks from watching."

"Watching you do *what?* Are you saying?—" Mariah jumped up. *"I did no such thing!"*

"You better stick with me and Sally, honey," Jacky said. "Or you're going to be one sorry little lady."

Mariah gasped. *"I haven't done anything wrong!"* she shouted. She couldn't believe what she was hearing. She burst into tears and fled. She went home. The phone rang often; she let it roll over to the answering machine. Jacky, Silver, and the media. She didn't return any calls. She was busy being physically sick. The demands of the baby in her belly and stress proved too much for her system. She spent the afternoon huddled on the floor by the toilet waiting for the next surge of dry heaves.

The healthy anticipations of her pregnancy were being smothered by the horridness of recent events. Off and on all afternoon the doorbell rang. She crept up to peek cautiously out and saw TV news trucks. No, no! This couldn't be happening to her. She had never drawn any public attention in her life. Nor had she ever done anything criminal, ever. She wasn't capable of it. So why was this happening to her?

After dark she gathered up toiletries and clothes and stuffed them into her largest suitcase. She slipped out the back door, walked three blocks, then caught a cab to her Uncle Harry's apartment. A bachelor, he worked long hours behind a deli counter. At home he spent his time chain-smoking and playing with his model trains, whose tracks covered every room but the bath. "Gotta guard against the rust factor," he said.

Uncle Harry and she met seldom, twice a year at best. On the basis of such a sketchy relationship she loathed asking for sanctuary, but she had to get away from her apartment. Harry understood at once. Not for a moment did he link his niece with anything that had happened at J. D. Day Care. "You got yourself mixed up with a sick bitch. Maybe she's a killer, too. You're tangled up and it ain't gonna be easy getting untangled." He had sallow cheeks and a gravelly voice. She had never liked his stained hands or the smell of cigarettes around him. But when she looked into his pale blue eyes she saw the unmistakable affection for her that eradicated her minor complaints. "You sit tight here tomorrow," Harry ordered. "No door. No phone. At work I'll talk to Izzy. Izzy'll know a name. A name is what you need."

The name was Shelly Mortenstein. He was a senior partner in a major law firm. Mariah was in awe at the MacLean, Martello and Mortenstein, P. C. office furnishings: polished brass, waxed dark wood, and solid Scandinavian furniture good enough for a millionaire's living room. She was a little awed, too, by the sleek young women who manned the exits and entrances.

Shelly Mortenstein's administrative assistant introduced herself as Grace LeRoy. She was stylishly dressed and self-assured. She announced that Mr. Mortenstein was expecting her. After a short time, he came out of his office. He was a compact man in late middle age with graying hair that somehow suited him and added to his look of competence and success. It seemed to Mariah that he was everything she wasn't. He was rich, well-dressed, and confident. Within his lavishly furnished office, pictures of a striking younger wife and three college-age children suggested victories on the personal front as well. She felt intimidated.

At once he sensed it. He asked her if she wanted coffee. She hesitated.

His pepper-and-salt right eyebrow rose. Then he nodded knowingly. "We owe it to the world to express our desires, Ms. Erris." His smile, for all its control, was warm. She said she wanted a lemon seltzer.

"And so we begin . . ." he said softly.

He led; she responded. After an hour he raised a manicured hand and shrugged. "You're innocent of everything improper that happened at your day-care center."

"Of course I'm innocent!"

He leaned back and chuckled, nearly shaking the desk with his mirth. What amused him was something that as long as she sat on her perch of inexperience and naïveté she would never see. She now felt less intimidated. Intimidation had given way over the last minutes to envy. This man had so much—education, wealth, wisdom. He knew about this baffling world, grasped important concepts that she didn't, but knew existed just over the horizon of her understanding. "I simply can't believe this is happening to me," she said.

He smiled and the eyebrow went up again. "There's two ways this can go. One, the ongoing police investigation and its subsequent evaluation by the district attorney determine that there's insufficient evidence concerning the abuse and murder charges. Two, you admit to guilt and—"

"I didn't do anything!"

Shelly Mortenstein leaned forward, his smile warmer than ever. He paddled the air lightly with a horizontal palm. "Ms. Erris, please try to relax. Try to understand society's position. First it has a murdered child to contend with. A deed for which it clamors to assign responsibility and punishment. Furthermore, it has uncovered a situation of child abuse. I don't have to remind you, being in the line of work you are, that nowadays such abuse is hotter than making cookies in hell. Everyone's on the lookout for abusers. If crimes are committed, people expect someone must be punished for them."

Mariah bristled. "It shouldn't be me!"

"*Voilà!* There we have the reason to defend you, all the way to a trial, if necessary."

She couldn't keep herself from muttering, "I can't believe this!"

Another thing she couldn't believe was his fee, which was somewhere between the middle and high five figures, with no guarantees it wouldn't go higher. She told him she absolutely couldn't afford that much.

He nodded understandingly. "Nonetheless, that is my fee." The tone of his voice and angle of his head suggested he was demonstrating something more than the cost of first rate legal services. *We owe it to the world to express our desires.* He told her she needn't make a decision on the spot. She should go home and talk it over with friends and relatives.

Before opening his office door he said, "Until you make a decision about whether or not I'm to represent you, not a word to Mr. Silver, Jacquelyn DuMarr, or anyone else. Lie low. Gather your strength. Whatever happens, the next months will be times of testing—and hopefully growth—for you."

Mariah left distraught. She wanted Shelly Mortenstein to defend her. But she needed tens of thousands of dollars. What hope did she have of getting it? She remembered the silly stock certificates in her bureau drawer. What chance was there that they were worth even what she paid for them? Nonetheless, she dug them out and had her happy encounter with Jim Chesty.

When she got back to Uncle Harry's apartment, he was absorbed in his trains. He sat before a transformer whose console was worthy of a 747. As open coal cars clattered by, he absently flicked his cigarette at them. At least two were overflowing with butts and ashes. In a voice so low it seemed to come from her shoe tops she told him what had happened at the big law firm and with the stockbroker. "I'm sure Mr. Mortenstein would do a good job for me. But the only way I could afford him would be to sell all the EDI stock and everything else I own, which isn't much. That would leave me absolutely penniless, Harry."

"You could find somebody cheaper."

She hesitated. "I felt something when I was with that attorney. I don't know just what. I think he was . . . a wise man."

"So you want to hire him?"

"It's not possible. After I paid him I wouldn't have a thing left to my name."

Uncle Harry's eyes stayed on his switches and dials. He said nothing. By Mariah's count seven locomotives, cars clattering behind, came curving by her from all angles. "What you need is a loan," he said. "For, say, half the fee. The rest you get from selling a decent number of shares."

"I don't know any Waltons or Trumps to loan me that kind of money, Harry."

He shrugged his pinched shoulders. "You know me."

"*You're* going to loan me twenty-five thousand dollars?"

His thin smile showed teeth nearly green from tobacco. "What else does a guy fifty years old who never got married or bought a damned thing except money in the bank?"

"Harry, the way I'm going, it would take me a lifetime to pay you back." She laughed. "You wouldn't live to the end of my repayment schedule."

"Then we make a deal." One by one he shut down the trains till only one OH gauge Southern Missouri Line locomotive with its five cars was in motion. "Take a look at the loco, Mariah. What's wrong with it?"

As it swept past, his touch on the transformer slowed it. She studied it. On the next swing past she saw. "One of the drive wheels is loose," she said.

He shut down the console and turned to her. "They've found some spots on my lungs," he said.

Mariah started. "Oh, my God . . ."

"Nothing yet. But maybe before long . . ."

"Harry, you *have* to quit smoking. It's crazy to keep it up if—"

"I like smoking." As though to demonstrate, he took the cigarette out of his mouth and stuck that end in his nostril and inhaled that way. "It's what I do."

"But if you're starting to get spots, you *have* to quit." Mariah suddenly had forgotten all about her own problems.

"One thing I never wanted was to die alone," Harry said. "So here's the deal."

He proposed that should his spots in time turn to lung cancer she was to stop whatever she was doing, wherever she did it, and come back to nurse him day and night. He had lived in this apartment for thirty years. He wanted to die here as well. If he died quickly, she need only see to the funeral arrangements.

"What happens if you outlive *me*?" Mariah asked.

His sallow face seemed to settle like pale mud left by receding waters. "No way that happens," he said.

To Mariah it seemed he was being overgenerous. She tried to reduce the proposed loan by half. She could borrow the rest somewhere. He wouldn't budge. "You know what around-the-clock nursing costs? Twenty-five grand would be gone in no time. I ain't givin' away *nothing!*"

Mariah offered to write up a contract, provide for signatures and witnesses. He waved away her proposals of formality. "If I don't know my niece, I don't know nothing. Your word is as good as your heart." He held out his hand. "A shake is all the two of us need."

The next day the police found Mariah. A detective in a worn suit, a young officer, and his hard-eyed woman companion came to Uncle Harry's door. The homicide detective whose name was D'Orio did most of the talking. After introductions, the first thing he said was that Mariah had the right to have counsel present.

She thought of calling Shelly, but didn't want to bother him. In any case, she had done nothing wrong. She didn't mind answering their questions. She signed the release they gave her. It never occurred to her that they wouldn't be polite or pleasant. They gathered around her, sitting on chairs, Detective D'Orio directly in front of her and the two officers off to each side. He warned her that anything she said could be used against her. Just like in the movies.

"Ask me anything you want," she said confidently. She was happy to help them out in their investigation. The sooner the murderer was caught, the better. After some preliminary questions about personal data they moved right on to her activities the afternoon and evening of Dotty Orel's disappearance.

She interrupted them. "Why are you asking me about what *I* did? I didn't have anything to do with what happened to Dotty."

Detective D'Orio looked up from his notebook. He shoved the point of his pen toward her. "Just answer the questions, please." His eyes had a flinty look that Mariah didn't like. "Tell us what you did last Tuesday afternoon and evening."

Mariah found herself rattled under the stare of three pairs of hostile eyes. She stammered and had trouble remembering exactly what she had done and in what order. She told them about leaving the center and resting for a time on the park bench.

"Talk to anyone on your walk?" the detective asked in a clipped, suspicious voice. "Talk to anyone in the park?"

"Well, no. There wasn't anybody close by." Mariah frowned. She realized suddenly that they weren't just looking for general information. They thought she was guilty! That's why they were questioning her. How stupid had she been not to realize it. "I want to call my attorney!" she said suddenly.

The detective stared stonily at her. "You declined to exercise the right. And signed off on it."

"And we witnessed that." The woman officer carried the same air of threat and suspicion as her associates. Mariah couldn't know if they were bluffing about her rights or not. She was very frightened. It showed as their questioning continued. She stammered, stuttered, forgot, remembered, backtracked. Even under ordinary circumstances she could be made to feel guilty far too easily. Today's circumstances were far from ordinary. She could tell they didn't believe her.

The intensity of the questioning increased. To a degree the woman took Mariah's side, the two men attacking relentlessly. The pressure rose till Mariah thought she would explode into hysteria. "Just the same, a witness *saw* you with the Orel girl," Detective D'Orio said. "She was killed that evening. Why don't you tell us what *really* happened?"

"It'll make it easier on everybody," the woman officer said. "You, us, the kid's parents . . ."

"I told you everything that happened. I told you! *I told you!*"

Her descent into hysteria was rapid—and salutory, as Shelly Mortenstein explained a day later when the police decided to resume questioning Mariah. With a fatherly chuckle he added, "Another half-hour and they'd have had you confessing to murder, lewd photography, and disposing of Jimmy Hoffa's body." Mariah wasn't amused. She didn't like being reminded of her personality flaws.

Shelly was very much present at the next interrogation. Three detectives did the questioning. He was more than a match for them. As he headed them off, demanded they rephrase questions, and gently ridiculed certain lines of investigation Mariah grasped the extent of his experience and the grudging respect that he drew from the assembled lawmen. He didn't have to point out to her that she had made a serious error in talking to them without him.

Possibly a little tardily Shelly marched into Mariah's meager camp. Witnesses were questioned, evidence evaluated, and arrest warrants issued to her and Jacky. All this was so *wrong*, Mariah knew. Shelly shrugged that off. "It's a crazy world. You've been tried and convicted by the media already. You saw the papers: 'Porn Queens Off Tot?' The 'evidence' includes statements from two of the kids saying you were there when the camera was clicking and one who saw you removing the murder victim from the center not long before her death."

"I did not do anything! *Nothing!*" Her face was flushed.

Shelly shrugged. "Being innocent and proving it are two very different things." He looked at her quizzically. "As I *think* you're beginning to grasp. I'll handle everything. Don't worry. Now here's how I'm going to arrange your bail . . ."

Handling the bail and all that followed was a long complicated business, much of it technically legal and quite beyond Mariah. Shelly worked at distancing her defense from Jacky's as much as possible. He forbade her to talk to Jacky or Sally Silver. He sought to have the charges against Mariah dropped for insufficient evidence. When the judge refused, he tried to have the women tried separately. That didn't work either. Both he and Sally wanted to have the trial delayed, but Judge Rechter felt the heat of anti-abuse mania and the county's shock at the murder of a child, and ordered proceedings to continue.

The trial? For Mariah it was one long nightmare unrelieved by starting up wide awake in the middle of the night. It ground on and on. The prosecution made such dreadful charges, the defense countered. She and Jacky both took the stand where they suffered the professional abuse of the female prosecutors. Shelly surprised her with the quality and number of character witnesses testifying on her behalf. Though each was sharply crossexamined, her reputation came through largely unscathed.

The testimony of the accusing children was another matter. It was chilling to hear Olive Mornay and Setha Rannerjee swear with seeming certainty that Mariah had stood by while Jacky turned her camera on their nude bodies. And of course Elmore Thurgood still insisted he had seen Mariah help Dotty Orel over the fence to her death.

Audrey Orel wasted no media opportunities. When Mariah could bring herself to watch the news on any channel she could easily find the woman emoting in front of its cameras. Her theme with variations: whether or not Mariah and Jacky were found guilty she would personally wreak vengeance upon them. During one particularly dramatic interview she screamed, "If the law doesn't punish

them, I'll take revenge with these hands!" She held up two
tiny, inadequate ones before half collapsing into grieving
husband Truman's arms. Mariah swallowed. How could
she blame her with her daughter in the grave?

Shelly was gentle with Olive and Setha. The jury had
been shown photos of them posed naked together with
Eddy Swale; the girls had their sympathy. Mariah couldn't
see where Shelly was going with his questions. It took
her a while to understand why he was asking them about
her movements, position, clothes, what she said during
her supposed voyeurism. He was trying to draw them into
contradictions. After all, she hadn't *been* there. Shortly the
children were disagreeing over details. Olive burst into
tears after the seventh time that Shelly pointed out that
"her friend" Setha had said something quite different
about Ms. Erris. Mariah felt Shelly was being persuasive.
She wondered if the jury felt the same way, those nine
women and three men whose faces were inscrutable.

Shelly's questions to Elmore were aimed at establishing
the distance he stood from the fence when Dotty was
taken and to suggest to the jury that another woman
could have worn an outfit like Mariah's. Throughout,
he hammered at Mariah's attention and concern for the
children. He managed to make the boy agree that she was
by far J. D. Day Care's most compassionate staff member.

He put Mariah on the stand in an outfit that clearly
showed that she was four months pregnant. He fashioned
her testimony to illuminate her traditional beliefs, her
feelings about children and—she realized later—her
naïveté. He made it very obvious that she had no motive
to ever harm a child.

Without asking her, he had had some private conversa-
tions with Rudy. She didn't know what he'd said, but her
husband appeared every court day in his only suit and

sat supportively just behind her. His carefully prepared brief testimony described Mariah as a model wife and professional woman. She knew Rudy well enough to understand that Shelly had frightened him into mature behavior. Several months had to pass before it became clear to her what the attorney's threat had been.

While Shelly's defense was the result of thorough preparation and experience, Sally Silver's was emotional. He rushed off in different directions, never halting with one point long enough to make it convincing to the jurors. He harangued and emoted, suit coat off like some latter-day Clarence Darrow. He had made an effort to tone down Jacky's clothing, but her outfits still stuck out. His most valuable ally was Jacky herself whose self-confidence and brazen denials nearly convinced Mariah of her innocence. For long moments she found herself actually weighing Sally's hypothesis that the photos had been planted by persons unknown in an effort to assassinate Jacky's and Mariah's characters.

The summations brought to a conclusion the longest two weeks of Mariah's life. Her nerves were in tatters and her emotions so on the surface that events as trivial as running out of milk sent her into a tailspin of tears. The jury debated two days. Shelly summoned her from home to hear the verdict.

Looking down at nails, nibbled to the quick, Mariah heard the jury foreman announce the verdicts—Mariah innocent of child abuse, endangering minors, and murder; Jacky innocent of murder but guilty of the other charges. Mariah raised her face ceilingward and burst into tears of joy.

The heavy woman sprang to her feet, whirled and pointed to Mariah. "If I'm guilty, she's guilty," she shouted. *"She's guilty, too!"*

After the trial, Rudy left Mariah and didn't come back. Helga Holmann was a mutual friend who Rudy claimed "knew more about being a woman" than Mariah ever would. All Mariah knew about Helga was that she had a huge Teutonic bosom and a thick mane of blonde hair that looked as though it had to be wrestled rather than combed into place. She had found Helga cold and imagined her very likely calculating. Those thoughts did nothing to quiet her hurt. Numbed by the emotional assaults of the trial and the publicity, she hadn't the reserves to struggle against Helga to win Rudy back. Maybe if she had felt better about herself, she would have at least made him pay for his infidelity. As it was, she allowed him to arrange the divorce and set the terms. She didn't discuss the situation with Shelly—and paid the price: Rudy didn't give her a penny. He took the car and two end tables that he admitted Helga had always liked . . .

Later, Shelly told her that Rudy's daily court appearances had indeed resulted from fear. He had threatened the man. Should it just happen that Mariah needed a divorce lawyer, he told Rudy he'd take her case *pro bono*—no charge. Of course his private investigations had already revealed Rudy's adultery. Rudy guessed what Shelly knew. His imagination told him what the attorney could do with that information in front of a judge or jury. Shelly told him that if he behaved during his wife's trial it would be the last he'd see of him. Rudy for once in his life had sense enough to follow orders.

With Uncle Harry's help, Mariah moved into his apartment and stayed five months, long enough to give birth to Clarisse and begin bonding with her. Out of all the horrors of the last year had come this one grand blessing. She clutched the nursing child and closed her eyes to better savor her joy. When she wasn't treasuring Clarisse, she was planning her future.

With the cooperation of relatives, chiefly a distant cousin, Maureen, she flew to Ireland. Maureen and her family had a farm in County Donegal. There Mariah stayed, working in the fields and making quilts for her modest room and board. Under gray skies she found the rain washing away her wounds. The seasonal simplicity of farm life, the absence of urban confusions and strivings soothed her. She had unhurried time to spend with Clarisse. To bring herself into focus took four years. The misfortunes, centering around J. D. Day Care and what she now realized had been a bad marriage, receded, leaving her with something like peace of mind. The death of an in-law made more room available in the sprawling stone house; she was invited to stay on indefinitely, which she gratefully agreed to do. She had reached what she felt was a final, frank self-understanding: her personality wasn't made for American life. She felt she was too shy, unassertive and self-effacing to carve out a life for herself under her country's competitive rules.

No sooner had she settled herself and her daughter for an indefinite stay than the letter came from Uncle Harry. He had lung cancer. He hoped he didn't have to remind her about their deal.

Life wasn't going to give her an easy out.

It took Harry two years to die. Even in dying he gave. He gave her power of attorney over his small nest egg. And he talked to her about herself. Propped up in bed, ashen faced and puffing away defiantly, he repeatedly reminded her of her virtues and strengths. Life had dealt her some bad hands, he said, but that didn't mean she couldn't play the game. After he died, she should think about a career for herself. He had followed the trial and understood what a hot shot child care provider she was. He had talked to his broker. The child care boom was going to go on for a while. People were having more kids now. One salary didn't cut it any more. Day care had moved from luxury to necessity. She should go for it!

Mariah didn't. Not while Harry needed her, which he did more and more as the cancer accelerated. One day he was too weak to reach for the Camel straights pack on his bedside table. He refused the doctor's advice to use oxygen and died in a coughing fit three days later.

Many memories of Harry stayed with Mariah, particularly the most recent ones.

Go for it!

So she gathered herself once again, as she had done in Ireland, and went forth. To plan, to capitalize, to design a day-care center and a new life.

Seven

Mariah floundered up from her faint and found herself sprawled on her office couch. She felt defenseless and disheveled. Phil Fontenot stood by with a wet cloth in his hand. Oscar sat unmoving in her desk chair, the camera on his right shoulder pointing forward like an animal snout.

The letter! She sat up stiffly and looked around. The office door was closed. "Someone sent you a letter about me?" she asked in a shaking voice.

Fontenot sat beside her, too close for her taste. He ran both hands back over his white-streaked hair. "You're a lady with a past, it seems," he said.

"If you've read those clippings—or anything else—you've found out that I was acquitted of all charges."

Fontenot chuckled. He looked at her piercingly as a hawk over his heavy pointed nose. "How long do you think this place would survive if word got out that you were tried for child abuse and murder."

"I wasn't guilty," Mariah said determinedly.

Fontenot shrugged, as though guilt or innocence was beside the point. "While we were trying to bring you around, Oscar and I were talking things over. Well, I mean, *I* was talking. Oscar was listening and looking, as usual. What we figured was . . ." He waved his hand to include the whole Tot Lot. "We don't need this one. We've got so many others."

"You don't need this one?" Mariah frowned. "I don't quite understand."

"Our getting a letter doesn't mean we *have* to do anything about the Tot Lot. We can pretend we never got any letter. It's our right to do that."

Mariah looked at him uncertainly. "Well, that would really make me happy," she admitted.

"If I make you happy, you should make me happy," Fontenot said. He was staring intently at her, his black eyes burning.

Mariah grew very suspicious. *"How?"* she said pointedly.

"I have a feeling that underneath those loose clothes you have nice skin, a nice body . . ."

Mariah jumped to her feet. Her head spun from her recent faint. However, there was nothing wrong with her indignation. "And you want to get your hands on it? Is that right?"

"It did occur to me." Fontenot's eyes traveled the length of her.

Mariah turned toward silent Oscar. His hairless skull gleamed like a snow hill. "And what about him? He want to join in?"

"Oscar likes to watch. And tape."

Mariah pointed. "There's the door, guys. Use it!"

Fontenot made no move to get up. "Okay, so you're

a virtuous lady. We're impressed. Your point is made. Now—think about what you're doing."

"I have thought. I—" She staggered. She wasn't yet steady on her feet.

"You have plenty to spare of what I want, Ms. Sullivan. What you don't have plenty of is reputation. So I can sink you *easy*."

"I don't think you will. You must have some kind of a conscience," Mariah said. "You can't be as small-minded and sordid as you sound."

Oscar made a weird wheezing that Mariah understood was laughter.

Fontenot rose to his feet; Oscar did the same. "Think it over. No rush."

"No chance."

Fontenot moved close to her and stroked her bare forearm. "I'm willing to wait to touch skin like this."

She raised her foot and brought it down on his instep with her weight on her heel. His shout of pain was satisfyingly loud. She spun toward Oscar. "You want one, too, Daddy Warbucks?"

Oscar shook his head. His wide gray eyes shone with disturbing mirth.

Recovering, Fontenot's eyes were dark. "You got a couple days. That's it, Ms. Tot Lot! You can call me at the station."

Mariah controlled herself until they had gone. Then she staggered down onto the couch. Bad enough their lechery. But who had sent them the letter? She was sick thinking those two toads knew what had happened at J. D. Day Care. They could bring all the horrors of her past to life like summoned demons for public consumption.

Things were getting worse. A lot worse.

She needed time to think. But she couldn't gather her

thoughts. They coalesced then spun apart, the cycle repeated throughout the day.

Not until she was nearly ready for bed did she regain full control of herself. She saw what she was up against.

A woman somehow connected to the past was out to destroy her.

She didn't know what to do. She would have to think about it.

Undressing for bed, she took off her blouse and reached behind to unfasten her bra. Her fingers froze on its fasteners. She always used the inner eyes for a tight fit. The hooks were inserted in the outer ones. In a rush of humiliation and anger, she knew what had happened.

When she was unconscious that afternoon, Fontenot and his camera toad had stripped her to the waist and taped her topless!

She growled and hugged herself, rocking in search of calm. Loathing crawled over her like a disgusting snail. Those rotten bastards! . . .

It took her better than an hour to calm herself. Even then she couldn't sleep. Three times she got up to check on Clarisse, who dreamed on, oblivious to her mother's mental state.

Mariah was dismayed at how matters were unexpectedly unfolding. Who had left the messages and effigy at the Tot Lot? The same woman who had taken the letter to the TV station? She thought of the characters returning unexpectedly to her life, like actors in a play she had thought long over! The Orels, her ex-husband Rudy, her ex-boss Jacky. Were there to be more reappearances or would her clouded future feature more new, sinister players like Phil Fontenot?

She groaned up into the darkness.

It's all going to happen again!

* * *

In the morning she got Clarisse on the bus and then found herself running a little late. She rushed out to the van. A man was leaning against the driver's side door.

It was Rudy Erris.

"Gotcha!" he smiled.

Mariah's displeasure was partially smothered by her shock at the changes eight years had made in his appearance. His thick head of blond hair had thinned, as had his face. He still had his Hollywood model chin, tissue now stretched too tight across the bone. His face mirrored his voice: he was a frantic man under pressure further exposed by the eager forward slanting of his body as she approached. "I don't want to talk to you," she said.

"Got to." He didn't budge from his post by the door.

For a moment she thought about turning around, going inside, and calling the police. But her last waking thoughts before her uneasy night's sleep revolved around quickly getting to the bottom of who was harassing her. The sooner she figured out who was behind it, the better for her. Right now she was ready to put her money on Jacky DuMarr. Yet who could say this man who had unexpectedly reappeared in her life didn't know something about what was happening. "Why have you been calling me?" she asked.

"Maybe to talk about old times."

"Eight years is a long time. And some of those times weren't so good, in case you've forgotten."

"I'm a different guy now," he said.

"Well, you have a different wife, that's one thing that's different." Mariah fought to keep the acid of old hurts from her voice.

"Helga's been great. We're getting along real good."

"Why do you want to talk to me, Rudy?" she asked. "And why does it have to be face to face?"

His features shaded as though a hood had been drawn down over them. He swallowed, hesitated. For a moment she thought he was going to turn around and leave in silence. When he finally spoke, she suspected he was encouraged by the memory of her once having been most vulnerable to his persuasive skills. She took a moment to remind herself she wasn't the same pushover she had once been. His thinned face manufactured a smile. "Maybe you could use some . . . protection."

Mariah barely smothered her gasp. "What do you mean?"

"Well, you got a new place, that Tot Lot. Maybe you need somebody to look after it, like a watchman, guard. You know."

Some things slid together in Mariah's mind. How far could she take this? "What makes you think a day-care center needs 'protection'?"

He shrugged. "Maybe I got a hunch."

"And how much would this service cost me?" She put hands on hips, tilted her chin up aggressively.

"I need ten thousand bucks," he said.

Mariah snorted. "I could use ten, too." She knew how gangsters worked it. They broke your windows, then allowed you to pay them to make sure it wouldn't happen again. No thanks! "What things would you protect the Tot Lot from, Rudy? Scary messages, threats, dummies in trees, letters to TV stations telling about what happened at J. D. Day Care?"

He scowled, hesitated. "Maybe," he said.

Amid the stormy lake of Mariah's distress floated a small craft called *Relief. This* bozo was at the heart of her problems. He and his Helga. He was the reason she was waking up nights and worrying about the past. She edged closer to him. "Listen, Rudy, I know what you're doing and it's not going to work. Get out of my life. No more dirty tricks or I call the police. Got it?"

"You don't know—"

"I know enough. Now clean up your act or you'll be talking to the cops." She tried to push past him to the door. He grabbed her shoulder. "Let go of me!" she spat.

"I need ten thousand bucks!"

"So do I. Now get out of my way." She shoved past him, got in and started the van. She rolled down the window. She saw puzzlement on his face. He was wondering where the old malleable Mariah was. The answer was: almost all gone.

He leaned his head in through the window. "You get me that money, Mariah, or you'll be damned sorry!"

"No way, José. Get a job!"

She shifted to drive and jerked out of her parking space. In the mirror she saw Rudy standing in the middle of the street, waving his fist.

Just try one more thing, she thought. And *you'll* be sorry!

At the Tot Lot she had trouble concentrating. She kept thinking of her ex reduced by life and what she realized now was a weak character to shabby schemes of blackmail. Well, he *had* succeeded in upsetting her with his nasty little tricks. She wished she had confronted him before today. Had she, then her threats would have stopped him from sending Helga with the revealing letter to that lecher Phil Fontenot.

She didn't know what to do about Fontenot. What he knew about her past could certainly hurt the Tot Lot. Her best hope, she thought, was to stall him off until she figured out how to deal with him. That slug! How she had tossed and turned last night thinking of him and his mute sidekick staring at her bare breasts. How humiliating!

In the afternoon, Clarisse arrived on the bus. Mariah was reminded of another problem—or perhaps it was an opportunity. She closed her office door and sat her daughter down beside her. She had the girl's favorite molasses cookies and a glass of milk ready. "Good day at school, kid?" she said.

Clarisse nodded, mouth full. She swallowed. "I got to help pass out the language arts papers!"

"Good for you!" Mariah hugged the girl. "You know what?"

"What?"

"I wish I knew some nice grown-up guys."

Clarisse looked up at her. "You do?"

Mariah nodded. "Do you believe your Mom gets lonely more than once in a while?"

"Yeah?" Clarisse looked genuinely surprised.

"Um huh." Mariah drew a deep breath. "How about you, honey? Do you wish there was a grown-up man around?"

Clarisse looked puzzled.

"I mean a nice man who came and visited and, say, did fun things with us." Mariah felt her daughter quiver weakly like a newly captured small animal.

"Could that happen?" Her voice was trembling.

"It could. Mom's been thinking about it. Having a male friend would be nice for me, too. Sharing might make—I don't know—a nicer life, maybe."

Clarisse began to cry and threw thin arms around Mariah. She didn't speak, just cried.

Mariah stroked her hair, nearly moved to tears herself.

"Listen, sweet. It can't happen right away. It's not like I have Aladdin's lamp or the three wishes stone."

The girl nodded vigorously.

"But I'll *try* to make it happen."

"There's Mr. Scoffler, one of the teachers at my school. He's nice."

Mariah leaned down, lips almost to Clarisse's ear. She whispered, "I know you want a daddy."

Clarisse looked up, wet-eyed and fragile. "Only if it's okay with you," she sniffled.

The phone rang and Mariah picked it up, hearing the wolfish tones of Phil Fontenot. She told him she'd call him back shortly. She hurried back to Clarisse and stroked her back. "So here's the deal, munchkin. If I find somebody I think we'll both like, I'll make sure you meet him quick. Is that a deal?"

"When will it be?"

Mariah shook her head. "I don't know. Sometime soon, I hope." She gave her daughter a Kleenex and led her down the hall to Rochelle Camwell's group. Returning to her office, she wondered if she had done the smart thing. Good men were harder to find than honest politicians. She hadn't hit it lucky in eight years. Why should she in the next week or month?

With gritted teeth she returned Fontenot's call. In a low voice he asked if she had considered his offer.

"What I considered is what you two sickos did to me while I was out cold!" she shouted.

"That's Oscar's style, not mine," he said.

Mariah was appalled that he didn't even bother to deny what they had done. "You do a program on me and you can be sure I'll tell the world what you did!" She hung up. When the phone rang immediately she let it roll over

to the answering machine. Fontenot didn't bother to leave
a message. She knew he wasn't through with her yet, but
she had bought herself some time.

Since the first message had been soaped across the Tot
Lot windows Mariah only now felt she was getting the
situation under control. She had laid down the law to Rudy.
She knew him well enough. He lacked the nerve to continue
in his outrageous blackmail scheme in the face of her warning. That would end the unpleasant incidents and balm her
tattered nerves. She would think of some way to deal with
Fontenot. She even managed a smile.

Her good mood lasted until about eight o'clock that
evening when her door chimes rang. She was glad she
had put Clarisse down for the night because her visitor
was her ex-husband's wife, Helga. For a moment she
dreaded facing the woman. Then she thought again. Like
Rudy, Helga too needed a sharp warning about helping
him in his blackmail scheme. After all, it must have been
she who dropped the letter off at WLIT-TV.

The big woman gave Mariah no chance to get a word
in. She shoved her way into the condo. "Where is Rudy?
You have him here, don't you?"

"I have no idea where Rudy is," Mariah said. "And
I don't remember asking you in."

Helga's head turned like a satellite dish in search of
Rudy signals. As she stomped into the living room Mariah
tried to grasp something of the woman's act. She observed
the calculated desperation in Helga's movements and
wondered just what role she was trying to play.

The years the woman had spent with Rudy had thick-
ened her, the flesh oozing in to fill what had once been
voluptuous curves. Her formerly jutting cheeks, once her
face's most commanding feature, had been softened by
the infiltration of fat. How little it had taken to erode her

striking physical presence! Her eyes clued Mariah as to the direction of her performance. Their roaming about was supposed to be in search of Rudy. Her supposed motivation: the evil spirit of jealousy. Rudy had fooled around married to Mariah. She was to believe he was up to the same tricks again—this time with *her* the other woman. That approach certainly had an icy logic behind it. Mariah wouldn't put it past Rudy to stray again.

Helga wore a light checked jacket and jeans. Her blond hair needed a good combing. She kept running her thick fingers through it in stagey vexation. "I know he's here!" she said.

"He's not here, Helga. And don't pretend you thought he would be."

The big woman turned narrowed eyes at Mariah. "I've heard him trying to call you."

"So what? I didn't want to talk to him."

Helga stepped closer. "I know you met him this morning." She inclined her head toward the street. "Out front." She clutched Mariah's arm. "Don't deny it. I saw you."

Annoyed by her touch and her act, Mariah shook her hand away. "Are you trying to make me think you followed Rudy?"

Helga tossed her head. Her matted blond hair stirred heavily. "I came to tell you one thing." Her bloodshot eyes met Mariah's. "Keep away from him!"

Mariah laughed. "I don't buy your little act, Helga. I know what you two are up to."

"I saw you talking," Helga persisted. "It didn't look to me at all like you wanted him to go away."

"Stop it!" Mariah scowled. "I know you're trying to pressure me into giving Rudy money."

Helga seemed not to hear. "He wants to go back to you!" Desperation sharpened the edge of her voice.

"He wants to get money out of me, Helga. *You* want to get money out of me." Mariah stepped forward authoritatively. "I don't buy your jealousy act, okay? You go home and tell your husband that. I'll repeat for you what I told him this morning: one more dirty trick and I call the police!"

Helga's face twisted in confusion. "What are you two trying to do to me?" she asked in a small voice.

"Stop it, Helga!" Mariah moved to the door. "I've warned you. I warned Rudy. Now I'm asking you to leave. Go back to him and talk it over. Get smart and stay away from me!"

The large woman moved toward the door, then hesitated. "You stay away from my husband!" she ordered.

"Drop the dramatics. I told you: I don't buy it." Mariah shoved open the screen. "And make sure Rudy gets the word, in case he didn't this morning."

When Helga was gone, Mariah poured herself a lemonade and sat on the couch. Now there could be absolutely no misunderstanding. If Rudy and Helga had one ounce of common sense, they would give up their crazy scheme.

Her troubles were over.

Eight

About ten, just as she crawled into bed, the phone rang.
Something told her to let the answering machine pick up.
It was Fontenot. His message was short: call him. His
tone was edged with threat. She hoped he wasn't the
impatient type. She hadn't yet figured out how to deal
with *his* blackmail effort. One blackmailer at a time,
please. Damn Rudy and Helga for having given the slimy
toad that letter!

With a mind more at ease than it had been in a week,
she turned her attention to ways she might improve her
social life and, in time, provide herself with a husband
and Clarisse with a stepfather. Not easy. She thought of
the single men who brought their kids to the Tot Lot.
Most were younger than she, and none that appealing.
As she ran through that half dozen, she supposed she
understood why their wives had run off or they had been
divorced. She wouldn't want to live with any of them.

She could always try the electronically enhanced advertisements. Leave your voice-mail message with the local newspaper. *Hello, caller, I am a thirty-two-year-old divorcee with a seven-year-old daughter . . .* Didn't *that* sound like a turnoff? Or she could pay big money and go to a singles' matching outfit and make a video tape. *Hello, match-seeker, this comely package likes to make cookies, enjoys traditional jazz and the magic realism of Latin American writers. Does not enjoy one-night stands or creepos like you maybe are—if you're not married . . .*

She groaned and twisted under the covers. No, face to face was the best way. Give the instincts, the ole chemistry a chance to work. Who knew what would turn her on? Or him, whoever and wherever he might be. Another factor: would Clarisse like him?

She sighed. This was going to be tough. She promised herself to talk it all over with Rita McRae. Mariah was anxious to see how she'd *pooof* away this one.

At the Tot Lot the next morning, she got a call from Felicia Greene, Jacky's parole officer. The regularly scheduled Jacky-Felicia meeting would be held later that morning. "So I'll just kinda slip in that you talked to me," Felicia said. "And that some funny things have been going on at your Tot Lot."

"I'm not really sure you need to go to the trouble, Felicia. I think my ex-husband's the one responsible. And I've warned him. He's trying to pressure me into giving him money. His new wife's in on it, too."

The black woman chuckled. "So you do day care *and* detective work," she said.

"Well, it seems pretty plain that—"

"You take it from Felicia Greene, ain't *nothin'* in this world plain as it seems. I'll have a few words with Jacky about you, if you don't mind. Just in case she's even *thinkin'* about bothering you."

Mariah swallowed. "She won't like it."

Again the chuckle. "Lotta things in this world people don't like. Life goes on just the same." She paused. "Where you *been*, honey?"

Hanging up, Mariah told herself that wherever she had been, she wasn't there any longer. She wasn't nearly as naive and trusting as she once had been. She was better able to handle herself in this often threatening world. She swallowed. She wished she had reached the point of knowing how to stymie Phil Fontenot without going to bed with him. *Yuk!*

Later that morning, Fontenot phoned. Randi Monroe, who took the call in her toddler area, forwarded it to Mariah. "It doesn't pay to ignore me," he threatened.

"I wasn't ignoring you. I was thinking about the situation." True enough.

"Well? You want to know where I live?"

Mariah sensed his earnest lust and the sincerity of his threat, but wasn't sure how to diffuse either. She did *not* want him to broadcast her past. "I'd like to talk to you." She surprised herself. "Can I buy you lunch?"

There was a Chili's restaurant halfway between the TV station and the Tot Lot. He agreed to meet her there at 12:30. During the drive there, she wondered what she would say. Her composure wasn't helped by finding his cameraman Oscar with him, camera on shoulder, though not in use. He explained that Oscar and his equipment went nearly everywhere with him. She forced herself not to dwell on the possibility that the bald one and his magic eye accompanied him into the bedroom as well. She swallowed her certain knowledge that the two of them had taped her topless.

An unwanted margarita in front of her, she found herself appealing to both Fontenot's better instincts and to his concern for his own reputation. Think about it, she urged. If she had been found guilty eight years ago, his "exposé" might make some sense. But she hadn't. So why bother? Someone with his reputation must have bigger fish to fry. If he insisted on including the Tot Lot on one of his shows, she'd make her own charges of attempted coercion. The sexual-harassment-sensitive world would love to know he wanted her to trade sexual favors for his silence.

He gulped his drink. "My word against yours. Not just mine," he said. He nodded at a silent Oscar. "The O's word, too. Written, of course." He reached across the table and wrapped thin fingers around her forearm. "More. *We* got the camera. We got the station. We got the forum. This is the post-electronic age. We're heading toward 2000 A.D. We got watchers, not thinkers out there. We got the first and best word, Mariah Sullivan. You got what? *Rebuttal?* Viewers don't have the patience for rebuttal. TV is like a street fight. The sucker puncher wins! Get with it!"

Mariah was tired of people telling her to get with it, get hip, get with the program—whatever. "I'm well aware of the advantage you have over me," she said evenly. "I'm simply asking you not to exercise it."

Fontenot's deep-set eyes were shrouded as his thoughts migrated elsewhere. Instinctively Mariah knew where they had gone—to the video tape they had made of her naked breasts. At that moment she despised all men. His focus sharpened not on her face, but on her blouse and each of its pearly buttons. Color rose in her neck. "You are a . . . horrid man," she breathed.

Oscar grunted and heaved in his chair. He couldn't speak, but there was no misunderstanding his nod.

"Come across, Sullivan. Get off your moral high horse," Fontenot said. "One night, like in the fairy tales, is all I'll need. One night and one tape that nobody but me and Oscar will ever see."

Mariah jumped to her feet. The table teetered, drinks splashed. "There ought to be a law against people like you!" she cried. Her face was crimson.

"All the laws are *for* us," he smirked. "This is America. We got a Constitution."

Mariah snatched up her purse and strode angrily away. Fontenot's voice, though set low, still carried through the diners' chatter. "Tonight is *Inside Track* night. I don't hear from you this afternoon, you're on it. It's goodbye, Tot Lot!"

Mariah fled without looking back.

Back in her office she tried to contain her outrage. She phoned Rudy and got Helga. "I want you to know that malicious letter you carried to *Inside Track* might just cost me my career. I just want you to know what your greed and stupidity are going to do to me!" Her voice tottered on the edge of the canyon of tears.

"Rudy wouldn't do anything to hurt you," Helga said in a dogged voice. "I think he's still in love with you."

"Rudy's already threatened me. He wants money. And you're trying to help him get it. Well, you're not going to! So you've messed up my life for nothing!"

"Listen to me, you foolish woman!" Helga shouted. "If you don't keep away from Rudy, *more* bad things will happen to you! Do you understand me? Do you think being embarrassed on a news program is the worst thing that could happen to you?"

"How can you be so stupid as to threaten me?" Mariah asked. "You think I don't know what the law and the courts can do to a person? Can do to *you*?"

"Worse can happen to you!"

"You're not getting one cent out of me!" Mariah

slammed down the receiver. More threats, more mischief—or worse? They wouldn't dare!

She needed advice in the worst way. But whom to ask? And whom to trust? She paced her office. She felt the near future threatening to envelop her like a suffocating blanket. Damn Rudy and Helga! Damn Fontenot! She had to *do* something.

A half hour later she had an idea. She picked up the phone and dialed a number in Clarion City that she doubted she'd ever forget. She expected to hear the voice of stylish Grace LeRoy, Shelly Mortenstein's administrative assistant. But the speaker was a stranger who told her Grace was no longer with the firm and that Mr. Mortenstein was out of the office indefinitely. Could one of the other partners help her? She thought not and hung up.

That afternoon she made sure she visited all the day-care groups and took part in plays and games. She tried to savor the accomplishments and hard work that had brought the Tot Lot and her own career to this prosperity. She helped monitor the playground and stood amid the swirl of children dashing through the September sunlight, wondering if after this evening anything would be the same.

Back in her office, she found herself staring from time to time at the phone. Call Fontenot and beg? Never! Nor could she agree to his demands to play amateur porno star. Her remaining hope was his sense of decency.

She still could scarcely believe what was happening to her and the Tot Lot—thanks to her ex, his wife, and a lecherous TV reporter. She covered her face with her hands for a moment and bowed her head. She remembered the yellow modeling clay letters and groaned into the stillness of her office. Rudy's threat was coming true.

It's all going to happen again!

One thing about it all was different. She had a daughter. She had no choice but to prepare her in the event Fontenot carried through on his threat. After dinner she sat Clarisse on her lap and outlined what had happened eight years ago in terms her daughter could understand. She stressed that she had been mixed up with a bad woman, so she had to go on trial. Above all, she made the girl understand that she had done nothing wrong. And that the jury had agreed. Later that evening it was possible a TV reporter was going to talk about what had happened on his show.

"Why, Mom? What's he care?"

Mariah shrugged, as though the matter was trivial. "His business is trying to get people excited."

"Well, that's not fair!"

"No. And enough said." She slid Clarisse off her lap and sent her upstairs to comb and brush.

Mariah steeled herself and turned the TV to *Inside Track*, wondering with an accelerating heartbeat whether or not the bad old news would be made new again. Fontenot saved the Tot Lot for the program's last ten minutes. Leave it to him to find and borrow old videotapes from the days of the Clarion City trial. See Jacky Babette DuMarr with loud clothes, blond bob and voice shouting her innocence in front of the court house with a mouth opened wide enough to audition for *Jaws*! See in the background, but not far enough in it, mouse Mariah lingering with lifesaving lawyer! Blowup and freeze frame brought her, grainy but recognizable, into tens of thousands of Madison living rooms. Hear again Audrey Orel's promises of vengeance, then Jacky swearing in public that Mariah had squirmed free of justice!

Fontenot saved the worst for last. Somehow he had found and taped some of Jacky's lewd photos, private parts electronically masked. His voiceover cooed innuendos while Oscar's footage of the Tot Lot and Mariah rolled. "Has a capricious jury freed abuse and deadly violence to wander for years and now settle in to victimize Madison children?" he dared ask the world. Mariah jumped to her feet, tears springing to her eyes. How dare he!

How dare he ruin her life?

The phone began to ring. She moved to answer, then thought better of it. Let the machine handle it. She called to Clarisse, who was close to the upstairs extension, "Don't answer it!"

"Why not?"

"Because. I want to read to you."

"All right!"

Sprawled amid stuffed frogs, dinosaurs, bears, and bunnies Mariah read from *The Lion, the Witch and the Wardrobe* in what she felt was her normal voice. All the while the phone rang and quit and rang. When she inserted the book mark for the night, Clarisse looked up at her with a frown. "Why were you crying, Mom?"

There was no way to really fool a child—at least this one. "That stuff that I told you about was on TV just now."

"About the other day-care center a long time ago?"

"Yeah. They tried to make it sound as if I did something wrong."

"But you didn't. You told me you didn't."

"That's right."

Her daughter's frown faded. "Then everything'll be okay."

"If anybody says anything nasty to you about me, just ignore them."

"I'll deck 'em!"

"You'll do no such thing! Now forget about it. Lights out!"

She went to the kitchen, made a cup of instant coffee, and poured in a little Kahlua. The phone had stopped ringing for the moment. She saw eight messages on the counter and listened to them. Three were from parents who were immediately withdrawing their children from the Tot Lot. Her heart sank at hearing the frightened voices trying to wrap themselves in unfelt politeness. She would have to answer them first.

A younger Mariah Sullivan would not have had the assertiveness to return the calls. Even as it was, she felt the timid beast of hesitancy nibbling at her resolve. Her day-care center had been rejected. *She* had been rejected. Well, the rejecters were wrong and ought to know it.

Mrs. DeFranciso heard Mariah's voice and hung up with a curse. Mariah shuddered. She didn't deserve such contempt. She sniffled back tears. She was not going to let them break her with their thoughtless stupidity!

She phoned Oprah Grayson, a single Jamaican mother, and tried to explain that she had been innocent eight years ago; she was innocent now. There was no reason at all to pull her Fletcher out of the Tot Lot. At least the woman heard her out. She then asked questions that Mariah fielded smoothly. "I can't be letting little Fletch get into bad things, nuh?" she said in her near-patois.

"There is *nothing* bad going on at the Tot Lot, Oprah, I assure you."

"I be thinkin' on it. Be thinkin' what best for de bwoy. Good night to you now."

She called Cassandra and Nick Delos, two thirtyish professionals with two careers and two Volvos. The couple had often met with her to make "suggestions" about enriching their badly spoiled daughter Valerie's day-care experience. If they cared that much, why didn't one of them stay home and do it their way, Mariah often asked herself. Cassandra broke in on Mariah's explanations. "I can't forgive you for doing this to our daughter!" she shrieked. "We certainly *are* going to pull her out. Then we're going to send her to a child psychiatrist! God knows what sick harm you've done her." Down went the receiver with a slam.

"I'll be seeing a professional myself," Nick added on the extension. "My attorney. You can *count* on a lawsuit, Ms. Tot Lot!" And then he slammed Mariah away, too.

Mariah stood crimson-faced despite herself. She wondered how two relatively bright people could become so unhinged by a few minutes of TV. Could they believe what they had seen and heard was neutral, dispassionate, with no axes to grind? Surely not. Past that, did they put all their eggs of trust in the shabby basket of Phil Fontenot because he was sanctified by the glow of CRT phosphers? She had thought of telling them about her ex-husband Rudy's blackmail scheme and the letter Helga had carried to the TV station. She could have described the reporter's lewd proposition. She thought better of it. One didn't best answer accusations with personal attacks.

She noticed that her hands were shaking. She did not deserve this! She was *innocent*, just as she had been eight years ago. A warning bell rang. She had learned from the tragedy that innocence didn't mean she needn't offer a defense to a suspecting society. Sooner or later she'd have to find an attorney. That would be another thing that was "happening again," just as Rudy had promised in his note, now more stupid than sinister. She groaned and leaned against the smooth enamel. Damn him and Helga for doing this to her! For a moment she thought of a lawsuit herself. No, that wasn't her style. Rudy and Helga had no resources; they weren't worth suing.

She had five more phone calls to make to Tot Lot parents. Repeatedly, she found herself answering offensive questions through clenched teeth. She stood by her position: she was moral and honest and the Tot Lot was safe. There was no reason whatever for any parent to anticipate either abuse or violence. Hanging up after the last call, she sensed she wasn't handling the situation properly. She had too quickly become defensive. It was her personality again! Maybe it would have been better to have attacked Fontenot by tarring him with truth as he had smeared her with innuendo. She should have been more assertive—no, *aggressive*.

She wasn't the timid, innocent mouse she had once been. Yet she had to admit there remained further important internal work to be done.

The phone rang again. She hesitated, then answered. It was Audrey Orel, her voice chirping excitedly. "We saw that dreadful news program, Mariah!" she said.

Mariah steeled herself. "Yes?"

"Truman and I wanted you to know we didn't believe a single thing that reporter was suggesting."

Mariah sighed with relief.

"We're supporting you one hundred percent. And we'll say it to anyone who asks us."

For all her encouragement, there was something strained in her voice. Mariah knew what was causing it: memories of their dead Dotty now brought to life again like campfire ashes stirred with a stick. Her heart went out to the woman.

"Thanks for your support," Mariah said sincerely.

"Is there anything we can do?" Audrey asked.

"I'm afraid it's mostly my problem, Audrey. Thanks

so much just the same. I'll just have to wait until it all dies down." Because the Orels had shown trust and forgiveness by enrolling Christopher in the Tot Lot and knew the painful earlier history well, she told Audrey about Rudy's scheme and Fontenot's indecent proposal.

"So the two men and—what's her name?—*Helga* are behind everything!" She sounded relieved that Mariah had identified her tormentors.

"Absolutely. And I've warned the couple. Fontenot's done his worst. Now I just have to ride it out."

"God bless you!" Audrey said. "Jesus is at your side. I *sense* it. Everything's going to work out all right. Trust in God!"

"God bless *you* for sticking by me," Mariah said, and hung up.

It would help if Mariah did a little fast work. She called all the members of her staff. Only Randi Monroe had seen *Inside Track*. Randi was an unpolished woman, but unflappable. "That man Fontenot is one nasty S.O.B.," she said. "Trying to step between the cracks like he was. Lie without really lying." Mariah didn't have to question Randi's loyalty. She warned the others about the broadcast and explained the situation. She asked them to stand by her. They more than anyone knew nothing improper whatever was happening at the Tot Lot. She expected them to tell that simple truth to the parents or anyone else who asked. If they stood fast, the Tot Lot would pull through.

She dragged down her dusty Smith Corona and typed out a memo to parents. She tersely denied all of Fontenot's innuendos as "dangerous sensationalist rubbish." She pointed out that she had been found innocent eight years ago. She was innocent still. The Tot Lot was a service of the highest quality, as the last months had shown. She read it over four times and corrected for tone. She was the offended professional for whom even having to rebut such spurious suggestions was an insult. She would make copies at the Tot Lot and post them everywhere. When the reporters called—and didn't she know they would!—she and her staff members would read it as their statement. That should hold the vultures at bay. Above all, she would stay cool. As Audrey had assured her, everything was going to work out all right.

The next morning at work, she wasn't so sure. She had spoken to five wavering families the previous night and thought she had persuaded at least three to keep their children enrolled. Nonetheless, she had twelve absences in the morning group, including Fletcher Grayson. After the roles were taken she saw that not all of the missing belonged to parents to whom she had spoken, nor to those who had flat out said no more Tot Lot for their little ones. So kids had been pulled by families who hadn't bothered to contact her.

Not all the parents had seen *Inside Track*. Dropping off their kids, they revealed nothing more troubling was on their minds than Richard's cold or little Martina's allergies. She asked them to read her memo; it was very important. Not all bothered to take the time. Mariah didn't think much of that. She suspected they wanted to avoid exposure to any negative thoughts about the Tot Lot. Failed day care here would mean they'd have to find another site. That always took a while at this time of the year and was sure to be a hassle. She thought it would be better for some parents if, instead of themselves, they put their children first.

When the calls from newspaper and TV reporters came, she simply read the memo to them. She wasn't giving interviews. She held an impromptu meeting with her staff. She guaranteed them they would be approached by the professionally scandal-hungry. She couldn't tell them what to do. If they wanted to be famous for their fifteen minutes at Tot Lot expense, that decision was up to them. She guaranteed whatever they might say would be twisted, truncated, and tangled in ways they couldn't imagine.

And so she got through the Tot Lot's worst day. She knew tomorrow things had to be better. Tomorrow was Saturday.

She and Rita had arranged to spend the weekend touring the coast with their daughters. They piled the girls into Mariah's van and took them to Marine World. Mothers' treat was a first-class seafood dinner ''with wine,'' their code for expensive. Saturday was frantic, but enjoyable. When Clarisse and Jeeter were asleep in the adjacent motel room, Mariah bought Cokes from the vending machine. She and Rita sat down to chat. She told Rita everything that had happened eight years ago, then went on to tie it all in with recent events.

Rita nodded sympathetically throughout, making faces at the worst of it. When Mariah finished, her friend rose and hugged her hard for a long time. ''And I thought *I've* had troubles—I didn't know what troubles were!'' Her eyes widened at the thought. ''On trial for *murder?* For the love of God!''

''And now it's starting up again!''

Rita hooded her eyes and screwed up her face in thought. ''So it's Rudy who's done all the harm.''

''Sure. Trying to extort money out of me. Ten thousand dollars! As if I had it.''

''What about Jacky DuMarr?'' Rita asked. ''This stuff that's been happening sounds more up her alley. She's an evil woman. And she's threatened you, too.''

Mariah felt uneasy. She got up and poured more Coke. She didn't like her assumptions of Rudy's guilt shaken.

If he wasn't behind what had happened ... Well, why couldn't Rita be right? The woman who took the letter to the TV station *could* have been Jacky. She too was a blonde. Now she felt relieved that Parole Officer Felicia Greene was going to have a chat with her. That way both Rudy and Jacky would be warned. Fine! She had hedged all her bets.

She still couldn't greatly enjoy the rest of the weekend. Fallout from *Inside Track* surely hadn't completely settled. Who knew but that Fontenot was planning a follow-up. She sickened at the thought. She prayed the horrid man would go elsewhere in search of lives to ruin. She couldn't help wondering what the coming week would bring. Rita caught her mood and tried to cheer her up. She made the familiar thumb-to-forefinger gesture and raised her hand to her lips. She lowered it. This was all too serious to just *poooof* away!

Monday morning brought a parent visitor to the Tot Lot office bearing a troubled expression and a sheet of paper. It was Mickey Donaldson, the black attorney. Behind his gold-rimmed glasses his dark eyes were court-room somber. He gave Mariah the sheet. "Have you seen this?" he said.

She read it. It was a vilification of her! It accused her of having been intimately involved with Jacky DuMarr's child abuse and of having taken part in the murder of Dotty Orel. It claimed she had avoided justice with the help of a conniving attorney and "influence" with the court. It promised that she would brew fresh horrors at the Tot Lot. Any parents stupid enough to continue to send children to her could expect to be sorry. As she read, Mariah's hand grew unsteady. Before she finished, the paper was fluttering as though in a breeze. "This is ... horrid!" she said.

"Indeed . . ." Mickey studied her with the same detached gaze he used after finding the effigy hanging in the tree. He took the sheet back. "Every parent who has a child at the Tot Lot got one of these in the mail, as near as I can find out."

Mariah closed her eyes and pressed a palm to her forehead. Her entire body was trembling. *"Who sent them?"*

Mickey Donaldson waited until their eyes met. "An enemy of yours—or a friend of the parents?"

Mariah's eyes widened. "You believe this? You think whoever wrote this is your *friend?"* She was aware too late that she was shrieking. She snorted in a breath, desperate for self-control.

"Some of us saw *Inside Track* last week. Most didn't. Some saw your memo. Others didn't. But we've *all* seen this." He waved the paper.

Mariah remembered that Rudy or Jacky had broken into her office. She had assumed whichever had only left the message in modeling clay. With dismay she realized the intruder had used the copier to run off a set of the names and addresses of all Tot Lot families.

The attorney sat down and motioned for her to do the same. When she had composed herself, he asked, "Ms. Sullivan, what's going on here?"

She thought of keeping the greater part of her troubles to herself. Then she realized that was unwise. Maybe she was encouraged by the judicial seriousness in his dark eyes. She told Mickey about Jacky DuMarr, Rudy and Helga, and Phil Fontenot. When he asked her what had happened eight years ago, she told him she had been innocent and naive and had unknowingly fallen into Jacky's wicked company.

"And the child's murder?" he asked.

"Neither of us had anything to do with it. I swear!"

He nodded, seeming a judge with his graying temples and somber style. He gave no indication whether or not he believed her. "Some of us parents have talked. We're setting up a committee."

The committee would deliberate over Mariah's character and quiz children about their treatment at the Tot Lot. For the time being, its members would not withdraw their children. When Mariah protested, saying there was no foundation whatever in any of the charges, Attorney Donaldson looked skeptical. "That view is not held by all committee members." With a tight smile he added, "The jury is decidedly still out."

Nine

Mariah had another visitor in midafternoon. Jacky DuMarr's lean face was livid. A vein swelled in the middle of her flushed forehead. She barged into the office without permission, whirled and slammed the door. She stalked toward Mariah's desk, hands on prison-thinned hips. "What the *hell* are you doing talking to my parole officer?" Her brassy voice seemed to bounce from the walls like a trampoline artist.

Mariah drew a deep breath. "Last summer you asked for a job here. When I didn't give you one, you threatened me. I said as much to Felicia Greene."

" 'You said as—' What kind of stupid thing was that to do? I didn't mean nothing when I said that. Now, months later, you're bringing it up again and causing me all kinds of trouble!"

Mariah rose. "Well, you caused me enough trouble, didn't you? You caused me half a lifetime's worth. You're a felon. You make a threat, I take it seriously." She would *not* be intimidated by the woman. She remembered her long talk with Rita, who thought Jacky was a far more likely suspect than Rudy.

Jacky moved closer to the desk. Her swollen lips were set. Her black eyes darted angrily across Mariah's face. "I'm clean now. I don't need trouble from you. You run your lying mouth, I could go back inside." She put her palms on the desk and leaned toward Mariah. "You want to know what it's like in there. Huh? You want to *know?*"

"You should have thought about prison before you did what you did." Mariah stood her ground. Her days of being intimidated by Jacky Babette DuMarr were over!

"You stay away from my parole officer, lady."

"And if I don't, Jacky? What then?"

Jacky grinned, turned away, and paced. When she spun back, her gaunt face was determined. "I seen the TV last week. You're back to doing what you swore you never did with me." She smirked. "I always figured you offed Dotty Orel anyway."

"Don't say that!" Mariah shrieked. She groped for control, swallowing heavily. "Don't you try to turn things around again, Jacky," she said. "I'll tell you why I talked to Felicia Greene. Because I think you're behind the troubles the Tot Lot is having."

"Me?" Jacky looked startled.

"Why not? You've always resented my innocence. You gnawed on it all the years you were in prison. When I said I wouldn't hire you, you decided to get even. You knew everything that happened at J. D. Day Care. You could make sure 'it's all going to happen again' here at the Tot Lot, couldn't you?"

Jacky shook her head energetically. "Huh unh. *Huh unh!* You're thinking crazy. And considering your situation, you're thinking stupidly too. The TV and the papers are going after you. You're on thin ice, baby. One more little thing now could sink you." Threat laced her tone. She jabbed a finger at Mariah. "So you'd be smart to forget your wild idea about mixing my name in with what's going wrong here. You'd be smart, too, if you stayed away from the parole people. If you don't . . ." Her smile was sinister.

"Are you threatening me again?"

"I'm just saying lay off me. Go find another wild goose to chase. You don't, keep in mind I can hurt you big time!"

"*That* is a threat!" Mariah shouted.

"Whatever it is, keep it to yourself, Mariah Sullivan. Or you'll be sorry!" Jacky rushed out and slammed the door behind her.

Mariah watched through the window as the woman got behind the wheel of an ancient Impala. When she wheeled out of the drive, Mariah picked up the phone and dialed a number she had copied into her Day Planner. "Felicia Greene, please," she said.

She was going to stop trouble at the Tot Lot—*now!* And trouble was Jacky DuMarr.

Rita had been right!

At one-thirty she heard a tap on her office door. It was Truman Orel, slight, gray-eyed, and grinning. "Where do you want the aquarium?" he asked.

He had taken the afternoon off from his job. He and Audrey had talked the situation over and though Mariah had told them she couldn't use their help past publicly supporting her character, they nonetheless wanted to do something for the Tot Lot. Considering that some evenings he worked in a pet store, they decided that he ought to set up a twenty-gallon freshwater aquarium for the children's enjoyment. When Mariah began her effusive thanks, Truman turned his odd eyes toward her. "Don't thank us. Thank Jesus. It was He who told us what to do."

"Well . . . thank you for hearing Him," Mariah said awkwardly.

"Listen!" Truman ordered. "He might be speaking to you."

While Truman made several trips to his car, Mariah again marveled at the transformation of the Orels from vindictive, hurtful people to good solid citizens. Evangelical Christianity had certainly become a positive force in American society. If the Orels were typical of the improvement conversion brought, she couldn't fault the movement. How much forgiveness they had summoned! First enough to allow them to sign their son over to her five days a week. Now here was Truman doing another trustful deed.

She checked in on him later. He stood hands on hips admiring his handiwork, a handsome filled tank, complete with bubbling filter, plants, rocks, heater, hood, and fluorescent light. "Be back in a few days to put in the fish," he said.

"You have to let me give you some money for this, Truman," she said.

"Give it to the poor," he said.

She stepped closer and met his eyes. "I want to thank you again for the trust and confidence you and Audrey have in me," she said.

"Thank Jesus for it." He made an odd curtsy-like dip with his knees and hurried out. Play group children were already gathering around the tank. "Hey, there's nothin' *in* there!" a boy said with disappointment.

"Mr. Orel said the tank has to 'settle' before we can have fish," Mariah explained. She hurried off to her tablet

of Post-Its. She wrote on one *Please don't tap the tank!*
The kids were already doing it.

At three-thirty, Clarisse got off the blue bus. Her smile
said: I've got a secret! She wasn't about to share it with
Mariah. She gobbled her ritual milk and two cookies,
then hurried off to her play group.

An hour later there was a light knock at Mariah's office
door. A man stood there holding a Stop 'n' Shop bouquet
nestled neatly in cellophane. He was in his early forties,
tall, almost gangling. He wore round metal-rimmed
glasses and a crooked grin. His hairline was receding,
baring a narrow pinkish expanse. "Hi, I'm Bud Scoffler!"
He quickly stepped forward and presented the flowers
with a flourish. "These are for you!"

Mariah was baffled—and touched. She couldn't
remember the last time any man had brought her flowers.
It hadn't happened in the last ten years, that was for sure.
But . . . who was this guy? "Do I know you? Or . . .
should I know you?" She tried to sound pleasant.

Bud Scoffler wrinkled his smallish nose and frowned.
"Well, you *should* know of me, I think. And I'm sure
you should be expecting me," he said brightly.

"I see." She felt vaguely embarrassed.

Bud's grin was losing some of its wattage. "I understand you wanted to meet me." His brown brows arched
questioningly.

Separated threads gathered in Mariah's mind. They
quickly became a tight little cord leading to . . . *Clarisse!*
"Clarisse told you that!" she laughed. "You're one of
her teachers."

"She did." Bud's face colored. "She . . . *did* clear this
with you, didn't she? She said you were expecting me."

Mariah stepped forward. She held out her hand and
took the bouquet. She offered her hand to Bud. "Pleased

to meet you. Excuse my confusion. It's been a busy day."
That little imp Clarisse! They *would* have a private chat
quite soon.

Bud was the music teacher in Clarisse's school. He
liked the girl's spirit. "She stands out as a feisty little
lady, that's for sure," he said. He revealed she had spent
a bit of time talking to him about her mother. She told
him she had described him to Mariah. Not quite true. If
she remembered correctly, Clarisse had mentioned him
once and said he was "nice," no more than that. Bud
and Clarisse had plans to take Mariah out to dinner that
evening. He looked at her expectantly.

Clarisse appeared in the doorway, her grin wall-to-wall.
"You two look great together!" she said in TV sitcom-
ese.

Bud beckoned Clarisse forward. "This is quite a young
lady you have here, Mariah," he said.

"Now and then more than I can handle." Like now,
Mariah thought.

They settled on dinner at Mariah's, where she and
Clarisse would be on familiar turf. She would have a
chance to cook for another adult again. Her last such
efforts had been for Uncle Harry, whose appetite ran more
toward Camel straights than a decent meal. She stopped
by the fish store and the three of them clustered in the
kitchen while she made sweet and sour halibut over rice.
She threw together a green salad, apologizing for bottled
dressings.

Talk naturally ran to children and education. Safe,
familiar turf for both of them—and for Clarisse, who
even passed up her rationed one-a-night sitcom to join
in the conversation. Here was a young lady with a serious
vested interest.

As to Mariah's interest in Bud, she understood she was

in the presence of an intellectual of sorts. He was no stranger to good food and of course to music. He enjoyed making selections from Mariah's tapes and CDs. His tastes, like hers, were eclectic. His only requested replay was Dizzy Gillespie's *Manteca*. She certainly couldn't fault that. When it came time for Clarisse to go to bed, he offered to read to her. Mariah declined politely. "That's my job," she said.

After another episode of *The Lion, the Witch and the Wardrobe* and a good-night kiss, she made Bud and herself espressos. He took Rita's seat at the kitchen table. In some ways a definite improvement. It was nice to have a man in the house again. Clearly a better one than Rudy— by miles. But Rudy, she now understood, was a poor yardstick by which to measure masculine quality. They chatted, then moved to the living room. She was relieved to find he knew nothing about her Tot Lot troubles. What a relief not to have to think about her career and professional reputation for a while! She would let him in on her troubles if and when.

He chose some mood music and the two settled on the couch. He offered facts about himself; she filled in the rest with intuition. He had gone to the regional state university, earned a teaching certificate, and found a way to make a modest living. She sensed he was more of a reader and thinker underneath than she, and hadn't had much luck hooking up with one of his kind. He seemed gentle and respectful, but she cautioned herself about one of her former bad habits, seeing everyone at first in a rosy glow.

When it came time to change the CD, Bud held one up. "You like this?" It was Verdi's *La Traviata*.

"Yes. Those are just excerpts, though."

Bud smiled. "Want to hear heresy? Opera was written to be excerpted."

"I get the same feeling." Mariah knew the disk and what was coming: *Libiamo*. Alfredo's and Violetta's passionate affirmation of love and liquor, very much in that order. And that music! She had heard it often, but always alone. Not tonight.

Tenor and soprano took their turns, then the chorus with that *sound* pumping them along! Maybe it was the strain of the Tot Lot that loosened her emotions. Maybe it was having been manless for not months but years. No mistaking the catalyst, though. Verdi, *il maestro*. She turned to Bud whose eyes were hooded by a like reaction. By the time he finally opened them wider Mariah had leaned closer to fill his field of vision. Her heart was pounding even before they kissed.

In time they untangled themselves. By then Verdi et al. were well into Act Two. "Well!" she said in a voice husky with arousal. They had put hands as well as mouths on one another. Once having done that, it was hard to return to formality. She giggled. "That really wasn't me. It was Verdi."

"I'm sure he never felt as good to touch as you are." Bud groped for his glasses on the coffee table.

"I'm serious. I'm not really that easy." She worked on her hair. Bud had touseled it but good! She must look a fright.

He held her lightly by the shoulders. "Do you think Clarisse has a future as a matchmaker?"

"You mean, do we have a future?" She looked up at him, working now not on thought, but intuition. "I'm willing to go ahead if that's what you mean, Bud. To see you again. See how it goes. I don't think it'll be like

Verdi every minute, though. Sorry, but my system would overload."

"I can probably live with that." He grinned. She walked him out to his car. He kissed her lightly before getting behind the wheel. His last words for the evening: *"Ciao!"*

Mariah checked on Clarisse. She slept deeply, having done her handiwork. The little matchmaker. Getting ready for bed, Mariah came to several realizations. The first was that she had been lonelier than she imagined. Put a half decent man in her presence and—*whaamm!* That wasn't necessarily good, but it sure had been fun! Second, her emotions had been taking more of a beating than she realized in the twelve days since the first incident at the Tot Lot. They stretched out naked and exposed as raw flesh. She had been turned on by a piece of *music*, for goodness sake! Romantic music or not, that just shouldn't happen. She ought to have more self-control.

Winding down into sleep, she wondered if maybe she wasn't giving enough credit to Bud Scoffler. He certainly knew what to do with a woman in his arms. She wondered about his romantic history. Well, if she saw him enough she would get an idea about it. Women's instincts never failed in that area. She hoped she would see him again. A lot of things in this world went better by twos. The way her life was going, she could use an ally.

Tuesday morning, she was a little slow off the mark. Work and parenting more or less set one's habits. Last night's pleasant diversions had left her red-eyed and yawny. She shook off her lassitude. No way she was getting too old to have fun!

At the Tot Lot she kept an ear peeled for the phone. She was expecting a call. It didn't come till late morning. She welcomed hearing Felicia Greene's no-nonsense voice. "Did you get a chance to talk to Jacky as I asked you to?" Mariah said.

"You know it!"

"What happened?"

"I talked. She listened. She got mad." Felicia gave a whoop of laughter.

Mariah found herself unamused. "Did you warn her never to threaten me again?" she asked.

"I told her. Once more and she's lookin' for a bad review of her parole."

"What did she say?"

Felicia paused. "She says it was a bum rap. Said she don't give a fart in a tornado about you or that Tot Lot. She said you takin' a big advantage because she did time. *That's* what she said, since you asked."

"Just the same, she might well be behind the troubles I'm having here, Felicia. I want you to assure me that you've seen to it that they're over."

Felicia laughed again. "Assure you? The only thing I can 'assure' you of is that Jacky Babette DuMarr won't be threatening you no more. Whether that stops your troubles, who knows? Up to now I never did think that woman had anything to do with your Tot Lot. You got no evidence of any kind, that's for sure. Fact is, maybe you just made your troubles worse calling me like you did."

Mariah frowned. "Why do you say that, Felicia?"

"When Jacky left here, she was one mad lady."

"Should I care about that?"

"Care or don't care. I don't know." Felicia's voice took on a little edge. "Listen up now. I did my thing for you. Now I don't want to hear from you unless you see Jacky DuMarr break a window at your place or somethin'

like that. Felon who does her time clean and neat needs
a break now and then, too. Anyhow, I been thinkin' all
along she never did do nothing new to you. Later.'' She
hung up.

Well, Mariah thought, *she* was sure it was possible that
Jacky had done plenty of harm. Looking back to yesterday,
she was pleased with how she had handled her. She hadn't
stood for any mischief. Jacky had threatened her; she had
called her on it. She should handle all her affairs with
that kind of prompt assertiveness.

Bud Scoffler called to tell her again that he had enjoyed
his evening with her and Clarisse. ''With you more than
Clarisse, to be honest,'' he laughed. He asked about getting
together again. She was pleased, but put him off till the
weekend. She didn't want to have to handle two late
nights in one work week. After hanging up, she changed
her mind. She called him back and invited him to join
her and Clarisse at the local pizza joint. He might as well
see how they lived. Find out if he was interested in buying
into their ways.

She watched Clarisse during the meal. Her eyes
scarcely left Bud. One vote of approval there. Not the
deciding one, of course. Casting that was her privilege.
Half listening to Bud's small talk, she tried to pierce the
armor hiding the secrets of attraction between the newly
acquainted. Could Mariah Sullivan and Bud Scoffler
become an item? More than just that? She probed herself.
How did she feel about him? Aside from his kisses and
caresses, which she certainly had enjoyed, she wasn't sure
what she thought. Time would focus her feelings, she
hoped.

Bud had promised her a normal bedtime, but was easily
persuaded to hang around long enough to say good night
to Clarisse and have an espresso. When Mariah met his

eyes across the kitchen table she felt herself being stirred up again. No, not tonight, too! His crooked grin flashed. Was he having the same reaction? He took her hand and raised her gently from her chair. His arms were around her. His mouth lowered itself invitingly. "Just one kiss for goodbye," she breathed.

"We'll see."

In the end it was more like a dozen. After the final one he tried to urge her toward the living room couch. She slid deftly out of his arms. He couldn't hide the brief annoyance that darted like a bird across the brown sky of his eyes. You shouldn't stir them up unless you were willing to go ahead, Mariah reminded herself. She felt like a college freshman again, guarding the gates against horny youths. She pressed a gentle palm against his spread lips. " 'It's got to be more than just physical,' " she quoted an unknown source.

"Haven't you noticed, Mariah? It is."

Later in bed she wondered if she *had* noticed. She must be the cautious one of the pair. She had learned a lesson during the grand misfortune of Rudy Erris. Don't go too fast with a man.

Before she fell asleep, her conscience stirred. She owed Bud the facts about her past and what was happening at the Tot Lot. Even though she imagined the worst was over, some fallout still might descend on him. She should prepare him. Unprepared, even the most rational person could easily get the wrong idea about her. Well, next chance she got she would do it. She had done nothing of which to be ashamed. The current uproar would die down. All she had to do was hang in there and in time everything in her life would be okay.

Ten

At ten-thirty the phone in her Tot Lot office rang. It was Phil Fontenot. He must have read her mind. The first thing he said was, "Don't hang up on me. You might regret it."

"You won't be surprised that your broadcast has hurt my business considerably," Mariah said. "What you did was horrid and dishonest—"

"Sure. Yeah. Maybe." Mariah imagined the hawk-faced reporter's expression shifting to its usual contemptuousness. She sensed he despised people. If she had seen too little of the human race at its worse, he had seen too much. "Maybe you thought I was bluffing, Mariah? Didn't think I'd do what I said?"

"I thought you might think better of it. But I certainly didn't bet on it!"

He chuckled. "So we understand each other, after a fashion, don't we?"

"What do you want, Fontenot?"

"Our first deal fell through. I want to make another one."

Mariah drew in a deep breath. She sensed more danger angling toward her life. "I can't imagine what we have to discuss. You did what you threatened to do. You damaged my reputation and that of my day-care center. What deals do you have left to make?"

"I had a visitor yesterday. A very angry lady . . ."

Mariah listened with a sinking stomach. Jacky had gone straight from her parole officer to WLIT-TV and Fontenot. Her intent was straightforward: to further assassinate Mariah's character. She was eager to publicly swear that her former employee had cooperated with her in the pornographic photography. She also claimed to have information linking Mariah to Dotty Orel's murder.

"None of that's true!" Mariah's protest sounded like a desperate plea.

"Maybe. Maybe not."

"I'm nothing like Jacky DuMarr! I'm an honest, decent woman!"

"That's why I propose to help you, Mariah Sullivan."

Mariah closed her mouth in shock. "*Help* me? Does this have something to do with the deal you're talking about?"

"I'm talking about you doing a rebuttal on *Inside Track*. The public gets to hear your voice, see you in action at the Tot Lot."

"And what has to happen for me to get the truth told?"

"We've got to get organized. We have to agree on what ways to go with it. We need a strategy session. Come over to my place tonight. We'll plan it all out."

Mariah was suspicious at once. "And I suppose your cameraman will just *happen* to be there."

"Just me. You have my word. We got an *Inside Track*

show to plan. The public's got the right to hear your side."

"You haven't ever really listened when I tried to tell you my side—"

"Now I'm ready. The ratings have convinced me. See you at seven."

"Listen to me, Mr. Fontenot. I don't trust you. What happens if I don't show tonight?"

"That would be stupid. You know why?"

Mariah looked around her office, hesitating. "I give up," she said sourly. "Why?"

"This is your chance to turn it all around. Turn all the negatives into a big commercial for your place."

"And if I still won't come?"

"I think you will. See you at seven."

She thought it over the rest of the day. Maybe Fontenot *could* help her turn it all around. Maybe he couldn't. Just the same, the trip would be worthwhile if she could convince him not to put Jacky on *Inside Track*. Fontenot was a sensation-seeking sleaze; he would do whatever it took to raise his show's ratings, including putting Mariah in a positive spotlight. Then she hesitated. Was she letting an outsider dictate her plan rather than making one of her own? Could her old nemesis of too much trust in others be stalking her again? She mulled it over until after five, then settled on a single plan of action. She would try to make a deal with the man. If she couldn't do it, she was out of there. It was worth a try.

Fontenot lived in the city in an expensive condo high-rise on a bluff overlooking the river. The place had a lobby as big as a 1930s movie house and a security guard seated at a desk into which were set a half dozen TV monitors. He cleared her way. A high-speed elevator took her up to the seventeenth floor.

Fontenot welcomed her into a wide living room, one wall of which was glass. It faced the lights of downtown Madison. The clear night polished every distant gleaming bulb and tube, making the city shine. The view beyond and the rugs and furnishings within told her that her host, in the course of destroying people's lives and riding roughshod over the truth, had become a rich man. On the wall opposite the glass, a long narrow mirror caught the glitter and tossed it back with an icy hand.

Food and wine were spread out on a table in an array that spoke of caterer's arts. At her request Fontenot brought her an opened Perrier mineral water from the refrigerator. Champagne glass in hand, he beckoned her over to the glass expanse. "The first thing I want to do is apologize." He had softened his harsh voice. She saw that his custom-made suit had been chosen from a rod several pegs above his everyday wear. She resisted feeling flattered. For her part she had worn nothing special, the day's business suit, sensible low heels. She hadn't bothered to do her hair.

"For *which* of the cruel things you've done to me do you want to apologize?" she asked. She glanced sidelong at him, trying to gauge his seriousness, his direction.

"About letting Oscar talk me into taping you after you passed out," he said.

She felt herself coloring. "Fine. Apology accepted."

"Your breasts were . . . lovely. You have to excuse men's weakness and stupidity." In the dim light the streak in Fontenot's hair seemed to gleam whiter, almost phosphorescent. Mariah took a deep swallow of mineral water. She was thankful for the weak light. Otherwise he would have seen her face aflame. "Let's stick to real business, not monkey business, Mr. Fontenot."

"Phil, please, Mariah."

"I don't feel comfortable enough with you to use your

first name," Mariah said. "And considering the harm you've done me, no one would blame me."

He led her over to a low Danish style couch, before which papers were spread out on a coffee table under a halogen desk lamp. He had prepared several outlines and invited her to study them. While she did, he refilled his glass and brought her a plate of snacks. As she finished the mineral water, she found she had trouble concentrating. She closed her eyes and rubbed her forehead. A warm wave like a luscious dizziness passed over her. Was she getting sick? That was all she needed, at a moment when the possibility of turning a bad situation around was presenting itself.

She attempted to gather herself and went back to the papers. Fontenot settled down on the couch on the other edge of the pool of light. She tried to concentrate on the list of shots he wanted inside the Tot Lot. She pointed to two of them and leaned over toward him. "These won't work. We don't have any kind of formal classroom arrangement." She saw her hand was trembling. He reached out and lightly took her wrist to steady her. She was surprised at his cool, firm touch.

He said, "We need group shots, then, with you in an active role, teaching or leading singing or something else to touch the heart."

To touch the heart. *To touch the heart.* The phrase rang down the halls of Mariah's misbehaving mind. That's what she wanted. Someone to touch her heart. Someone more manly than pleasant, politely horny Bud Scoffler. But what was she thinking? Where had that thought come from? She felt a rush of warmth infuse her. It washed in on a wave of adventurousness that defied the mindset of her ordinary days . . .

Fontenot had raised her hand to his mouth. His lips were cool. Almost without thinking, she caught his earlobe in her mouth, felt the nubble of gristle between her teeth as she bit down gently. He shoved his fingers between her teeth. She tongued their tips. Then his lips were on hers. Her head spun. What was happening to her?

Fontenot had slipped out of his jacket. She went for his tie, then it was off, too, snaking down and away. She smelled expensive aftershave. She slid her palms down over his forehead, covering his eyes. His prominent nose protruded between her thumbs. "My hooded hawk!" she murmured. "No flying till I give the order!" She couldn't believe her own words, much less her actions. She went to work on his buttons, jerked his shirt from his belt. She freed it from his arms and tossed it away. He peeled her jacket down off her shoulders, pinioned her arms with it, and pressed open-mouthed kisses on her slack mouth. She shrugged off the jacket and unbuttoned her blouse. She cupped her bra and offered her breasts to him. "You have the nerve to touch these while I'm awake?" she teased.

He reached around her toward the hooks that had betrayed his earlier voyeurism. She playfully batted his hands away. "No. You first!" she ordered. She snatched at the bottom of his T-shirt, jerked it up. Umh! Hairy chest, decent pecs, tiny nipples. She explored them with her mouth. She used her eye teeth. He groaned. She wasn't gentle with him.

Her newly purple world swirled and they tottered together like exhausted marathon dancers in the middle of his vast Oriental carpet. Hands on her shoulders, he shoved her down to her knees. She felt the soft nap of the rug under her kneecaps. She knew what he wanted, and maybe she wanted it, too. She nibbled his belt, tasted the finish of expensive leather. The eye of his monogrammed buckle winked *F* in small diamonds.

Then she heard the noise.

It sounded loud as a fire siren despite her befuddled mind. Even her raging lust couldn't smother it. She froze.

A momentary metallic clatter, it told much. It said . . . *Camera!*

She jumped to her feet, reeling toward the distant wall. "Sullivan!" Fontenot moved in pursuit.

She dodged him clusmily, but well enough to get him off balance. She staggered around him. He lunged for her, his clutching fingers brushing her hip. She snatched a metallic sculpture off a table and staggered closer to the mirror. She whirled the weighty metal with all the strength in her left arm, then let it fly. The two-way mirror shattered, shards falling like glittering rain. Her lusty euphoria evaporated in the heat of shock and anger. There stood Oscar in a mini-studio designed for the recording of his master's conquests and other scurrilous eavesdropping. His camera was on a tripod, long-range lens protruding like a thick finger.

Mariah staggered as lightheadedness swept over her. She understood only then that Fontenot had drugged her mineral water. Some kind of alkaloid or hallucinogenic, no doubt. She tried to shake off her disorientation. She felt his hand on her shoulder. He spun her around. "Don't stop now!" he said. His eyes blazed with arousal.

She wavered for a moment, then thought of the camera and a leering Oscar behind it. And the drug! They said everything about what Fontenot was and would always be. You could not make deals with such a man. You couldn't trust him one inch. And you surely couldn't let him touch you! She cried out wordlessly and slammed the heel of her bare foot down on his naked instep. He howled and limped back. She ran for her clothes. When she had them she headed for the door. She would take her chances of embarrassment in the hall.

"Don't even talk to me!" she screamed at him.

"Jacky DuMarr will be featured on *Inside Track* tomorrow night," he intoned. "Tough T-bone for the Tot Lot!"

"The police will want to hear about you drugging me!" Clutching her clothes in front of her, she groped awkwardly for the knob.

"I'm *sure* you'll want to call them," he said facetiously. "That's what you want: police attention in Madison, just like you had in Clarion City. Particularly when we have tape of you undressing me."

"The drug—"

"*What* drug? There was no drug." He waved his arm slowly from side to side like a working conjurer. "See the news tomorrow! 'Tot Lot owner found in love nest!' Hardly a fit woman to manage the lives of young children, is what the world will think." He reached past her and opened the door. When she stepped through it he shoved her hard. "Beat it, babe! You're done in this town. I'll make *sure* of that!"

She stumbled, falling facedown on the hall carpet. By the time she rose to her feet, his door was closed and she was in tears. She wrapped her clothing clumsily around her, feeling more a naked waif than a humiliated professional woman. She found a janitor's closet and dressed herself.

Driving home she was in a turmoil, alternately sobbing and cursing. She gathered her wits well enough to pay Mrs. Fields, the baby-sitter, and check on Clarisse. Then the tears came washing back and she had to huddle for a moment on the floor of the upstairs hall. When she eventually felt sure that she wasn't going to descend into hysterics, she hurried to the bathroom and took a long, hot shower. She was washing Fontenot away in more ways than one. She promised herself never to see or talk to him again. He was simply too wicked for her.

Robed, her hair in a towel, she went to her modest liquor chache and poured herself a double Kahlua. She took it to bed and pulled the covers up to her waist. She felt drained. Her head ached. God knew what the reporter had tricked her into putting into her body. Hadn't she behaved like? . . . There was nothing wrong with passion, but to be set up and *used* by that man was so degrading! She took no comfort in having been reminded that she still had plenty of desire in her. How he had misdirected it! She groaned, sinking back onto the pillows. She summed up the evening—and the coming TV fallout featuring a mendacious Jacky DuMarr—and didn't like the total one bit.

Her troubles were worsening.

Past that rudimentary understanding was an insight more painful than the drug-induced flash about Bud Scoffler's overall inadequacy. She had prided herself on her personal growth over the last eight years. The problem, her insight whispered, was that she hadn't come far enough to handle these new troubles. She still wasn't assertive enough. She still too often reacted rather than acted. Bad habits! But tough ones from which to wean herself. She shuddered. *It's all going to happen again* could become a dark reality not just for what might be done to the Tot Lot, but for the destruction looming before her very life. It took three hours of tossing and two more Kahluas before she admitted the truth.

She needed help.

After nine the next morning she was on the phone to

Clarion City, the law offices of MacLean, Martello and Mortenstein. The unfamiliar woman's voice told her that Mr. Mortenstein was still out of the office indefinitely. Mariah said she wanted to see him on a personal matter. The woman gave her his home phone number. She called and got one of Shelly's sons. She told him she wanted to talk to his father. Was he there?

"He's in Cedars of Sinai," the boy said. "You want the visiting hours? I know them by heart."

After making arrangements for Rita to pick up Clarisse and tape the evening's *Inside Track*, Mariah left the Tot Lot early and began the two hundred mile drive to Clarion. Along the way she found her brain darted between last night and the present. She saw flashes of the reporter's chest, hairs curled tightly in the shallow channel between his pectorals. She glimpsed her chemically induced abandon, saw herself sloe-eyed and heavy-breasted in the mirror behind which skulked Oscar. She felt again her shock and anger. To her disamy, arousal twisted to life momentarily like a faint musky scent on the wind. She cried out hoarsely, the car swerving under her unsteady hand. Loathing for Fontenot surged up even more strongly than her humiliation. He had barely failed to achieve his fleshy conquest. Tonight, with Jacky DuMarr's help, he would console himself by destroying what remained of her reputation. She had no one to blame but her own too trustful self for getting into last night's situation. *When* was she going to learn? It had better be soon!

She cut that kind of thinking short. Her fault? Hardly! Fontenot was a cruel, heartless man. He had taken every chance to destroy her reputation and possess her body. She doubted she had ever hated anyone in her life. She had never lined up folks and called some enemies. She knew why: timid people lacked the courage to hate and to admit to having enemies. This evening with the tires buzzing on the interstate she felt that shackle of timidity fall away to join so many on the road of the months behind her. She admitted—more, *wallowed* in—loathing Phil Fontenot with all her heart. And here came something else new, to her surprise.

She wanted revenge!

She found the hospital and got Shelly's room number, wondering what ailed him. She got a shock when she walked into his room. Nobody ever looked good in a hospital, but Shelly was deathly pale. He had that washed out look of the unwell, though she saw no tubes running in and out of him or signs of surgery. He was hooked up to a monitor whose CRT showed what looked like his heartbeat. A stylish woman sat in a chair with a book on her lap. The diamond on the hand atop the pages was as big as a hazelnut. Mariah remembered her face from the photograph on Shelly's desk years back. She was his wife. She quit reading as Mariah stepped into the private room and introduced herself. "I'm sorry to bother you, Mrs. Mortenstein," she said. "I drove all the way from Madison today to talk to your husband."

Shelly lay motionless with his eyes closed. His formerly graying hair had shaded to snow. At the sound of Mariah's voice his lashes fluttered. His eyes opened sluggishly. His formerly piercing glance had lost much of its command. At that moment Mariah understood the man was dying. Dismay ran through her like flash flood waters.

Despite his condition, she saw recognition in his eyes. No, more than that. *Expectation!* Had he known that one day she would return? His dry lips moved. "Unfinished business," he said. He shifted his head on the pillow. "Give us a minute, Naomi. This is . . . my once and future client."

"I remember her case." His wife got up, smiled, and walked out.

"Sit," Shelly said. "Talk."

She told him everything, finishing with, "I came for some help." Her face must have revealed her distress about his health because he said, "Don't worry. We'll come up with something. We always do."

"*You* always do, Shelly."

"From here on it's going to be up to you." His voice grew stronger. He squirmed higher and Mariah adjusted his pillow so he could sit up. He touched his chest. "The ticker's going, going, about gone."

"I'm so sorry." She felt her eyes misting. She owed so much to this man!

His gaze met hers. "I have a feeling you've come a long way since those days you wouldn't dare ask for a lemon seltzer."

"Thanks. I—"

"From the look of you I'd say you're about fifty percent of the way to getting control of your life."

Mariah closed her mouth and swallowed. A worse evaluation than she had anticipated. "I can't help it if someone is trying to destroy me!" Shelly's presence made that hard reality sound like an excuse.

"Your day-care center and reputation seem to be the targets, not you directly."

"Who do you think is doing it? Why?"

His shoulder under the hospital gown twitched in a shrug. "Whoever, whyever, the problem is, you're not doing the right things to find out. Running around making accusations won't do it. Neither will trying to make deals with a poor excuse for a TV journalist."

"I know I need help," Mariah admitted. "That's why I came."

Shelly flinched. Color drained from his face. Mariah looked around anxiously. If he was having an attack . . . His eyes closed for a long moment. When they opened, she could see the pain there as though written in text across the black gleam of his pupils. ''I'm about past giving people help.'' His lips trembled in a feeble grin. ''But lucky for you, not completely past it. I know a guy in Madison you should talk to. His name is Yuri Nevsky. Call the firm, ask for Louise. She still has my black book. She'll give you the number. Tell Nevsky, Shelly sent you.'' He relaxed, as though what little he said had exhausted him. ''Beat it! Send Naomi back in. I want her here when I die.''

''Shelly, don't . . .''

His eyebrow arched—that familiar gesture! ''Don't say 'die'? Or don't die?''

''Neither!'' Mariah felt tears welling in her eyes.

''Mariah, listen to Shelly's last words to you. This 'challenge' you're facing is your second chance to get your life right. You don't meet it, you won't get another one.''

''But what should I *do*, Shelly?'' She felt guilty imploring a dying man.

He rolled his eyes. ''Oye! Still you don't know?'' He fixed her with a glance close in intensity to those of eight years ago. ''What do you do? *You don't be so nice!* Go see Nevsky. Now call Naomi. *Mazel tov!*''

Mariah wept over Shelly Mortenstein for the first fifty miles of her return journey. The rest she spent trying to order her thoughts and make a plan. She failed. Back in Madison, Rita and the two girls were asleep. She ran the tape of the *Inside Track* broadcast. It went much as she had dreaded. There was Jacky, nearly as loud and vulgar as in her heyday. The veneer of prison-commanded humility had peeled off under the heat of TV lights and the masses' attention. She made her nearly libelous statements: Mariah had played a role in the loathsome photography; it was a distinct possibility that the same thing could happen at the Tot Lot; there were "facts" that if uncovered might link her former employee with the death of Dotty Orel.

And there was Fontenot, leading the former felon forward to the edge of libel, stirring in his own innuendoes and posing "questions that the public wants answered." The pair left the Tot Lot's good name well below that of Oliver Twist's orphanage. The pair was ludicrous and unbelievable—but only to Mariah, who knew them and what they were trying to do. To the average viewers? What could they think about the Tot Lot, except that it was the Day-Care Center from Hell? She covered her face and sighed deeply. The hour was late. She was exhausted.

She felt she could be excused for bawling her head off.

Eleven

There were more calls for her on her home answering machine from distraught parents and reporters. She wouldn't bother with them for now.

She got to the Tot Lot early. She took each staff member aside as soon as she appeared. She told them all about *Inside Track*. For the first time she told them about the bargain Fontenot had tried to strike with her. She added that he had tried to drug her when all else failed. They mustn't believe Jacky; she had wanted a job there at the Tot Lot, wasn't hired, and was now trying to get even. And once again Mariah assured them that she was blameless. Someone was out to wreck the Tot Lot and her career. She didn't know who or why.

Hearing her voice, she wondered if it didn't sound as though she was patching together something out of cobwebs and dew that only the most gullible would accept. She studied her employees as she spoke. All of them nodded, seemingly believing.

Later in the morning, Nikki Herakis, Rochelle's assistant, slipped in looking nervous. "I probably shouldn't say this, Ms. Sullivan, but . . ." She shrugged and ran her hands through her heavy black hair. "Molly Dolman's been talking about you to the rest of us."

"What's she been saying?"

"Well, her uncle watched *Inside Track* and he said . . ."

Molly Dolman's uncle seemed to be an evil-spirited, suspicious man with too much influence on his niece. Molly had some education and varied life experiences. Mariah was surprised that she would be susceptible to . . . suggestions. Molly had been sounding out the others, wondering what they thought.

"And what *do* they think, Nikki?" Mariah asked. "And please be honest."

Nikki frowned. "Well, it's not really that easy to tell, but—well, you can count on Rochelle, for sure! She says somebody has it in for you and that the media are blowing it up, like, all out of sight."

"What about Randi? I notice she's still willing to bring her two kids in with her."

Nikki screwed up her face. "She's been saying she trusts you, Ms. Sullivan, but if she wasn't so broke . . ."

"She might leave us."

"I guess."

"I'll have another chat with her. I'd hate to lose her. What about Grace and Deidre?"

"They both told me their husbands are keeping an eye on the situation. They're not convinced of anything yet."

Mariah nodded. She managed a smile. "And what about you, Nikki?"

Nikki stroked her hair. "I don't have any doubts about you, Ms. Sullivan . . ." She paused.

"I hear a 'but' coming," Mariah said.

"My mother says I should quit," the girl blurted. "She says if one more thing goes wrong here, I'd never be able to do anything in child care again."

"And what do *you* say?"

"I'm staying. But, Ms. Sullivan, I want to be honest with you, I'm not saying for how long!"

In the noon hour she got a visit from Mickey Donaldson in his role as chairman of the nameless parents' committee in whose hands the fate of the Tot Lot lay. He was sober-faced as usual. His gold-rimmed glasses glittered as icily as his questions. The bottom line was that the committee wanted her reactions to the *Inside Track* broadcast.

"I categorically deny every lie and innuendo!" Mariah stood up, annoyance coming to the surface. "I wouldn't have believed that an attorney like yourself would be so quick to condemn me without hearing my side of things. That toad Fontenot told me that in a world with TV in it there was no rebuttal—unless they allowed it. I'd hate to think he's right."

Attorney Donaldson nodded. "The committee is considering having you speak to them about the situation."

"There isn't any 'situation!'" Mariah snapped. "Some nasty people have gotten together to cause me trouble. And they're doing a great job! Just the same, I'm keeping the Tot Lot open until the public comes to its senses."

She couldn't read the attorney's tight smile. "I'll report that to the committee," he said.

He was about to leave when shy Truman Orel appeared in the doorway, a large plastic bag filled with tropical fish in his hand. "Guests for your wet hotel," he said.

"You're so kind to do this, Truman," Mariah said.

Recognizing Donaldson, Truman said, "You committee people should come to your senses real quick about this young lady."

The attorney frowned. "I don't believe I know you."

"You know my wife, Audrey Orel. She's on the committee. She's told you the same thing I have. And that's that Mariah Sullivan here is the salt of the earth. She wouldn't hurt a fly, never mind a toddler."

Mariah sent up a silent prayer for the Orels. *Listen to him, Mickey Donaldson.*

"Indeed," Mickey said noncommittally. "I appreciate your vote of confidence, but I'm afraid the situation isn't quite that straightforward."

"Ahhh!" Truman waved a slender hand in disgust and off he went with his fish.

After Donaldson left, Mariah sat trembling at her desk. She sensed the situation slipping away from her. She opened her Day Planner and turned to the phone number she had copied down during her call to Shelly's law firm. Yuri Nevsky.

She telephoned him. Nevsky was noncommittal until she mentioned Shelly Mortenstein's name. Then his tone changed completely. They set up a meeting in his office for one-thirty. "Most of the crowd's gone by then," Nevsky said, puzzling her.

"Tell me what you look like," he said.

Her misgivings grew, but she told him. She clock-watched till one-fifteen.

She drove down Dowager Drive, slowing as the street numbers climbed toward 1380. She was on the lookout for an office building among the franchise restaurants. All she saw was a Wendy's. She pulled into the lot, hoping to ask directions. She saw the restaurant's number was 1380. This was Nevsky's office?

When she walked in, a man at a small corner table gave her a smile and beckoned discreetly. She moved toward him. He was older than she had expected, likely in his early fifties. His wiry beard was shot through with gray. He was bald on top. He had high Slavic cheekbones and the barest Oriental tilt to his eyes. He stood as she came closer. Now she saw his lined face's prominent feature was its look of battered determination. This man had fought battles and lost his share, but was undefeated.

He had bought her a cup of coffee. The paper cup had a lid. Creamers and sugar packets lay beside the cup. She thanked him and offered him her hand. "Mariah Sullivan."

"Who has problems, if Shelly sent you." His hand was gentle and dry.

She told him about Shelly's heart. His face sank and his eyes grew distant. "He was one of the good guys."

"He's not dead yet, Mr. Nevsky."

"I heard from Naomi this morning. He died around midnight last night. Just a while after you left, I guess."

Mariah had no control over the tears that started down her face. Nevsky offered her Wendy's napkins. She blew and sniffled. Working with her coffee gave her more time to control herself. She glanced at him, saw his patient smile.

"Just ease into it when you're ready," he said.

"Maybe you could go first?" Mariah's voice shook. "That would give me another minute or two. What do you do? Why did Shelly give me your name?"

Nevsky shrugged. "A lot to tell, but nothing much relevant now. I'm semi-retired from getting paid to help people with problems. Once in a while I take on a client. Sometimes for money. Sometimes for free." Studying his worn face, Mariah knew there was a great deal that she wasn't going to hear.

"I don't have much money," she said. "I run a day-care center . . ." She got it all out while Nevsky sat silently, save for an occasional question. He drank two cups of coffee while she scarcely touched hers. Now and then his eyes moved to her face as she shared what he must have felt was a revealing fact about herself. When she finished, he held up his palms questioningly. "So . . . now what?"

Mariah frowned. "I hoped you might tell me that."

Nevsky nodded absently, rose, and turned to face out the window toward the traffic stream. He stood taller than she had guessed, about six-two. He was slender, but had good shoulders. She imagined at one time he might have been a bit of a ladies' man. She also imagined he was resourceful. She hoped so.

After a few moments, he turned back to her. "You want any food? You ought to eat lunch. Advice is easier to digst when your stomach is already working."

"I haven't had much appetite lately."

He nodded and leaned forward. "Mariah Sullivan, your problem is made up of two parts, like everybody else's." He pointed at her. "You." His index finger swung toward the window. "And them."

As Nevsky explained Mariah had to admire his insight. He had gotten a good read on her personality, its strengths and shortcomings. If she wanted to find out who was trying to destroy the Tot Lot and her reputation, she had to be more active, he said. They could work on that together. As to her suspects, he frowned and shook his head. "Maybe you want to think harder about who it might be. Who might be holding a grudge against you."

"It can only be one of a very few people, because whoever it is knows what happened eight years ago."

"Fontenot found out a lot about you. It's all public information. Why couldn't somebody else do that?"

"Yuri, I'm not sure who would want—"

"That's why I'm asking you to think about it. Not now. Mull it over when you have time."

"I'm sure it's a woman, a blonde, I think. A woman likely did the sewing on that horrid effigy. A blonde dropped off the tip that got Fontenot started."

Nevsky nodded. "Could be. As I said, don't be in a hurry to make a decision."

Hesitantly she agreed. "What else?"

"I have to do some thinking," Nevsky said.

"Could you think about Phil Fontenot? He's tried his best to make me notorious. Then tried to take advantage of me."

Nevsky's grin was spiced with cunning. "I've already thought about him. Say the word and I'll get him off your back and maybe some other people's."

Mariah frowned. "How in the world are you going to do that?"

"Two men I know owe me a favor. They're big men with bad tempers."

"But . . ."

Nevsky touched her hand, resting on the table. "You're going to do things in a more assertive way, right? Do you have any tender feelings toward Fontenot?"

"None! He's been loathsome." Mariah recalled her epiphany on the road to Clarion City. "I hate him! I consider him my true enemy. And his mute flunky Oscar's just as bad."

Nevsky got up and offered his hand. "Think of that decision as the first one of the coming best part of your life."

* * *

Mariah hadn't been back at the Tot Lot twenty minutes when Rita called. Her voice was tight. "I just picked up a copy of the *Declarer*. There's a picture there of you. I have a feeling it's in all the main and satellite Madison newspapers, too."

Dread welled up in Mariah. "What kind of picture of me, Rita?" she nearly shouted.

"It's you talking to that woman, Jacky DuMarr, on your porch. The caption is—well, awful. It identifies her as a convicted child abuse felon and your former employer. The rest of it suggests you two might be in cahoots again. Oh, Mariah, it's *awful!*"

Mariah rushed out and bought a paper. The photo was even worse than she expected. The photographer had used a telephoto lens and caught them at a moment when it appeared as though they were both leaning forward in deep conspiracy, when in fact they had been arguing.

She grabbed the phone book, then the phone. She called the *Declarer* news office. "I'd like to know the source of one of the photos in your paper today." She gave the woman the information. She was put on hold; light rock favorites played into her impatient ear. Finally the woman came back on the line. "It was mailed anonymously to the news director along with some of the information from which the caption was written." Was there anything else she'd like to know?

Mariah hung up. Her fingers still clutched the receiver. She was fuming with anger and humiliation. In a few minutes those emotions partially cooled. She found herself wondering . . . who did she know was good with a camera?

The answer came at once. Rudy Erris.

Possibly she had made a mistake thinking Jacky DuMarr was behind her troubles. Rita had been most convincing in her arguments about her former boss's guilt. Fleetingly she admitted the possibility that she had turned a largely neutral Jacky against her with her determined accusations, sending her into Fontenot's camp. Well, anyone could make mistakes.

Her tormentors had been Rudy and Helga, after all.

How often years ago had she seen Rudy hunched over his tripod-mounted 35mm SLR, telephoto lens sticking out like a snout? He had pointed it at mountain scenery, clusters of friends, and of course at her. So had he done it most recently that morning she had stood on her porch with Jacky? It was entirely possible.

He had ignored her warnings, her threats to go to the police. How desperate he must be for money to persevere in this obscene way! By now he had bypassed mere blackmail, crossing the line into vendetta. She knew how his mind worked: he could be nasty when crossed. In a sense it all fit together. A blond woman had delivered the letter to the TV station. Once again she came back to Helga. Had to be, if Jacky was innocent after all. The messenger couldn't have been Audrey Orel, the only other woman linked to the past. Audrey had come in peace bearing the olive branch of her child. And Audrey wasn't a blonde.

Then her memory summoned up Nevsky's voice: the harasser didn't necessarily have to be connected with the past.

She had warned Rudy that if he continued in his vindictive campaign she would call the police. Well, he had done just that! She went to the phone and picked up the receiver. She hesitated. Did she *really* want to call them? What kind of reception would she find, considering her growing notoriety? Would reporters follow in the police wake? More of *that* kind of publicity she could do without.

She put down the receiver, then jerked it up again. The number she keyed in was Nevsky's.

They met again at Wendy's. He had seen the photo. "Nasty work," he called it. He grunted. His high cheekbones seemed more angular above his briefly pursed lips. He sat back and wrapped his right hand around his paper coffee cup. "Now you're back to thinking it's your ex again?"

She nodded. "He and his lady friend."

Nevsky frowned. "You spend any time thinking who else might be out to get you? Maybe other people who've threatened you? Somebody else you made angry?"

"Oh, no, there's nobody like that," Mariah said quickly. She wanted to get on to dealing with Rudy. More, she wanted to bring this extending nightmare to a quick end.

Nevsky grunted. "Okay, if you say so. Let's give some thought to what you promised yourself: a new order for Mariah Sullivan. How are you going to do things from here on out?"

Mariah thought for a moment. She remembered Shelly suggesting she was only halfway to being a complete person. And Nevsky had pretty much agreed, without beating her over the head with it. She drew a deep breath. "I take the initiative. I try to handle the ball. I don't think I rely on the police in this situation."

Nevsky nodded. "Very good!"

"So I know I have to do something," Mariah said. "Just what do you suggest?"

"How about some food. Brainstorming goes better—"

"Don't tell me, Yuri," Mariah said. "It's easier to brainstorm when your stomach is digesting. You just like fast food! Big philosopher!"

"So have a salad. Me for a Dave's Deluxe."

Mariah snickered. He was amusing. She wondered about his history. That face! He hadn't spent his life sitting around an office, she didn't think. No wedding ring. Right now for her he was a bit of a mystery man. They didn't talk much over their meal. Both were deep in thought. Finally Nevsky wiped his hands, drew a deep breath, and said, "What do you think of this idea?"

Roper Reynolds was a police patrolman by day. Like many officers, he moonlighted doing odd security stints, served as a bodyguard or handled other quasi-enforcement work for cash. All this Nevsky had explained before setting up her rendezvous with Roper, Saturday afternoon in a mall coffee shop not far from Rudy's rented house. She knew Roper from Nevsky's description even before he introduced himself. He was a carefully barbered, square-faced man in his early forties. He looked clean somehow. Maybe it was the blond hair and lineless face. She trusted him.

On the way to Rudy's rented house she asked him about Nevsky. He seemed reluctant to answer. "Yuri stays out of the spotlight these days," Roper said.

"Well, what about when he was in the spotlight?" Mariah insisted.

The cop hesitated. "He was a low-profile private eye. He had a partner, a lady lawyer, lived in a big old house. Then he took some hits, racked up some losses."

"He said he's semi-retired. What does that mean, exactly?"

Roper turned his shadowed face toward hers. "Why don't you ask him?"

"Was he married to the lawyer?"

"Not to her. To some other woman, years back." He

coughed. "That's all I know." He changed the subject to reviewing the "MO," as he called it, once they were inside Rudy's and Helga's house.

They found the house set back on a corner lot. It was a rambling Victorian wreck. Paint peeled from its columns and cornices. Some of its high windows had been broken and patched with transparent plastic sheets. It was an eerie place. Mariah was glad to have company.

Rudy answered the door. He was surprised to see that she wasn't alone. She introduced Roper as "a friend." Helga stood right behind Rudy in the small entrance hall, on guard against intrusions into her romantic fiefdom. Suspicion flamed in her fleshy face. Rudy led them into a drafty living room where pieces of dark turn-of-the-century wooden and marble furniture squatted like beasts in the shadows. He sat down on a sagging fringed couch, eager to begin the conversation. Mariah was amused to see how effectively she had set him up. It was a new feeling for her. There was something exhilarating about being on the offensive in life, even in a small way. "You been thinking about making me that loan?" Rudy prompted.

Helga interrupted. "I don't think that's why she came here. She came to see *you*. She's not done with you yet, and you're too dumb to know it."

Mariah said, "Helga, I assure you, whatever was between Rudy and me is over. *Well* over."

"Why don't you stay the hell out of here then?" Helga's complexion had ruddied, likely for the length of Mariah's stay.

"She came to talk business," Rudy said. He pumped some confidence into his Hollywood pretty face.

Mariah leaned forward toward him. "I'm not really here to talk about giving you money, Rudy. I want to talk about that photo of me and Jacky DuMarr that you took and sent to all the papers."

He looked at her blankly. "What's this? I don't know anything about any photo—"

"I told you!" Helga cried. "She's just looking for ways to get close to you."

"Let's everybody stay calm," Roper said. Mariah guessed he was no stranger to domestic disputes. He got up. "I'd like to have a look at your photography setup, Mr. Erris," he said. "Lab, cameras, whatnot."

Rudy frowned. "What's going on here?"

"Roper's interested in photography. I told him you're quite a picture taker." Mariah managed a convincing smile. "Show him your stuff."

"What if I don't want to show him?"

Oh, yes, that old belligerence. Mariah remembered it well. Mr. Bullheaded himself hadn't changed. Just *try* to make him do something . . .

"I'll just have a look on my own," Roper said. He started toward the next room. Mariah noticed his body was square and powerful.

Rudy looked indignantly at Mariah. "Who is this guy? What's with the camera angle?"

"She's hoping I'll go after him so she can talk to you in private," Helga said. "No way, Rudy!"

"Helga, quit acting!" Mariah ordered. "I told you both earlier that I know what you're trying to do to me. Make my life so miserable I come across with ten thousand dollars."

"You're mixed up big time, Mariah," Rudy said. He started after Roper. "Hey, pal, you didn't get invited on the ninety-nine-cent tour."

"Well, I'll look around just the same, if it's all right with you." Roper pushed ahead.

Rudy put his hand on Roper's shoulder. "Huh uh!"

Roper spun around so quickly that Mariah gasped. He shifted his weight somehow and with arms and legs moving swiftly spun Rudy around, collared him, and shoved him head first against the wall. Rudy's head met hard plaster. Holding the stunned man in a half nelson, Roper said softly, "You just let me go my way, okay?"

Roper's transit of the sizable house—fifteen rooms at least—was paced and thorough. While he searched, Rudy shook off his semiconsciousness. Helga pressed a cold face cloth to the lump on his head. "I'm going to call the police," she said.

Rudy stirred excitedly. "No police, for God's sake. I don't need the law snooping around my life!"

Mariah guessed he didn't want to answer the charges she'd make if the police showed up. She *knew* the two of them were somehow involved in her troubles.

Roper caught Mariah's eye and shook his head. He had found nothing. He sat down beside Rudy, who was propped on the couch. "Where's the camera equipment, friend?" he said.

"Who is this guy, Mariah?" Rudy asked.

"I told you. A friend."

Rudy's mouth opened to deliver one of his rude retorts. He closed it, thinking better of making Roper angry. His pale face now colored. "I pawned it," he said in a small voice.

Helga nodded. "We needed money. We have debts."

Roper glanced at Mariah, looking for guidance.

"I don't believe you!" she said. "You have all your cameras hidden somewhere."

"Why don't you get out of here?" Helga asked. "You and your strong-arm man. Stay away from my Rudy!"

Rudy looked baffled. "I don't know what you're up to, Mariah."

"Where did you pawn your equipment?" Mariah asked.

"I don't have to tell you!" Rudy said.

Roper snatched Rudy's shoulders and jerked him up off the couch. "Tell her anyway," he breathed. "Just to show me you're a real cooperative guy." Rudy told him in a frightened rush of words. Helga went to her purse and produced the pawn tickets.

"It's time to go," Roper said to Mariah.

They held a debriefing at the mall coffee shop. She gave him the hundred dollars she had promised him. "You didn't get much for your money," he said. "I'm sorry about that."

She smiled tightly. "I liked the way you handled Rudy. That's really the *only* way to handle him. I tried appealing to his good sense. I don't think he has any."

"The trick is not to get carried away with handling people rough. It can be like dope." Roper sat back and sipped his soda.

Mariah pressed her palm wearily to her forehead. "I don't know about Rudy now. I really don't."

"The woman didn't like you much," Roper said. "She thinks you're after her man."

"I was *married* to her man, Roper. I had enough of him. She won't believe it, though."

Roper looked thoughtfully toward the ceiling. "You know what? My cop gut feeling says you can forget about your ex as a suspect. But . . . the woman. Mariah, she's jealous. Hell, she hated you!"

Twelve

She drove home wondering if she had been only half right about the Rudy-Helga axis. Rudy had undoubtedly told his new wife about the misadventures of his old one. Why wouldn't she use them to destroy Mariah, whom she still saw as a threat to her happiness. The real threat to Helga of course was handsome Rudy and his straying ways. Was Helga responsible, Helga . . . alone? Could be.

She went to Rita's house to pick up Clarisse. Her friend was waiting with a sly smile. She shooed the kids off to play a while longer. "I gather you didn't see the local news this evening."

Mariah shook her head.

"I guess there's rough justice in this world after all. Want a cuppa?" She waved toward her coffee maker.

"Sure. What was on the news that I should really care about?"

"A brawl in a restaurant." Rita tittered, on the verge of a giggle.

"Oh? Who was involved?"

"Two of your *very* good friends, one of whom is a local celebrity. Phil Fontenot and his sleazy sidekick Mr. Oscar Something. Mr. F. got his face smashed in pretty good, teeth out, black eyes. He got his leg broken, too. Ditto Oscar."

"Oh, my God! I didn't think they were the brawling type. Sneaking and peeping were more their line."

"Two witnesses plus the offended parties swore Fontenot started it." Rita paused. "Isn't that *wonderful?*"

Mariah wondered about that. For a brief moment she felt concern for Fontenot. Then she caught herself. He hadn't cared about *her* pain, about what he had done to her reputation. He hadn't cared that he tried to drug her and use her body for his scum bag. Oh, she had too much of her share of woman's stock in trade—compassion! She had always been too feeling, too caring, too overflowing with empathy. Let there be a new order there, too! She was too much a woman to ever lose her tenderness. Just the same, she needed the spine it took to call for retribution when it was earned. She suddenly realized that Nevsky had arranged for Fontenot's public beating, damaging the reporter's reputation as well as his body. Good! She would save her tender feelings for those deserving them from here on out!

"*Inside Track* is going to be taken over temporarily by Chan Lee," Rita said. "She's a comer. Besides, they've got too many Anglo men with hairpieces on WLIT. I'm betting she'll do a better job than Fontenot."

"That's all good news." Mariah grinned.

"Hey, Mariah!" Rita made her thumb-and-forefinger

gesture. She puckered her lips. ''*Poooof* to Fontenot and Co.!''

Mariah didn't gloat on the way home. She did, however, feel a surge of satisfaction that carried her beyond readying Clarisse for bed and reading to her. It finally fully diminished when she found her answering machine held a half-dozen messages from reporters wanting her comments on the damaging photograph. She wouldn't be commenting, giving substance to that horrid, libelous thing. She supposed Jacky would talk to any reporter who'd listen, further vilifying her. Possibly later she would make some kind of statement. She ought to defend the Tot Lot. Nor had she forgotten the threats of the yuppy couple Cassandra and Nick Delos with their misguided outrage and sincere threat of a lawsuit. She ought to get an attorney, too. She very much wished Shelly was still alive to help her. How selfish of her to think that!

Among the reporters' inquiries were messages from two Tot Lot parents. They had withdrawn their children. She sighed. Every defection eroded her hopes of keeping the day-care center open.

For the first time since trouble had once again descended on her, she thought the worst might be over. With Fontenot silent and Jacky certain to trip herself up eventually, maybe things were going to quiet down. The public had a short memory. As to the ad hoc Tot Lot committee, she could readily defend herself before it. Maybe she had reached a position where she need no longer worry about who had harassed her. Whoever it was had done his worst, and the Tot Lot was still open. She found herself crossing her fingers. Let it remain that way!

Let nothing more go wrong!

She had a disturbing dream whose details escaped her after she started awake. It left her with an elusive impression that, after all, she ought to try to identify her persecutor. She supposed her mind was processing what Nevsky had suggested: look for other suspects. Awake, she had no luck coming up with a name or names. Jacky, Rudy, and Helga still led her suspects parade, with Helga now at its head. Nonetheless, she was niggled by the shifting nocturnal vision that refused to come into focus.

When Bud Scoffler surprised her with a phone call early Sunday morning, she found her reaction to him uneven. Her emotions had somehow been affected during her interlude of drug-driven passion in Fontenot's apartment. Sexual passion such as she had never felt, not with Rudy or anyone else. She recalled wanting more manly companionship than she had found to date. Bud had taken the brunt of her hallucinatory criticism. But had that been fair?

His plan for the day wasn't the passion-arousing kind. It included Clarisse, seats at the symphony orchestra's matinee, and a meal at a Mongolian restaurant newly opened in the next borough. Throughout the afternoon, he praised Clarisse's developed ear and palate, and her mom for having exposed her to culture and cuisine. That brought the conversation around to mothers. He lived with his. And from there to what his mother had seen in the paper—the photo of Mariah with Jacky and its accusatory caption.

"Mother wondered what that was all about." He pushed his palm back across his receding hairline to the back of his scalp. She sensed he was agitated.

"And what about you, Bud? Did you wonder, too?" He frowned. "Of course."

"I don't think you should have." Mariah felt her annoyance rising. "Do you really believe I could have done the things I've been accused of?"

Clarisse intruded into the conversation. "My Mom didn't do anything. I tell them that in school all the time!"

Mariah cleaned her daughter's lips with her napkin a little more vigorously than necessary. A signal to shut up, please. She stared at Bud. "Do you think such a person as I've been described as being would have a child like Clarisse?"

"N-no. I suppose not." He was hesitant. Mariah found that irritating.

"I think our afternoon should draw to a close." She hated to say it. During the concert the ear of her eroticism had heard not the tired warhorse of Beethoven's *Leonore* No. 3, but the strains of *Libiamo* . . . She had thought of consummation. Oh, she had been without a man for so long! Rita had been primed to take Clarisse on short notice. But no, it wouldn't be Bud's lucky day. The stars of trust and desire were misaligned.

She didn't hurry their goodbyes, though. Bud *was* a good kisser. She sent him on his way with reassuring but in no way humble words for his mother. Time would tell about Mariah's relationship with him. She didn't want to think that one libelous photograph had the potency to knock him right out of her life. If so, what kind of a guy was he?

On Monday morning a visitor came to her Tot Lot office. Her name was Cynthia Tran. Her card announced that she was with the Madison Day-Care Regulatory Board. Her title was Evaluator. Behind octagonal glasses, her Oriental eyes were swift and sharp.

"What brings you here, Ms. Tran?" she asked. In fact she had dreaded for some time the possibility of the arrival of officialdom on her doorstep. The Tot Lot had simply received too much bad publicity. That it was all unde-served made little difference. Truth wasn't what got attention these days. It was sensation.

Cynthia Tran nodded curtly and unzipped an expensive, soft briefcase. "We have been preparing a review of your facility and your qualifications for some time," she began.

"I'm sure it started with the first *Inside Track* broadcast."

Again the curt nod. "Yes."

"Well, you can be sure that I'll have plenty to say—"

"But that is not what brought me here today," interrupted Ms. Tran. "Evaluating this facility and its management is a fairly time-consuming process."

"Then, what *did* bring you here?"

"This." Cynthia slid a sheet out of the briefcase. She smiled apologetically. "Or more precisely, the letter from which this copy was made. It was mailed to my superior, Mr. Marvin Browne, chairman of the Madison County Day-Care Regulatory Board."

Mariah scanned the lines below the inside address with increasing shock.

MY DAUGHTER IS ENROLLED IN THE TOT LOT DAY-CARE CENTER. WHEN I SAW ALL THE NEWS ABOUT IT AND THAT MARIAH SULLIVAN RUNS IT, I GOT NERVOUS. I WAS WORRIED ABOUT WHAT MIGHT BE GOING ON THERE. I TALKED TO MY DAUGHTER AND MADE HER TELL ME THE TRUTH. MISTER CHAIRMAN, I WANT YOU TO KNOW MY DAUGHTER *SWORE* THAT MS. SULLIVAN TOOK SOME OF THE KIDS INTO HER OFFICE AND MADE THEM STRIP AND POSE. THEN SHE TOOK PICTURES OF THEM JUST LIKE THEY SAY SHE DID YEARS BACK AT HER LAST DAY-CARE CENTER. AND SHE TOUCHED THEIR PRIVATE PARTS. I'M GOING TO PULL MY DAUGHTER OUT OF THERE, BUT I WANT YOU TO KNOW

WHAT GOES ON AT THE TOT LOT. AND I WANT YOU TO
STOP IT—NOW!

The letter wasn't signed. Mariah was aware her face
was ashen. When she began to speak, she felt as though
two hands had gripped her throat. "This is a lie. All of
it."

Cynthia Tran nodded perfunctorily. "Yes, you must
deny it, of course. No one would admit to such behavior."

"I'm not admitting to it because I didn't do it!" Mariah
said angrily.

"My visit today is official. It's my bureau's responsibility to investigate such charges as are made in this letter."

"But it's not signed. Anyone could have written it,
whether or not that person has a child enrolled."

"In that case our investigation will reveal as much. In
the meantime our regulations require us to do two things
in concert with our investigation. The first I've already
done: inform you of the nature of the charges behind the
investigation. The second is to notify all parents about
the charges." Cynthia crossed her knees primly and
smoothed her skirt over them. When she looked back at
Mariah's face, her eyes had taken on a steely look that
she guessed masked loathing. She squirmed inwardly. She
didn't deserve this! Regardless of her personal opinions,
Cynthia's tones remained determinedly businesslike.
"And to tell the parents that they may be asked to make
statements in connection with the charges."

"No child has been abused here!"

"We are required to do one more thing in connection
with the public interest," Cynthia went on. "We must
issue a public statement that an investigation of the Tot
Lot is under way."

Mariah cringed inwardly. How many more blows could

the Tot Lot take before its walls fell down? How much more did parents need to hear before all the remaining kids were pulled out? She thought of Shelly's and Nevsky's counsel. That encouraged her to spin her mind free of her pervading feelings of helplessness. Dwelling on injustice was her old way of thinking. A lot of what happened in the world was unfair. One had to fight it, not just feel wronged. She must act, not just react. She gathered her strength and stood, towering well above the short, seated Vietnamese woman. "I have a statement for you to take back to your people, Ms. Tran—besides telling them that everything in this letter is a lie. Tell them that I'll be in touch with my attorney about a very large libel suit against whomever wrote this letter. If we find out who is responsible, that person won't be left with a dime!"

Cynthia slid a Mont Blanc pen from her briefcase and made a note on a small clipboard. "Duly noted," she intoned. She looked up. "The bureau will need the mailing list for the current Tot Lot families."

"Do you know someone broke into this office, made a copy of that list, and sent every parent a letter filled with spurious charges?"

Cynthia's brow rose above her octagonal glasses. "I did not know that." She made another note.

"Someone's trying to destroy this day-care center and my reputation along with it!" Mariah said. "I wasn't guilty of anything eight years ago and I'm not guilty now!"

A curt nod. "The bureau will schedule an interview with you at the appropriate time."

Mariah felt her anger rise. "Why do you jump when some weirdo sends you a crank letter—then make me sit and wait before I can give my side of things?"

"Rules," Cynthia said.

"Your rules suck." Mariah surprised herself with her crudity.

Ms. Tran overlooked it. "You're not required to give us the list. But it's simpler just to do it than make us get a court order—which of course we *will* do."

Mariah felt somehow refreshed by her lingering anger. "Does that take care of your official business, Ms. Tran?"

"I believe so. Once I have the list."

Mariah opened her files and pulled out a copy of the parent list. She gave it to her visitor. "Then I believe you should leave. Have a good day."

She struggled to keep her emotional balance in the wake of Cynthia Tran's visit. She had to *act*. This was no time to sit and fret about what had just happened and could happen.

She phoned Attorney Donaldson, chairman of the ad hoc parents' committee. She crisply told him about the letter to the regulatory board and Cynthia's visit. She wanted to go on record at once, she said, to make it clear that the charges in the letter were false. She wanted the committee's help in finding out which parent—if any—had sent the letter. She doubted any parent had done it. She wanted everyone to understand that someone was conducting an unprincipled vendetta against the Tot Lot and her. She was pleased to find nothing pleading or submissive in her tone. She simply said her piece and hung up.

Her next call was to Nevsky. "I want to talk to you," she said.

"What about? You're on your own. I did my little piece for you."

"For which I thank you." She thought it unwise to

spell out Fontenot's misfortunes over the phone. "Just the same, I still need about ten minutes of your time. Where do you live? I'll come over."

"It's not a great place to entertain." His voice turned hesitant.

"What's the deal, Nevsky? You live in a cardboard box?"

"Next best thing. Basement apartment. I'd rather meet you at Wendy's."

"Give me your address!" she ordered.

Pause. "Hey, it's not a great place to entertain, okay?"

"Address?"

"138A Sunset Avenue."

"Like I said, I just need about ten minutes of your time," she said. At the noon hour she left the Tot Lot, stopped by a deli and loaded up on the sandwiches and coffee on which she had a feeling Nevsky lived. The 138 part of the address belonged to an impressive Tudor style mansion. To find "A" she had to walk down a side driveway and under a stone arch. It led to a rough stone corridor above the big house's rear cement deck. At the end of the corridor on the left was a screen door. There was no doorbell. The screen door had a spider-shaped hole in its mesh. Real spiders had left furry egg cases at the ends of the lintel. She clattered the screen open and knocked on the heavy wooden door leading into the basement.

As she stood for a moment, shifting her grip on the bag, she reminded herself that she really needn't have made this visit. What she needed to know she could have found out from Nevsky on the phone in a few minutes. That way, of course, she couldn't have seen where he lived.

He was right. It wasn't much. Two small rooms with

a kitchenette and bath. The place was permeated with the smell of mildew. Its white walk of dormant summer-summoned stains wriggled low on the walls. Nevsky lived like a monk. A few books lay on tables. He had no TV or radio that she could see. The phone was the only concession to the electronic age. Furniture was cheap and worn.

He read her inquiring glance as plainly as a billboard. "I've pretty much got past having things," he said.

"Oh?" There was a statement you didn't hear every day. "And how did you come to this exalted state?"

He told her something of his past, palmier days, more social life, more comings and goings. He hinted, without boasting, at some special, dangerous adventures in pursuit of the "help" he had once sold—on a grander scale than he was offering her. He mentioned a woman named Charity with whom he had shared his life, but not his bed. Then things had angled down rather sharply . . .

"I'd think you could still handle—well, more in life," Mariah said.

He smiled, his slightly tilted eyes closing with deeply felt humor. "Possibly I could. Possibly I will again. Mariah, it's the way of the Russian to withdraw to private places after soul-trying events to think and seek an adjustment with greater things."

"You mean with God?"

"I mean to realign one's place among the mysteries."

"So you're doing that here? That's why you live here—in this dump?"

"Some Russians go to monasteries or to holy men. Starets they call them. I came here."

This line of talk led Mariah on to most unfamiliar ground. Thinking about her spirit or soul or whatever made her feel most uncomfortable. She wasn't much for church goings on. She was ready to drop the topic—and fast. Then Nevsky said, "So you see, you and I have come to the same point in our lives."

"I don't understand." She busied herself with the bag, unpacking, searching the kitchenette for dishes. Why did she feel so nervous?

"Life has brought me to a difficult point along my own track," Nevsky went on. "It's done the same to you along a quite different one. Each of us needs to re-center ourselves among the mysteries if we're to go on in a positive way. A way clear of error."

"I don't know what you're talking about, Yuri." She unwrapped the pastrami sandwiches. "You do something wrong? Get over it!"

"Maybe you can't put words to your shortcomings. But I think you understand something about them. My old chum Shelly—may he rest in peace—couldn't have passed up a chance to suggest you had to work on yourself . . ."

Mariah swallowed. She remembered Shelly's words. *I'd say you're about fifty percent of the way to getting control of your life.* And hadn't she lamented that situation? Hadn't she told herself there was so much to be done? Now she thought for the first time: wasn't there *too* much to be done? At least more than she knew how to do.

Nevsky offered her the other chair. "Mariah, we allow things to happen to us. We open up the door and they come in. What we both have to do is close the doors that we've allowed to open through timidity or poor judgment or mistrust or whatever, and open new ones."

She laughed nervously and looked sidelong at him. She almost wanted to see a smile. But his high-cheeked face was set seriously. "Things aren't what they seem," he said. "Mysteries penetrate everything. We have to reattune ourselves to them. That's why I'm holed up here. I can be free to think."

"What did you do wrong that takes so much thinking?"

"Nothing so much wrong as ill-advised. Anyway, it doesn't concern you, I'm happy to say."

"You told me I had to act more, not be so passive. Is that what I'm supposed to do to 'reattune' myself?"

"Partly." Nevsky spooned mustard over his pastrami with a flimsy plastic knife. "The rest is more subtle. It's about accepting your weakness and looking for strength in mysteries."

Mariah slapped the table. "*What* are you talking about?"

"Personal salvation . . ."

She left Nevsky's apartment with what she had gone to get, the name of a reliable attorney. She couldn't hope to find another like Shelly. Nevsky was reassuring. He told her she didn't want another Shelly. She wanted a more flamboyant character. Hence Frederick Folsom, "Frenetic Freddy," as Nevsky called him. What else she left the mildewy apartment with she wasn't sure. Had the Russian-American been talking nonsense, or was there something important in what he had said for Mariah Sullivan? *Looking for strength in mysteries . . .* She certainly didn't know about all that. She smiled. She saw Shelly Mortenstein's fine hand in all this. Had he known all along what she needed and a man who could lead her to it?

Frederick Folsom was delighted to shoulder her problems—for a fee, of course. One she sensed was smaller than it might have been if she hadn't come recommended by Nevsky. Frenetic Freddy was dressed according to the styles of Las Vegas, Los Angeles, or New York, one of those male couture centers. He looked like a combination of a racetrack tout and an MTV rock zombie—wide stripes in his pants, a cartoon on a tie almost big enough to use as a tablecloth, striped suspenders, and a shock of white-blond hair dryer-blown into a cloud.

"Consider yourself out of the loop from hereon out, sweets. I make the statements," Frenetic Freddy said. "I hold the news conferences. Send the swill gatherers straight to me. You have no comment, no comment, *no comment*. Clear your every word with me."

"What about the ad hoc committee at the Tot Lot?"

"You have no comment. No comment . . ." he repeated. "Me, I'm going to have plenty of comments. I'm going to threaten enough suits to open a men's store. We're gonna start shutting a lot of people up! We're gonna back them off like the lion tamer in the Barnum and Bailey cage!" He threw an arm over her shoulder. "Meantime, bust your buns to find these loonies who're succeeding in making your life crazy, whoever they are. Call the cops, the PIs, the freakin' National Guard. Meantime, I'll hold the fort."

He ushered her out of his private office. "Say hello to Nevsky for me, sweets," he said in parting. "There's a guy who's *muy hombre*, when he's not off studying his navel."

Mariah left Folsom's office with a spinning head. She had so much on her mind now! She sensed she wouldn't be able to sort everything out, not with the pressures of running the Tot Lot and parenting Clarisse. Just the same, she sensed a rising pressure to do just that. Further, she sensed the increasing need to sort *herself* out. No matter Nevsky's precise meanings—if there were any—the overall guiding principle couldn't be disputed. As he might put it: she was walking in error. And would until she completed the changes in her inaccurate thinking.

She groaned above the van radio's rock. She couldn't see how she could do all that! She needed strength and resourcefulness that she wasn't sure she had. What she had to do loomed like a mountain seen from foothills. Too much. *Too much!*

She worried the rest of the day about where she was and what to do. Not surprisingly, her sleep was trouble- and dream-filled. When she started awake, it was with a mumbled cry of revelation. She sucked in deep breaths and looked up at the shadowed ceiling. Yes, yes . . . Maybe this was all going to be easier than she thought. Because she had found an answer of sorts. It came in a dream that seemed as real as they were ugly. They were . . .

The Groomes!

The Tot Lot had been open only a few weeks, she recalled, reeling her mind into the past. Had routines been established, Mariah undoubtedly would have spotted Scotty Groome right away. Even so, she noticed him first the day he had limped out to the playground. She hurried over to him, a thin five-year-old, and looked down at his narrow freckled face. She smiled and touched his shoulder. He flinched. That meant nothing at the time. What she remembered was that he didn't smile back. She asked him why he limped. He lisped that he had twisted his ankle. "Did it running around," he muttered. She led him down to the sand pile where orange and yellow plastic trucks and earthmovers stood like the originals on a sprawling construction site. "You stay here and play, Scotty. Don't try to run around."

When he moved to sit down on the sand he winced. "You must have given yourself quite a twist," she said. "Let me see."

"No!" He covered his sock with a little hand. "It's okay. I'm okay."

She forgot about the incident until the next week, when she walked by the water fountain where Scotty was bent over drinking. Another boy stood behind him, waiting. He playfully grabbed Scotty's loose shirttail and flipped it up. Scotty's back was covered with small bruises. Some were purple, others yellowed by passing time. She asked him to come to her office. She offered him a cookie. He refused it. He was nervous. She tried chatting with him, but he didn't respond. He sat on the edge of his small chair, looking like a racer poised at the starting line.

"How did you get those bruises on your back, Scotty?" she asked.

"Fightin'," he said at once.

"Fighting with whom?"

"Just . . . fightin'."

Mariah sat silently for a moment. What now? She had an idea. She turned to her desk and pulled out the Groome folder. She wrote a brief note to Edna and Cliff Groome, whom she had to admit she didn't remember. She said she was concerned about their son's fighting; that it could cause him possibly serious injury. She hoped they could put a stop to it before something worse happened. She sent the note home with him but received no reply.

She then made it a point to go by Rochelle Camwell's room daily to check on Scotty. He seemed all right. Mariah asked efficient Rochelle what she thought about the boy. "Quiet, listless, not great in social skills." She shrugged. "What about him?"

"I think he might be abused," Mariah said softly.

"I'll keep an eye on him."

A week later Rochelle caught her in the hall. Her matronly face was white with anger. "The S.O.B.s! They're marking him under his clothes. There're red marks on the backs of his legs. Looks like a can opener point or an ice pick." She clutched Mariah's forearm. "When I asked Scotty what they were, he didn't answer."

Mariah felt a flow of white anger. She went to the phone and called the Groomes. She left a message on their machine. No response. She tried again the next day. Same result. The next morning she waited under the portico for Scotty's arrival. He got out of a rusty VW bug. A woman was waving him on his way. Mariah walked around to the driver's door. The occupant was a girl of about nineteen. She had very bad skin and a cigarette in her hand. "Mrs. Groome?" Mariah asked.

"Nah! I just drive the little jerk in. They pay okay for it."

"Will one of the Groomes pick him up?"

"Nah! They got somebody else to do that. Hey, the Groomes are busy people. Dig it!" She clunked the VW into gear and scooted off.

At an earlier time in her life, Mariah might have avoided a confrontation. No longer. She and Rochelle arranged a visit to the Groome home at dinnertime. They lived in an immaculately manicured single-level ranch. A Volvo and a Saab paired in the driveway. The door chimes pealed "Come Back to Sorrento." A blonde in an expensive business suit opened the door and stood staring at them through the storm door. "Yes?"

"Mrs. Groome?"

"Yes."

Mariah introduced herself and Rochelle. "We'd like to talk to you about Scotty."

Edna Groome turned back toward the interior. "Yo, Cliff, the day care is here." Her suit flattered her generous curves. On her left wrist she wore gold bracelets and a diamond-decorated watch. Cliff strode up. He was at least six-four, with shoulders like an action adventure movie's leading man. He wore designer sweats. "Yeah?" he said.

"Could we come in?" Rochelle asked. "What we have to say the neighbors needn't overhear."

"They're not the nosy type. Why don't you tell us what's on your mind?" Cliff had perfect teeth and the close shave that only a barber could provide. Neither made any move to allow their visitors inside.

Well, she hadn't come this far to stop short, Mariah told herself. "We've come to ask you about the different marks on Scotty's body. Bruises, punctures . . ." She let her voice trail off. She might as well have been speaking Urdu for all the signs of understanding she got from the Groomes.

"Marks?" Cliff asked in a puzzled voice. "He's a little boy. He falls down, gets up, falls down again."

Edna's toned face angled into a heavy frown. "Are you implying something about Scotty? About us?"

Mariah kept her voice steady. "We've come to ask you how he got the marks on his body. The ones he has now and the other ones he's had since we began to notice them."

"Beat it," Cliff said without emotion. "We don't need you here. We pay our bill. You take care of our kid. That's it." He stepped back from the door, preparing to close it.

Mariah folded her arms. "You'd do well to talk to us. If you don't, I guarantee you'll be talking with someone from the child welfare agencies."

"Why in the world would you tell them about us?"

"I wouldn't dare make any charges or suggestions that you could run to attorneys with," Mariah said. "You just guess what I mean. Talk to me or talk to child welfare."

Cliff's face reddened. "Your talking to them would be

a mistake. A giant mistake. One I think you'd be *very sorry* you ever made." He and his wife stepped back as though on cue, and shut the door in the two women's faces.

The next day Mariah made the appropriate phone calls. There was an elaborate ritual of investigating a charge of child abuse. She was happy to leave it in the hands of the professionals. Three days later, Scotty didn't appear at the Tot Lot. Or on any of the following days.

Three weeks later, her office phone rang. She recognized the polished voice of Edna Groome. "We're thinking about you a lot lately, Tot Lot lady. We're thinking about how much trouble you started for us."

"You started it yourself when you—"

"We owe you big time already. If things keep going the way they are, you're going to be one *sorry* lady." She hung up.

Mariah's hands were shaking.

Six months later she got a call from welfare services. The previous day, Scotty had been removed from his parents' custody. She received the call with a pounding heart. In the shadows she saw hulking Cliff. Her anxiety worsened when he called her the next day. "Start worrying, Tot Lot. Because you have a lot to worry about now. Because of you our son is gone."

"Excuse me! Because of *you*, not me."

"We'll pick our time, our place, and our way," Cliff said. "Have a pleasant day."

That had been months ago. Afterward she had been shaken for some time, watching her back and dreading unexpected phone calls. Then she reasoned that at the bottom of their hearts, the Groomes were cowards. How else could they abuse their son? After that the couple slipped into the back of her mind.

Now they were very much in the front of it. And Mariah had a plan. Her days of pussyfooting around problems were over. She imagined she understood what Nevsky meant. She had to act, not sit back. She called Roper Reynolds. "Want to earn another hundred bucks?" she asked.

She arranged an after-school play for Clarisse and met Roper after closing the Tot Lot. On the drive to the Groome home she filled him in on Edna and Cliff. "One of America's fun couples," the cop muttered.

"He's pretty big," she said.

"Cowards come in all sizes."

The Groome chimes must have been programmable. Now they pealed, "O Solo Mio." Edna answered. To her coutured look was added a flattering suntan. "You!" she said. "Of all the nerve . . ."

"We'd like to visit for a bit." Roper grabbed the handle and opened the storm door as Mariah pushed in past Edna. "Hey, what the hell—" the stylish woman protested.

"We're just making a little social call, Mrs. Groome," Roper said. "Mariah wants to talk to you."

"Cliff!" Edna backed away as Mariah walked into the pristine living room. Its expensive Orientals were newly vacuumed. The antique furniture was polished and perfect. She saw no dust, dirt, or disorder. This had never been an environment in which to raise a child.

Tanned Cliff appeared in an electric blue jogging outfit and pump sneakers. He glowered at Mariah. "Look who's here!" he said. "I can't believe it!"

"They pushed their way in here," Edna said.

"Just to say something to you. Then we'll be out of here." Mariah made herself step closer to Edna. "I'm here to warn you about what you've been doing to me and the Tot Lot."

Edna's face broke into a grin. "What *we're* doing? You mean what *you're* doing. You're doing what you accused us of doing—abusing. Pot calling the kettle black!" White moths of saliva flew from Edna's mouth. "Think we don't eat up everything they're saying about you? It's sweet after what you did to us."

"You two arranged everything," Mariah said. "It's taken me a while to figure it all out. I'm here to say stop it!"

"And just what do you think we're doing?" Edna asked.

"Getting your revenge!" Mariah cried. "You blamed me for the loss of your son. Now you're trying to get even, just the way you promised!"

"Nice try," Cliff said. "We only just heard about your problems a couple of days ago."

"You mean about a month ago. When you started to cause them."

Edna's eyes widened. "You honestly believe we're responsible?"

"I'm *sure* you are."

"Guess where we've been for the last two months?" Edna said. "Florida!"

"With plenty of witnesses," Cliff said.

Edna was about to say something. Cliff cut her off with an abrupt gesture. He pointed at Roper. "And who's this, Sullivan? Your bodyguard?"

"A friend."

Cliff said, "Well, I have somebody I want you to meet." He pointed behind them.

Mariah turned. She heard a *thhwupp*. She spun back to see that Cliff had punched a distracted Roper in the stomach. The cop staggered. Mariah screamed as Cliff waded in, fists big as ham hocks. Roper tottered backward, trying to get his hands up. Cliff muttered through clenched teeth. "Yeah, push your way in here! Dummies! You don't have a legal leg to stand on." He cursed violently. His fists quick as mousetraps punished stunned Roper's face and body. *Thwuupp, thwuupp!*

Mariah screamed again, feeling helpless and frightened. No! She had to *do* something. Without thinking, she flung herself on Cliff's back. He'd been well named. His back was like a cliff and about as easy to hang onto. He tried to shrug her off. She wrapped her arms around his neck, trying to pull him back. He heaved her nearly off. Into her midsection he drove an elbow as punishing as a log in a torrent. The wind knocked out of her, Mariah sank to her knees, sucking desperately for breath, fearing she had been horribly injured.

While she knelt frightened and gasping, Edna moved in and kicked her in the ribs with pointed-tip shoes. Edna hissed, "You bitch, Sullivan! You deserve this!" She drew back her leg again. Mariah couldn't stand. She managed to topple over. The second kick struck her hip. She couldn't get her wind! Edna circled toward her head. She was going to kick Mariah in the face! She pressed her nose to the carpet just in time. The kick glanced off the top of her skull. Still breathless, she couldn't cry out.

Above and behind her she heard more curses and blows. Then those sounds stopped until the only thing that reached her ears was the ragged rush of Cliff's breath. Edna kicked Mariah's head again. Lights flashed and redness invaded her sight. She swam toward unconsciousness, then recovered. She felt Cliff's arm around her waist. He pulled her to her feet. Each gasping breath gouged her with pain. She groaned.

"Some bodyguard you got!" Cliff sneered. "Not even watching for a sucker punch."

Tears of agony ran from Mariah's eyes. Through them

she saw Roper sprawled motionless faceup on the carpet. Blood ran from his left nostril. "You murdered him!" she panted.

Cliff chuckled. "No way! He's down for the count, that's all." He grabbed her roughly by the shoulders. Edna pressed in, her face inches from Mariah's. "You came back to us!" she gloated. "After what you did, you came *back*, asking for it."

"And pushed your way in, you and your goon," Cliff said. His voice took on a singsong innocence. "All we did was defend our hearth and home."

"Let me go," Mariah panted. She was smeared with tears and still in pain from Edna's kicks to her head. She thought a rib was broken. Everything had gone so wrong!

Cliff dragged her across the room and threw her down on the couch. He towered over her. "Now we got you. What do we do with you?" He made a fist and looked at it.

"Beat her pretty white face in!" Edna suggested.

Cliff's handsome smile was chilling. "I can feel the bones behind that sweet face breaking like eggshells." He grabbed Mariah's shoulder and sat her up straight. His huge fist descended slowly to touch the tip of her nose. "One punch and you could look like a pug who stayed with the ring too long."

Dread rose in Mariah's heart. For the moment she forgot her pain. She thought of horrible harm, reconstructive cosmetic surgery. "You can't just beat me up!"

"Oh, we can't?" Cliff said. "It's our two words against yours." He cuffed the side of Mariah's head. Pain flared up from her skull's bruises. She trembled, and not just from the pain. "If you disfigure me, you'll pay an enormous price." She played her only trump. "My bodyguard happens to be an off-duty cop."

A shadow passed over Cliff's chiseled face. He weighed the pleasure of revenge against the danger of society's reprisal. Disappointment dimmed his glittering eyes like a shade drawn down a window.

Edna came to the same conclusion. "Give her just *one* more!" she urged. "For Scotty!"

Cliff drew back his hand deliberately. He was gauging how hard to hit her. Mariah couldn't raise her hands in time to block the blow. His open-handed slap fell like fire on the left side of her face. She screamed.

Cliff grabbed her arm and jerked her off the couch. He rushed her toward the door. Edna opened it. He sent her tumbling off the porch onto the grass. She stumbled and fell. It had begun to rain. Her stockings and dress were smeared and torn. Her palms were greased with grass. She twisted up to a sitting position in time to see Cliff drag Roper out and dump him on the matted lawn beside her.

"Come again any time," he said.

Thirteen

She sat across the unadorned table from Nevsky. He listened without comment while she told him what had happened to her and Roper at the Groome home. She carried witness to the disaster on her body. The left side of her face was heavily bruised, her eye partially shut. She had knots on her skull and a broken rib that clicked every time she drew a deep breath—which she seldom did now. "It was all a terrible mistake, Yuri!" she said.

He nodded noncommittally. He rested his elbows on the table and leaned forward onto his cupped palms, his graying beard protruding over his hands. "The real mistake you made was in trying to be rational, to sit down and figure it out. Real revelations originate in magic. That's why you ran off half-cocked."

She glowered. She had come for practical advice such as he had previously given her. Now here he was starting in with the weirdness again. Her whole world was crumbling and he was talking magic. "Magic isn't my strong suit," she said crisply.

He tossed off a shrug. "Have you completely forgotten what I said about seeking strength in mysteries?"

"I don't understand when you talk like that!" she said. "Look at me! I nearly got killed trying to save my reputation and my day-care center. And you sit there and talk about 'mysteries.'" Her swollen face throbbed with the pulse of her agitation. She felt an inch from either tears or rage.

He got up and made more coffee, giving her a chance to cool down. He brought her a fresh cup and said, "How would you describe the situation, Mariah?"

"The situation is awful! Worse than before I went to the Groomes. Frenetic Freddy advised me not to press any charges against them. The publicity would hurt me. That didn't work. The *Groomes* reported Roper and I forced our way in and tried to rough them up. The media slanted everything to make them look like heroes defending their turf against an all-but-convicted child abuser. All lies, but the media has me in their sights and they're going to keep firing as long as there's new ammunition. Nobody bothered to research the Groomes and find out they're *real* child abusers!" She shook her head. It hurt. "The Tot Lot's lost about half its enrollment. I'm now running in the red. *Everything's* gone wrong."

"And you're completely at a loss about how to handle it."

"That's why I came here, Yuri. To get some help. Not talk about 'magic' and 'mysteries.'" She didn't tell him about how she had to battle to overcome her self-consciousness, considering her face's appearance, to even make the trip across town.

Nevsky chuckled. "Why not talk about mysteries, when they're all around us?"

"Yuri!"

He sighed. "Turning one's back on rationality isn't an easy concept to grasp, but it's harder when you resist, Mariah."

He could be so annoying! "How about some more *practical* advice?"

"Open up your thinking. You're too locked in on reasoning. Entertain new, wild options. Allow mystery to enter in." He raised his cup in emphasis. "I don't think what's happening to you is exactly what it seems."

"Could you say something I understand?" Mariah growled.

"All right. I will. Invite me for dinner."

Later she wondered if she had wanted him to ask something like that. She wasn't sure what to make of him or how she felt about him. One thing: he was interesting and a little mysterious, speaking of mysteries. Romance? With twenty years between them? She doubted it. Right then she hadn't the energy or focus to contemplate romance. Then she thought of Clarisse, fatherless, and wasn't so sure how she felt.

Her whole world was falling apart and she didn't know how to stop it.

That afternoon, Frenetic Freddy called her. He had attended a meeting of the Tot Lot parents' ad hoc committee. "Got a lot of silly, scared people in that bunch, Mariah," he said. "But you got one friend there at least."

"I can't imagine who."

"Black guy. Glasses. Kept talking about evidence. 'We have no evidence, evidence, *evidence*,' he kept saying."

Mickey Donaldson. Who would have thought him a friend?

"And you got some kind words from a Mrs. Orel."

"I'd forgotten she was on the committee. *She*'s in my corner—at least for now."

"I told them somebody had it in for you," Freddy said. "The big smear attempt from somebody getting even. I kept telling them you didn't do anything."

"They believe you?"

"Who knows?"

"Where are they, Freddy? What do they want to do?"

"Some want to sue. Some just to boycott you. Others aren't sure. Hey, you want my gut feeling?"

"I guess."

"In the end, they're all going to dump the Tot Lot."

"Oh, Lord . . ."

"The letter that was supposed to have come from a parent?" Freddy said. "About you taking pictures of kids? They can't find out who sent it."

"That's because no parent did it!"

"They're looking for a name to put on it."

"They won't find one! What about Cassandra and Nick Delos?" Mariah asked. "That letter I got from their attorney?"

"I called the outfit, talked countersuit. That'll put some sand in their clockwork for a while."

"Good!" At least there was some good news.

"Then we got that Dragon Lady, Ms. Tran," Freddy went on. "She's gonna put the nail in your coffin with her interviews. She's talkin' to everybody, scaring them half to death." He coughed nervously. "Kid, it doesn't look good."

It didn't look any better by Saturday. Nor did she. Her face was less swollen, her eye fully open. But the downside was that some of the purple had yellowed. What she looked like was beyond the power of makeup to hide. She didn't even try. The rib was the worst. When she moved or was forced to breathe deeply it darted with pain.

Since her last visit to Nevsky's mildewy basement apartment, she had alternated between dismissing his mystic mumblings and trying to shove her thinking in new directions. She surely wasn't certain precisely what he was trying to tell her. Nonetheless, as she made pastry for the evening's apple tart some different ideas arrived with force enough to still the marble rolling pin under her palms. Those ideas boiled down to one word.

Why?

Why was the pattern of scandal and shame from eight years being repeated? *Why* was the Tot Lot being made to relive the horror of J. D. Day Care? *Why* was she being vilified as a new version of Jacky DuMarr? All along, her only thought about the motivation of her tormentor was revenge against her. All her suspects had their reasons to want to get even: fat Delsy Comorra, who blamed Mariah for the failure of her wretched day-care center; Rudy, who was attempting blackmail; Helga, who was needlessly jealous; and Jacky, who had thought Mariah ought to hire her "for old time's sake." All had denied her accusations. She had believed none of them. Now she wondered. Could they *all* be innocent?

If someone else was enraged enough to go to the extremes required to ruin her reputation and destroy her business, that person must be living in a rage of hate. Then why didn't he or she physically attack her? Why not simply . . . kill her? She swallowed and looked up from the spreading circle of dough. A chill breeze seemed to stir through her condo. Why pussyfoot around with notes and effigies and photographs? Why try to visit so much notoriety on the Tot Lot? Why not just do away with Mariah Sullivan? She took her thinking down a still darker path. Maybe she *was* to be killed—but not until she had been publicly and emotionally tortured. Not until she was the same ragged wreck she had been eight years ago.

A discovery of sorts, then, was distilled from the mash of her tumbled thoughts: the tormentor's motivation was deeper than it seemed. Yet just what it was she couldn't pin down.

When Nevsky arrived shortly after six, she intended to share her ideas with him. But Clarisse, like iron to male magnet, sat beside him and wouldn't be dislodged. He didn't make it any easier by practicing his repertoire of sleight-of-hand tricks. He pulled quarters from her ears and made them disappear in a flick of fingers. "This one was taught to me under the oath of secrecy by the Sultan of the Perilous Peninsula," he fibbed. Clarisse ate it up.

At dinner Clarisse monopolized the conversation, talking mostly about herself. Mariah supposed it was good for her to talk, but there was a limit. She finally shushed the girl and asked Nevsky how Roper was doing. He reported that the biggest injury was to the cop's pride and reputation. His fellow officers were ribbing him without mercy over his having been such an easy K.O. "His head and his belly are sore," Nevsky said. "He says he's a better cop for it. He said forget about paying him. He did a lousy job."

Mariah made a note to send Roper a card—and further apologies for getting him into that stupid mess. Hefting her Day Planner caused her to twist. Her broken rib grated and she grimaced. The pain reminded her of how bad she looked—something like a cross between a kung fu match loser and a dental patient after a full-mouth extraction.

It took forever to get Clarisse to bed. Firm words were required. Mariah was about to crank out espresso for two when the chimes rang. It was Bud Scoffler, dressed in a suit and tie. He slipped in before she could say anything. "I wonder if we could have a chat?" he asked.

"I'm sorry. I have company. Come, join us," Mariah said. He stared at her damaged face, but said nothing. "It's not pretty, is it?" she asked. She thought he would ask what had happened to her, but instead he looked away. He was obviously disturbed by her injuries. Well, that made two of them. She led him into the kitchen and introduced him to Yuri. She noted the small scowl creasing Bud's brow. "Why are you here, Mr. Nevsky?" he asked.

"Name's Yuri. Got invited. More than I can say for you." Nevsky had always struck Mariah as an affable sort. She hadn't expected abrasiveness from him. Men! Hormones!

Bud sat. "Do you mind if I ask what your relationship with Mariah is?" he asked.

"Bud, that's not your affair!" Mariah's indignation rose.

Nevsky nodded his craggy head in agreement. "It isn't, but . . ." He shrugged. "If you must know, I'm Mariah's starets, her spiritual counselor."

Mariah's mouth closed. *That* was how he saw their relationship?

Bud leaned toward Nevsky, the balding facing the bald. "She and I are an item," he said.

"Mariah is an item all by herself." Nevsky grinned.

Bud blinked. He wasn't sure what Nevsky meant. He sat back. Mariah could almost hear him thinking. He nodded and turned toward Mariah. "I wanted to talk with you about some things."

Mariah sensed he was somehow confessing. "About what?" she asked.

"Mother saw an article about you and some goon breaking into a couple's home and assaulting them. She thought I ought to find out directly from you about what went on."

"Mariah and Roper were breaking and entering," Nevsky volunteered. "The Groomes surprised them and defended their property."

"Yuri!" Mariah squawked.

Nevsky nodded slyly and winked. "Here's a tip." He motioned Bud closer. "She's setting you and your mother up for the same thing!"

Bud was puzzled. His brow wrinkled below his thinning hairline. The lenses of his metal-rimmed glasses suddenly seemed opaque. For the first time it occurred to Mariah that maybe he wasn't that bright. A good kisser and music lover—*Libiamo!* But . . . maybe short on smarts. Then there was the issue of trust that had arisen a few days earlier. Surely he couldn't believe Nevsky's blarney for one second. "Bud, ignore Yuri. Join us. We were just going to have an espresso."

The three of them proved to be an odd trio. Conversation was stilted, at best. Mariah didn't want to drag out the dirtiest of her linen in front of Bud, though discussing her worst problems with Nevsky came easily. She supposed that was because he was more like a father to her. So they torturously trod the trying conversational plain of current events and entertainment. She had the feeling each man was simply trying to outwait the other.

About eleven o'clock Bud turned to her with some impatience. "Well, what about that business in the paper and on TV, you fighting with that couple?" He studied her damaged face afresh. Mariah nearly cringed under his critical scrutiny. "It's pretty clear you were smacked a few times."

Mariah's eyes narrowed. Didn't he remember how badly she had taken his earlier suspicions? "I'll say this once, Bud, and then I don't want to hear anything more about it. The media got it all wrong."

"But—how could they?" He seemed genuinely baffled, as though the nightly news was unimpeachable.

Nevsky got up. "Bedtime for the middle-aged," he said. "I'm outta here."

At the door, Mariah barely had time to say, "I'm sorry. I really hadn't expected him."

"Your regular guy?" Nevsky's angular face revealed nothing.

"No, not really. He's—well, I'm not sure. Yuri, I still have to talk to you about what I figured out. I let my mind wander free and—"

"Good night, Mariah," he said.

She watched him get into his borrowed car, some kind of rundown Detroit junk. When she turned back toward the kitchen she understood she wasn't in a good mood. She couldn't read Nevsky! One minute he seemed her ally. The next, an irritable stranger.

She had Bud out of there in fifteen minutes.

Going to bed, she thought, *I haven't a clue about what I'm doing—anywhere in my life.*

Mariah spent Sunday thinking about her public and personal lives and wasn't comforted. She tried to take her idea further that there was more motivation to what was happening at the Tot Lot than just the destruction of her reputation and career. But her concentration wasn't up to it. She sensed she was in the chase for something important, but couldn't run it to earth. She phoned Nevsky, but got no answer. Maybe that was for the best. She wasn't sure what she wanted to say to him.

Clarisse announced over her brunch tuna sandwich and soup, "Mr. Nevsky was funny. How does he do all those tricks?"

"Beats me. Moms don't know everything."

"I think I like him better than Mr. Scoffler."

Mariah wondered if she felt the same way. If so, was that the smart way to feel? She sighed. She was wandering in the wilderness.

It was a good day to have a daughter; they could go shopping. They went to the mall and looked for some outfits for Clarisse. Even at her age, the assertive little lady had clear ideas about what she wanted to wear. She also had a taste for secondhand clothes. The mall part of the excursion wasn't that productive. But visits to Nearly New and the Salvation Army Thrift Store sent them home with bulging used plastic bags.

There was a message from Bud on her answering machine. He was wondering when they could get together again. Was that the voice of his mother she heard muffled far in the background? Mariah couldn't catch her exact words, but her tone was suspicious and critical. Rita had told her to watch out for men who lived with their mothers. They were poor risks, her friend had said. Risk? Well, she hadn't invested that much in Bud. There was no harm in having men friends that you weren't going to rush to the altar with right away, for heaven's sake. Lighten up, she told herself.

She might have lightened up if she hadn't gone food shopping with Clarisse and come back to find spray-painted graffiti marring the front of her townhouse just below the front windows. The ugly black letters read: LEAVE, ABUSER!

Her stomach twisted sickly. She suspected that this defacement hadn't been the doing of her unknown tormentor. It had the look of neighborly work. Such neighbors a woman could well do without. She felt shame first, though she knew outrage should be her ruling emotion. She had done nothing to be ashamed of. She swallowed her welling anger and found it as bitter as vinegar.

No hoping that sharp-eyed Clarisse would miss the lumpish letters. "Mommy! Look! What's that mean?"

"That means somebody doesn't like me because they think I did things I didn't."

"The same way they are at school sometimes?"

She touched her child's shoulder and knelt beside her. "Have they been really mean to you and you haven't been telling me?" She studied the girl's clouded gaze.

"Once in a while. But if they are, I punch them!"

"Clarisse!"

"Or I tell the teacher." She scowled. "They're more scared of *me!*"

Mariah was touched. Who knew where her daughter had gotten her spunk? Wherever, it was coming in more than handy. Just the same, her child shouldn't have to endure such insults. It wasn't fair! Anger clogged her throat like a cancer. As she led the girl inside she assured her that before long all this "nonsense" would come to an end.

To satisfy herself and defuse her anger, she made a big production out of washing away the ugly message. She used a bucket, soap and water, sponge, paint remover, short step ladder, and enough rags to stuff a half dozen pillows. She asked Clarisse to help her, too. From time

to time she paused and turned with her hands on her hips
to stare at the fronts of the other condos in her cul-de-
sac. She wondered if someone so stupid as to have defaced
her home would feel the tiniest crumb of shame to see
her and her daughter spray and scrub. Well, she would
do her best to make them feel *some*, at least.

Their efforts didn't quite clear the vinyl siding. She
couldn't remove a faint smear that took some studying
to be read. Good enough. She felt better for having done
something. No neighbor came forth to offer either sympathy or insults.

There was a small crisis at the Tot Lot the next day, a
cloudy October Monday. Molly Dolman, heeding the
advice of her nasty-minded uncle, had resigned. With the
reduced enrollment cutting income, there was no way
Mariah could fill the woman's slot. That meant she would
have to supervise the oldest children herself and take
over Molly's chores. She gathered her loyal troops, solid
Rochelle Camwell and her assistant Nikki Herakis, Deidre, Grace and Randi Monroe who, though wavering,
needed the money and a day site for her two toddlers.
She found out just exactly what other duties Molly had
handled and wrote them in her Day Planner. Later she
would enter them on her daily schedule.

She saw her employees' eyes on her damaged face and
sensed their eagerness to hear her side of the Groome
story. She told them that the violence had largely been the
abusive couple's work. As always the media had leaped
toward the seamier side like crazed wolves, questioning
Mariah's stability and trustworthiness. As she thanked
each staff member individually for her continued loyalty,
she studied eyes for signs of wavering. *I hope you don't
leave me*, she thought. *But if you do, I'll manage—somehow.* Though she wondered very much if she could.

There was so much going on! The seemingly incessant gong of the media, still for a moment, had been struck again by the Groomes. It reverberated through her days, reached her neighbors, her clients, her poor daughter. Then there were her suspicions, shooting off this way and that like wild skyrockets, missing every target despite the determination of her aim. Now she was left with . . . Helga, she supposed, motivated by jealousy. But she wasn't sure . . .

And what about Nevsky, nibbling at the edge of her personality with his talk about mysteries and suggesting temporary retreat from rationality? She was such a practical person! She hadn't time for thoughts about leaps to the intuitive or whatever. Or about her spirit. Heavens, she didn't even know if she had a spirit!

She was in a tailspin about the Tot Lot. So many kids had been withdrawn. Others could well follow. The parents' committee could simply recommend the withdrawal of every child, if it so chose. And well it might.

Everything swam and dodged before her, like Truman Orel's tropical fish in their tank. The real problem was that she couldn't bring all her troubles into a single focus. She didn't know how to order them, never mind how to attack. She had flown off in search of her tormentor and found failure on every front: Delsy Comorra, Rudy, Jacky DuMarr, the Groomes. All but Helga seemed innocent. And who knew but that she was, too. In short, she didn't know how to answer her own question, the one she sensed held the answer to all her troubles and possibly the identity of her tormentor: *Why?*

She didn't know if she ever would be able to answer that question on her own. She felt that afternoon as if she was twisting in the wind of her bewilderment like the horrid effigy in the Tot Lot tree.

But then the package came.

Its flap was sealed with transparent tape. The address was block lettered, characterless. No return address. She pulled the tab, exposing the mailer's shadowy innards. She parted the padded paper and peered in.

She saw a tot's shoe. She pulled out the scuffed girl's pump. Right foot.

Someone was returning a shoe that arrived at someone's home by mistake. She looked inside the mailer. There was no note to help her match the shoe up with the proper child. Annoying! She slid the shoe back into the mailer and tossed it onto a shelf. Leave it to kids to lose coats, hats, books, socks. Why not shoes? She'd check around and see if anyone had lost a shoe in the last week.

She didn't know her memory was chewing on that tough, scuffed morsel. The results of the internal research were delivered as she was touching up her hair in the staff bathroom. Her comb hand froze. She saw the color draining from a face that too faithfully reflected the wounds and strains of the last month. Her expression of uneasy amazement fit too well amid the newish lines and smudges. She said to the mirror, "No! It couldn't be. *It could not be.*"

She wanted to leave the Tot Lot at once to go and check. But with the staff losses she didn't have her former scheduling flexibility. She had to stick it out until nearly six. Then with Clarisse belted beside her, she sped home through rush-hour traffic. Keeping her cool, she set the girl to sorting laundry while she went up the ladder to the storage area over the bedroom. She pulled down a cardboard carton and put it on the bed. She stared at it.

I thought I'd never open you again, she thought.

She was aware her heart pounded. She heard the heavy rustle of anxious breath in her nostrils. She cooed softly to herself as she attacked the strapping tape with scissors. "No, no, no, no . . ."

Her stomach tightened as she saw again the file folders. They held eight-year-old yellowing newspaper articles, legal papers, trial records, all documents from a time of terrible trouble. *Let it not be*, she said to herself. She pulled out the folders holding the newspaper clippings. How quickly they had turned jaundiced and brittle! She began to go through them. Her hands trembled. Where was it? Probably somewhere in the middle, after those on the scandal at J. D. Day Care and before the ones on the trial.

She pulled out a likely stack and held it. She closed her eyes and took a deep breath. *Don't get carried away*, she thought. *You're not sure of anything yet.* She sought to center herself before looking at the articles about the discovery of Dotty Orel's corpse. There was one photo she remembered. If she could spot that . . .

There!

On a stretcher was a small shape, torso and face covered with a blanket to hide the horrible wounds that opened like mouths on her head and chest. From below the blanket hem protruded two thin legs. The feet were clad in anklets. On one foot was a shoe.

Mariah squinted and turned the newsprint to the best angle under the light. The shoe . . . She had imagined she recognized it. Now came the critical moment of examination, the test of memory. Her memory hadn't failed. With that understanding a chill crept over her body as though her bedroom had become a meat locker.

In the mailer at the Tot Lot was the mate to the shoe on dead Dotty Orel's left foot!

Her tormentor was the person who had murdered Dotty Orel!

Fourteen

Mariah's emotional uproar threatened to completely overwhelm her. Yet as moments passed she realized she had trodden this path too often over the last three weeks. Too familiar were the shakiness in the knees, the inward trembling, the dread that loomed vast and sinister far beyond her small span of control. On those swift emotional rapids floated the familiar urge to look for help, maybe even to beg for it. Wasn't all that getting a bit *old* by now, she asked herself, to her own surprise. Wasn't it time to listen to the late Shelly, Nevsky and her own heart? Hadn't the time come at last to help herself?

Yes! It had. It certainly had.

She fed Clarisse and rolled up the girl's Ninja Turtles sleeping bag, packed her Glow Worm, and scooted her into the van. The early November twilight began to fall. "Mom, where are we going?" she asked.

"Lake Liberty."

"Why?"

"I need to think."

Rita had showed her the lake in midsummer, boasting of its large public beach. From that sandy swath Mariah had looked around the wooded shore, where the cottages of the well-to-do nestled amid oak and pine. At the lake's far end rose a promontory called Indian Leap. Mariah had never granted herself her wish to look out on the lake from that high land. Tonight she would do it. She didn't ask herself why now of all times. She just kept driving.

There were lights dotting the shore. Even this late in the season lake-loving cottage owners sat before stone fireplaces and Scandinavian stoves to eke out a few more evenings in residence. Spots of illumination on the water pooled dark and viscous as oil. She turned into the look-out's small unpaved parking lot. Engine off and brake on. She rolled down the window despite the evening chill. She listened intently, but heard nothing. That suited her immensely. She sat gazing down at the lake, drawing deep breaths, waiting for Clarisse to fall asleep. She was the last, sweetest distraction . . .

When the girl's breathing grew smooth and regular Mariah opened herself to the peace and silence. It was a strange feeling to try to center herself away from the shocks of the last weeks and the florid emotional banners she had waved willy-nilly at every fresh misfortune. The attempt was a novel mental exercise that called for a conjurer's trick—suspension of time and situation. Succeeding would bring distance and with it the perspective she so badly needed.

Shortly she noticed that time's passage didn't seem so important here. Minutes rolled to hours then to a shifting murk unworthy of her attention. Without directly dwelling on troubling matters, she found ideas presenting themselves clad as certainties. She came to understand why the shoe had been sent to her.

To break her.

To finish the artfully begun scheme that had already taken her and the Tot Lot to the brink. Hadn't her intuition nearly tumbled at the start when she beheld the dangling effigy in the Tot Lot oak? Her imagination had leaped back over the years to suggest that the murderer had resurfaced. Too bad she hadn't heeded her intuition. Now she had been given what someone hoped would be a last little push. The well worn child's pump was intended to send her over the edge to panic and destruction, the Tot Lot careening down with her.

Well, it wasn't going to work!

Sitting as she was in darkness, in a near trance, she found that the search for motivation now failed to command her feverish attention. For the moment she wouldn't worry about why. Instead she would figure out how to turn the scuffed leather shoe into the magic slipper that would in the end save her reputation and her life . . .

If she hadn't realized that sea changes were beginning deep within her, her reaction to an unexpected visit from Phil Fontenot would have nicely cued her. She had hurried from one of the Tot Lot play areas back to her office to pick up some notes and found him in a chair, an aluminum crutch tilted across his thigh. His hawklike nose had been crushed. He had to breathe through an open mouth that disclosed the too perfect alignment of upper and lower temporary bridges. They replaced his formerly expensively capped teeth. His face was a palette of yellows and fading purples.

She didn't betray her surprise. Instead, she said casually, "Where's Oscar?"

"Hospital. Needs more surgery on his leg."

"What can I do for you?" she asked evenly. "I'm busy with my sinking ship. The one you torpedoed."

"So you got even." The beating he had taken had stolen much of the arrogance from his eyes and tone.

"Got even? I'm not sure I understand."

"You set us up. In the restaurant. Those were professionals."

"I heard you were brawling. That's all I know. I'm sorry you got hurt." This last was in a way half true. Too bad he and Oscar were feeling pain and suffering. But the point that she consciously focused on for the first time was that a man like Phil Fontenot could learn decency in no other way. And she, too gentle and empathetic by far, had no other means with which to deal with him. Hadn't she tried gentle persuasion, appeals to his better side, turning the other cheek?

"You set us up," he repeated. His voice was leaden with certainty.

She walked over to stand directly in front of him. He couldn't rise to tower over her. She stared down into his eyes. "I have no idea what you're talking about, Fontenot." She kept staring, waiting for his reaction. When it came, it wasn't in his voice. It was a shift in his expression, his dark glance.

There she read . . . fear. He was afraid of her. Afraid of Mariah Sullivan!

Having shoved in vain against him and his media power, she was for the moment astonished at the change in him. It had seemed her destiny to heave the boulder of his destructive attention forever uphill, like Sisyphus, never to find relief from its crushing weight. And there it was! She felt lightened, released.

"I don't know how you did it, but it was you," he said doggedly. "You sent those hoods . . ."

She folded her arms. "I resent your accusations! You have hundreds of enemies—and deserve every one. Why single me out?"

"Intuition."

"Well, your intuition is off the air—like you are. Why did you come here? What do you want now? To do me more harm?"

He shook his head. Even the small grin brought a wince to his badly damaged face. "I wouldn't dare," he whispered.

"So why *did* you come?"

"To see if what I thought was true," he said.

"And what do you think?" she asked hotly.

"It's a definite," Phil Fontenot said.

After he scuttled out on his crutch, Mariah tried to pin down how she felt about what she indirectly had asked be done to him. Her thoughts shifted until she felt she had glimpsed a whole new level of human activity. She understood there were ways of getting things done that weren't taught in school or approved by media, government, or the pulpit. It was a world of action, not endless balanced analyses and parliamentary procedures. It was one where permission was never asked, a place unwarmed by the suns of empathy and pity. Despite the public rhetoric of the moment, she knew that glimpsed world wasn't one where women flourished. Particularly one like her, still colored with the chalk of naïveté and by far too softhearted. Nonetheless, she had passed through the portal and now felt that new land's seductiveness. She understood that her continuing to act there promised great risks. At the same time, if she was to save herself and her career she couldn't turn back. She could no longer afford to be the bleating frightened child. She couldn't go on dodging and flinching.

She had to charge!

By juggling the Tot Lot schedule, she managed to free herself for two hours during the day. She hoped that that would give her enough time at the Madison police headquarters. It had taken some fast—albeit vague— talking to get an appointment with a detective, a Lieutenant Jimmy Griefe.

Mariah's face had largely cleared of its yellowish bruises. She had carefully applied light makeup that morning and spent more time than usual on her hair. She chose an outfit that showed her figure, too. A woman going to war brought along her own kinds of weapons. She carried only a purse and Dotty Orel's shoe in a manila envelope.

Jimmy Griefe was in his late forties. His face was flattish, like a plank. Out of it his lumpish features stuck like rooty knots. His hair was thinning. While shaving he had missed some spots under his chin. He had the look of a man a stride or two behind the parade of his life's finances. He wore a plain wedding band. On his desk was a family photo featuring more children than Mariah could count with just a glance. Here was a devoted husband and father. Just the kind of cop she had hoped for! Maybe this would go well.

He sat her at a chair beside his steel desk. From a heap of papers he pulled a scribbled note no doubt left by the officer with whom she had spoken on the phone. "You want to talk about . . . a serial child killer, Ms. Sullivan?" he asked with a frown.

"It's an idea I want to share with you, lieutenant," Mariah said. "Depending on what you think, you might want to talk to the police in Clarion City."

"Why don't you tell me what's on your mind," he said.

His ash-gray eyes didn't look all that friendly. Well, she was the *new* Mariah. She wasn't going to be badgered by a bit of beetling brow! She had prepared herself for this interview. From her briefcase she pulled the opened mailer. She put it on the desk and slid out the battered pump. "It was this that got me thinking . . ." she began.

Where her idea had come from—and when—she wasn't sure. Suddenly it had just been *there* in her head. Chalk it up to one of the "mysteries" that Nevsky promoted, but never described. Once the grain of sand was lodged in her attention she added layers to it like an industrious oyster. She was certain that Dotty Orel's death had nothing to do with J. D. Day Care. The victim just happened to be enrolled there. The murderer had swooped down like a hawk and snatched her. She could have been any child lost for a few moments in a mall, on an outing, on a deserted stretch of beach. Nonetheless, in the killer's mind there was a connection to the Tot Lot. Hadn't the shoe been the latest in a long string of threats and warnings beginning nearly a month ago with the soaped message? While her tormentor and the murderer didn't have to be the same person, it now made sense that they were. What didn't make sense was why the killer was trying to put her reputation and the Tot Lot's on the skids to destruction.

No matter that everything didn't quite fit. Her next thought had been whether or not Dotty Orel had been the killer's sole victim. Had other children in the Clarion City area been murdered in a similar way? Had an article of clothing—

their right shoe, perhaps—been removed as a grisly souvenir? Maybe the police could check the records and find out. If Dotty Orel's murderer was a serial killer, the police would want to find and convict him as soon as possible. They would become her allies. The killer would be stopped—before he destroyed her and the Tot Lot.

She explained all this to Jimmy Griefe. She concluded by saying, "All you have to do is check to see if any other Clarion City children were abducted and killed the way Dotty Orel was. If there weren't any, I'm wrong. If there were, well, then the Clarion City police can start investigating—"

"I appreciate your coming in to share your theory, Ms. Sullivan." The lieutenant got up in a way that made it quite clear that the interview was over.

Mariah sat as unmoving as a boulder. She steadfastly held his gaze. "Well, what do you think about what I said?" she asked.

"What do I think?" His smile was narrow, unpleasant even, his teeth short and spade-shaped. "I think your theories are interesting."

Mariah frowned. She wasn't sure what she had expected from this lieutenant. But his near indifference was certainly not it. Even though he was standing expectantly beside her chair, she still sat. Stubbornness was another character trait that she should cultivate. She was sick of being so damned agreeable! "Does 'interesting' mean you'll start the wheels of an investigation turning?"

"Of course."

"Can I ask when and how?"

His ash gray eyes met hers. "I can't share police procedures with you."

Why did he seem so cold and distant? "Can I call you for information on how it's going?"

"Sure. Call." He hesitated. "You'll have to excuse me. I have a meeting."

Mariah got up. She reached for the pump. Lieutenant Griefe reached out and gripped her forearm, guiding it back to her side. "You better leave that," he said. "It could be useful."

She nodded. There was nothing more she could do with it, that was for sure.

A few shallow pleasantries from Griefe and she was out the door and back onto the street. She stood in the shadow of police headquarters, turned and looked back. She shook her head. Her intuition whispered that hadn't gone well at all.

She hadn't the faintest reason why.

Despite her seemingly abrupt treatment at Lieutenant Griefe's hands, toward the end of the next day Mariah had no trouble picking up the phone to check on police progress. Griefe wasn't at his desk, so she left her name and requested that he return her call. She didn't hear from him.

Thursday afternoon, the phone rang while she was seated at her desk. As she picked up the receiver she noticed the calendar. It had been four weeks since her harassment had begun. Four weeks! It seemed like four years, considering all the stress and sea changes. She felt that she had undergone a transformation of sorts. The only thing that remained the same in her life seemed to be her name. "Tot Lot. Day care *extraordinaire!*" she said. "Mariah Sullivan speaking."

"You have your nerve saying that!" It was a high-pitched male voice, edged up half an octave by emotional pressure. "This is Delmar Bronk. We had a child in the Tot Lot."

Mariah plundered her memory and came up with the

Bronks, Delmar and Debbie, a bland couple, she round and red-nosed, he thin as a tomato stake, pale-handed and grinny. "Yes, Mr. Bronk?"

"We know what you did to Tessie. She told us."

Mariah's heart thumped like a conga. Tessie Bronk? A little bug-eyed five-year-old redhead with the overbite of a shark and her father's ready grin. The couple had pulled her out of the Tot Lot last week. "Mr. Bronk, nothing was done to Tessie that wasn't done to every other child enrolled here."

"You better not mean that, or your goddamned Tot Lot is hell for every child in it!"

Mariah drew a deep breath. "Why don't you just tell me what the problem is."

As he did Mariah felt her inner self being squeezed as though under a giant press. Under intense and probably leading questioning by a frightened mother and father, Tessie had told them that she had been "touched" by Mariah and her staff. Delmar Bronk could scarcely put words to his shock, outrage, and disgust. He had no trouble, however, with heaping threats on Mariah ranging from physical violence to a lawsuit. "Debbie and I talked it over," he said. "And we agreed that the best way to fight you is to put you out of business. We're going to use what you did to Tessie as a weapon against you. Of course that'll mean subjecting Tessie to a lot of unwanted attention. But it's the price we're prepared to pay when we go public."

"Go public?" Mariah asked. "Do you mind if I ask what you mean by that?"

"We're going to the media on this, you witch! We're going to close you down!"

Along with the shock and dismay that flowed through her, Mariah felt a sensation of déjà vu. "Mr. Bronk, I suggest you watch what you say and to whom you say it." She was heartened by the icy calm in her voice. "I'm going to give you the name of my attorney. I suggest you call him and discuss the legal implications of what you're threatening to do. If you don't you'll be hearing from him shortly!" She hung up and called Frenetic Freddy and told him about the Bronks.

"They wanna be famous by Friday, kiddo," he said. "Happens all the time. People think cameras, lights, the big broadcast! Makes them feel important, like celebrities. I'll give them a call, try to quiet them down."

"If you can't . . ."

"Then you're in it even deeper, kiddo." Freddy's voice dropped an octave. "You having any luck finding out who's responsible for all this? I mean, I'm a hell of a lawyer, but I'm not Gunga Din. And they're already coming over the walls, you know what I mean?"

"I have some new ideas. The police are working on them."

"Right on! I can hold the fort—for a while."

An hour later she phoned Lieutenant Griefe again. He wasn't at his desk. Yes, he had gotten her last message. He was very busy with his caseload. Certainly he would get back to her as soon as possible.

He hadn't called back by the time Mariah left the office.

So she was surprised to answer a knock on her condo's front door that evening to find Griefe standing there with a woman officer he introduced as Claire Gordon. She wore her black hair short and had a protruding jaw that gave her the look of a terrier. She didn't smile. "I'd like to ask you some questions, Ms. Sullivan," Griefe said.

"Sure! Whatever it takes. And please, call me Mariah."

Neither cop responded to her friendly overture. She sat

them on the couch and ordered Clarisse upstairs, door closed, please. Big-people conversation.

Officer Gordon opened a notebook. The lieutenant leaned forward, as stony-faced as ever. His gnarled root features seemed more prominent in the weak living room light. "Ms. Sullivan, I'd like you to tell me again about your receipt of the shoe . . ."

Mariah began by answering his questions quickly and precisely. She badly wanted attention focused on the Dotty Orel murder. She still sensed that finding the killer would save her reputation and livelihood. But when the questioning veered toward her actions in events eight years old, she found her tongue growing sluggish. Suspicion reared up like a spooked horse. "Why are you asking about *me*, lieutenant? The shoe isn't about me. It's about whomever killed Dotty Orel."

The lieutenant leaned forward, his spade-shaped teeth exposed in a thin smile. "Maybe *you* killed her, Ms. Sullivan," he said softly.

Mariah spoke in a rush, words pumped out by the pressure of suddenly exploding emotions. "I was acquitted of that crime!" she cried.

He nodded. "Sometimes juries make mistakes," he said.

Mariah jumped to her feet. "What grounds do you have for saying such a thing?"

Griefe folded his arms and stared stonily at her, as though she was a prisoner in the dock. How could she not have read his hostility all along? The lieutenant's eyes narrowed. "Does the name Eddy Swale mean anything to you?"

How could she ever forget little Eddy Swale, who had caught cold while standing around naked at Jacky DuMarr's lewd bidding? "I know who he is," she said.

"Did you know he's my nephew?" Lieutenant Griefe asked.

Mariah gasped. At that moment she saw the man as though for the first time. All his family devotion, which she had hoped would be assets to her, had turned to horrid liabilities. His *nephew* had fallen into Jacky DuMarr's hands! And hadn't Mariah been tried with her? Despite her shock she kept her wits and held her voice even. "Then you know all about the trial. You're well aware that I was acquitted—"

"I don't give a damn about your acquittal!" he said loudly. "I thought then that you were guilty; I still think you are. That yid shyster you hired to defend you hypnotized the jury. My nephew was messed up for life and all the satisfaction our family got was your lady friend gets a slap on the wrist. And you walk."

"*What* is going on in your head, lieutenant?" Mariah cried. "Why would I have come to you now with the dead girl's shoe if I had been responsible? What possible reason would I have? I came to you for *help*."

"The criminal mind—"

"I don't have a criminal mind, Lieutenant Griefe, you do! If you had one ounce of smarts you'd do as I asked you to and open an investigation in Clarion City for a possible serial murderer. Don't you realize other lives could be at risk?" Mariah raised flattened palms, as though asking toddlers gathered in their reading ring to get up and get moving. "I don't have anything more to say to you two. If you need anything else from me, I'll want my attorney present. Now get out!"

Griefe rose slowly and Officer Gordon followed. "You'll be hearing from me again," he said.

"Do the taxpayers a favor and make some calls to Clarion City," Mariah said.

"If I do, they'll be about you," he said darkly.

She held herself together until they were out the door and inside their car before she released her tears of frustration. "You idiot cop! Don't you know what I need? I need *help!*"

A noise to her right whirled her around. Clarisse stood in her nightgown, her Glow-Worm under her arm. Snail tracks of tears on her smooth cheeks proved she had been eavesdropping. "I'll help you, Mommy. I'll do anything you want!"

After calming and bedding her daughter, Mariah poured herself a glass of Kahlua. She felt oddly focused. What bothered her now was Griefe's stupidity, not her own feelings of helplessness. She wasn't helpless. She didn't have to cooperate with the police. She could use Freddy as a buffer. If the police wouldn't be on her team, she'd go on without them. She'd find the killer herself! Only when finally falling asleep did it occur to her that she had told Griefe off. Casting her memory back over the months, the years, she couldn't remember when she had told *anyone* off.

In the middle of the night, she bolted up from a deep sleep, sweating and shaking. After eight years they were after her again! For a while she wrestled old phantoms and dreads. Then she steadied herself. Oh, Mariah, come on, she told herself. Be a big girl. She slid her back up against the bed board and patted the covers down over her thighs. She calmed herself with deep breaths, summoning her new resourcefulness. Jimmy Griefe was a jerk. Let him try to make a case against her. They hadn't done it eight years ago. They couldn't do it now.

The next morning, Freddy called. His usually bubbly tones had gone flat. He had talked his way into the Bronks' trailer home and warned them about making slanderous statements that could lead to lawsuits. "So sue us!" Delmar said, waving his hands around at their cheap, meager possessions. The Bronks spent every penny of both paychecks. "They got nothin'," Freddy summed up.

Then he explained what the Bronks' plans were. Having nothing, they were trying to hop aboard the sensation train. They intended to use the Tot Lot's damaged reputation as a springboard into a seamy fabrication about their daughter's abuse at the hands of Mariah and her staff. They were looking for an agent, book and movie deals. They had already hired "a shyster that makes *me* look like a Supreme Court justice," Freddy said. At one time Mariah might have wondered how people could do such things as trade a daughter's well-being for a fistful of dollars. One of her recent enlightening realizations was that people did whatever they could get away with. And they got away with plenty.

"Guess what they're going to do," Freddy said.

"I can't imagine."

"Hold a press conference. I tried everything I could think of to stop them," Freddy said. "Nothing worked. The only thing they got to sell is their daughter's innocence. So they're going to do it."

He was getting press releases ready that denied all the Bronks' charges and promised lawsuits that they would never file. When the time came, he'd arrange Mariah's own press conference, at which she would defend herself. He regained some of his old energy. "Hey, kiddo, hang in there. The Bronks don't have the staying power. They'll flatten like a leaking tire. Be cool."

Mariah said she'd do her best. "This isn't easy," she said.

"Hell, no. Remember the old days when people got tried in court instead of on TV?"

She gathered her staff once again and told them what the Bronks planned to do. She looked around at the familiar faces—Rochelle Camwell, the Tot Lot's middle-aged steady flywheel, Randi Monroe, loyal through the necessity of having two children enrolled tuition-free, and Nikki Herakis, the bright assistant whose parents would pull her out at the next "incident," which seemed imminent. Finally there were Grace Kleingold and Deidre Williamson, family women who had been unwilling to believe the charges against Mariah. Backing them at home stood two solid husbands.

Chatty blond Grace couldn't wait for a chance to talk. "The Bronks are going to say that you and we, the *staff*, abused Tessie?" she asked.

"So it seems," Mariah said.

Grace frowned. "My Saul isn't going to like this."

"Neither is *my* husband," Deidre said.

"This whole business over the last month has been like a cancer." Rochelle levered her big body to the front of the group. "It just keeps spreading. I think it's time we put a stop to it at once."

Everyone looked at her expectantly.

Rochelle approached Mariah and put her arm over her shoulder. "This poor woman has done nothing but suffer attacks. And we haven't really stood behind her, have we?"

There was a chorus of sheepish Nos. Not everyone met Rochelle's glance.

"So we're human, ladies." Rochelle shrugged her wide shoulders. "We're not heroine types. We didn't get really excited until now. Until the crazies started pointing fingers at *us*. So, that's what it took to get us behind Mariah. Time's come for *all* of us to fight back . . ." She hesitated. "But I don't know just how."

Suddenly, Mariah had an idea. She stood up and waved her arms, excited. "Hey, listen, ladies," she ordered. "You all know about that parents' committee they've set up. They've been nosing all around. You all know the questions they've been asking. It's time for them to admit there isn't any abuse here. We and the committee should all get together to tell the world everything's A-okay here at the Tot Lot. This time we'll *invite* the media in . . ."

"I don't know . . ." Rochelle's worried expression surprised Mariah. The older woman was usually so enthusiastic, so positive. Why was she balking now?

The others took up her idea in a more positive mood. The more they talked, the better Mariah's idea seemed. She assigned Rochelle to meet with attorney Mickey Henderson to propose the idea. If he agreed it was worth discussing, he could take it to the committee for further action. When Rochelle hesitated still, to Mariah's further surprise, she had to cajole her until she couldn't say no.

When their meeting broke up, she took Rochelle aside. "What's wrong?" she asked her.

The older woman's look was distant, absent even. She was silent a long moment. "Oh, Mariah, I don't know. My instincts, I guess. They're saying maybe you should be playing it safer—*we* should be playing it safer. Not taking so many chances. Not flying willy-nilly at a doubting public."

"I've always played it too safe, Rochelle. It's why my life has gone the way it has, the reason I want to change."

"Hmm . . ." Rochelle wasn't pleased.

Well, it wasn't Mariah's job to please her. Trying that had helped lay the foundation beneath her past troubles. "Live with it," she said softly. "It's the new order."

Toward evening, Mariah's determination was solid. She thought of the Bronks trying to make profitable the bogus destruction of their daughter's innocence. How grasping and covetous of them to go that route! She couldn't stop them, so she had to fight them—and hard! She couldn't afford to be nice about it! She gasped at the thought.

Hadn't that been what Shelly had said to her on his deathbed?

Little by little she was getting the messages. Would she get them all? And would it be soon enough?

CHAPTER 77

Fifteen

Friday evening, Mariah disconnected her phone and kept the TV off. Saturday morning, she didn't buy a newspaper. She didn't want to hear first or second hand what lies the Bronks had broadcast at their news conference. She could pretty much guess what they had claimed. As she and Clarisse left the condo about 10:00 A.M., she found two women reporters waiting in ambush. They scampered forward. Into the face of their insistent questions she said twice, "Contact my attorney for my comment. Frederick Folsom, 555-9087." Then she and Clarisse were in her van and away.

Their first stop was the East Side Deli, where they provisioned. Next was a certain basement apartment . . . When Nevsky opened the door, Mariah sang out, "It's picnic we-a-th-er!"

"A gray November day is picnic weather?"

"Come with us and you'll see."

He came along, but Mariah found his Slavic face as

hard to read as Sanskrit. Their try at small talk didn't go well. No need to worry about silence amid their trio, though. Clarisse was on, with a vengeance, filled with chatter and questions. She begged Nevsky for more sleight-of-hand. Mariah wondered what it would be like to mother a shy child.

She wheeled through the university gates and made her way around to the back of the campus, where the greenhouse was. "I think we'll dine in the Desert Room today," she said.

The university greenhouse was divided into six sections, opening like spokes from the central hub of the entrance hall. Climates within the sections varied from tropical rain forest to desert. Here and there students bustled about, pruning and fertilizing. In the hub, seedlings grew in peat pots; water dripped from marble cherubs' mouths. The air was moist and rich with the smell of growth.

The Desert Room had benches tucked away among the barrel cactuses, rocks, and arid earth. Mariah found a low weathered plank table on which she unpacked their brunch—warm bagels, cream cheese speckled with lox, pastrami sandwiches, chips and dips, sauerkraut and pickles. "Health food!" she said brightly.

"Coronary specialist's delight," Nevsky said.

"I love pickles!" Clarisse cried.

Mariah whispered to Nevsky, "That's why I bought two extra."

After they ate, Mariah found a student willing to give Clarisse a greenhouse tour. Returning to Nevsky, she began to tell him about her inner changes and what they had led her to do. As she talked, she sensed she was seeking his approval.

He nodded. "Action becomes you," he said.

"For some women it's moonlight. Me, it's action."

"You're plenty good-looking outside, Mariah. But it's inside where we win or lose our battles." Nevsky attacked the last half of his pastrami on rye.

He had a strong jaw and clearly enjoyed eating. How did he stay so thin, Mariah wondered. "Don't you ever say something that isn't philosophical, Yuri?" she asked. "Like 'Have a nice day'? Or 'I shop a lot at Marshalls'?"

He smiled around a filled mouth. He chewed and swallowed. "Everything has meaning. Can I help it if I try to understand what it is?"

"I think I've figured us out. We're *complete* opposites." Mariah drew a deep breath of the dry air and went for it. "I guess that's why I'm attracted to you." She surprised herself. Had she really meant to say that? Did she really believe it?

"I'm very flattered, but I've retired from romance," Nevsky said. Was there a trace of smile behind that stray strand of pastrami?

"But not from friendship, I hope."

His shoulders moved noncommittally.

"That guy who was over at my house the other night. Bud? He's not my main man or anything," Mariah said. "In fact, he's the *only* man besides you that I've seen socially in more than six years. And him only two, three times." She swallowed. "I'd rather see just you." She held her breath. Look at her, here among cactuses and sand—the aggressor! What had happened to the tongue-tied shy one she had been? She knew: she didn't have *time* for that Mariah any more. She had to rush ahead now and not worry about loose ends. There were long-overdue gains that needed to be made on all fronts.

Nevsky turned on the bench and lightly took her hands.

She liked the warmth of his skin. He might be graying, but he wasn't old. "I'm flattered," he said. "But—"

"Are you going to 'but' me to death, Yuri Nevsky? Like some kind of . . . old goat?" She couldn't help but grin.

"You're still in trouble. You have to get out before you can think of . . ." He smiled. "Anything else at all."

"You've helped me. With Fontenot. With my thinking. I *am* getting out, aren't I?"

"You're making progress, Mariah. But I think the biggest tests are still out there somewhere on the horizon."

She gasped. "My God! How can you say that after—"

"Why don't you bring me all the way up to date," he suggested.

She told him everything, right up through the Bronks' press conference. He nodded several times. When she finished, she asked, "So what do I do?"

He looked surprised. "You still asking for advice, Mariah Sullivan? You don't really need it. I think you know what you have to do."

"I do?"

He nodded. "Let's switch roles. *You* tell *me* for a change. Give me the action plan." He was grinning. She liked the way the laugh lines emerged around his eyes.

She sat back and looked around the Desert Room, then up through the plastic panels above which November clouds scudded by. She thought a long while, letting intuition assemble the ideas that had tumbled through her mind. She spoke carefully. "I defend my reputation and the Tot Lot's. That means I work with Rochelle and the committee. We try to counter all the negative media coverage with a news conference of our own."

"Worth a try," Nevsky said. "Good. What else?"

She frowned, suddenly feeling herself reluctant to speak. Speaking would make the dangerous challenge more real. Eventually she vocalized it: *"I have to find out who's doing this to me!"*

"Yeah. And here's a suggestion that I'm sure you've already considered."

She looked at him questioningly.

"Find the other right shoes."

Through the rest of their midday together, Mariah resisted her old impulse to pick Nevsky's brain. Her compulsion to seek seeming certainty died hard, even though she was coming to suspect there was no certainty in anything. In the sloping driveway by his mildewy apartment, he thanked her for the food and companionship. "I can use both," he said.

"I thought it was more the food that you needed."

"We all need more than bread." He blew her a kiss through the open van window. "My treat next time."

She wasn't sure what she had accomplished with him. Expressed her interest, showed he was worth the commitment of her energy and a few dollars, she supposed. Whatever her message, it was a pretty safe one. She wasn't adept at taking wild risks just yet. Someday maybe. She would have appreciated a little more response out of the man. She sensed that wasn't his style. He wasn't like Rudy or Bud. He was a bit of a hybrid. Head ruled heart with him. And she sensed he had *lived*. Dangerous adventures could greatly alter a person.

There was a message on her answering machine from Rochelle. The tone of her voice edged toward sullen. Mariah remembered she hadn't been in favor of working with the committee toward a news conference. She had wanted Mariah to take a more conservative approach. Nonetheless, the older woman had talked to Mickey Hen-

derson. The committee was meeting that night. She and
Mariah were invited. "They want to talk about what they
believe and what they want to do about it," the tape told
her.

Rita took Clarisse for the evening—to Jeeter's
delight—and gave Mariah a big hug in the doorway. "The
very best of luck, sweet!" she said. "You're due for
some."

The meeting was in the game room of the Henderson
home. Mariah got a surprise when she walked down the
stairs. There were only six parents in the room besides
Mickey. Mariah knew only one of them well. Audrey
Orel.

The wren-like woman hurried up to her. "God bless
you, Mariah! This is all going to work out. Don't you
worry!" She gave Mariah's arm a nervous squeeze. Her
inward snort packed more energy than usual.

The small attendance was clearly an embarrassment to
the attorney. He hurried to explain it. "The committee
reached a conclusion by vote on Thursday evening." He
pushed his gold-rimmed glasses higher on his nose. "It
was decided that all the charges against Ms. Sullivan and
the Tot Lot staff were without merit."

"And so they should have decided!" Randi Monroe
said loudly. "I never heard such a load of crap in my
life!" She looked down at her two children. "And if these
littles understood everything, they'd agree with me one
hundred percent!"

Attorney Henderson looked sourly at Randi and
coughed. "And after the vote was taken, the other five
members of the committee chose to resign to better carry
on their campaign against the Tot Lot."

"You mean the vote was only six to five in favor of
me?" Mariah asked loudly.

"Emotions ran high," the attorney replied.

Mamta Bannershee, one of the six parents, said in her singsong accent, "I thought maybe there be fights."

Mariah tried to take the pulse of the group's commitment, but couldn't. What she did find out was that the Bronks had spared neither Tessie nor the Tot Lot at their news conference the previous evening. That included trotting out their "abused" daughter before TV lights, swearing vengeance, and exhorting officials and the law to descend on the Tot Lot and close it "before worse happens," a disgusted Audrey Orel reported.

Though unsure of the group's mood, Mariah decided to plunge ahead and propose that they hold their own pro-Tot Lot news conference. Of course she got an immediate second from Randi. Then she looked around at the seven faces, hoping to see enthusiasm and commitment to justice. Both looked in short supply—until little Audrey, more nervous and wired than ever, jumped up and shouted, "Well, let's get behind her, all right? We all agreed that Mariah Sullivan is a fine woman, a wonderful child care provider, and a first-rate human being. She has a history that wasn't much of her making. Do you remember us all saying that? *Do* you?" The little woman looked around accusingly.

She drew some grudging acknowledgments.

"Then for goodness' sakes let's do something to help her and the Tot Lot. Let's stand up in public and say we believe in Mariah Sullivan. It's only right!"

It took better than two hours to persuade the six and Mickey Henderson to agree to stand before the media and simply tell the truth. Once committed, the attorney got behind the project. His law practice had a public relations firm. They could help expedite matters.

"For everything but the TV," Mariah ordered. "I want to handle that myself."

She was excited. At last she was going to use the media to support her and the Tot Lot. She phoned WLIT-TV and said she wanted to get in touch with Chan Lee, the woman who had replaced Phil Fontenot. She had her choice of Fax or voice mail. She picked voice mail. The newscaster returned her call Sunday evening.

Mariah's motives were a calculated gamble. She guessed Chan Lee was ambitious. She gussed the woman was looking for ways to make herself more visible. Most of all she guessed that Ms. Lee wanted Phil Fontenot's job permanently. Wonderful! Mariah would do what she could to make that happen.

Chan Lee's voice was soft, carrying an edge of intelligence. By way of greeting, she said, "You're very much in the news these days, Ms. Sullivan."

"And hoping for a little more exposure . . ."

How fast things could come together these days! Mickey Henderson was an efficient man. He oversaw the preparation of the news releases denying all Tot Lot-related charges and innuendoes. Chan Lee had imagination. She thought the news conference should take place in no other place than the Tot Lot. "And should include a little tour of the facility," she suggested.

"Are you for me or against me?" Mariah asked her.

"I'm against anything that Phil Fontenot started," Chan said.

Mariah asked her staff about how they felt about facing reporters. Randi was happy to show up. "I'm bringing my two little ones, too," she said. "And we're all going to say this is the best day-care center in America!" Nikki, Deidre, and Grace declined. Rochelle hesitated. What a change of heart she'd had since Mariah began to launch her counterattacks. What had got into the woman?

After the children left late Tuesday afternoon, Mariah paced in her office. Clarisse hunched over a coloring book. *This is all going to go all right*, she told herself. *The Tot Lot is going to be all right. I am going to get through this after all.*

The phone rang. It was Cynthia Tran of the Madison Day Care Regulatory Board. She wanted to set up an interview with Mariah for the next day. "Can't, Cynthia," Mariah said. She was pleased at her businesslike tone. "I'm holding a press conference tonight. I'll be bushed tomorrow. You ought to tune in. WLIT's covering it." She added brightly, "Chan Lee's agreed to play a key role."

"It would be wise not to delay our meeting in light of—"

"In light of *what?*" I *dare* you to allude to any culpability on my part, Mariah thought.

"The pressure that my bureau is feeling from outside," Cynthia said diplomatically.

"Thursday noon, then. I hope you don't mind if my attorney sits in."

"Ah, well."

"Yes?" Mariah insisted.

"I believe that is permitted."

"Nice talking to you, Cynthia." Mariah hung up.

An hour before the eight o'clock press conference, Nevsky and Roper showed up uninvited. "What can I do for you gentlemen?" she asked with a smile.

"Let us watch the doors for you," Nevsky said. "We'll keep out the rubberneckers and freaks. Give us a couple of your staff to help filter the parents through."

Good idea, Mariah guessed. Things she never thought

about. Seeing Roper again brought back her chagrin over
their misadventure at the Groome home. "You've healed
pretty well, Roper," she said.

"Likewise." He grinned sheepishly.

Mariah had checked the mirror at least three times daily
over the last two weeks to see how the healing process
was coming along. At noon that day she noticed with
relief that the last yellowish bruise had finally faded. Her
broken rib no longer clicked and pained. Thank goodness!
She well knew her physical appearance before camera
lenses and reporters' eyes was critical.

She wasn't used to gussying herself up to make an
impression, but she was learning. She had done her best
for her first meeting with Griefe—for all the good it had
done her. Well, if ever the time had come to look good,
it was tonight. She had ordered her hair cut and layered
to give her a more professional look and bought a classy
suit that murmured in wool, "Take me seriously, please."
For once she had ignored the price tag.

She had hung the suit in her office during the workday,
donning it and touching up her makeup only minutes
before Nevsky's arrival. He had seen her at her most
attractive, but she knew her appearance didn't mean as
much to him as what went on in her head. That was what
women were *supposed* to want in a man. Why then did
she find that reality so challenging, at times even intim-
idating? No matter. She found Nevsky's presence encour-
aging both professionally and privately.

Frenetic Freddy showed up a half hour before what he
insisted on calling "Show time!" He had outdone himself
this time. Tonight he sported a shiny suit that reminded
Mariah of a magician's outfit, except that its pants flared
at the bottom and its vest was paisley. He had given up
his customary braces in favor of a narrow belt. An ancient

Egyptian-looking medallion cut from dull stone hung around his neck on a matching paisley ribbon. He briefed her. She had the stage. Use it. Prepared remarks were a must. Explain all attacks on the Tot Lot, rebutting each. Keep it short. This was the media age. Take questions; he'd tell her which to answer. He'd handle the most blatantly unfair ones himself.

"I am going to owe you a *lot* of money after all this is over, Freddy," Mariah said.

He shook his head. His white blond hair, tastefully permed, scarcely stirred. He said, "Not tonight. Tonight I should pay *you*. You know what this kind of publicity is worth? I couldn't afford to pay for the kind of advertising I'm gonna get." He nudged her ribs none too gently— on her good side, thank heavens. "Make sure you let me talk some."

She wondered more how she would ever shut him up.

Audrey Orel found her just past seven-thirty. She wore an expensive dress and pearls. Her husband, Truman, was at her side, in his own quiet way supportive of her and Mariah. He nodded encouragement, his face looking as soft as kneaded dough. His eyes slid away from Mariah toward his wife.

"I want a chance to speak up for you tonight in public!" Audrey chirped. "You make sure I get it, Mariah Sullivan."

Mariah swallowed swelling emotions. The past had been forgotten. Audrey was firmly on her side. Before Mariah could reply, Chan Lee appeared. She was smaller than Mariah had imagined and had an aggressive stride. Her cheeks angled like blades. Her teeth had been expensively capped. "You set for the tour, Mariah?" she asked. Not waiting for an answer, she waved in her cameramen.

"This is as good a place to start as any, guys. Mariah, you want to do the honors?"

As Mariah turned toward the cameras, a scowling Truman led his wife off. Truman had told her while floating his bag of tropical fish that he wasn't the kind of guy who relished media attention. He didn't know how she could bear the public scrutiny she had received up to now. Remembering his kindness in setting up the aquarium reminded her she had never properly thanked him for trusting her enough to enroll his son in the Tot Lot. She hoped Audrey had told him how grateful she was. Again she marveled at how their apparent spiritual rebirth had improved them as human beings.

The news conference passed in a rush. She had no time for self-consciousness; too much was at stake. Before lights and lenses, she made her cool professional statement. She presented her evidence of an unknown tormentor. She stylishly disposed of the Brocks' charges, inviting them to continue at the risk of being exposed as shallow, desperate people trying to trade their daughter's peace and future for the silver pieces of media attention.

She steered completely clear of the issue of Dotty Orel's death. Not because she feared it, but because she didn't want to warn the murderer that she had gone to the police, had been rebuffed, and was planning to take solo action of some kind. If murder came up in questioning, she had conspired with Freddy to confine it to the past.

She looked over the crowd, saw her few fearless staff members, Attorney Mickey Henderson smiling encouragingly, Mamta Bannershee and other supportive members of the ad hoc committee. The remaining Tot Lot parents' curious stares told her they hadn't made up their minds.

With Freddy's help, she handled Chan Lee's skeptical

questions calmly and efficiently. When she faltered even momentarily there was Freddy, loud and abrasive, defending her like a bear his cub. Then they took on the other media's reporters whose questions were calculated to offend, accuse, and enrage. Mariah skated over them well enough with Freddy's help. He proved a bit of a showman, drawing sympathetic laughter with his caustic counters and disbelieving double takes.

Before the reporters' questioning had ended, Audrey Orel jumped up and hurried forward. A TV staffer stuck a mike toward her mouth. "I want to tell everybody what a fine person Mariah Sullivan is and how much she cares about children," she said. "I want you to know *I'm* the mother of the child who was murdered eight years ago. Dotty was in Mariah's old day-care center at the time she was killed. Just the same, we enrolled our only son in her new one!" And off she went on themes of trust and confidence. The reporters stared: they hadn't dreamed that any couple would take such a risk, even though Audrey attributed much to celestial powers. In the face of their skepticism she said loudly, "And we're certain our Christopher is in *no danger whatever* under Mariah's care." She was nearly eloquent. Her normal birdlike movements, amplified for the benefit of the cameras, made her seem not only more worthy of sympathy but more believable as well.

Freddy's showman's instincts made him end the news conference on Audrey's high note. He cut off questioning and hurried Mariah away and back to her office. Nevsky and Roper fell in behind them and held off pursuit.

Nevsky closed the office door behind their little group and leaned casually against it. Freddy crowed, "A great victory for you, Mariah. A Desert Storm!" In elation he hopped from foot to foot. His perfectly polished shoes gleamed.

She and the three men adjourned to a restaurant across town. Mariah found herself famished. They ordered pizza and beer and debriefed. They agreed it had been long past time for her to have a positive media opportunity. All felt the news conference had gone well. Tot Lot critics would have some tough gristle to chew through—Mariah disclosing publicly that she was the target of some nut and Audrey speaking eloquently on her behalf. Most importantly, she had stood up bravely under the reporters' assault. This time she didn't take it. She dished it out!

And it had felt *good!*

In time she and Nevsky were alone, the last of a pitcher of beer between them. "So what do you *really* think, my moody Russian?" she asked. The late hour and his age had chiseled fleshy brackets around his mouth. His forehead was cut with wrinkles. He looked wise, but Mariah sensed he wouldn't want to hear that.

He swirled the beer in his nearly empty glass. "I think you're coming along, finding your way among the mysteries."

She bristled at that old refrain. "The only 'mysterious' experience I had was sitting in my van by Liberty Lake in the middle of the night. And even then I don't know just what happened—if anything."

He nodded. "That's why they call them mysteries. They dodge definition like minnows."

"What else?" she asked. "I mean about me and the Tot Lot, not about . . . that other stuff."

He looked up from his glass and caught her in the direct spotlight of his full attention. "I think you're growing as a person." He smiled. "And I'm proud of you. Things are happening for your benefit, just as they should. It seems you're tested, you grow, then you're tested again.''

"I've had about enough testing!" Mariah announced.

Nevsky rested his hand lightly on hers, warmth above the cool tabletop. His eyes danced. ''You know what they say: no pain, no gain.''

Mariah dislodged her hand from under his. ''Up to now, at least, you've spared me platitudes. I might not have understood what you've been talking about, but at least what you said was original!''

"Mariah, you understand what I've been saying. You just don't like the sound of it.''

"Well, that's my privilege, isn't it?''

He nodded. ''Listen for a minute. Think of who you were eight years ago.''

She made a face.

"Kind of a frightened, naive little mouse, right?''

She nodded.

"Now look at you. A woman with some spine, one starting to get a grip on what this world is really like. Would you want to go back to being the old Mariah again?''

"Of course not.''

"You wouldn't be the Mariah you are now if you hadn't gone through what you have. You didn't like what happened to you. You almost lost your mind. But every time you came through it and got stronger—''

"All right. Okay. Now I'm strong and I'm fighting back at whoever's trying to destroy me and my day-care center.'' She drank the last of her beer. ''And maybe I'm even winning!''

"You are.'' Nevsky leaned forward. ''That's why whoever it is that's responsible for your troubles is now sure to play his highest card.''

* * *

Thursday at noon, Cynthia Tran had a different bearing than during her first visit. Mariah guessed she had seen some part of the news conference. It helped her growing confidence to again have Frenetic Freddy at her side. "Today I'm just a 'show' shyster," he explained before Cynthia's arrival. "Just like a piece of furniture. You can handle this slant yourself."

And in fact, she did answer Cynthia's penetrating, in-depth questions without difficulty. Behind Mariah's thinking was the refrain *I'm winning*. It gave luster to her expression and confidence to her voice. She recalled what Nevsky had said. She had been given challenge after challenge; she had met them all. Not always cleanly or with style, and sometimes with luck and help from others. But she had met them nonetheless. As the hour she had allotted her visitor came to an end, she gave her a master key. She was welcome to go anywhere in the building she wished. Mariah also gave her a list of her appointments with other Tot Lot staff members. "I'll be here, of course, Cynthia, but with the children. I'll be happy to answer more questions as long as they don't interfere with my afternoon responsibilities." She got up. Freddy rose, too. The interview was over.

How much better she was getting at handling life's little challenges!

How badly, too, she needed every small victory.

Toward the end of the afternoon, Cynthia returned to Mariah's office. She asked if she could plug her laptop PC into the phone line. She wanted to get her report into her bureau promptly. She explained that her colleagues had gathered information "elsewhere," which Mariah took to mean from her false accusers. Soon bureaucrats would begin to discuss whether or not to pull the Tot Lot's license.

"There's absolutely no reason for that to happen!" Mariah said testily. "And you know it, Cynthia."

Behind octagonal lenses, an impenetrable sheen covered the Oriental woman's brown eyes. "This case is unusual, Ms. Sullivan. Right now its final disposition is most unclear to me."

Despite Cynthia's doubts, Mariah felt she was still pretty much on a roll. She encouraged herself to go with it. She phoned Bud Scoffler and invited him to dinner that evening. "And bring your mother," she ordered.

Ms. Sophia Scoffler proved to be well behind the times insofar as her hair, clothes, and opinions went. She wore her bottle blondish hair in a French twist decades out of fashion. Her blouse and skirt were dark and cut conservatively. With her girth she had the look of a little Queen Victoria. Bud waited on her as though she was the original item. While he bustled, the woman eyed Mariah with the steely glance of the doting mother, asking that age-old question: could you *possibly* be good enough for my son? Though Mariah knew she had invited Widow Scoffler to meet her, she couldn't put into exact words what else she sought. Something like . . . had Bud been crippled inwardly by this hefty lady or had his independence survived?

Bud suggested that Clarisse, as bubbly and forward as ever, call Sophia "Mother Scoffler." "I think that's *most* premature, Randolph," she said.

So Bud's given name was Randolph. He was right not to use it, Mariah giggled inwardly. *Randolph!*

She had gone to more trouble with dinner than she should have, paying a fortune for a salmon and poaching it. She found some dill in a specialty grocery and made

a sauce. Her side dishes were boiled potatoes and arti-
chokes for Clarisse, who loved to peel them down.

Sophia Scoffler could scarcely restrain herself past her
first few bites. "I hope you'll explain to us the trouble
you're having with your day-care center and reputation,
Mariah," she said. "And about your tainting at your former place of employment."

Instead of the outrage and embarrassment that he ought
to now be showing, Bud instead leaned forward like a
drawing room character in the denouement of an old
mystery novel. His mother had charged him with doubt.
He too wanted explanations, amplifications. Worse than
that, they both wanted *certainty*. When had Mariah come
to understand that in life there was no certainty? Had it
been when she was talking to Nevsky, or had he just been
the catalyst for that somehow most humbling discovery.

"My mom didn't do anything bad!" Clarisse said defiantly. A swell of pride ran through Mariah. What Bud
needed was about twenty percent of that child's faith.

"I understand quite differently, young lady," Sophia
said.

"Possibly you *mis*understand, Mrs. Scoffler." Mariah put
down her fork. She wondered if her invitation to the Scofflers
was for no other purpose than to bring her to this moment
of confrontation. Who knew? Mysteries, as Nevsky would
say. She sensed the spontaneity in her current way of doing
things was a definite improvement on her former reserved
ways. "I and my day-care center have been targets for some
kind of lunatic. The same lunatic, I might add, who murdered
a little girl eight years ago."

Bud made a startled noise in his throat. His eyes widened. "The same person?"

"So it seems. Whoever it is sent me ... evidence to
prove it. I chose not to make that part of it public."

Sophia snorted. "This is most unbelievable!"

"Believe it, Mrs. Scoffler!" Mariah ordered. "Because it's the truth."

The older woman's eyes narrowed. "I see . . ."

"*What* do you see?" Mariah asked.

"I see the lengths to which you'll go to keep the hood over my Randolph's eyes."

"Mother—"

"Of all the lies you've told him—"

Mariah jumped to her feet. "I have never told him—"

"This last is the *most* preposterous," Sophia went on. "A long-gone murderer stalking you like some Son of Sam." She turned a skeptical glance full on Mariah's face. Her fleshy cheeks were reddened with the effort to keep her "boy," pushing forty-five as Mariah remembered, at her side. Mariah in turn looked at Bud. Last chance, Buddy, she thought. Come to my defense. For an instant she had hope. He opened his mouth. Right then Sophia turned her iron glare on him. His jaw slackened as though a powerful drug had been blasted into his bloodstream. His lips closed without having shaped a word.

Mariah remained standing. She shrugged broadly. "I see no reason for me to stand here and listen to you call me a liar, Mrs. Scoffler. I'd like to ask you and Bud to leave now." She stared pointedly at him. "Another thing I'd like would be not to hear from you again, Bud."

He shook his head, his expression disbelieving. "You're being unreasonable, Mariah. I haven't done anything to deserve this kind of treatment."

"Oh?" Mariah put a palm to her hip. "The foundation of love is trust, Bud. You're supposed to believe in me. You're supposed to take *my* word—not your mother's! Get the picture?"

"Randolph!" No marine drill instructor's recruit snap-

ped to attention any faster than Bud Scoffler did at his
mother's command. Sophia observed, "The time for talk
has come to an end."

"Too bad. I thought maybe there was a chance a real
dialogue had just started. One that might have included,
oh, let's say, topics like dominated, emotionally crippled
sons." Mariah's tone was sharp. Bud winced but kept
moving.

Mother and son trooped out of the condo together. Not
surprisingly, Sophia led and Bud followed.

Wasn't she telling people off these days! Mariah
thought. It was about time. She was proud of herself,
albeit emotionally drained. But she didn't cry in front
of Clarisse. She ambled into the bathroom and sobbed
stealthily into a damp bath towel. She told herself she
had done the right thing. She *knew* she had. But it still
hurt. After her daughter was asleep, she went to the phone.
She thought she'd call Nevsky. But she changed her mind.
She had won a sort of victory this evening. One that,
despite its pain, she ought to spend time savoring. Alone.

Before sleep, she grasped the inevitability of what had
happened between her and Bud. She had sensed his depen-
dency probably from the moment Rita had warned her
about men over thirty who still lived with their mothers.
Yet she had been pushed to try with him: Clarisse wanted
a father. And she wanted some companionship and—darn
it!—some loving! So she did still. And so did Clarisse.
Somehow it would all work out. She would *make* it work
out.

Sixteen

In the morning, she called police headquarters and asked to speak to Lieutenant Griefe. She hoped he had been in touch with his colleagues in Clarion City. Not to ask about *her*, as he had threatened, but about the possibility of a serial child killer having gone about his grisly business over the last years. She found herself on the line with Griefe's sidekick, Officer Gordon, no less stiff-jawed and suspicious than her boss. She told Mariah that Griefe wasn't available.

"Do you know if he did any checking in Clarion City, Officer Gordon?" Mariah asked.

"Negative."

"*Is* he going to check? Or is he going to kiss me off because his nephew happened to have the bad luck to be enrolled in J. D. Day Care?" Why not speak her mind, Mariah asked herself. It was the least she could do, even though her frankness had seemingly no effect on Ms. Gordon.

"Your suspicions aren't a high priority in this office, Ms. Sullivan. We're up to here with serious crimes from yesterday and the day before." Mariah sensed the woman was about to hang up. As a parting shot, the officer couldn't resist saying, "Doesn't seem like you need any help. I saw your news conference."

"That was held in defense of my reputation and the Tot Lot's—nothing more!" Mariah bristled. "It didn't help me in finding the identity of a possible child killer. You'll remember I didn't mention my theory in public. I thought it was smarter not to give away my suspicions. The killer might guess that we're on to him."

"We?" Contempt fairly dripped from the word.

Mariah imagined Ms. Gordon's heavy jaw set above her uniform's starched blouse collar. She sighed. "If you won't help me, I don't have any choice but to try to find the killer myself."

"Maybe you should just look in the mirror."

Mariah's rage, born of years of suffering and a new strength of purpose, exploded in a curse. Who was this thickheaded cop, to think she had *ever* laid a murderous hand on any child? All she was doing was parroting her equally thickheaded boss. As she began to tell Officer Gordon these things, the woman hung up. Mariah stood, breathing hard, dead receiver in hand, still red-faced with anger. Instead of embarrassment she felt flushed with pride. Don't mess with me, she thought. Don't mess with the *new* Mariah!

As the adrenaline of verbal combat drained, it occurred to her that she had been crude and tactless. If she was transforming her personality, those characteristics weren't becoming ones to add. Or practical. After all, she might one day really need the police.

She didn't realize it would be that afternoon.

The phone rang in her office. In response to her determinedly cheerful greeting she heard a distant, rustling voice. It said, "One of the Tot Lot children is going to die!"

Her fingers gripped the phone anxiously. "What—are you saying?"

"One will die!"

She couldn't identify the voice. It was airy, sexless. Terrifying! "You're the person who's done all this to me—"

"Yes."

"Why? *Why?*"

The caller hung up.

Mariah put down the receiver and sank into a chair. She held herself until her heart slowed. She looked around her office, as though to gain strength from familiar surroundings. *When* was all this going to end? How much more could she take? Death eight years ago. Now death again? *Again?*

She called 911. Shortly a cruiser arrived. Another officer team, this one far more polite than Griefe and Gordon, asked questions and took notes. Mariah read their earnest faces. They knew about the Tot Lot's troubles, but didn't let that affect their work either way. One of them would stay through the children's departures. They'd pass along their information to their superiors. There would be an investigation . . .

Maybe there would be, if Lieutenant Griefe didn't get involved.

The woman officer, "Call me Elspeth," was clear-eyed and competent. She spoke quietly to Mariah while her partner radioed the dispatcher. "Today's Friday. If I were you, I think this threat would make me close the place starting Monday, Ms. Sullivan."

"I was thinking exactly the same thing."

Mariah gathered her staff and told them about the threat. They got excited. It took twenty minutes to answer their frightened questions and calm them down. She told them she was going to close the Tot Lot. That meant some tasks had to be done right away. They needed a printed announcement to be distributed to parents when they picked up their kids. Parents who had no children in the center that day had to be phoned and warned of the closing. She wanted her staff to come in next week for a few days at least to clean up the place and tie up administrative loose ends. They agreed to do so. Nikki Herakis said, "Do you think the Tot Lot will ever reopen, Mariah?"

"That depends."

"On what?"

"On how good a detective I can be," Mariah said.

That afternoon she made some phone calls to Clarion City. To her surprise, she was remembered. She made an appointment for eight o'clock Saturday morning, the earliest she could manage. That meant a sleepover for Clarisse at Rita's—God bless the woman! At five Saturday morning, Mariah was on the road. She avoided dwelling on the fate of the Tot Lot now that it was no longer producing an income. With a bottom line of zero, it couldn't survive long. She nudged the accelerator down a hair.

Her destination: Clarion City Police Plaza. Her contact was her old enemy, Detective Joe D'Orio.

She found him in his office, around the corner from where it had been eight years before. He wore jeans and a golf shirt. The years had brought gray to his sideburns and chipped some of the flint from his eyes. He had done her a favor coming in on a Saturday. He leaned back in his chair, his hands behind his head, and picked up the conversation where they had left it on the phone. "So you think there were other kids killed earlier in this town? . . ."

She summed up her suspicions: the harassment, the shoe in the mail, events not quite duplicating but certainly paralleling those of eight years ago, when both she and he had played different roles. D'Orio leaned forward now, all attentive. "I hear you. I *hear* you." He nodded thoughtfully. "One thing a cop hates is an open case. And he *really* hates when a kid is offed and somebody gets away with it." He glared at her. "So back then we tried to pin it on you and Jacky DuMarr. Didn't go. After that we had no other suspects. I checked the file after your call. Case is still open." He got up and walked around his desk. "But let's tell it like it is, Mariah. It ain't a high priority no more, if I make my point."

Mariah looked up at his face, run to lines and fat pockets. "Well, what am I going to do? I told you I got on the wrong side of my local police. And it wasn't my fault! Just the same, they won't help me. And neither will you!"

"Take it easy."

"How can I? Somebody wants to kill one of the kids from my day-care center!"

D'Orio drew his palm slowly down his face. He was looking for the right thing to say. He straightened his shoulders. "Okay, listen. I don't want to have to deal with your buddy Griefe. I don't know him. I want to keep it that way. He's got a bug up his ass about you. I can't do anything about it."

Mariah pointed an accusing finger at him. "You're saying you don't *care* enough to find out if other kids were killed by the same maniac."

"Didn't say that."

"What *did* you say?"

He waved away her question. "I have higher priorities. That's an old case. I got new cases." He scowled. "Crime never sleeps."

Mariah's frustration brought her to her feet. "Griefe won't help me. *You* won't help me. You won't even talk to the man. So what can I do to find out if other children were killed by the same person?"

D'Orio smiled broadly and held up an index finger. "You can listen up. We got a computer . . ."

He took twenty minutes to explain how to search the database and showed her in what ways the records were incomplete. "You don't get the whole picture. You get about eighty percent of it," he said. "But that's better than nothing. And you get it fast. Then you gotta go to the files for the kind of details you want. Shoes on or off and such."

Fast or not, it took her three hours to find fifteen unsolved cases involving murdered children dating from both before and after Dotty Orel's brutal slaying. Then she had to go to the files. They were in an underground complex in the next building. File cabinets, many dating from the days of wood, filled six floors. She got in with a pass given to her by D'Orio, now long gone to his Saturday foursome. "The Golden Leaves Classic!" he had grinned on his way out the door. "Good hunting. Let me know how you do."

A soft-spoken woman officer in the records building lobby gave her a typed sheet explaining the filing system. If Mariah had any questions, she was to come back and ask.

Mariah tried to work fast, but it wasn't easy. She had to haul out file folders by the dozens. She cut her hands on paper and cardboard. Grit found her pores. She dealt out photos like so many decks of cards, looking, looking . . .

And in time, finding.

By the time she had slammed the last file drawer home, six hours had passed. There was sweat high on her brow. Her hands trembled with excitement. Three girls and two boys had been killed like Dotty Orel, with some kind of machete or cleaver. The deaths were two years apart almost to the day, in different boroughs of Clarion City. Each time, one shoe had been removed from the victim. Since Dotty, no others had died in the same way. Or at least Mariah could find no records of similar tragedies. D'Orio had said only eighty percent of cases had been entered into the computer. So she couldn't be absolutely sure. Nonetheless . . .

She gathered that the similarity of the murders had escaped police attention because the unfortunates had largely been black or Puerto Rican. She wasn't so naive not to know that it took ten deaths in the ghetto to get the same notice as one in the suburbs.

She sensed she had found something beyond the confirmation of her serial killer theory. But even during the two-hour drive back to Madison, she couldn't get a grip on it. Well, she had no more time for speculations. She had made progress, and had a great deal more to make before the weekend was out!

Late that afternoon, she took Rita into her confidence and explained what she was going to do. She wanted her friend to continue to watch Clarisse for the rest of the weekend. Rita agreed, but she was clearly uneasy. "Isn't there some other way to handle it? That maybe isn't so . . . risky?"

"Can't think of how. And still get it done and over with quickly, hopefully before another child dies. One who spent time under *my* care."

"The police?"

"Griefe hates me. Period."

"What about this Nevsky guy?" Rita asked. "Can't he take care of things for you?"

Mariah smiled. "I think—no, I'm *sure*—he'd want me to handle it myself."

Rita frowned. "What kind of friend is that?"

"A very different one." Why was she grinning so, Mariah wondered. Nevsky had encouraged her to solve her own problems. To help do it he had in a sense hung her out high and dry. And here she was, cherishing him for it!

After touching base with Clarisse, she returned home and dressed in black sneakers and jeans. She pulled on a dark brown sweater and knit hat. She wasn't playing ninja; she just didn't want to stand out. Then she got into Rita's Detroit Unnoticeable, which she had swapped for the van for the rest of the weekend.

Her challenge was a simple one: *find the missing shoes!*

When she found them, she would have found the killer.

She had her short list of suspects. She was going to march right down it and see what she could uncover. She knew she was making a lot of assumptions that she couldn't truly back up. Among them was that the killer kept the shoes at home. Another was that she would be able to complete her searches by late Sunday evening. Okay, so she needed a little luck, she told herself. Well, somebody said luck was a residual of good design. And she liked her design. To her astonishment, the exhilaration of chancy action charged her like an exotic drug. Go get 'em, Sullivan!

She started on that rainy late Saturday afternoon with the home of Jacky DuMarr, who was now living with her sister. She had gotten her old boss's address from Felicia Greene some time before. Felicia, who thought Jacky's crimes were behind her. The woman was a lot more sure of that than Mariah was. She drove to Jacky's sister's address. It was the top half of a wooden duplex. Driveways poked straight back on either side of the building. No cars were in either one. No lights burned on the second level.

She walked around to the back and found wooden porches and stairs. Clothing hung on sheltered lines. She started up the back stairs and found a boy of about seven sitting in the middle of the second flight. He was playing with a sand bucket filled with mud, which he was smearing on his shoes. He looked up, unafraid. ''Who you lookin' for, lady?''

''Jacky DuMarr.''

''They ain't here. They all went out. I seen 'em.'' He muddied his shoes further.

Mariah smiled. ''Thank you. You're a pretty sharp little guy to know so much about what's going on where you live.''

''Yeah!'' He grinned and stirred his mud.

''If Jacky's not home I'm going to have to go up and leave a note.''

''I'll give it to her,'' he said.

''I'd rather leave it myself,'' Mariah said.

The boy quit stirring the mud and looked up with a pair of closely set suspicious eyes. ''Five bucks I tell you where the key is.''

Mariah started to protest, then cut herself short. She swallowed, tossing earlier assumptions to the breeze. ''And that buys a zipper for your mouth, kid.''

''A deal.''

''I didn't come to steal anything.''

He shrugged. She didn't like his tight little smile. It belonged on the face of the shifty, opportunistic thirty-year-old he would undoubtedly grow up to be. She reached in her pocket for some bills and felt conspiracy descend like a fog . . .

The inside of Jacky's sister's apartment smelled of stale cigarettes and the sweat of a male not fond of baths. There were only three rooms, a kitchen and a bath. And not a lot of furniture in them. Who knew how much time she had. She had to move quickly, yet check every bureau, cabinet, drawer, shelf, nook, and cranny.

She covered them all, but found no shoes. In what must have been Jacky's bedroom she found three sealed cardboard boxes. She had pulled on a pair of gloves before taking the key from its hiding place, so she didn't hesitate to fetch a kitchen knife and slice the tape. Inside she found clothes, some bric-a-brac, and . . . shoes. Her heart pounded and she drew in her breath in a sharp gasp. *Maybe* . . . Despite her excitement, determined rummaging produced only Jacky's out-of-style dress heels.

She checked the bathroom and kitchen a second time, now peering inside larger boxes of detergent and health aids. Nothing. In the other bedroom closet, she found a hatch leading up to a crawlspace. She had to check it. She dragged a kitchen stool under the hatch and pushed it up. She peered up into the gloom and glimpsed some kind of trunk. She groaned to realize she would have to climb up to get a look. If she didn't, she couldn't be *sure*. She pushed the hatch fully open. Arms on each side of the opening, she struggled to lift herself up the rest of the way.

Her upper body strength had never been great. Now she regretted her sedentary life. She thought her arms were going to pull loose from her shoulders as she clumsily levered herself up into the crawlspace. Once there, she bent to avoid the roof supports. She was breathing heavily and had begun to sweat. November or not, it was warm up there. She found a switch and threw it to light the single dangling bulb. She had to walk carefully on the edges of the ceiling joists. One poorly aimed step and her foot would plunge through the thin wallboard below.

She made a clumsy crisscross of the confining space. She looked in vain for shoes tucked down between boards and paper-backed insulation. She angled over to the trunk, which she now saw had Jacky's name stenciled on it. Clenching her teeth, she thumbed the fake brass studs. The tongues popped up. She nudged the shaped stud above the heavy centered lock. It moved. She eased up the boxy lid, breath catching in her throat.

More clothes! What had she expected? How many dozen flashy outfits had she seen Jacky wear? She wouldn't have thrown them away just because she had been imprisoned. Mariah began to carefully search through the folded clothing.

Until she heard Jacky's unmistakable braying voice!

With a gasp she looked up. There was a louvered open-ing in the eaves of the house to provide air circulation. Jacky was still outside, no doubt having just arrived home by car. A chill traveled up Mariah's spine. This wasn't the place to lose it, she told herself. She fought to control her rising panic.

Time to get out!

She made herself take the time to quickly check the rest of the trunk's contents. No children's shoes, dammit! She closed the trunk and fastened down its latches, then tightrope-walked the beam leading to the opening in the ceiling. She scrambled down to the stool and reached up to slide the hatchway back in place. Stool in one hand, she raced back toward the kitchen. She snatched up the knife she had used to open the boxes, replacing the stool and knife in the kitchen. Hearing voices on the landing, she thanked heaven that Jacky was a big woman and wouldn't be bounding the stairs in great strides.

She opened the door onto the porch, stepped out, and eased the latch home. She was glad to see an early November dusk falling. Grateful for the sneakers she wore, she scampered across the porch and down the stairs until she was below the apartment's sight lines. Then she slowed, walking casually down the rest of the way. She realized she was soaked with sweat. There was an alley straight ahead. She moved toward it. She paused for a moment beside a rusty dumpster and looked back. Lights went on in Jacky's sister's apartment. She heard no outcries. For the moment at least, no one had seen her or suspected her visit.

In the distant driveway gloom, she spotted the boy with his bucket of mud. He stared after her, confidant or betrayer she couldn't guess.

She hoped she never saw him again.

She pulled out a Kleenex and dried her brow and upper lip. Her heart had finally moved back to idle. Plenty of excitement for you, Mariah Sullivan. But no shoes.

She found her way to Rita's car. Walking along, she thought for a moment that maybe she had gone crazy, taking such a risk for mere suspicions. She thought not. If she was mad, she reasoned, it was an intoxicating madness. That of those who finally act after so many years of timidity.

It was nearly dark when she reached her next stop, Rudy's and Helga's cavernous rented house, where Roper had roughed up her ex-husband—to her delight. She saw no lights within. Empty garage doors gaped. The Errises were out. Her luck was holding. She parked in the next block and circled back, staying in the shadows. She pushed through some bushes, angled behind the neighbor's garage, and stepped through onto the lawn behind the old towering house. There were three doors facing away from the street. She tried all three. Locked. She didn't want to go up on the front porch; a streetlight illuminated it too well.

She began to feel anxious. There was much space to be searched and the Errises could return at any time. She knew she was foolhardy to persist in this way. But she wasn't going to turn back. She had spent too many years never driving toward her desires. Turning back now would remind her of those bad old days and the meek Mariah who had suffered through them.

She found a basement hatchway and heaved up one of two rusty metal doors. It clicked into its open position. She descended the half dozen wooden stairs and faced the solid basement door, reaching out and groping for the knob. It was covered with rust. She turned it and dug her shoulder into the splintery wood. It didn't open. She had the feeling, though, that it might if forced. She heaved again so hard that her healing rib throbbed. The latch loosened, the door groaned open, and she stumbled forward into the basement. She climbed back up the stairs and closed the hatch, then the wooden door behind her.

She smelled mildew and the limy scent of damp whitewash. From her pocket she took a mini flashlight. Preferred by housebreakers everywhere, she thought. She moved silently through what looked like a root cellar, then another room filled with shelves and wine racks where dust as thick as cotton lay on everything.

She searched every square foot of the vast basement. Good thing it had been cleaned out long ago. It held no furniture or stored possessions. Only the natural stone walls with their coating of peeling whitewash could conceal any shoes hidden behind the many niches. She hadn't time to wriggle every protruding uneven boulder. She turned the beam of her light above to the heavy floor supports in search of packages tucked away. Nothing . . . Enough for the basement, though doubt that she had made a thorough search remained. She had to get upstairs.

On the first floor the shadowy beasts of Victorian furniture made her uneasy. She moved quickly to open the many thick cabinet doors and drawers. Her probing light found heaps of folded linen carrying the ghostly scents of spent sachets. She thought of the dead, generations stretching out into the past, strung out in the Dance of Death. Ladies in hoop skirts, men in boiled collars, hand in hand. The dead . . . Hairs rose on the back of her head. She whimpered, then seized control of herself. Keep going, she ordered. You have a lot of work to do.

Closets revealed antique clothing hung in dry rotting profusion. In the first she reached her hand between garments to part them. They fell to tatters and dust at her touch. She cried out squeamishly and beat her suddenly powdered hands against her thighs. From then on she contented herself with searching only the shelves and corners of the remaining closets.

As she continued her investigations, she found the number of rooms daunting. Maybe it would be better to first search those rooms that contained likely hiding places. If she didn't find anything there, she'd take the rest of the rooms in random order. However she handled her search, she told herself, she would continue until she was successful, had finished the job, or was interrupted by the Errises' return. She hadn't time to get tired or to be afraid. After all, what was there to fear except shadows and times past?

She didn't discipline herself well. She kept being drawn aside by inviting cupboards that proved to be stacked not with incriminating evidence but with unused china and cooking utensils. She stood on chairs to better peer in vain among dishes, silver, and pots. Then a low cabinet would catch her eye, then a cedar chest . . .

She lost track of time. Eventually she found her way to the second floor. A quick count disclosed six rooms: a study, stripped library, and bedrooms. Not too much furniture. Not a lot of hiding places—thank goodness! She opened a half dozen doors in search of the Errises' bedroom. She found it less by sight than smell. It was the faint scent of a familiar Avon perfume that led her away from dust and dryness toward the last door on the left of the long, darkly carpeted hall.

The moment she threw open the door, she heard the noise.

No mistaking it. It was a footfall on a creaky stair. Her knees turned watery and began to tremble. The Errises had returned! And one of them was coming up the long staircase.

Had they heard her, despite her stealth?

She had to hide somewhere! She darted back down the hall and into the library. She found a towering armoire. Its high wide double doors were inviting. Her light revealed a protruding key. She spun one and swung its door open. She climbed up, ducking below an empty hanger rod, and pulled the door toward her, leaving just a slit from which she had an angled glimpse of the hall.

She saw a flickering golden glow brighten the gloom. What was *that?* Again hairs stirred on her neck. Her hand on the door trembled despite the strength of her grip. The light grew brighter. It came from one of the kerosene lamps she had glimpsed on the first floor. She had thought them mere antiques—ornaments. The lamp was in the left hand of a woman wearing a beige blouse and dark woolen skirt. A large leather sack purse hung by a strap from her shoulder. Her face was turned toward the far side of the hall. Nonetheless, there was no mistaking the blond hair. Helga! Mariah's stare was torn from Helga's head by the gleam at her side. No matter Mariah's brief glimpse, there was no mistaking what the woman held in her right hand.

A large chef's cleaver!

Just such a weapon had been used to slaughter Dotty Orel—and five other children!

Mariah's blood turned to ice as she grasped the danger into which she had blundered. Despite her fear, her mind raced along. Everything made sense! Helga had been odd from the start. Deranged, murderous actions couldn't be put past her. Mariah wondered where Rudy was, and if Helga played her deadly games only when alone. She held her breath, put a determined rein on her fear, and listened intently.

Helga bustled around her bedroom. Mariah heard a toilet flush and then tap water running briefly. Mariah found her posture causing a cramp on her cracked rib side. She straightened just a bit to ease the discomfort. Doing so, she tipped the shelf above her with the top of her head. Some sort of metallic object toppled off the shelf, to fall at her feet with a clatter as loud as thunder. She stifled her gasp. *Oh, no!*

Helga's movements stopped abruptly. Her footsteps told Mariah that she was coming back down the hall. Now she had stopped and gone into a bedroom. With a sinking heart Mariah realized the woman was searching each room for the source of the crash. And she had a cleaver.

A cleaver!

She shook off her imagination's horrors of impending

doom and quashed her panic with steely mental toughness. She had to do something—fast! She thought of climbing out of her hiding place and trying to find another. But she was certain to make noise. And where could she hide in a few moments that Helga and her cleaver couldn't find her? She flashed her light around the inside of the armoire. What she hoped to find she couldn't guess. A secret passage? The way to Narnia?

She turned her light on the old lock set in the door in front of her. It had an antique mechanism. From the back of the lock casing stuck a short square stud. She turned it with her thumb and forefinger. She pushed at the door. It was now locked. All right! She twisted the stud back the other way. She nudged the door open, reached out, and groped for the key. She found it, pulled it silently out of the keyhole and dropped it into her pocket. She reclosed the door and twisted the stud back to lock it.

Then she stood unmoving and waited.

In moments she heard Helga in the doorway. Her silence was more ominous than any threat she might have uttered. It was now obvious to Mariah that the woman's jealousy was the tip of an iceberg of mental troubles. She was easily insane enough to be both Dotty's killer and Mariah's tormentor. And dumb Rudy was tangled in some way into her snarl of madness and murder.

Through a narrow slit high in the armoire Mariah saw the light from the kerosene lamp. Helga had entered the room! The lamp and the cleaver were the calling cards of her lunacy. Mariah was sweating now. Her knees shook. She was afraid they might make her sway and blunder into the side of her small protective chamber. She heard Helga first go to the room's three closets, jerking each door open in turn.

Then her steps turned toward the armoire. The light in

the thin slit grew stronger. Soon she was standing right in front of Mariah's hiding place, not four feet from her. Mariah tried not to breathe. In the silence she heard Helga's breath. Did she imagine lunacy echoing in each weighty exhalation?

Helga spun the key in the other door and swung it open. She hesitated, no doubt peering inside, then pushed the door closed and relocked it. Further hesitation as she found no key in Mariah's door. Mariah felt the slight tremble as the woman fingered the door flange in search of leverage. She labored intently for a long moment.

Then Mariah heard a sound that brought a cry to her lips that she barely smothered. Helga was pulling the *other* key from its lock! Of course it would work in Mariah's door! She stood rigid as Helga tried the key. It rattled about only inches from Mariah's hip as Helga tried to force it to turn. It didn't. It didn't fit. Thank goodness!

There was a long pause, neither woman moving. In moments Helga was on her way, figuring no doubt that if the armoire door was locked, no one could be in there. Mariah didn't move until she heard the other woman's footsteps move off down the hall into the remaining rooms, then down the stairs.

As she calmed, Mariah realized that she hadn't just been lucky. She had been *dumb* lucky. She had been gifted with the discovery that Helga Holmann Erris was her deadly nemesis. She smothered her instinctive thoughts of now rushing from the house as fast as she could. She dared not leave right away. She had been given a break. It was time to take advantage of it. Time to nail Helga down with some hard evidence.

She crept out of the closet and moved silently to the head of the stairs. She noticed a side door. She peered out a window and saw that the door opened onto a long porch. In the moonlit gloom, she thought she saw stairs leading down to the ground. That would be her exit when she chose to leave. Which wasn't quite yet . . .

She listened hard for sounds downstairs from Helga. She heard nothing. Maybe the woman was waiting for her to reveal herself. Then she would make her move, cleaver in hand and a mad fire in her eyes. Mariah could play a waiting game. She sat down on the top stair and calmed herself. Not four minutes later she heard an outside door open, then the screen slam shut. She rushed to a front window and saw shadowy Helga heading for the rear driveway. She had left the house!

Mariah grinned in the darkness. Her close call had been worth all the risk. Now she had all the time in the world to find the shoes.

She knew they had to be here.

In the end they weren't hidden all that well. In the back of Helga's bedroom cabinet behind a heap of hats and scarves she found a wrinkled plastic grocery bag. She opened it in triumph and pity.

Inside were five pathetic little right shoes.

She felt a swell of sorrow for the lives torn from small bodies so long before their time. Helga, Helga, the monster . . . She bowed her head and closed her eyes for a long moment. Though unseeing, she glimpsed something of the danger and randomness of life. Everything was up for grabs. How could one hope for salvation in reason? One had to turn elsewhere for that. To God? To gods? To mysteries? She thought of Nevsky. For the first time, she grasped something of what he meant. So much lay behind the scrim curtain woven of the senses' input. Behind it lay the *real* stage, where meanings played their parts.

In time she rose from her reverie. Thankful for her gloves, she reclosed the bag and put it back just where she had found it.

I have a suspect. I have evidence.

I am almost out of the woods—at last!

Seventeen

Nevsky phoned at ten Sunday morning. Mariah was bubbling over with all she had to tell him, but she managed to control herself. He asked if she and Clarisse owned ice skates. When she said they did, he invited her to pick him up in a half hour. She realized he didn't own a car. He had borrowed one to visit her. Somehow she wasn't surprised he was carless. If he could do without a TV, he could do without anything.

She thought he would guide her toward a public skating rink and its crowds. Instead his directions led them to the university, across its playing fields, to the rink. It was closed, she realized, seeing no cars. She turned a puzzled glance toward him. "I have ways," he said, and ordered her around to the delivery entrance. He rang the bell. Shortly, the wide service door slid up on heavy tracks. Standing in the doorway was a bullet-headed bald man in his sixties with ox-wide shoulders.

Yuri embraced him. More than you've ever done to

me, Mariah thought. The two men spouted rapid-fire Russian at each other, then Yuri introduced her to Sergei Isadorovich, the rink's janitor. He beamed, flashing two gold incisors. His accent was so thick she scarcely understood his "You vill haff such skating . . ."

Within, Clarisse squealed at the sight of the empty ice. "All for just *us?*" She hopped up and down. From her lips came her version of Sergei's accent: "We *vill* haff such skating!"

And they did. The rink was cool and still. High above hung colored banners commemorating championship hockey victories. Empty wooden bleachers led down to a rubberized walkway following the curve of high transparent plastic panels. Beyond, the ice lay as smooth and clean as glass. Mariah was a fair skater, Nevsky a bit of a showoff with his little jumps and spins, and Clarisse a novice. It was to her that they both soon turned their attentions. Each took a hand and the three of them slowly circled the ice. "*Slide*, honey. Don't just run on your skates," Mariah urged.

On they went in the cool stillness. It would have been nice to skate in silence, Mariah thought, but there was no reason to quiet her daughter's happy chatter. She had endured psychological abuse at school thanks to the troubles at the Tot Lot. Mariah more than owed her a few hours of attention. Guilt, every mother's bugaboo, reared up, even though the threats to her reputation, business, and now to one of *her* children deserved the greater part of her attention over the last forty days.

In time Clarisse tired. They put her in the penalty box. Mariah and Nevsky stroked over the ice hand in hand. She closed her eyes and sailed. She loved the *crissssss* of the ice beneath her blade edges, the cool breeze on her face. She almost hated to leave the dreamy, gliding world, but she had to bring Nevsky up to date. She told her whole story in a rush. She had no time to hear his reaction. Clarisse had wobbled back out on the ice, ready for more attention.

Après skate was held at a quiet bar near Nevsky's apartment. He ordered hot chocolate for Clarisse, then introduced Mariah to something called a "Jamaican Coffee," a brew of coffee, cordials, rum, brandy, and whipped cream. At this early Sunday hour it went to her head like a left hook.

She became aware of how much she yet had to say to this man with his angular cheeks, deep Slavic eyes, and indirect way of doing things. Much about her situation and maybe just as much about their personal one. For example, did they even *have* a situation? Or had Mariah woven a cloth of fantasy from webs of her own loneliness, her child's basic needs, and the recent strain born of her harassment and testing? She didn't know. She needed to talk. As luck would have it, Nevsky said he had an appointment.

"Yuri, I have so much to *say* to you," she said, sorry at once for the naked pleading in her tone. That wasn't the new Mariah.

"We'll get together again." He smiled. "I didn't know you liked skating so much."

"I love it!" Clarisse interrupted with a brown-smeared mouth. "And so does Mom!"

Mariah shook her head with resignation. This wasn't going to be her day. Yesterday had been her day.

When Nevsky opened the door to get out of the van in front of his building, she touched his arm. "Yuri, what should I do with everything I've found out?" she asked.

He looked her in the eyes. "Push it. Push it *hard!*"

Early Sunday afternoon, her thoughts, spurred by the

Jamaican Coffee, moved back and forth over just what to do with the previous night's discoveries and just what she had a right to expect from Nevsky. She imagined he ought to have given her more of his time to help her sift through her options. He owed her that. Or did he? Like a will-o'-the-wisp, he was of her life, yet not of it. She paced and looked out at her cul-de-sac. The day had turned cold and blustery. Kiddies' Day-Glo hoods were up. Teens, gloveless and hatless as always, backed into the breeze.

She pondered on. She *was* getting to know Nevsky a little. She was beginning to understand how he operated. Possibly his cutting short what had promised to be a whole day with her and Clarisse had been extemporized. He had not really had an appointment. Yet he wasn't one to run from a problem—not that guy! If he had indeed deliberately sent her home alone, the reason was that he wanted her to decide on her own what to do and how.

After all, it *was* her life, wasn't it?

By the time she found her way to bed, she was ready with a plan. A sense of urgency hung over her. Helga absolutely had to be arrested before she carried out her threat to kill a child. Mariah's closing the Tot Lot guaranteed nothing. A former enrolled child could be found and murdered far from day care. She made fists and raised them to the dark. "Never!" she cried into the stillness. No Tot Lot child would die!

She phoned police headquarters in the morning and left a message for Elspeth, the officer who had advised her to close the Tot Lot. Midmorning, Elspeth called back, and Mariah arranged a meeting during the officer's lunch break. Over ham and cheese sandwiches and yogurts she explained that a serial child killer was the person making the threats. She tied in Dotty Orel and the shoes. She stopped short of revealing what she had found out Saturday night.

Elspeth had taken off her cap. She wore her hair up in a short braid. She spooned up blueberry yogurt while Mariah rushed on. Her waving spoon cut Mariah short. "Why are you telling me all this, Ms. Sullivan?"

"Good reasons, I think. Did you do as I asked when we last talked? Did you tell Detective Griefe that one of the children's lives had been threatened?"

"Well, yes, I got word to him . . . ." Elspeth frowned. "So?"

"Did he do anything?"

"I'm . . . not sure." Elspeth's wide eyes were that startling light blue that had always made Mariah think of a separate, superior race of humans. Now they narrowed just a bit. Elspeth was not stupid.

"I'll be candid," Mariah said, deciding to rush ahead. "He had a relative enrolled in my last day-care center."

"Uh-oh!"

"Yeah. He still thinks I was guilty—of something." Mariah swallowed heavily but kept her eyes on Elspeth's face. "He thinks maybe I killed the girl . . ." She hesitated, wondering if the lady cop was following her.

"I saw some of those awful news broadcasts," Elspeth said. "You mean Dotty Orel?" She left the spoon in her unfinished yogurt. "Maybe it would be better if you just told me what's on your mind, Ms. Sullivan."

Mariah leaned forward. "I've found out who the killer is," she said softly.

Elspeth's eyebrows rose. "Tell me who and how."

Mariah did and Elspeth listened intently. She smiled. "And the shoes were there. You didn't . . . put them there?"

"I most certainly did not!" Mariah was ready to career

into rage until she noticed Elspeth's smile widen. She had only been teasing. A bad move by an inexperienced officer.

"I'm sorry, Mariah. That wasn't the best timing in the world." Elspeth put her hand on Mariah's elbow. "What do you want me to do?" she asked.

"Is there anybody at headquarters besides Griefe you can tell about what I found out?"

She shook her head. "It's Griefe's case. Anybody I tell has to go to him with what they know."

"You must understand I'm worried he won't do anything," Mariah said. "Because he won't believe anything I tell him."

"I'll talk to him myself," Elspeth said. "He'll listen."

"I'm not sure about that." Mariah drew a heavy breath. "So that's why I want you to listen carefully to what I'm going to say. It's this: tell him that if he doesn't do anything on his own, I'll force him to."

Elspeth frowned. "How?"

"I won't tell you."

"I'm not sure all this is a good idea."

"It won't be a good idea if one of my tots is murdered either." Mariah touched the other woman's hand. "I want an arrest today!"

"Hey, I can't promise that," Elspeth protested. "Griefe might not be around. There's *procedure!*"

"Tomorrow then, Elspeth. Tomorrow at the latest."

"I can't promise—"

"Promise that you'll call me then and report progress. I *have* to know what's going on."

Elspeth tried to hide her wince. She realized she had allowed Mariah to entangle her. A more experienced officer would have known how to handle the desperate type that Mariah had become. Mariah saw in the high blue lakes of Elspeth's eyes the desire to back out; that desire warred with her obvious compassion. As though reading her mind, Mariah knew she was thinking *just this once.*

"You'll hear from me, Mariah." Elspeth held up a hand in a halting gesture. "But whatever happens, don't do anything crazy!"

"We'll see," Mariah said.

She scarcely had time to mull over her lunch meeting. The moment she got back to the Tot Lot, Grace Kleingold and Deidre Williamson came to her. They intended to resign. Over the weekend they had talked over the death threat with their husbands. The possibility being connected with the murder of a child once under their supervision was more than they wanted their reputations to have to bear. They were sorry, but . . .

Mariah surprised them with a smile. She waved at two chairs. "Have a seat, ladies, and I'll tell you a tale of serial murder and guilt . . ."

They heard her out, then Grace said, "You mean they're about to arrest this Helga woman and maybe your ex? You mean this is all almost *over?*"

"Yes!" Mariah answered, jumping over possible difficulties. "And not only that. The public is going to find out what Helga did to me. There's going to be a big wave of support for me and the Tot Lot. And enrollments are going to go up! I know it. I'll be getting more of the kind of free, positive publicity that's due me—finally. I need you both to stay on. In the end I'm going to have to hire more people, maybe put a big extension on the building. I know it!"

Deidre pursed her lips. "Aren't you getting a *teeny* little bit ahead of yourself, Mariah?"

"I *saw* Helga with the cleaver. I found the shoes. Never

mind how the details finally fall out. This thing is almost over!"

To Mariah's disappointment, the two women said that, having seen her through the toughest times, they had earned the right to sit on the sidelines for a while. They were going to join their husbands on a Myrtle Beach golf vacation for a week or so. By the time they came back, the Tot Lot would be booming, assuming Mariah had it all figured right. They'd ask for their jobs back then. They understood they ran the risk of her not rehiring them.

Mariah then went to her remaining staff, Rochelle Camwell, Randi Monroe, and Nikki Herakis and explained why the crisis was at long last about over. As always Randi had her two children, Gert and Dan, with her. It had been them rather than any commitment to the Tot Lot that had kept her on duty. Now she faced Mariah with a frown on her usually untroubled brow. "I can't come in any more, Mariah. Not until an arrest is made. If the woman you suspect promised to kill one of our kids, it could be one of these two." She pointed at hers. "I'm going to get out of town. I'll come back when she's in jail."

Mariah shrugged. "Fair enough. It won't be long. By tomorrow night."

Nikki shook her head. "Ms. Sullivan, my parents . . . Last night they laid down the law. They don't want me here anymore, not with death threats out on the kids. I'll have to stay away, too." Her young face brightened. "But only until everything clears up. I'll explain what you just said to Mom and Dad and I'm sure they'll—"

"Nikki, it's okay. Don't worry. We're just talking hours here, not weeks." Mariah smiled. "You'll be back with us before you know you left."

Once steady but now wavering Rochelle shrugged as though in the face of an inevitable unpleasantness. "So it's just you and me, boss, left to do all the cleanup. If I had kids here or parents there, I'd be gone, too, I suppose." Her smile was a bit forced. "So I guess I'm the old warhorse. I'm the one who just has to stick it out." She put an arm over Mariah's shoulders, tilted her blond head till her hair brushed the younger woman's cheek. Mariah felt a welling of complex emotions. Thank goodness for stout people like Rochelle. Despite her recent unexpected sullenness over Mariah's strategy and a few complaints, she was a solid trooper all right. "I'll see the Tot Lot to the end of the tunnel," Rochelle said. "All the way through to new beginnings!"

Late afternoon, Mariah got a call from Elspeth. She had spoken to Griefe.

"What'd he say?" Mariah asked.

The officer hesitated. "Bunch of stuff about you. None of it real positive."

"I told you!" Mariah said. "So . . . is he going to have Helga and Rudy arrested?"

"He said he'd look into it."

"That's all?"

"Mariah—"

"Did you tell him I'd *force* him to do something, Elspeth?"

"No."

"If Helga isn't in jail before tomorrow night, I have no choice but—"

"Mariah, be reasonable," Elspeth pleaded. "I'm just a beat officer. Griefe outranks me much. Plus, I'm out of my jurisdiction. I'm right on the edge of making big problems for myself!"

Mariah was sympathetic. Officer Elspeth was an empathetic soul and a good cop. Just the same, Mariah *had* to exert her will. Her whole new life was riding on removing a murderer from society. Always before, when push had come to shove, it was she who had been shoved. It was long past time to shove back. "Elspeth, just do that *one* thing for me and I'll get off your back. Tell Griefe that if he doesn't act, I'll force him to. And never mind how."

"Mariah—"

"Do it—*please!*" She hung up, her emotions twisting. The woman had been caring and helpful, yet Mariah was putting her on the rack. Well, it wasn't much of a rack. And from Mariah's new, more assertive point of view, it wouldn't hurt Elspeth—or Griefe, for that matter—to act on her behalf. After all, arresting a serial murderer who had eluded discovery, never mind arrest, would be a feather in the knotty-faced detective's cap.

The next day, she and Rochelle started to clean up the Tot Lot. The uniform of the day was informal. Mariah wore a worn khaki jumpsuit, her hair up and tied with a scarf. Rochelle wore a linen Mother Hubbard cap "that you mustn't ever admit you saw on me," she ordered. The older woman bubbled with enthusiasm about the "post-whacko" Tot Lot, as she called it. She saw the period of strain as having strengthened their little institution and brought a rough maturity to its staff. She was betting only Deidre and Grace wouldn't be back at work on Monday. She shared some reorganizational ideas that had been in the back of her mind for months. Maybe it was now time to get some of them going. What did Mariah think of . . . ?

Mariah's problem was, she couldn't give Rochelle her full attention. It was divided between her and the telephone on which she expected a call from police headquarters. One that didn't come. Well, she simply wasn't going to wait for her evening deadline's arrival. She picked up the phone herself over the course of the afternoon to leave three messages for Officer Elspeth. None were returned.

At five, a grimy and weary Rochelle decided to go home. Mariah was left alone, faced with a quandary. There was only one way to resolve it. She phoned the Erris home. She held her breath at the ring. Someone picked up. "Helga Erris speaking," Helga said.

Mariah's heart pounded. Murderer of children! Still walking free! She slid the receiver softly into its cradle. So . . . either Officer Elspeth hadn't carried her warning to Griefe or she had and he had chosen to ignore it. For whatever reason, Mariah's deadline had passed. Now it was time to show them she wasn't bluffing.

She picked up the phone and called Chan Lee. Two hours later Chan returned her call. "What's up?" the reporter asked.

"How'd you like to be the one to break the news about a serial child killer? And put the heat on the police to arrest her?"

Chan was silent for a moment. "I guess we have to talk, don't we?"

"And soon. We have an unknown child marked for death, as you TV types like to say. And a murderer just waiting to be arrested."

Chan was interested enough to come over to Mariah's condo alone that Tuesday evening. She pulled up in her white Lexus, vanity plate C. LEE. Mariah then thought of Fontenot, another ostentatious spender. Were these the new aristocrats, these ambitious, hard-nosed types riding their media steeds roughshod over compassion and reality? She would have to ask Nevsky's opinion—when her life was on an even keel again.

She leveled with Chan over their first espresso: she

wanted the police to act; she needed the reporter's help. Chan nodded. "I know Griefe. He doesn't like us pulling his chain."

Mariah cocked her head, worried for a moment. "So? . . ."

Chan's eyes nearly closed as she flashed a mischievous grin. "So we pull his a little harder when we can. Up to now we haven't had much of a chance. Looks like that's going to change."

Chan laid out how she thought things ought to go. No news conference this time. She wanted the *Inside Track* exclusive. She had the perfect role for Mariah: a desperate professional woman and single mother forced to play detective because of police department intransigence. A woman struggling against time and the threat of death to save her reputation and her day-care center. They outlined some questions that would give Mariah a chance to unload all her suspicions. The reporter lowered her cup and looked intently at Mariah. "You know, we're running a big libel risk with all this. Let's . . . do a little rethinking."

They settled on a more cautious but no less revealing approach. Mariah would report only what she had done and seen, beginning with her receipt in the mail of Dotty Orel's shoe, continuing with her trip to the Clarion City police archives, her observation of Helga with lamp and cleaver, and her discovery of the missing right shoes. Wrapping it up, Chan shook her head. "You're still riding the whirlwind with this deal, Sullivan. Anything could come out of it. You could be sued. You could be hassled for breaking and entering. You could end up on every Madison cop's black list." She scowled. "And I could be in for some heavy sailing, too. I could go on . . ."

"Don't. I have big problems with my entire life," Mariah said. "Now I find out the woman who's caused them has killed five kids and promised to kill another. No kind of safe, reasonable action is going to save me. I've been trying that for *weeks*. All I did was embarrass myself and make things worse—never mind getting drugged and nearly raped by your colleague Fontenot. It's time to roll the dice, win or lose." She surprised herself with that speech. Where had it come from? The right side of her brain? Or was it the left? Or was its source one of the mysteries that so delighted Nevsky? Again she thought of the scrim of the sense's information behind which the real, subtle play of life was acted.

Chan drained her third espresso and got up to leave. Mariah said, "You've been more than helpful to me. I greatly appreciate it."

"It's a scratch-my-back-your-back kind of thing," the reporter said. "The ratings for your news conference went through the roof. Who knows why? Maybe because day care is such a big business now. And there are abusers out there. It's the fascination of it, the this-could-be-my-kid's-day-care-outfit deal. Everybody wondering if you're guilty or not. I looked at the stats of calls and letters. A lot of people are rooting for you."

"I want the police in my corner. I want Helga in jail."

"I'm going to have to juggle the schedule to get you on tomorrow night," Chan Lee said, now in a tactical mode. "There are going to be some unhappy campers."

"I appreciate—"

"We have a death threat," Chan said absently. "That carries a lot of weight with the bosses. Not even those hard-assed moneygrubbers want to see another kid get butchered." She slipped into her coat. When she turned back, a bright smile lit her face. "I'll take my turn at thanking, Sullivan. Thank *you! Inside Track* is mine now.

The station managers saw I was doing a better job than Fontenot. They fired him and Oscar."

Mariah smiled inwardly. There was some rough justice in this world. She remembered Fontenot in her office, cane in hand and fear in his eyes. She had never wanted anyone to fear her. But he had reason to, hadn't he? His body was broken, though it would heal well enough, and now his job was gone. It was a brutal world. She understood she didn't have to apologize for her victories. "I'm not sorry he's gone, Chan."

"Nor am I," the reporter said. She added in a low, private voice, "All the worst rumors about him were true."

Mariah had trouble sleeping that night. Her whole world was descending into turmoil. Those things to which she had clung, her regular schedule, her expected responsibilities, her paced and even life had disintegrated bit by bit over the last month and a half. She had been harassed and psychologically tortured like a bull in the corrida. Not surprising, then, that she wasn't who she had been.

She couldn't grasp precisely how she had changed. She had been given nothing more than little glimpses of her retooled identity, tiny flashes of insight like lightning bugs on an August evening. Words couldn't pin down who she was now, or that sensation she had of living a life teetering on the edge between victory and disaster.

Nor could she grip all the strings. There were too many now: the Bronks and their slanderous claims, Cynthia Tran and her phalanx of day-care regulators, the Cassandra and Nick Delos lawsuit, the Tot Lot ad hoc committee, paying her staff, meeting overhead, affording her lawyer . . . The list of obstacles went on and on. When the dust settled, she'd see where she was.

She felt she was barely outrunning an avalanche. Helga had to be arrested—and soon!

Wednesday morning she listened to the radio and TV. There were no reports of any murdered children. Thank God! She brought Rita in as a clothing consultant to help her pick out an interview outfit. Mariah had caught on: physical appearance was eighty percent of everything. Which viewers were going to bother to dig down into meanings? The suit she'd worn at the press conference had served its purpose and couldn't be seen again. She mustn't seem penurious; rather more established and professional. "I need to wear something to help me throw down the gauntlet to the whole Madison Police Department," she told her friend.

"How about a suit of armor?" Rita asked.

Jeeter and Clarisse in tow, they found three pricey wool dresses. Rita held them up. "Number One says: 'I have always been an innocent woman,'" she suggested. "Number Two says: 'I'm empowered but new to it.' Number Three: 'I'm solid, but I sometimes take crazy risks.' Which is it?"

Mariah smiled. "Pretty much the three parts I've played in my life up to now, Rita. There's nothing else I can do but wear Number Three."

"Go for it!"

Mariah took Clarisse to the TV station. She wanted her to watch from behind the cameras. This was big stuff in both their lives and she didn't want the child to miss any of it. She took care to explain to her that there was no real telling if what she was going to do on *Inside Track* would solve their problems, but it was worth a chance. In the grown-up world, you made your best effort, then took your chances. The girl seemed to understand.

Mariah surprised herself with her composure. No matter

the camera's glowing red lights, she formed her sentences with care under Chan's cunning cuing. The questions allowed her to covertly make herself the heroine of the tale, one who took risks to uncover a murderer threatening one of her Tot Lot children. She was no longer Tongue-tied Tess, or the long-ago little wraith in the shadow of the bombastic Jacky DuMarr. Smoothly and persuasively, she told her story. She did not make a single charge. It fell to Chan to wonder aloud "if the police are going to take action on this" and "what are city officials going to do to remove the cloud of threat over the long-suffering Tot Lot and its tough, courageous owner?"

Mariah took Clarisse to King Cone for her choice, a two-scoop chocolate fudge. While she ate, Mariah phoned Rita. "How'd I do?" she asked.

"Fantastic! You should be on stage, kid!"

"Sure." She hesitated. "Rita, do you think I managed to get Helga and Rudy arrested?"

"I'd bet the ranch on it."

When she got home, she found four reporters' cars along the curb and a man on her doorstep. From a distance, she thought the shadowed form might be Nevsky. Wishful thinking. She saw gaiters and stylish polka-dot slacks. It was Frenetic Freddy. The moment she recognized him, the reporters realized she was home. They tumbled out of their cars like circus clowns. Freddy had time to say only, "You are one ballsy, crazy woman! You're full-time work for any shyster crazy enough to get hooked up with you!" Then he shoved her and Clarisse in through the door. "And don't come out!" he ordered. "I'll handle the Huns."

He held the reporters at bay while Mariah got Clarisse ready for bed. The phone was promising to ring all night, so she turned it over to the answering machine. Let them jabber onto tape. She had just put on the water for instant coffee when Freddy opened the door just enough to shove in a long box. A reporter tried to follow it, but Freddy gave him the low shoulder and knocked him back. Mariah slammed the door.

The box was from a specialty florist and fruit store, the expensive kind that stayed open all night. She put the box on the kitchen table beside the BLESS THIS MESS ceramic tile. Lifting the lid freed sweet odors that swirled like perfume in the dry kitchen air. Cut flowers! But from who?

She found the card, tore it open. *Great performance!* it said, and was signed *Nevsky*.

She closed her eyes, drew in deep breaths of sweet-scented air. She lifted out an iris, at least two thousand miles from where it had been cut. She cupped the blooms in spread hands and gently crushed them. The fluids from ruptured petals streaked her fingers. The scent rose thicker than fog. She sighed. Am I in love in the middle of my troubles? How could she answer that question with so much to sort out? And why Nevsky, a man she really didn't understand, didn't know very well, who was too old for her?

Her reverie was interrupted by Freddy, who had chased away the reporters. "Coffee!" he ordered. "And a shot in it if you got it."

She fortified him. He started to lecture her about failing to inform him about what she intended to do in front of the TV cameras. If she had, he could have talked her out of it. "Too wild and crazy!" he lamented.

The door chimes sounded. Freddy motioned her to sit. He slid in the chain lock and opened the door a crack. He turned back toward her. "You want to deal with the law at this hour?"

"Who is it?"

Freddy asked; she heard the answer: Lieutenant Griefe and his female clone, Officer Gordon.

Talk about fast results! Mariah swallowed her uneasiness and told Freddy to let them in.

The couple was stone-faced, he more narrow-eyed than ever. Before they could say anything, Mariah said, "I'd like you to meet my attorney, Mr. Folsom."

Griefe blinked. Mariah wondered if it was in displeasure at Freddy's presence. She had stirred up a hornets' nest, but it was good to have a bee screen when the swarm arrived.

"Is this a social or business call?" Freddy asked. He touched his head. "I got to know which hat to wear."

"And whether to charge me or not," Mariah giggled. Nervously, she was sure. She was also sure her mirth bothered Griefe and Gordon. Why not bother them? They had caused her much distress with their intransigence.

"Let's call it social," Griefe said. "Save the lady a few bucks."

"Fine. What's on your mind?" Mariah asked.

"That stunt you pulled on that TV show, Ms. Sullivan. What were you trying to prove?" Griefe didn't want an answer. He hurried on. "When people like you play detective, they make it tough on us real cops. Then they get on TV to malign us—"

"My client did no such thing," Freddy interrupted. "She simply stated the facts as she saw them."

Griefe turned a look of contempt at the flamboyant Freddy. "People who run their mouths and shysters who protect them—"

"You don't like the Constitution, get it amended," Freddy said.

Griefe turned away from Freddy's irritating grin. He

sat back in his corner of the couch. His lips twitched in a dim approximation of a smile. "Thing is, people aren't so smart. They get TV and movie trash mixed up with real life. People like you, Ms. Sullivan, get up and run their mouths. And all of a sudden, everything is simple. Why don't you cops get off your asses and arrest the criminals out there?" His voice was raised in a sarcastic whine. His gray-eyed glower found Mariah's face. "Are you following me here?"

"I'm listening," Mariah said.

"I know Officer Gordon is following me." He looked at his sidekick. "Aren't you?"

"They should know how they can mess everything up for us, Jimmy," Gordon said.

Seeing that Griefe was about to continue his lecture on the difficulties of conscientious police work, she interrupted. "Lieutenant Griefe, you wouldn't do a thing to help me. You don't like me and you don't believe anything I say. I told Officer Elspeth to explain how I felt—"

"She did. She's a rookie. She didn't know better. She got a warning that cost her. She'll think about you every month when she looks at a smaller paycheck."

Mariah felt a distant surge of her old guilt. She turned the valve and shut it off. "I'm sorry she's been treated unfairly. Just the same, I had every right to do what I could to get movement on the Tot Lot case. And I think you know all that. So why don't you tell me why you came here and I'll do everything I can to help you from here on out."

Griefe turned to Gordon. "She thinks we came here for her help!"

"Cops have thick skins, but they're not space capsule reentry shields, are they?" Gordon asked. Ventriloquist and dummy.

"Fine. If you don't want my help, what do you want?" Mariah asked.

Griefe eyed Freddy. "We wanted to tell you about some things that *could* happen becuase of the unwise thing you did earlier this evening. It could happen that no cop will want to help you now." Another glance at Freddy. "I'm saying *could*, not will. It could happen that anything to do with clearing up whatever's going on at the Tot Lot will become a low priority. It could happen that police friends at the Madison Day Care Regulatory Board will take action on your case, pull your license, and close you down once and for all."

Mariah steadied her voice. "I think I understand what you're saying."

"If you find yourself in trouble, it could happen that you'll be there by yourself," Gordon said.

Mariah rose. "I see where we all stand this evening. Do you have anything else to add?"

The cops got up, too. Griefe stared at her. "You made yourself a tough row to hoe, Sullivan."

When they were at the door, Mariah said, "Question?"

Griefe nodded.

"Did the Madison police arrest Helga and Rudy Erris this evening?"

His sour face shifted to a snarl. "Yes. Goddamn you!"

Eighteen

Clarisse woke up in the middle of the night with a bad cold. Mariah hadn't been able to sleep, so great was her exultation. It was almost nice to have company, even if it meant fussing with hot water and lemon juice and dishing up sympathy in Mom-sized portions at three-thirty in the morning. Helga was in jail. *Helga was in jail!* The wicked witch was dead!

The police would work it out. They would grill her and Rudy like burgers until every last detail of the death of five children was known and her lunacies were as exposed as a ruptured hive. When Clarisse was momentarily at rest, Mariah went down to check the answering machine for calls from reporters that she could ignore. As she'd hoped, there were also a half dozen messages from parents who wanted information about the Tot Lot. They were thinking about enrolling their children! Yes! She made a note to send them brochures. The power of the media had thrown some stardust over her, the brave

heroine single-handedly running evil Helga to earth. Some
of the glitter had fallen to the Tot Lot too.

Up for the day, she spent the time between Clarisse's
bedroom and the kitchen table, where she pondered Tot
Lot spring enrollments and possible expansion. She
resolved to stay home with her sick child. She had mountains of neglected housework to do that she could now
handle with a light heart. She called Rochelle and told
her to carry on with the Tot Lot cleanup as well as she
could. She'd be in tomorrow. The blonde seemed oddly
disappointed. Probably didn't want to have to work alone,
willing as she was.

Toward midmorning, reporters appeared, chomping at
the bit for interviews. She wouldn't open the door to
them. She gave them Freddy's name and number. The
phone rang often and the answering machine filtered the
calls. The only ones she answered were from Tot Lot
parents wondering when she was going to open up again.
Evidently, news of Helga's and Rudy's arrest had been
detailed on the morning news. There had been footage
of them in handcuffs, unflatteringly illuminated by TV
camera spotlights. "A sleazy looking couple if there ever
was one," a caller said. Amen to that, Mariah thought,
shoving the vacuum wand into neglected corners.

Between chores, she read to Clarisse and gave her hot
broth for her health and ice cream for her morale. Finding
her asleep in midafternoon, she settled down for a couple
of hours of business planning: the immediate and more
distant future of the Tot Lot. She planned to reopen January 1. That would allow time for most of the excitement
to die down and for her to get to all the parents who had
enrolled children before the trouble began. They would
be given a reenrollment option. If they declined, it seemed
there were plenty of other kids available to fill the vacanc-

ies. Next year she would seriously consider adding a wing to the building. She had allowed space for it in the original design. The afternoon flew.

She gave Clarisse soup and she asked for chicken. That meant she was already on the mend. No school for her tomorrow, Friday, then the weekend to complete recovery. Sick kids weren't so bad when they didn't have fevers. Mariah and Clarisse both turned their bedside lamps off early that evening. Mariah had been so excited to notice that she was emotionally and physically exhausted, like a marathon runner tottering to the tape. She was glad she had turned off the phone. She needed time in the land of dreams.

She was going to wake up in a far better world than yesterday's.

In the morning, she took Clarisse with her to the Tot Lot. She found two reporters waiting outside. She pulled Clarisse past them, "no commenting" all the way into the building. She made sure the door was locked behind her.

"Mom, those reporters are really pushy!" Clarisse complained.

"They have their purposes." Mariah felt a swell of uneasiness at her own smugness. One should never crow. As the Greeks had pointed out, that brought retribution from the gods.

She told Clarisse to occupy herself with something while she and Rochelle continued cleaning up. Maybe the girl could even help out later, depending on her energy level. Mariah discovered that Rochelle had made great strides in her solo efforts. She thanked her profusely and apologized for having to stay home.

Rochelle cocked her head and looked at Mariah with

a queer grin. "You've had bigger fish to fry it seems than worrying about cobwebs in high corners," she said.

"I guess." She looked at her loyal middle-aged worker. Today she had abandoned her Mother Hubbard cap. She wore her blond hair in a bun. Made her look a little like Helga, at least to Mariah, who couldn't get the other woman out of her mind. "Well, I'm out of the woods at last, Rochelle."

"Are you?" Her expression was genuinely quizzical.

"Well . . . *of course.* Don't you think so?" This obliqueness wasn't like Rochelle at all. She was a most direct woman. Right now, Mariah's steadied nerves didn't need fresh irritations.

"I'm not saying I don't," Rochelle said. "It's just that this whole business has been going on for so long, I can't believe it's over."

Mariah thought she saw something hesitant in Rochelle's wide face, something held back. "Do you know something I don't?" she asked.

Rochelle shook her head. "Nothing I can put my finger on."

Mariah leaned forward, concern edging her voice. "What do you mean?" she asked.

Rochelle shrugged. "It's nothing, Mariah. Some things you just can't be sure of, that's all." Her smile was queerly distant.

Mariah realized for the first time she didn't know Rochelle all that well. Her inscrutability was a side of her she'd never seen up to now. She promised herself to meet the woman socially over the next year and find out just what she was like. She shook off distant foreboding. Everything was all right.

Rochelle had made a list of some cleaning products

needing replacement. Mariah hadn't paid the wholesaler who delivered so she didn't dare place another order. She took the list and went to ask Clarisse if she wanted to go to the supermarket, one of her favorite adventures. She found the child curled up asleep on one of the futons in the nap room. Let her stay, she thought. Clarisse needed the rest. She asked Rochelle if she would keep an eye on the girl, then got in the van and started for the store.

On the way, it occurred to her that she hadn't thanked Nevsky for the flowers. How thoughtless of her! Of all the people who deserved her gratitude . . . She pulled off into a convenience store parking lot, but when she called him, his line was busy. She sat fidgeting a few minutes, then tried again. Still busy. One more try, she promised herself. If she couldn't get through this time, she'd wait till later.

He answered on the first ring. ''Been trying to get you,'' he said in a rush. ''Called your house and—''

''Well, you've got me, Yuri. First thing is I want to thank you for the flowers. They were—well, much more than I expected.''

''We better save our mutual admiration for later.''

She noticed the tension edging his voice. ''Why? What's wrong?''

Nevsky told her he had friends in police headquarters. ''Chatty buddies,'' he called them. He had put them on notice to find out how the interrogation of Helga and Rudy had been going. One had just called him.

''Well, what did he say? Did she confess?''

''*Au contraire*, as the French say.'' Nevsky's voice dropped. ''The night you say you saw Helga, she was at a party with your ex-husband. They have ten witnesses.''

''I . . . don't understand.''

''Neither do I. The shoes are legit. Belonged to murdered kids. So the cops are checking on where the Errises were when the first child was killed twelve years or so ago. My buddy told me Helga claimed she was in London and can prove it." He paused. "Are you with me, Mariah? It doesn't look like she's guilty."

Mariah couldn't speak. Her knees weakened and she sagged against the pay phone's aluminum hood. "Yuri . . ." she gasped. That news meant so many things—all her suppositions were wrong, all her expectations of escape from the careening emotional ride of the last forty-five days were crushed, all the best of her future had been thrown into doubt! There was worse, though. *Worse!*

A child murderer was still free.

And another child was to die!

"Where are you?" Nevsky asked. "I know you're not home. And you're not at the Tot Lot—"

"How do you know that?"

"I just phoned there."

"Didn't Rochelle tell you where I'd gone?"

"Nobody answered."

Shock passed through Mariah's body like electricity. She had set the phones to ring in every room. Rochelle should have been in one of them. Even if she had gone out, the phones' ringing would have awakened Clarisse. The little imp wouldn't have been able to resist answering. Dread followed her shock like thunder after lightning. She slammed the receiver into its cradle and bolted for the van.

Hand on the door latch, she was struck by a sudden revelation. She bit back a high note of keening despair. A blonde who had very likely lived in Clarion City and knew what had happened to Mariah eight years ago had been behind all her torment. The same blonde had been stalking the Erris home with a cleaver and a kerosene lamp. Now Mariah remembered she had never really seen the madwoman's face. She had only *assumed* it was Helga. But it hadn't been Helga at all. It had been the *other* blonde in her life. The one she saw every working day. The one who had seemed faithful and true. The one who had never failed to mention her loyalty and how she shouldered more than her share of Tot Lot responsibilities. The one she had never once suspected.

Rochelle Camwell!

Mariah had known all the facts, but hadn't ever put them together—until now. Hadn't Rochelle told her she had come from Clarion City? Rochelle had surely followed all of Mariah's past distress through media reports and her present torturing from firsthand observation. She was perfectly positioned to know just how to tighten the screws to further her lunatic plans. And Mariah hadn't tumbled, even as recently as an hour ago when she had noticed Rochelle looked a little like Helga. The older woman had been vaguely threatening her with Helga's possible innocence. *Possible!* She had known Helga was innocent all along! Because *she herself* was guilty.

How cunningly the woman had masked her true nature! Sympathetic as a sister, she had accompanied Mariah on her fool's errand to the Groome home and seemingly shared her outrage over the couple's abuse. She, the murderer of five children! Mariah couldn't forget Rochelle's speeches urging her to fight on when the great tidal wave of her troubles was at its height. Only her hesitancy over Mariah's holding the news conference in cooperation with the parents' ad hoc committee signaled her true nature. That and the sudden surliness accompanying it. How could Mariah not have understood that those reactions had originated in the fear that she might somehow right her sinking ship by uncovering the traitorous worm within?

Grasping Rochelle's monstrousness, she began to draw more conclusions. Earlier, Rochelle must have seen her go to police headquarters with the mailer in which Dotty Orel's shoe had been sent. She had assumed Mariah would be crushed, destroyed by the sight of the pitiful little item. That hadn't happened. She had badly underestimated the new Mariah's toughness. It followed, then, that the reason for her night visit to the Erris home had been to *hide* the shoes. To get rid of condemning evidence. In her large purse she had carried the grocery bag. It had been where Mariah had found it only for a few minutes!

And Rochelle was with her child! Why did no one answer the phone?

She ran two red lights and nearly sideswiped a bus on her frantic return to the Tot Lot. Even as she flew down the road, speed limit long abandoned, she thought herself moving at a tortoise pace. After what seemed hours, she skidded into the day-care center's drive, eyes on the building. How could she tell from the outside what had happened within? She had to go in just as she was, with no weapon except a mother's despair and fury.

She bolted for the door, fumbled frantically with the damned key. She hurried inside, shouting, "Rochelle, Clarisse!"

Silence.

She ran toward the nap room where she had last seen her daughter. It was empty. She screamed, "Clarisse, are you here? *Clarisse!*"

She hurried back to the crawl and bawl area, where Rochelle had been working. Inside the door she pulled up with a hoarse cry.

Rochelle lay crumpled on the floor, blood running from her head. Mariah spun around to discover what had transpired. She saw no one.

Why had the monster Rochelle been hurt? For an instant Mariah felt elation. The wicked woman had been struck down. Clarisse was safe!

But where was she?

She hurried to Rochelle's inert form. Knowing her guilt, Mariah was repulsed by her face, even veiled by unconsciousness as it was. If she wasn't dead, Mariah wanted to throttle her until she was. All the torment and distress this woman had caused her! She hesitated, her hands curling and uncurling like a strangler's. Then her eyes caught on something.

On the fallen woman's back a note had been taped. She knelt to read it. The few words devoured her attention.

I HAVE CLARISSE. SHE WILL BE THE ONE TO DIE.

Mariah blinked. She stared blankly at the paper for a heartbeat. Then she understood! She screamed. Rochelle wasn't guilty. *Rochelle wasn't guilty.* It was someone else! She tore wildly at her hair. For the love of God, who was doing this to her—and now to her daughter? She stared wide-eyed at the prostrate Rochelle. She scrambled to her feet, wanting to do something, but not knowing what. If Rochelle lived, Mariah swore the woman would never know from her own lips to what stupid conclusions she had jumped. Not *ever*.

She whirled. She had to find Clarisse! ''Where are you, sweet?'' she shouted. She ran into the hall, flew to every Tot Lot room. Clarisse wasn't there.

Clarisse had been kidnapped!

Battling churning emotions, she barely controlled herself. She went back to Rochelle, bent over and looked at her head. The wound wasn't as bad as she had at first thought. She touched the woman's neck, felt a faint pulse. Alive! She knelt and pressed her forehead to Rochelle's barely moving chest. I am so sorry about my wild suspicions, she thought. You deserved my trust. You earned it every day. Now, dear, you must *not* die on me! Her eyes moved back to the long wound. The skull had been bruised, the skin torn more than cut. Nonetheless, Mariah was chilled. She guessed what had been used to fell Rochelle.

The back of a cleaver.

She hurried to the phone and dialed 911. She shrilled her information into the beeping line, ending with "And my child's been kidnapped!"

She rushed back to Rochelle with a wet washcloth and tried to revive her, but the woman lay unmoving, her breathing slow and shallow. Mariah groaned in frustration. Rochelle would know who had attacked her. She would know who had tormented Mariah for nearly two months. "Wake up!" she cried. But Rochelle didn't move.

She ran for a cup of cool water and poured it over the prone woman's forehead. Still she didn't regain consciousness. Mariah cursed her impotence, rose from her knees and began to pace. *Where* were the police?

She heard a siren. A patrol car skidded to a stop in the driveway. Two officers scrambled out. She was heartened to see Elspeth was one of them. She rushed to her and began to blurt out what had happened. The cop pushed by her. "Take us to the injured woman, please, Ms. Sullivan," she ordered. Her partner wasn't the pleasant officer who had been with her previously. This man was tired-eyed and craggy-faced. On the streets and through squad car windows he had seen it all. It dawned on Mariah that

Elspeth had been reassigned to a tougher senior officer because of what she had done on her behalf. The male cop said, "Get us to the injured woman, please."

"My Clarisse has been kidnapped!" Mariah shouted.

"One thing at a time, ma'am."

After checking Rochelle, they radioed for an ambulance. Mariah jabbered at them about what had happened, scarcely realizing what she was saying. They paid no attention to her, busy as they were with first aid for the wounded woman.

"Please bring her to," Mariah begged. "I *have* to know who did this to her. Who took my child!"

Bent over Rochelle, they ignored her, mumbling to one another about "stabilizing her condition."

"Please get her conscious!" Mariah begged.

"Let us alone to do our job!" Elspeth ordered. "Or we'll cuff you to the cruiser."

Mariah paced like an asylum inmate, imagining the sequence of coming events. The two cops had to finish with Rochelle and put her in the ambulance when it finally arrived. Out would come their notebooks. The questions would start. A horrid thought came to her. Considering the disaster of her relationship with the police over the last two days, they might choose to think *she* was guilty of assaulting Rochelle and arrest her. She had been falsely accused before, hadn't she? If not that, maybe to pay Mariah back for failing to cooperate with her, Elspeth might see to it that at the very least she was held for a few hours.

Then what would happen to Clarisse?

Mariah was frantic. Years ago she would have been frozen by her emotions. Now only one thought came into her mind: *do something!*

The first thing she had to do was get away from the police.

The ambulance came. The two officers and the paramedics gathered beside Rochelle. Mariah chose that moment for her exit. She moved quietly out of the building and slid quickly behind the wheel of her van. She released the emergency brake, glided down the slight slope of the drive, and didn't start the engine until she was well down the street.

She stopped at a pay phone and called Lieutenant Griefe. To her immense relief, he was at his desk and took her call. He told her that their conversation was being recorded. Sure enough, she heard periodic beepings. Between bursts of sniffling she poured out a terse summary of her situation.

"Your daughter was kidnapped, you're saying?" His voice was calm, fatherly.

"Yes, yes. Lieutenant Griefe, you have to help me. The *police* have to help me!" She wanted so badly to rely on him, to get the force on her side.

"Well, sure. We'll help you. But kidnapping isn't my department, Mariah. I have other responsibilities."

"I understand that. But you must be able to do *something*."

"Where are you? I'll send Officer Gordon over. She can get all the facts, get the ball rolling."

"But you know the facts. All that's been done to me. Whoever's behind all that has now kidnapped my child. *And is going to murder her!*"

"You don't want to talk to Gordon?"

"It's not that. It's—I don't have *time*, lieutenant. It might already be too late."

"Let me give you the name of somebody in missing persons."

Mariah's frustration rose up like a volcano from the Pacific floor. A flash of understanding lit the landscape of her mind.

Griefe wasn't going to help her.

He was doing just what he said he would do—turning a cold shoulder to her desperate plea. He was running his tape so that if she ever dared accuse him of not helping her, he would play it back. Its message would be straightforward: he had tried to help her through channels, the bureaucratic way. And no one in the bureaucracy would ever fault him for it. She let the receiver drift back into its cradle, as though on its own. He didn't choose to help her. He had made sure Officer Elspeth didn't dare to.

She would get no help from the police.

Alone now, her fears flooded in like heavy tar, threatening to immobilize her. She fought them, organizing her resistance around one idea. *She would have to be the one to find her daughter.* No one else could do it before the cleaver gnawed the child's flesh and bone. She wailed at the windshield at the thought of harm coming to Clarisse's little body. Even now she might be too late. Her darling, her *life* could have already been hacked away.

She glimpsed herself in the rearview mirror. Was that her face? Where had her youth gone? Where was the easygoing smile? The woman in the mirror carried weight on her back and sorrow in her heart. She wasn't sweet. She wasn't nice. She was a desperate mother with whom to reckon.

Her imagination soared off toward regions where it had never dwelled. Powered by the engine of her desperation, it ranged in all directions, guided by nothing more than her intuition. Ideas floated into her mind and began to coalesce in a place far from regimented reason and logic. Eight years ago, a dark-haired woman dressed like herself had kidnapped and murdered Dotty Orel. A blonde had taken the libelous note about her to Phil Fontenot. A blonde had carried the lamp and cleaver right past her staring eyes. None of the women she suspected, blond or brunette, had been guilty.

But there was one woman in from the start of all this whom she had ignored. One who seemingly had no motive.

Couldn't a brunette wear a wig? Couldn't a motive be uncovered?

She spun the van around and pulled into a mall parking lot. She sat concentrating intensely. Go ahead, she urged herself, challenging both her memory and her imagination. Initially the idea was a bit of gossamer, a fluttering web in the breeze. Then it gathered strength and snagged on another idea. It began to bear the weight of her suspicions. Yes, yes, it could be . . .

She took her telephone credit card to the kiosk. Thank goodness she remembered Truman Orel's employer was Multi-Standard Electronics. And she also remembered what Audrey had said when she appeared to enroll her son in the Tot Lot. She said Truman had been transferred from corporate headquarters in Clarion City to the Madison branch office.

She got the Multi-Standard corporate office number from information. She keyed it in and asked for the human resources department. A young woman who said she was Claire asked how she could be of help. Mariah took a deep breath. "This is Jolene Bonaparte from HR at the Madison Office. We're tidying up our records, boss's orders. I need some information about one of our people who used to work there. Now he's with us, came here maybe a year and a half ago. Really great employee and a hard, hard worker. Can you help me out, Claire?" Mariah held her breath.

"Well, sure, long as it's nothing, like, confidential, you know. If it is, I'll have to ask Mr. Pearlman and—"

"Nothing like confidential," Mariah interrupted. "Could you check your files for an Orel, Truman. All I need is the reason for transfer."

"Oh, just that? I knew Truman. We *all* knew him. Great guy. We miss him. I don't have to look in his file. We used to tease him about why he wanted a transfer."

"And why did he?" Mariah's heart was in her throat. She couldn't swallow.

"His wife made him, he told us."

"Thanks so much!" Mariah said in a rush. She hung up, her breath coming in short, shallow gasps.

Audrey Orel had made Truman transfer to Madison so that she could follow Mariah to her new city. She had enrolled her son in the Tot Lot to misdirect everyone. What she really wanted was a chance to kill again, but not until she had tangled Mariah in her snares for the second time. Why, Mariah didn't know. How could she pierce the motivations of a madwoman? Because if what Mariah believed was true . . .

Audrey Orel had murdered her own daughter. Dotty Orel's murderer was her own mother!

She sensed everything didn't fit. But she couldn't take the time to fully complete the puzzle. She didn't have the time!

She snatched her briefcase from the back seat and pulled out her list of parents' names and addresses. Finding the Orels', she turned back into traffic. Her heart pounded. Excitement brought perspiration to her temples. She turned off the van's heater.

For a moment, she was torn between ignoring the speed limit and all traffic signs and signals and the dread of being stopped and so delayed. She thought: my child's life is at stake. Go! She pushed the accelerator down. From then on she only slowed to avoid accidents. She covered the miles to her destination in a few wild minutes. As she drove, a litany rose up from her innermost heart: please let Clarisse not be hurt, *please* let Clarisse not be hurt . . .

The Orels lived in a common split-level ranch on a street filled with them. Theirs was white, their lawn a bit rattier than those of their neighbors. As she swung into the drive, her eyes moved across the house. All its curtains and drapes were closed. A battered Chevy Nova sat under the carport. Audrey's car.

Mariah didn't know just what she was going to do—except not hesitate. She leaped out of the van and ran to the front door. She thumbed the chime button and heard it ring within.

No one answered. She heard no sounds of life.

Something told her Audrey was inside. She went around to the kitchen door and peered in past an edge of curtain. Nothing moved. She knocked loudly without results. She would not be put off. She twisted the knob. Locked. She went to a nearby flower bed, gone late-November brown and stiff. She kicked loose an angled decorative brick and snatched it up. With it she smashed the kitchen door glass, reached through, and twirled the lock knob. She threw the door open and charged into the kitchen. "Clarisse! Audrey! It's Mariah Sullivan," she shouted, her voice shaky. She so much wanted to hear her daughter reply!

Silence.

"Audrey!" No response. Mariah had made so many bad guesses in the last weeks. First this person was guilty, then that one. Then none of them. Now she had the right person, but was her feeling about Audrey's whereabouts going to be yet one more bad guess? All right, she'd search every room. It wasn't a big place. Just the same, she was aware of time flying, bearing away with it Clarisse's chances of survival.

She started with the small dining room. No place to hide there. Coat closet by the living room. She opened it. Coats, boots, hats on the shelf. "Audrey! It's Mariah Sullivan!" she shouted. "Are you here?" On the walls she saw plaques and posters praising Jesus. On the TV were photos of Truman, Audrey, and Christopher in family poses. No photo of poor dead Dotty.

She climbed to the second floor. In the master bedroom she saw half-filled suitcases on the bed. She had interrupted someone packing. She looked at the clothing. Audrey.

Then she heard a sound below.

In a way, it brought her to her senses. It dawned on her that she might be alone in the house with a cleaver-swinging woman with five murders to her credit. Clarisse possibly becoming a sixth victim allowed Mariah no time for paralysis or even caution. Thinking vaguely of defense, she snatched a pillow off the bed in the larger of the two bedrooms and flew down the stairs three at a time. She heard a louder noise. It came from the basement.

Mariah hurtled into the kitchen just as Audrey burst out of hiding, up the basement stairway. She didn't have her cleaver. She shrieked at seeing Mariah, who threw down her pillow. "Audrey Orel. *Stop!*"

Audrey's birdlike face was pale and wide-eyed. A low whimper escaped her clenched teeth. She bolted for the kitchen door. Mariah hesitated. She wasn't sure what to

do. "Stop!" she shouted. Audrey didn't stop. Her hand
was already on the knob, turning it.

Desperate, Mariah lunged forward and grabbed the
woman's arm, pulling her hand off the knob.

"No! Let me go!" Audrey squirmed and kicked at
Mariah's legs.

Mariah had no idea how to fight or subdue a criminal.
She grabbed the smaller woman by the shoulders and
shoved against her. Their legs tangled and they thumped
down together to the vinyl tiled floor. Audrey squealed
as the wind was knocked out of her.

Mariah took the opportunity to kneel beside her and
push both palms against her forehead so she couldn't get
up. In a few moments, the smaller woman had recovered
her breath. She looked up at Mariah with wide, frightened
eyes. From them tears began to leak. "Let me leave here
now!" Her eyes bloomed with naked pleading. She sat
up halfway. "I haven't done anything!"

"Oh, yeah?" Mariah moved her hands to Audrey's shoulders. She shoved her back down against the floor. She
remembered her little girl fights of long ago and squirmed
up onto Audrey's rib cage and sat. "Where's my daughter?
Where's Clarisse?" she shouted. Audrey's instant descent
into weeping chilled Mariah's heart. "If you've already
killed her, if she's down in that basement . . ." The thought
wrenched Mariah like a physical blow. She nearly collapsed
into trembling. She sucked in heavy breaths and clenched
her teeth. She had to hold on!

Audrey blubbered and shook her head. She nearly
gagged on her tears. "No, no. She isn't . . ."

Mariah thought she would go mad with the delay. What
had this woman done with Clarisse? She snatched
Audrey's hair with both hands and started slamming the

back of her head against the floor. Audrey howled in pain. Mariah let go. She had to get a grip on herself! She sat back on her haunches, taking some of the weight off Audrey's thin chest. "Talk to me!" she ordered.

Audrey's smeared white face seemed naked now. Mariah was startled by its haggard exhaustion. She drew a shocked breath. That face confessed . . . secrets. Had she never seen that before amid the constant nervous chirping turned desperately pious over recent years? But *what* secrets dwelled within the tiny heart upon which she now pressed? Her instincts told her that no matter the danger in which Audrey had put Clarisse, the moment had come to listen. "Talk, Audrey!" she ordered again.

"My Dotty was a sweet child, you know." Her snuffling inhalation was a weak whisper in her nostrils.

Mariah stared down. Dotty was eight years dead. Sweet or not, she didn't matter now. Beneath her, Audrey quaked and jerked as though in a fit's grip. Was she an epileptic, then? Oh, Lord, help me not to lose her now, Mariah thought, to unconsciousness or madness. She understood that something like catharsis now swept through the tiny, strained body beneath her. Tense and hyper for . . . how long, now that Mariah thought of it. Tense when they had first met, super-tense after the passage of eight years. Why so tightly strung, Audrey? Puzzlement swept over Mariah. "Talk," she urged more gently. "For the love of God!"

Drool escaped Audrey's mouth. Mariah nudged her captive's shoulder with a fist to awaken her from her daze. Audrey began to blink rapidly in her normal way. When she spoke, her voice was a dry rasp. "Do you believe in the devil, Mariah?

Mariah was about to blurt "Of course not!" Then for some reason she thought of Nevsky, his mysteries. Who knew where they reached. Maybe into matters of faith, good and evil. "It doesn't matter what I believe," she replied.

"I think the devil visited us when Dotty was maybe three years old. He touched our little family. He touched Truman. And Tru tries so hard to be a good man." Audrey trembled more lightly, as though the discharging catharsis was now diminishing. Her tone turned dreamy, almost reminiscent. "And I tried hard to help him be a good man. Even though I knew I didn't understand all he did, I knew it couldn't be very bad. He isn't a bad man."

Mariah resisted the urge to scream at her to get to the point. If she did bully the little woman further, she dreaded losing her completely—well before she had the faintest clue about what she was trying to say. She got off her chest and sat beside her, looking down at her pale, drawn face smeared now with fresh tears and drool. "Before we were married I think Tru might have done some things that weren't right. I don't mean real bad things ..." Audrey said.

"Audrey, about Dotty and the devil?" Mariah prompted.

Audrey frowned and the damage of time showed clearly on her face. Mariah was shocked at the depth and number of her wrinkles. The little woman had never frowned in Mariah's presence. Possibly until this moment she had never frowned outside of her home. Audrey Orel clutched her secrets close to the heart. "Tru wasn't quite right with her. Or me. He did things to us. Oh, I don't mean *bad* things."

Mariah groaned inwardly. Truman . . . The quiet, polite man bearing gifts of benign tropical fish. She suspected he had indeed done bad things. She took a guess. "He hit you. He hit Dotty," she said.

Audrey nodded weakly. "It was the devil in him. He fought him. He's a brave man. But not strong enough . . ."

Mariah had to get some answers. She heaved in a heavy breath and spoke the unspeakable. "How did Truman make you dress up as me and take Dotty? How did he make you . . . kill your own child?"

Audrey howled and began to scramble to her feet. Mariah threw herself on her, dragging her back down to the floor. "No, Audrey, you're staying here until you tell me everything!" Mariah too was in despair—over time passing and Clarisse somewhere in grave danger—or by now very possibly dead.

"I didn't kill Dotty. It wasn't Tru either. *It wasn't Tru!*"

"Then *who* did it? Who killed her? Who delivered those horrid notes and sent lying letters about me? Who caused me no end of anxiety and fear? Who snatched my Clarisse?"

Audrey's eyes rolled alarmingly. Mariah sensed she was skewing off toward a fit and had no idea what to do. "I needed Jesus' help those years," Audrey said. "For me and Christopher and Tru," she said dreamily. "Jesus was my strength. We all needed His help and protection."

"To protect you from *who?*" Mariah was vexed, her patience disintegrating.

"Her."

"Her? What *her?*"

"The woman who did things to Dotty. The one I had to protect Christopher from. The one I *tried* to protect Tru from. I sent up so *many* prayers for Tru."

"Who is she?" Mariah asked. "Do I know her?"

"No."

"Audrey . . ."

"She made me sew together that horrible dummy she made Truman hang."

Mariah was growing desperate. She tried a different angle. "Where's Truman, Audrey?"

Her shrug was a pathetic twitch. "Gone. Somewhere. He'll never be back."

"Where's Christopher?"

Audrey smiled, momentarily serene. "Away. In Chicago with relatives. He's safe. I put him on a flight day before yesterday."

"Why?"

"Because I knew that never mind the note she sent you about killing any child, the one she wanted to kill was Christopher!"

Mariah wasn't getting this. What kind of hold did this unknown woman have on Audrey and her soft-spoken husband? "How did you know that?"

"Because she killed Dotty."

Mariah gasped. A dreadful joke was being played on her, the horrid punch line eight years in the making. "You're telling me ... You're telling me this crazy woman who killed Dotty, when she couldn't find Christopher picked *my* child instead?"

Nineteen

Audrey couldn't look Mariah in the face, or speak. She only nodded her assent.

Mariah wailed and clenched her fists beside her cheeks. Then she glowered down at the prostrate woman. "So you *knew* who killed Dotty eight years ago. *Didn't you?*" Her hand flew to Audrey's shoulder. Into it she dug in her nails. "Answer me!"

Audrey squealed. "Yes! Yes, I did."

"Why didn't you tell the police that? *Why did you make me go through what I did?*"

Audrey's white face twisted with anguish. "I felt so *awful* about that. And about the things she made me say about you. So awful! That's why when I got the chance I enrolled Christopher with you in the Tot Lot. I wouldn't have him go anywhere else. That's why I spoke up for you at the news conference and every other chance I got. *I felt so guilty!*"

Mariah lowered her face till it was inches from prostate

Audrey's. "You followed me to Madison from Clarion City. You made Truman transfer from corporate headquarters to a field office."

Audrey's head shook rapidly in denial. "It wasn't me made him do that. It was *her*."

Mariah howled in frustration and bewilderment. "What 'her'? Who is this woman?" She stared at pitiful Audrey. "Truman has a mistress, right? Who is she?"

Audrey shook her head wildly. "The evil woman. The devil!"

"A relative then? Somebody in your family?"

Her eyes cast down, Audrey shook her head.

Mariah had no more time for this crazy guessing game. She curled her nails in front of Audrey's wide eyes. "Tell me right now where my daughter is. Or I'll be the last person you'll ever see!"

Audrey's eyes closed. She began to tremble. "All the years . . . all the lying. I can't anymore . . ."

"Audrey! *Where's Clarisse?*"

Audrey trembled more wildly, as though in the grip of a monstrous ague that might carry her away. Mariah dug the tips of her nails into both of Audrey's cheeks. The woman's eyes started open at the pain. "Audrey!" Mariah shouted. *"Where is Clarisse?"*

"She took her to Fin and Feather, the pet shop," Audrey gasped. "It's closed. They're in court over something. That's where Tru used to work evenings. So she has the key."

Mariah pried the address from the frail woman's trembling lips. "Why did she take Clarisse there?"

Audrey rose to her knees, now wheezing and sighing with tears. "So she could see all the nice animals before . . ." She looked away. Her wail stirred the thin hair on the back of Mariah's neck. Again her imagination discharged the nightmare vision of a descending cleaver splitting defenseless pink flesh.

"Audrey, how long ago did they leave?"

"About a half hour."

Maria flew toward the door. So much *time* had passed. "Wait!"

Mariah spun back. Audrey's hand flew toward the knife rack. For an instant, Mariah thought the disturbed woman was going to attack her. But she shoved the long boning knife toward her, handle-first. "Take this. And do me a favor: kill her if you can!"

Mariah's head spun in a wash of dread. Now it didn't matter who the lunatic relative or Truman's mistress was. All that mattered was that Mariah reach her before the worst happened—if it wasn't already too late. She thought of calling the police. No—if they came at all they would pull up in squad cars and yell through bullhorns. Clarisse's captor would surely be provoked to kill her.

Just the same, she did take the few seconds needed to slide by a drive-in phone. She called Nevsky, told him where she was going and why. Before he could answer, she told him to get there as quick as he could. Then she hung up. After several minutes back on the road, she remembered he didn't have a car. And cabs were few in his part of the city.

It was as though all these events were unfolding according to Nevsky's design. He had urged her all along to become fully responsible for her own problems. Now here was the worst of them all—Clarisse in mortal peril and Mariah on her own! Of course this all couldn't be laid at the Russian's feet. Nevsky wasn't a wizard controlling time and chance with spells. Nonetheless, she dared not wait for help. She had to go ahead. She looked again at herself in the rearview mirror. Was that Mariah Sullivan? The determination in the lines on her face was written even larger than when she had been on the way to the Orel home. She again tossed aside concerns for traffic laws. When she wasn't stopped, she thought about how luck favors the daring.

She squealed around the corner of Fin and Feather's storefront block. There it was! Across the street. Its two wide windows were soaped into solid white curtains. CLOSED UNTIL FURTHER NOTICE read the large sign covering the door top to bottom. Mariah hit the brakes and made a U-turn. There was an alley behind Fin and Feather's shop row. She headed toward it.

The alley was narrow, no-parking-except-while-unloading signs everywhere. It was after six, so traffic back here had ended for the day. She jerked to a stop, quickly killed the engine, and threw open the door. When she slid down to the cement her knees were shaky. Standing panting beside the van in search of stability and maybe nerve, she remembered something. She had left Audrey's knife on the van seat. She thought of leaving it behind. The only thing she did well with a knife was slice onions for Clarisse's burgers. Well, it was big enough to scare with, even if she had never struck a violent blow in her life. She opened a few blouse buttons and gingerly slid the boning knife behind the fabric until the point caught and held in her bra.

From the moment she had pried the twisted, incomplete tale out of Audrey Orel she had dreaded that she would be too late to save her daughter. So close now, she had no time or patience with spy-like reconnoiters. She had to go into Fin and Feather and take her chances. She guessed the woman had her cleaver with her. She had used it on Rochelle. Given the chance, she would surely use it on Mariah.

To her great surprise she wasn't afraid. What was at stake—Clarisse's life, if she *was* still alive—allowed no margin for fear of her own death. Her job was to get the girl out of there safely any way she could. Failing that, she would die in her daughter's place if it had to be that way. She looked up at the darkening November sky and sucked in a breath that made her lungs ache.

That she felt no fear surprised her not as much as what she did feel.

Fury.

Fury not only at the woman inside the pet store who had tormented her for more than seven weeks, but rage at her own old ways and her old personality that had brought her to this place alone under the worst circumstances. She had thought her catharsis complete, but it hadn't been. Events, time, and personality had gathered together like lowering black clouds shaping a final tornado. Its funnel was about to touch the earth.

Right now! And who could guess its path of destruction.

She hurried down the alley, her breathing shallow. Which building belonged to Fin and Feather? She saw sodden cardboard boxes piled by a dumpster. Their curling stickers read LIVE TROPICAL FISH. Here.

She reached the heavily armored rear door. Handleless, its only noticeable feature was the coppery disk of a lock for which she had no key. She glanced down the wall. The grime-smeared window was barred. Her attention swung back to the door. She put the fingertips of both hands under the thin narrow flange and tugged. The door swung open a crack. She knew why Clarisse's captor had thrown the lock.

To allow a speedy exit after she cut the child to pieces.

On silent feet, Mariah entered the store, leaving the door slightly ajar behind her. She was in a storage room.

Despite the shop being closed to customers, its shelves were well stocked with sacks of dog food, aquarium gravel, leashes, and doggy pillows. She heard the yapping of pups and birdsong beyond the spring-hinged wooden door before her.

She strained her ears in hope of hearing voices—Clarisse's above all.

And she did hear a voice! But it was an unfamiliar woman's high-pitched nasal whine, unpleasant under normal circumstances, awful indeed at this moment. It went on and on in an uninterrupted, disturbing monotone. Who was talking? Who was this woman who had eluded Mariah's awkward, amateurish detective work? This woman who strode like a colossus over the Orels' small household.

There was a small plastic window in the door ahead. It was scratched and smeared. Through its distorting lens she glimpsed the pet shop display and sales area. It was larger than she had expected. She glimpsed animal cages and stocked aquariums of all sizes. At the front of the store, she caught a glimpse of the woman whose voice she heard. She wore a dark brown jacket, gray skirt, and a semi-cloche hat over heavy blond hair. The hat's curving knitted fabric partially hid her face. Through the smeared plastic, Mariah glimpsed a strong chin and reddened lips. She didn't recognize her.

Where was Clarisse? Alive, or . . . ?

She didn't dare wait to see whether or not her child appeared. She had to go in there and find out what had happened. If Clarisse was alive, Mariah had to free her. If she was dead . . .

Either her murderer or Mariah wouldn't leave this place alive.

She eased open the door and ducked into the main

room. She squatted down below the level of tables stacked with pet supplies. The droning voice was louder now. Its words swam together like the tropical fish she was astonished to find the woman describing nonstop. "At breeding time the leopard catfish female's belly turns red and the first ray of her pectoral fin—that's the one sticking out of the middle of her back—turns red, too—"

"I don't want to know any more about fish!"

Clarisse's voice. *She was alive!* Mariah clenched her fists with joy, closed her eyes, and sent up a silent prayer of thanks.

She knew what she had to do: get between her daughter and the murderer. Clarisse could scamper to safety out the rear door while Mariah blocked pursuit. She proceeded carefully forward. She glimpsed Clarisse's head for a moment. It looked unmarked. Did Mariah deserve such good fortune? Please, let it be so!

She retreated, then advanced behind a different row of shelves. Now she saw the woman's right side—and the cleaver hanging down in her hand. A chill blew like Arctic wind through her nerves. She couldn't lose her courage!

Nonetheless she hesitated, looked down at the floorboards, saw the grime caught in their cracks. Beyond her field of vision the woman droned on about the habits of freshwater scavengers. The benign topic heightened rather than lessened her menace.

She was a lunatic.

Drawing shaky breaths, Mariah understood she couldn't hesitate any longer. She had to charge!

Get between them, she reminded herself. Just get between them, and Clarisse would have an excellent chance of escaping out of the shop. After she had run to safety, Mariah would quickly follow.

Clarisse squealed with fright. Mariah was electrified.

She tensed her muscles and sprang forward. "Run, Clarisse. *Run!*" she shouted, charging ahead. Eyes on her daughter, she saw with shock that the child would not be able to run far.

She was buckled into a large dog's harness to prevent her escape. An eight-foot woven nylon leash ran from it to her captor's hand. The leash loop was around her wrist. The woman's other hand held the cleaver upraised to either frighten Clarisse or destroy her.

She whirled toward the rushing Mariah and swung the cleaver down. Mariah heard her daughter's terrified scream. "Mom. *Mom!*" Mariah evaded the blow, only to feel an elbow and forearm dig into her neck. Far down her back she felt the cleaver's spent weight. Her assailant staggered backward, kept on her feet only by Clarisse's weight at the other end of the leash.

Mariah went for the woman's face with her nails. She howled with wordless loathing at what she saw—false lashes crumbed with mascara, thick lips pasted with scarlet liner, and heavy powdered jowls beneath which lay a closely shaven but unmistakable beard.

She was attacking a man! One who in his long years of delusion periodically imagined he was a woman.

It was Truman Orel.

With the flash of recognition came answers fast as thought could bring them. He had abused and murdered Dotty, his own daughter, to cap his string of killings. Then he had either lost his nerve or his insanity had abated. After eight years of slumber the evil awoke, maybe stirred by learning that Mariah had opened the Tot Lot. His scheming meshed with his total domination of his wife to permit them to enroll Christopher. From that day forth his threats and sabotage had been designed to turn the Tot Lot into a place of chaos like J. D. Day Care in its final days. Then would come the conditions under which best to kill. This time he would of course choose his son, closing the final, darkest chapter of an obscene family saga. Now all Mariah's misbehaving pieces fit. It had been he who had followed her to police headquarters, he who had stalked the halls of the Erris home to plant the evidence implicating Helga.

"Poor woman, to be here now, Mariah Sullivan," he piped in his feminine treble. "I'm telling you that, woman to woman."

"Unggh!" Mariah's nails ripped curls of flesh from his cheeks and tufts from his eyebrows. The force of their struggle slid his blond wig askew. He howled with unexpected pain and heaved her off. She spun down hard. Her head glanced against the metal leg of an aquarium stand. Lights flashed and rockets burst inside her skull. She rolled desperately aside as he came at her, cleaver high.

"No!" Clarisse screamed, heaving herself wildly against the harness, causing Truman to step off balance. Aim ruined, his blow went awry. The cleaver struck the leg of the cast-iron stand, throwing off sparks.

Mariah scrambled to her feet. He rushed at her, jerking Clarisse after him. The girl was pulled off her feet, a dragging dead weight. She screamed in fright, further catalyzing Mariah's desperate courage. He wildly swung the cleaver parallel to the floor. She jumped back, felt the blade brush her blouse. The wild blow found the glass of a three-hundred-gallon display tank. Glass crumbled and saltwater, sand, aquatic ornaments, and flailing fish surged over the floor.

Mariah retreated over the watery ruins. Truman stalked her, turning often to look at Clarisse, who now stumbled behind him. Mariah stared resolutely at his oncoming bleeding face. "The police are on their way," she lied. "You have nothing to gain by killing either of us."

"And nothing to lose. *Nothing!*"

"You're a very sick man, Truman. You've done such awful things. Think of your dead daughter, the other children you slaughtered. Think of what kind of life you made your wife live, pushing her to the edge of what any human should be asked to endure. Never mind what you did to me!"

"Constance didn't intend to kill you. Or your child. It wasn't in her plan."

"Your name's not Constance—it's Truman!" Mariah shouted.

"I'm Constance! Constant as the sky. Constant as the constellations."

"No, you're not!"

"Now you're both here." Truman's giggle was idiotic, but more terrifying than all his threats. It spoke of a mind cut loose from his moorings, as doomed and dangerous as a rudderless freighter on stormy Lake Superior. He shrugged. "It'll just end up being a simple case of . . . death by default."

"Truman . . ." Mariah looked past the madman. Clarisse had snatched up a broken shard of glass. She was sawing frantically at the tough nylon leash. Maybe she could get loose!

Desperate to keep his attention, Mariah snatched up the closest thing at hand, a small pouch of blue gravel, and threw it at him. It struck his padded chest with no effect. She retreated, drawing him after her, throwing boxes of dog treats, cat dishes, anything small enough to be snatched up and tossed. Anything to grip his attention.

With a howl, he made a sudden rush at her. She flinched

and darted aside. Behind him Clarisse was jerked off her feet. When she stumbled up again, the front of her dress was soaked black from the slide across the watery floor. With dismay Mariah saw the girl had dropped her piece of glass. Cat quick, she picked another out of a puddle and resumed sawing on the leash, her face burning with desperate concentration.

Still facing Mariah, Truman said, "Not both of you together. One at a time. The girl and then the mother."

"*No!*" Mariah screamed. "Kill me first!"

Clarisse tensed. If Truman came after her, she was ready to run as far as the leash would allow. How long could the girl hope to avoid him, Mariah asked herself. Seconds at best. He was turning toward the child!

Mariah shoved a hand down into the front of her blouse. "Truman! I have a knife!"

He whirled back. She realized she had made a serious mistake. She should have waited until his back was turned, then she could have attacked. Her stupidity had turned the weapon into a mere threat that he would now eliminate. Sure enough, he turned away from the girl and readied to charge her.

Behind him, quick-witted Clarisse, taking advantage of her size, dodged under the legs of a huge display tank, then out again. The leash was now looped around a cast-iron leg bearing several thousand pounds. When Truman sprang forward, anticipating only Clarisse's weight behind him, he jerked his arm as he had earlier. He assumed that effort would easily pull her off her feet and allow him to reach Mariah.

His arm was brought up short with a savage jerk. He howled and threw down the cleaver. His freed right hand groped his tortured shoulder.

Mariah hesitated. She wasn't a killer. She didn't have

a killer's instincts. She was a woman, and without the capacity for hateful violence. She had missed her chance to strike him. Her second mistake . . .

Truman recovered himself and snatched up his weapon. Mariah had lost what might have been her only chance. She backed away, completely at a loss for what to do. She understood that though she had changed so much recently, the metal of her reformed personality required a final annealing in the hot fire of violence.

In defense of her child and her own life, she had to strike a mortal blow.

Truman spun back toward Clarisse, tangled to the tank by the leash. She had given up her mobility to save her mother. Now she had to bear the blow of the upraised cleaver that would kill her at once. She was still sawing at the leash, frayed now from her earlier efforts and the mighty tug just given it. She sawed on determinedly as Truman descended on her like an avenging devil.

"Clarisse!" The scream was torn from Mariah's mouth.

The girl ducked the cleaver blow—then darted. She was free! The leash had been severed.

"Run out of here!" Mariah shouted. "The back door's open. Get the police. *Run!*"

Mariah's heart leapt. Her daughter was going to escape! She thrust out the knife toward Truman and waved it. *"Truman!"* He whirled back to face what could have been her attack. To Clarisse, she shouted again. "Run!"

The girl ran—but not toward the back of the store. She went to the puppy and kitten cages and threw open their latches. She was so quick! In moments, she had freed more than thirty yapping, cavorting critters. They came frolicking through the puddles. "Sic 'em!" the girl shouted. "Sic the bad man!"

"Clarisse, I am ordering you to get out of here!" Mariah

shouted, though she realized then that nothing she could say would make her daughter leave without her.

Freed of the burden on the end of his left arm, Truman had begun to stalk her. Puppies short on training but long on affection pranced on their hindquarters and pawed his legs and hers. Chows and miniature terriers, dachshunds and Dobermans. From the corner of her eye, Mariah saw a kitten. Small animals were everywhere. "Clarisse!" she howled, but the girl ignored her. Oh, Lord, she was going to get herself murdered after all! Both of them were going to die!

But not without a fight, she swore to herself.

Truman cocked his cleaver arm and advanced. His face was a smear of reds, bloody scratches and a paste of lipstick. Through the sweaty, scarlet ruin peered gray eyes far removed from the world of reason. He charged, and Mariah bolted. The cleaver found her rear, a grazing near miss. Pain seared as she was cut. Adrenaline pumped through her. She dodged behind a display of waist-high tanks. He circled. She circled the opposite way. Behind him, Clarisse was smashing aquariums with the corner of a small stand. Water poured out, now more than ankle deep. Fish flopped; dogs darted, jumped, and yapped. Kittens mewed.

He tried circling back. So did Mariah. With a grunt, he began to topple the tanks and push his way through. Mariah flailed at his arms with the knife in both hands, but missed. She was too clumsy with it and too far away. Now he was through and after her again. In a frighteningly swift lunge he reached her leg with the cleaver. She felt it cut through her skirt, leaving a dull ache in her leg. Looking down, she saw blood dribbling down her leg. Rather than crippling her, the blow had charged her with still more energy.

She dodged behind a display of forty-pound pet food sacks. He clambered over them, emitting a weird, eerie sound from high in his throat: *Eeee-eee-eee-eee!* He was past talking, she realized. Something had snapped. Audrey had spoken of his gradual descent into disintegration. Now its final stages were being acted out. And she, Mariah, was to witness and suffer them.

Backing away, she found herself being edged into a corner. A stone of dread settled into her stomach. She spun, looking for escape. Her arm swept along a shelf. Tiny aquariums and snifters with their Siamese fighting fish went crashing down into the widening puddles. She glimpsed stacked sacks of dog chow at her back. She was trapped! She spun back. Truman was advancing, carefully now. His absent gray eyes shone like sinister beacons. He held the cleaver in both hands like an executioner before the block. Mariah felt a scream welling up within her.

He had her. She couldn't get by him!

He charged the last few feet. And stepped on a German shepherd pup. It squealed in pain as his weight collapsed its legs. Its body rolled under the sole of his shoe. For a moment he was off balance. Mariah darted past him. She smelled his sour sweat as she lashed at his ribs with her knife. She felt the blade grate over bone. He screamed, but wasn't slowed—or badly hurt. Despite her desperate situation, she found herself grimacing at the pain she caused him. Oh, she wasn't *made* to hurt or kill!

He splashed after her, dogs dancing around his feet. Retreating with her eyes riveted on his advancing form, she couldn't watch her step. She stumbled over a toppled aquarium stand, went twisting down to all fours. Panic flooded her throat as he rushed at her. She threw herself aside as the cleaver swung by her to clash on metal. His free hand grabbed her right forearm. Instinctively, she thrust the tip of the knife deep into his wrist.

He howled and let her go. His other hand swung the cleaver wildly in rage and pain. The wind and flash of it passed inches before her squinting eyes. She shoved the knife savagely into his upper arm. It dug in. He screamed. Her squeamishness had fled. In its place came a mad glee at having truly hurt him. She knew her face was an ugly twisted snarl. Why not? She was fighting for her life!

Elated by her transformation, she completely failed to see his next blow. His left elbow caught her on the side of the face and knocked her spinning. She tried to break her fall, but her hand slipped in the water. Her head splashed down onto the floor. Inches from her face, a finny tropical banged the puddled planks in suffocating fury.

She tried to scramble up, but wasn't quick enough. Truman's foot, heavy as a storybook giant's, pressed her down on her stomach and drove the wind out of her. He loomed above her, the cleaver upraised in both hands. He was going to split her head like a piece of firewood under a maul.

She was going to die amid puppies and puddles.

She saw swift motion to her right. It was Clarisse, holding a kitty in both hands. She flung it right into Truman's smeared scarlet face. As frightened kittens do, it sank its claws into what it could—in this case, Truman's cheeks and forehead. It hung from his face. He screamed, trying to pull the feline free, but its little claws held like hooks.

Then Clarisse threw a second kitten on him.

Mariah gasped desperately for wind and struggled to her knees. At that moment she felt herself begin the final act of an agonizing eight-year odyssey. An act that would

validate her maturity and speed her along to a more promising destiny. She carefully put the knife in both hands
and gripped it tight. As Truman cleared his ripped face
of kittens, she thrust the blade into his stomach up to the
hilt.

And left it there.

Ignoring his wild screams, she snatched at her daughter's wrist, caught it, and dragged Clarisse through water,
dying fish, and scampering animals toward the back of
the shop.

They burst out the rear door into the alley, already at
a sprint. Just then, a car squealed around the corner and
headed for them. It slid to a stop. Its lights blinded Mariah.
She knew who it had to be—Audrey, having had yet
another change of heart. She would once again stand by
her man—her *mad* man. And Mariah had left the knife
in him.

The car's doors opened. She heard a familiar voice—
that of Officer Roper Reynolds, her rent-a-cop! He came
around the side of the car, jabbering into a walkie-talkie.
Something about kidnap victim freed and in custody of
parent.

In her confusion, Mariah didn't immediately recognize
the other man. Clarisse did. "It's Mr. Nevsky!" she
screeched. She took a flying leap into his arms. He had
no choice but to grab and hold her. "You shoulda seen
how we handled this crazy guy who wanted to kill us!"
Clarisse crowed.

"Oh yeah?" Nevsky said quietly. And abruptly he held
an armful of weeping little girl.

"Oh, Lord!" Mariah hurried to her daughter. Nevsky
continued to hold her. He tilted his head toward Fin and
Feather. "What happened in there?" he asked.

"I—I defended Clarisse and myself." Mariah's voice

shook. "I stabbed him." Her memory, sharp as a diamond cutter's chisel, served up the moment she had thrust the blade into the madman's stomach. Her victory intertwined with the distress of inflicting pain. She shuddered and groaned. For a moment she thought her knees were going to fail her.

"Who was it?"

"Truman Orel. He killed his daughter eight years ago when J. D. Day Care was a mess." Mariah's voice was shrill in her own ears. She couldn't help it! "He messed up the Tot Lot much the same way and was planning on killing his son. Thanks to his loony wife, he had to settle for my child." She drew a deep breath in an effort to settle herself. Nevsky's face was shadowed, turned as it was away from the headlights. She stepped close to him. "Did you have even the faintest notion of all this?" To her surprise, she found her tone accusing. She knew her ragged nerves couldn't be trusted, but she imagined he had arrived late by design, not chance. He had forced her to handle this most dangerous situation on her own, even though it might have cost her her life. She squinted, trying to make out his features. "*Did* you know?"

"I did my best to get here, Mariah," Nevsky said. "That we didn't make it sooner wasn't from lack of trying. It just wasn't to be, that's all. It was written that this was to be *your* night, sink or swim." Clarisse's bawling had given way to sniffling. She put her arms around Nevsky's neck with no intention of letting go.

"You could say the way things ended up working out for me was just . . . a mystery," Mariah said sourly.

"You could."

Neither of them smiled.

Twenty

While Mariah attempted to compose herself, Nevsky and Roper moved quickly into Fin and Feather to tend to Truman Orel. Roper's walkie-talkie quickly summoned a patrol car and an ambulance.

Nevsky ran interference while Mariah made her statement to the police. Halfway through it Frenetic Freddy, notified earlier by the Russian, arrived, brash, bold, and as flashily dressed as ever. In later weeks, Mariah wondered why Nevsky had chosen to call the attorney. Had he guessed Mariah would be able to use one? Or had he *known* what was going to happen? She supposed that was impossible. Nevsky wasn't a wizard. Or was he?

The curious thing was that she could never bring herself to completely believe what Nevsky said about simply having arrived too late to help her. If he had figured out Truman Orel was her tormentor and hadn't told her, then she couldn't forgive him. Not if he knowingly allowed her to single-handedly face a cleaver-wielding, cross-dressing madman. Though she kept her feelings to herself—after all, she had no evidence on which to base them—they nonetheless tempered her affection for the bearded Russian and quieted her earlier romantic interest.

Maybe it was just as well. Over the next months, her energies and attention were largely devoted to damage control and repair of the Tot Lot's reputation, to say nothing of her own. Two days after her encounter with Truman Orel, she arranged another news conference. Complete with a black eye suffered during the encounter and limping from the wound in her thigh, she described the full arsenal of his harassment over the last two months. She didn't spare the details of their struggle in the pet shop. After all, she had faced death with the odds against her. Desperate courage and a resourceful child were honest, high-class fodder for the media animal. Earning respect and public admiration was small enough compensation for beholding her daughter in mortal peril and for being close to death herself.

She was invited to appear on local media talk shows. She accepted the TV offers first. They put her and Clarisse before hundreds of thousands of eyes. And didn't the kid love it! She who so liked to be in charge had the chance to stand front and center. Mariah gave her free rein, considering what the girl had been through, starting with the abuse she had suffered under her classmates and finishing with her near brush with death. Later Mariah might have to do some downsizing of the kid's ego. But for now, let her enjoy her brief celebrity and heroism. On the radio, Clarisse delighted in taking calls from other kids and answering their questions. One interviewer whispered to Mariah, "Hey, you got a little ham bone there!"

Child had survived the ordeal better than mother. Too frequently Mariah's sleep was broken by nightmares peopled by those who had tormented her: Jacky DuMarr, the Errises, horrid Fontenot and his cameraman flunky, and the scarlet smear of the face of "Constance." *Constant as the constellations.* Awake, she sometimes found her attention wandering previously walked painful paths where she relived the emotions of those troubled travels. She groaned aloud and sighed. People looked at her oddly and possibly understood. Time, she hoped, would dissipate the potency of those disturbing waking reveries.

She had to deal with the pending lawsuits filed against her. Her public vindication brought an end to most of them. She was particularly glad to find that Cassandra and Nick Delos had quickly dropped their budding legal action. When they asked to readmit their spoiled Valerie to the Tot Lot, Mariah refused. "To be candid, she borders on the unmanageable," she told the pompous Nick. A bit of an exaggeration. But she owed them something, even though she wasn't a spiteful woman. However, she was now the kind who would get in her licks when someone deserved them.

She was delighted to hear from the other parents who had pulled their kids and now wanted them back in again. Among them was Oprah Grayson, who wasn't too proud to admit that she had panicked when she withdrew her Fletcher so quickly. "Serve me right if now you close de gate on my bhoy."

"For you and Fletcher, the gate's always open."

"Be seein' you den. Please no more smash up de school."

"No more . . . I certainly hope not!"

Without raising a finger, Mariah torpedoed the sensationalist hopes of Delmar and Debbie Bronk, who had unscrupulously sought to capitalize on their innocent Tessie's nearness to rumored scandal. The newspaper reported that the TV miniseries based on ''her story'' had quietly been dropped. The Bronks, she was happy to read, were planning to leave the city.

Cynthia Tran phoned, all lighthearted and happy-voiced, as though overnight her Day-Care Regulatory Board had become as well-intentioned and openhanded as a charitable foundation. She cheerily reported that the board's overall Tot Lot findings had been positive. Mariah swallowed the despair that Cynthia's visits and alarming efficiency had brought to her life. She was noisily grateful over the news of officialdom's verdict. Incense not the bureaucrat, she thought, their power is great. One day the Tot Lot's license would come up for renewal. ''If there's anything more I can do for you . . .'' Cynthia added. Were they worried about some kind of lawsuit? Well, not from Mariah Sullivan. She had seen enough of courtrooms and lawyers to last a lifetime.

She reopened the Tot Lot in January with mostly new staff members. Deidre and Grace had decided to find easier part-time jobs; Nikki chose to go on to college. Mariah lost loyal Randi Monroe and her two children. She had found a man, quickly married him, and moved to New Mexico.

Thank goodness Rochelle had stayed. She swore it took more than a konk on the head to keep her away from ''her children.'' To Mariah's embarrassment, she admitted that her recent sullenness originated in the fear that Mariah no longer needed her, not in the lethal conspiracy Mariah had imagined. She had felt threatened by her boss's new assertiveness. After all, she had enjoyed her role as counselor and de facto decision-maker for much of the center's operation. She dreaded Mariah taking over everything. Mariah reassured her that she was now more indispensable than ever. She never confessed her morbid flight of fancy that had for less than an hour branded the steady, reliable woman a child murderer. She kept that piece of humble pie in the front of the freezer of her memory. She could thaw it out any time she felt too arrogant and sure of herself. Though she hoped there would be far *more* such instances than there had been in the first thirty years of her life.

Many of the children in the January enrollment were new. Some parents had simply given up on the Tot Lot during its time of troubles and wouldn't be returning their kids. But in the wings were other moms and dads who were impressed enough by Mariah's courageous stand in the face of torment, harassment, and physical danger to feel honored to put their children under her care. The waiting list was longer than it had been in September, before all the trouble had started.

She would have to think seriously about adding that new wing.

She had kept a careful eye on Clarisse for aftereffects of the traumatic ordeal. There seemed to be few. Clarisse asked what had happened to "that crazy man." Mariah told her he had indeed been crazy and been put in a mental institution. She asked Mariah if she wished he had died from his wound. She answered that she never had wanted to kill him or anyone. But that she would do the same thing again to defend her child's life and her own. At every opportunity, she told Clarisse that she had been a very brave girl and that she was *very* proud of her.

It was Clarisse, she supposed, who kept Nevsky in her life. She asked that the three of them spend time together. Mariah did what she could to accommodate her child without compromising her own diverging interests. They went on outings to the zoo and to indoor swimming pools. Sunday morning skating with Sergei's cooperation was still popular. She found herself avoiding moments alone with Nevsky, though, and would keep doing so until she felt she had more control over herself.

Nevsky, Nevsky . . . She hadn't yet been able to figure him out, though she was wise enough to know he had set her on the last, steepest rails up which she had labored to her final metamorphosis. Curious how he seemed a stranger now. She knew why. She was a different person. She saw the world—him included—differently than when she had first met him.

Back when she had scoffed at his talk of mysteries.

Now the entire world seemed mysterious. Had she never realized its immense complexity? Had she not seen how nothing, once examined, was readily explained? To find irrefutable evidence of that look no further than frogs or leaves, never mind humanity. Meanings lurked like schools of fish beneath the placid waves of reality. Having herself changed, her surroundings no longer fit her earlier conceptions. Everything needed to be looked at afresh.

That would keep her busy and out of trouble for a while.

HAUTALA'S HORROR AND
SUPERNATURAL SUSPENSE

GHOST LIGHT (4320, $4.99)
Alex Harris is searching for his kidnapped children, but only the ghost of their dead mother can save them from his murderous rage.

DARK SILENCE (3923, $5.99)
Dianne Fraser is trying desperately to keep her family — and her own sanity — from being pulled apart by the malevolent forces that haunt the abandoned mill on their property.

COLD WHISPER (3464, $5.95)
Tully can make Sarah's every wish come true, but Sarah lives in teror because Tully doesn't understand that some wishes aren't meant to come true.

LITTLE BROTHERS (4020, $4.50)
The "little brothers" have returned, and this time there will be no escape for the boy who saw them kill his mother.

NIGHT STONE (3681, $4.99)
Their new house was a place of darkness, shadows, long-buried secrets, and a force of unspeakable evil.

MOONBOG (3356, $4.95)
Someone — or something — is killing the children in the little town of Holland, Maine.

MOONDEATH (1844, $3.95)
When the full moon rises in Cooper Falls, a beast driven by bloodlust and savage evil stalks the night.

Available wherever paperbacks are sold, or order direct from the Publisher. Send cover price plus 50¢ per copy for mailing and handling to Penguin USA, P.O. Box 999, c/o Dept. 17109, Bergenfield, NJ 07621. Residents of New York and Tennessee must include sales tax. DO NOT SEND CASH.